The Shape of Darkness

Judy Tucker

Also by Judy Tucker

BOILING POINT
(#2 in the Jack Grady Mystery Series)

RUN!
(#3 in the Jack Grady Mystery Series)

PRESSURE POINTS!
(#4 in the Jack Grady Mystery Series)

ISBN:1480067881
ISBN-13:9781480067882

To My Family

I

PROLOGUE

The big cactuses have shape, even in the darkness. She can see just enough to avoid them. But there are smaller ones everywhere. And bushes. They catch at her skin like claws.

There! Dodge to the right... Too late. Thorns tear her shoulder.

She collides with a branch, something tall and prickly, shoves it aside. It snaps back and hits her in the face.

One bare foot lands on the edge of a rock, and she almost cries out—clamps her mouth shut, swallows the sound. She can't help herself; her eyes go to her wounded foot. She's done. Just give in. But when she raises her head, there it is: the path, lined with low, small lights.

She meets it halfway up its length, struggles along its pebbled surface, managing a shambling, lurching run. Then, finally, up one step, another. She stumbles the last few feet, punches the lighted button, holds it down. The screams burst out of her.

Jill starts awake. Is that the doorbell?

The sound is distant, way up at the front of the house. Charlie hasn't even rolled over, and Sophie can sleep through anything. Jill pulls on a robe. She can't remember the last time someone rang their bell in the middle of the night.

1

She's almost at the door when she hears the other sound.

Coyotes.

No...

Human.

She rushes across the entryway, hits the switch for the porch light, and peers out through the small window at the top of the door.

It's a girl, looking up at Jill through the glass. She's standing so close to the house that all Jill registers at first is an open, contorted mouth, wide eyes... Oh, God! She's naked, covered with blood. Her shrieks are a continuous siren.

Jill can't make her fingers work. They're stuttering all over the keypad. Then her training kicks in, calming her hands, and she manages to get the buttons right. Alarm off.

With a soft moan, the girl crumples, collapsing onto the porch.

Jill pulls open the door...

1

Grady finds them in the family room. The girl on the puffy beige linen sofa has cropped blonde hair so thick it's almost fur. He can't tell if the color is real, but she has the right skin for it. Her nose is small and turned up, and her tear-filled eyes are a startling shade of blue. She is curled into herself, but one slender foot peeks out from under the yellow cotton robe. Her toenails are painted: pale pink.

She's survived initial questioning, and now she is being, well, watched. The coffee table is littered with soggy tissues. Jill's left arm is placed protectively around her shoulders. The place is outfitted like the American dream, with a pool table, several sofas and a movie-sized flat-screen TV. A young deputy stands awkwardly in the corner.

Jill hands the girl another tissue, gives Grady a look that could be anger, could be a challenge, could be... Hell, he's never been good at reading his ex-wife. Why should that change now?

Shit, thinks Grady. Why am I here? And what the fuck am I supposed to do?

#

He was lost in an ice field when the phone rang, his left foot frozen, gray with cold, right toes numb. Using his ice axe to crawl back to camp.

He heard it distantly. BRRING. Once, twice...

His sheet was on the floor. The swamp cooler poured its damp, icy air into the room, blowing the curtains out the open window. His ancient German shepherd, lying in the pool of moonlight by the side of the bed, groaned.

He grabbed the receiver.

"Jack?" Female. Worried. And just about the last voice he expected to hear coming out of the dark. A sudden roar drowned her out. Fuckin' motorcycles. Grady lurched across the room and slammed the window. Damn Saturday nights.

"I have a situation here," she was saying. "I, um, need your help."

For what he couldn't imagine. He looked at the lighted dial of the bedside clock. 3:00 a.m. Pushing it for Scotch and too early for coffee. You have a husband, he thought, let him help. But what he said was, "Can't it wait till morning?"

"No. That won't work." A pause. "People have been trying to reach you."

"Shit." Grady rummaged through the mess on the top of his nightstand, finally flicked on the light. Aw, jeez, why did he have 100 goddamn watts overhead? He pulled open the drawer. There they were: pager flashing, cell phone dead—as usual.

The pager held two numbers. One of the gatehouses. Pergama. And... The cops? Yup. Sheriff's department. "Jill? What the hell's going on?"

"Someone's dead."

Grady found a phone battery that still had some life in it. He pulled on his jeans, bumped a foot into Bear, rubbed the dog's ears in apology. His gun went on his belt, a Wildcats cap on his head. He grabbed a bottle of water to fight dehydration, thought about taking a beer to fight whatever demon he was fighting this week, but decided that even he couldn't be that stupid.

It was almost cool when he opened the door. Tucson in June.

Bearable only in the pit of the night. The days were like living in a goddamn blow dryer, winds sucking the moisture out of even the youngest skin. And hot as hell. The world crackled.

He worked his cell phone as he drove the ten miles up into the foothills, but the desk jockey at the sheriff's department just gave him some bureaucratic crap. And the gatehouse was a constant busy.

As he neared Pergama, he could see that the big gates were closed. And they were never closed. Like the other gated communities in town, Pergama was generally content with wooden traffic-control arms. But now someone had apparently decided that even the welded steel barricades weren't enough. Two sheriff's cars, lights flashing, blocked the road just inside the entrance.

They got the gates open, and backed up one of the black-and-whites enough to let him squeak by. He grabbed one of the uniforms, learned the perp was unknown and there were deputies out beating the cactus. That meant calling the homeowners' association president and getting her to activate the phone tree. Pergama's families lived within the electronic arms of their alarm systems, but walked their dogs at any hour. No one needed a hostage situation.

As he entered the gatehouse, Erwin started talking. The cops wanted to know, the guard said, who'd come in the gate since he'd taken over at midnight. No one except the Phelps coming home late all dressed up, he'd told them. Things were real quiet.

Grady listened with one ear while he checked the night's log. Nothing remarkable. "Lock it down," he said. And he was back in the car driving up the road as the gates slid shut.

He had never seen the place so bright. Landscaping that mimics untouched desert was status in Tucson. The more expensive the neighborhood, the scarcer the lawns, the thicker the cactus, and the blacker the night. Normally, only a few tasteful lights near gateposts pierced Pergama's darkness. But now—spotlights glared from garages and rooflines, pools glowed. He should have known: the telephone tree could never keep up with the grapevine. In the projects, time hung heavy, so people watched TV and gossiped. Here, they planned exotic trips and talked about neighbors they might not even see from one season to the next.

Jill's house was a mile up—five speed bumps and a right turn, Sophie liked to say. Leave it to a kid several years too young to drive to come up with the easiest way to get people to her home. Sophie was neat, Grady thought. Had Jill's looks, her dad's energy, and a sense of humor all her own. If he'd had a kid, he could have done worse than Sophie.

The place he was heading for was next to Jill's, one house farther in off Pergama's main drag. He vaguely remembered something about people from the Midwest. Maybe part-time residents? Hard to believe that so many people could afford to buy and maintain five or six thousand square feet of house plus pool just to camp out for a few months between November and May.

#

Now, Grady sweeps the crumpled tissues aside and sits down on the coffee table facing the two women. He's a big guy, but the piece is solid. It'll hold.

He's still wondering what his role is in all this. Making it up as he goes along.

"I hear you've had a rough night," he says to the girl. She begins sobbing, so he reaches behind him and pulls a fresh tissue out of the box, hands it to her and waits.

"I...uh...I already did..." she finally manages to get out. "I told them."

"Them?"

"Your colleagues."

"The sheriff's people. Well, that's good, and it's something you had to do, but they're not my colleagues. I work for the people who live here."

"You work for the Nelsons?" More sobbing.

Jill gives her a comforting pat. "He's director of security," she interjects, "for Pergama and three or four other gated communities around town."

Actually, it's five, Grady thinks. Even so, not exactly an impressive gig. "I'm not the law," he says, "but the Nelsons and their neighbors have put me in something like an official position. I know the gist of what you told the sheriff's people, but they're pretty busy right now. And I'd rather hear your story from you."

Grady waits. The girl sobs.

"You're Winnie Pearson." He finally prompts. "And you're a guest of the Nelsons."

She shakes her head.

"She's house sitting," Jill interjects. "Mary's niece. From Wisconsin."

"Michigan," Winnie Pearson says between sobs.

"How long have your aunt and uncle been gone?"

"Three days. They told security I'd be staying here and left a key for me up at the gate."

"When will they be back?"

"October."

"How can I reach them?"

Jill again. "You can't. Not easily." She holds a tissue up to Winnie's nose. "Ed and Mary are on one of those once-in-a-lifetime treks in the Himalayas. Ed came in to get his teeth cleaned before they left, and I suggested maybe sixty-eight was a bit old for Nepal. But the family dentist has little influence in these things, even when she's their next door neighbor."

"So the Nelsons are in Nepal."

Jill shakes her head. "Probably still in the air. It's a lot of connections and some layovers."

"I could look," Winnie manages to get out. "There's an itinerary." Then she breaks down again.

"Later," Grady says. "Right now, let's talk about what happened. Take a deep breath, try to relax and tell me."

Winnie literally pulls herself together, gathering the stray foot under the yellow wrap, tugging the robe tightly closed around her neck, curling under the fabric like a sheltering tent.

"I watched TV," she begins. "Uncle Ed and Aunt Mary have this great system, just like a theater. I made myself dinner, and had a glass of wine—not from the wine cellar—I opened one of the bottles that Aunt Mary keeps in the small cooler behind the bar." She gestures toward the corner where a wet bar holds enough liquor to keep a drinking man busy for weeks.

"You watched TV until...?"

"I don't know. Maybe midnight. It didn't really matter since I didn't need to get up any special time."

"You're on vacation?"

"Sort of. More of a respite really. That's what Aunt Mary called it. She said I needed a break from life."

"And life's in Michigan?"

The girl nods. "I'm from a suburb north of Detroit. But I've been going to school in Ann Arbor."

Talking about the ordinary facts of her life has calmed her down. Her voice is stronger. The tears have stopped. Grady pushes on.

"So you stopped watching TV about midnight. What did you do then?"

"Went to bed."

"Straight to bed?"

"Well, I brushed my teeth... stuff like that."

"And then you went to sleep."

"Right away. I usually don't. I always read to get sleepy. But I must have been more tired than I knew. I just went out. In fact, I sort of woke up once and realized I'd left the light on, the one on the nightstand, but I fell asleep again before I could turn it off."

"So you're sleeping."

"Yes."

"And then?"

"I woke up. I started to roll over to go back to sleep. And then I noticed."

"Noticed?"

"The bedside light was off. Maybe the bulb burned out, I told myself. Maybe the plug's loose. Maybe there's been a power outage—although I couldn't think why."

From time to time she visibly struggles to stay in control. Her voice deepens, becomes richer, as she talks. She isn't as young as he first thought, as much of a child as her manner suggests. He pegs her age at mid-20s, maybe as old as 27 or 28. Still a kid by his standards, but he can remember when he thought 35 was middle-aged and 47, the number of candles on his last cake (if he'd had a cake), was all but deceased.

He waits.

"I just lay there. I'd think about getting up and turning a light on, but then I thought, what if... I told myself I was just being silly. But I couldn't shake the feeling that... that something was wrong. It felt like danger."

"Like danger?"

"The air. The air felt like danger." She takes a deep, shuddering breath. Jill's arm tightens around her shoulders. "Then I heard the noise."

"What kind of noise?"

"One of those you almost think you don't hear, so that you can tell yourself it's the house settling or the snow falling off the roof—well, that happens in Michigan. And then I heard it again. It was a muffled, round sort of sound. It didn't have any sharp edges. Maybe that's why it was so hard to hear."

"What did you do?"

"Nothing. I kept lying there with my heart pounding. I didn't dare move. I tried to breathe as quietly as I could. There was a phone on the nightstand, but I was afraid to use it. I thought I'd just be still, and whoever it was would leave and when it got light I'd call 9-1-1."

"So you're lying there."

"Yes."

"Any idea what time it was?"

"No."

"But something happened."

She nods. "A light went on. I was in the guest room. I thought using the master bedroom would be rude even though Aunt Mary said I should. So I was in the guest room. It's down the back hall, off the living room."

"Where was the light coming from?"

"I couldn't tell. But I could see enough to tell that my door was open—the one into the hall."

"You'd closed it?"

"Uh huh. Like a hotel, I guess. I didn't think about it, just closed it automatically when I went to bed."

"So you knew someone was there."

"I tried to tell myself that maybe they'd left some lights on a timer. People do that. But why would a timer turn anything on in the middle of the night?"

"What did you do then?"

"Nothing. I was paralyzed. I couldn't have moved if I'd wanted to."

Her voice breaks. She pauses, visibly shaken.

"Then someone rattled the door."

Puzzled, Grady looks at her. "I thought..."

"One of the French doors. Someone was on the little patio outside my room. Pulling the knob so hard it shook the glass. I could see the beam of a flashlight."

"And you reacted."

"God, yes. I couldn't help it. I screamed, I was screaming, I kept screaming. I ran out, into the hall. I thought I'd run to the front door and get to a neighbor's. Or hide. Or something. I had to get out."

"So you were running."

"I was running down the hall, and I ran into the living room, and a light was on there, not really bright, just a table lamp, but I could see that one of the patio doors leading to the back yard was wide open so I ran the other way across the room—toward the entry hall—and I fell over it."

Grady is silent, encouraging her to go on.

"I tripped and landed right on top of it."

"It?"

"You know." Her voice is little more than a whisper. "The body." She pulls her legs up to her chest, wraps her arms around them, bends her head, burying her face. "I didn't even know he was dead. I just saw these staring eyes and all the blood and I got up as fast as I could. It was hard to get up. It felt like I was tangled in him."

Jill explains. "She hit her head and twisted her ankle."

"Finally I was on my feet and I ran out the front door to the nearest house. I rang the bell. I guess I was screaming."

Jill nods. "She was naked and covered with blood. Absolutely hysterical."

Grady looks at the girl. "Naked?"

Winnie meets his gaze. "I sleep that way."

He turns again to Jill. "So you called 9-1-1."

"Charlie did. I pulled her inside and wrapped her in my robe. She was scratched up—I think she must have crashed into a bush or two. But she was mostly just upset. I cleaned her up and put some ice on her ankle. Then the sheriff came…"

"And they brought you back over here."

The girl's face is buried again, her words muffled by her arms. "Yes. They did."

"And they asked you to look at the body."

"They made me."

"And you couldn't identify him."

"I don't know him."

"You've never seen him before."

Winnie looks up, straight at Grady, her astonishing baby blue eyes fixed on his bleary brown ones. "I've never seen him before in my life."

2

Grady doesn't say anything. He lets the silence settle in between them. He waits for the girl to elaborate. He waits to see if she'll repeat her statement the way nervous witnesses often do, reciting the same phrase over and over as if no one has heard it the first time.

But she doesn't say another word. Her eyes, still resting on his, fill with tears.

"Aren't we done here, Jack? The detectives already know all this." The edge in Jill's voice says she's impatient with him, her tenderness reserved for the girl. Maybe she expected him to instantly fix things. Somehow make the whole mess go away. Clearly, he hasn't lived up to expectations. That's nothing new.

Grady turns back to Winnie. "What about the alarm?"

"The alarm?"

"It didn't go off?"

"No."

Grady waits again. Finally, he breaks the silence. "The Nelsons do have one. I saw the keypad by the door."

"I think I forgot." Winnie's voice is tiny. She's back to sounding fifteen. "They left me instructions, but I'm not used to it. I did set it earlier in the evening, but then I went outside because there are so many stars here and I wanted to see them, and when I came back in I guess I forgot."

"You guess?"

"I'm pretty sure."

Jill breaks in. "Look, Jack, it took you forever to get here. And now you're just playing cop."

Winnie objects softly. "I don't mind. He's nice."

Jill doesn't comment. She simply glares.

Grady gives up. He reminds himself that although the guy in the living room is dead, there doesn't appear to be any imminent danger to anyone living. Jill is probably right. Once a cop, always poking into other people's business. He isn't sure where the sheriff's job ends and his begins, but whatever he's supposed to do, it can probably wait until morning.

He stands up. "I guess we're done here," he says. "Sleep well, Miss Pearson."

"Thank you, Mr. Grady," she says, and, unmistakably, she smiles.

It is one of those smiles, childish and sensual at the same time. She has small teeth, and they reinforce the impression of innocence. She has a small round chin and a dimple in each cheek. The word that comes to mind (although it is a word he detests) is adorable. He has to admit it. Winnie Pearson is adorable.

"Good night, Jack." Jill says it as if adjourning a meeting.

In the living room, the crime scene crew is dusting everything that doesn't move, including the corpse. The man is on his back, naked, uncircumcised penis flopping over a swath of black curly hair that runs down his chest into his crotch. Grady reminds himself that they always say you can't tell in the flaccid state, but, still, the guy was well endowed.

Reasonably fit, not a lot of body fat. About six feet, maybe 180 pounds, mid-to-late 20s. He has hair almost rock star length, a full beard, an olive complexion, brown eyes and an extra opening sliced into his neck. There is a lot of blood. It has soaked the carpet, sprayed on furniture. A muddled red trail leads toward the front door.

What look to be the man's clothes lie in a blood-spattered pile nearby. Grady can see denim, a black t-shirt, and underneath it all, a pair of Nikes, once gray with black trim, now painted with red.

A female deputy is perched over the body, tweezers deployed. Andy Davis seems to be in charge. He looks the same as ever, sagging jowls peppered with a day's worth of stubble, white short-sleeved shirt popping its buttons over his gut. As he spots Grady, he runs his hand through his thinning hair. "Hey," he says, "you smoke these days?"

Grady has to admit that he does. His usual excuse is that he finds slapping on a patch to be unsatisfactory, post-coitally speaking. Truth is, it's been a while since there was much coital activity in his life. But the nicotine habit does help him fit in with some segments of law enforcement. "Promised the wife I wouldn't buy 'em," Davis says. "So I have to bum 'em."

They adjourn to the front porch—if porch is the right word for the patio-sized area paved with flagstones and adorned with potted palms. Two wide steps lead down to the driveway.

Only 4:30 a.m., but night is already fading behind the black outlines of nearby peaks.

Pergama is tucked into the Catalina Mountains. Few of the lots are flat. Houses are creatively—and expensively—designed to accommodate hills and washes. Several rest on huge pillars.

This deep into the foothills, wildlife abounds. Homeowners boast about the deer and javelina and moan about the skunks and scorpions. Grady's first challenge on the job was a bear that moved into Sungate, Pergama's sister community a few miles to the west. A woman going out to take a morning dip discovered it sitting on the steps of her swimming pool. Lighting up, Grady and Davis watch a bob cat slink across the street, heading home after a night's hunting.

"Stinks in there," Davis says. "Smells like a butcher shop that oughta be condemned."

"Looks like a weird one."

"Ain't they all. Fuckin' people going around killing other fuckin' people. Usually people they know and love."

"You think she knew him?"

"Says she didn't. No reason at this point to believe she did."

"No reason to believe she didn't."

"Huh. Niece comes to visit and offs her boyfriend in the living room."

"Something like that."

"Except she didn't kill him."

Grady knows what Davis is driving at. "He's a big guy."

"And she's a little girl."

"How'd they get in?"

"Could have been one of those doors to the back patios. They gotta couple sliders. And, yeah, they have those fancy extra locks like all of 'em up here. But the girl—she was in, she was out, she was looking at the city lights. She doesn't remember whether she used the fuckin' safety locks or not when she came inside for good."

But if the perp got in that way, was already in, with the door to Winnie's room open, why the flashlight outside, the rattling of the patio door? It makes no sense. He and Andy both know it, and they're both thinking the same thing. Scared people get confused. And if she was going to make up a story, she could do a whole lot better than that. Fuck. He wouldn't want to be the lead on this one.

Davis stubs out his cigarette, pockets the butt and holds out his hand for another one. "So how's life treating you?"

"Can't complain."

"And it wouldn't do any good if you did, huh? I know how that goes."

"This where she came out?" Grady indicates the entry behind them, the wide-open double doors they've been careful not to touch.

"Yeah. You can see the trail."

"Cause of death looks pretty clear."

Davis nods. "You could say."

"Got a weapon?"

"Big butcher knife lying right next to the body. Would fit one of the empty slots in the knife block. Matches the rest of the set. Some of that pricey crap my wife's always going on about."

"Not a lot of help there."

"No shit, Sherlock. The forensics boys will go over it for prints, but I'd bet my left ball it was wiped."

The birds are waking up now, making a racket in the nearby mesquites. Davis puffs away. "How's Gina?"

"About the same, I guess. We don't hear from her much."

Davis shakes his head. "Shit," he says, and Grady knows he is cursing in sympathy. "She was such a pretty girl, too. We used to go to those association picnics. Frannie would be sitting with your mom. And Gina would be running around with the rest of the kids, all of them swarming over the swings and the jungle gym. But it was always Gina who'd be kind of organizing them, even the ones bigger than her, making sure nobody got too amped up, or hurt."

That was a long time ago. Grady flashes on the last time he saw his niece two, three months ago. She was sitting at his mother's kitchen table when he got there one Saturday morning, dropping off a supply of asthma drugs. Her hair was a black that looked painted on, with pale roots peeking through. She wore a man's sleeveless white undershirt, and she was the kind of thing that came from drugs at best and drugs plus HIV at worst. She was smoking a cigarette, and his mom just sat there smiling at her, tubing plugged into her nostrils, oxygen concentrator humming away in the corner. Grady grabbed the cigarette from Gina's hand right in the middle of her "Hi" to him and flung it out the back door. All of that, in a split second, is what he thinks. "She was a nice kid," is what he says.

One of the uniforms, a guy who looks barely old enough to drive, calls Davis away, and Grady pushes back the thoughts of Gina. A moment later, a black-and-white pulls up in front of the entry, and Jill and Winnie come out and are swooped into the back seat.

"Going home," Jill says to Grady as they go by. "We'll deal with her stuff later."

Grady watches as the car carries them the few hundred yards down one driveway and up the next to Jill's front door. He turns again to Davis. He knows that to Andy he's a civilian these days, just a kind of rent-a-cop, knows he's pushing, but he has to ask.

"When you were talking about the knife block, you said 'one of the empty slots'."

"Yeah." Davis stubs out his cigarette, regards the butt lying on the flagstone, finally bends over, picks it up and puts it in his jacket pocket with the first. "There were two. But the other one was for a little knife. Not a monster like our guy used. Where is it? We dunno."

Could be in a drawer, Grady thinks. Could have been tossed out with the garbage years ago. Why do they care? But Davis isn't talking.

Grady lights up one last cigarette and takes a drag. He's always thought that eventually he'd get used to the money up here, but he never has. More cars, refrigerators, home theaters and (almost) swimming pools than people. And all of it accessible via only one road, one gate.

So how'd they get in—the dead guy and whoever cut him? Not on foot. It looks easy on a map—just hike a couple of miles through a bordering neighborhood, climb the wall. But Pergama itself is a risky obstacle course: dark yards packed with nearly impassable desert landscaping, oddly shaped pools surrounded by their own fences, motion-activated security lights—and more than a few large dogs.

No, they came in through the gate. And they didn't do it on the graveyard shift. Erwin is no mental giant, but he's deadly serious about his job.

So who was on duty right before Erwin? Though he glanced at the log sheets, Grady doesn't remember. And it doesn't matter. Davis and his boys will check it out. As far as the cops are concerned, gated communities are a joke. The barriers are flimsy. The guards are low paid and lazy, don't keep good records. But the detectives will at least go through the motions.

The sun is now a fiery red glow behind the Rincon Mountains

17

on the east. Summer has been official for less than a week, but the Old Pueblo has been baking for more than a month. Grady has heard that herds of javelina, extended families up to twenty strong, have been spotted crossing the road leading to one of the foothills resorts, looking for water.

He feels hot already. He climbs into his car and sees his cell phone lying there, envelope icon blinking, letting him know he has messages.

It's Doris Asprey. Twice. He punches in her number. He has to hold a meeting, the homeowners' association president says. Today. This morning, in fact. To reassure people that they are safe (and, Grady thinks, that one little murder will not affect property values).

Grady buttonholes Davis and trades a pack of smokes for a promise that Andy will show up and say a few words. Then he drives down to the gatehouse. The black-and-whites are still positioned inside the big gates. Three TV news vans idle outside.

As Grady gets out of his car, the reporters rush the gates, shoving microphones through, calling out questions. "Who's the victim? Is there a suspect? Have there been any arrests? Is there a manhunt?" Grady was never a spokesman for the department, never had anything to do with the press in that way, but when he had his problem, he was an easy target. They kept talking cover-up and referring to "the rot that sets in when things are kept from the public." But if they were looking for something explosive, they never found it. Without a bigger story, he fell off TV news, then off the front page, then out of sight. Nothing ever happened, except he left the force. And that was inevitable. He enjoys ignoring them now.

He talks to Erwin, tells him to let residents through. He takes gatehouse coffee to the guys manning the black-and-whites and reminds them that Pergama is private property, the press has no right to come in. Then he drives the half block to the clubhouse and sleeps in his car until it's time for the meeting.

3

No one has told Sophie what's going on. There have been no screaming sirens. And Sophie isn't roused by more subtle disturbances. So when she finds her mom sitting at the kitchen table staring out over the patio, beyond the swimming pool, up at the mountains, she's puzzled. Today is Sunday. Her mother sleeps in on Sundays, and when she does get up, she always has a coffee mug in one hand and a section of newspaper in the other. This morning, the coffeepot is empty. And *The New York Times* is nowhere in sight.

Even odder, the counter is littered with dirty cups and crumpled paper napkins.

Sophie pours herself a glass of orange juice and walks up next to her mother. She stands there for a moment, sipping her juice and trying to see what is so mesmerizing.

Finally, her mom sighs. "Hi, sweetie," she says. And she goes back to watching the mountain.

Sophie flops down in one of the kitchen chairs, swivels it around, and begins running her ring finger around the rim of her glass. It makes a high-pitched whistle, a smooth, wet sound.

Her mother sighs again. She keeps her eyes on the mountain. "We have a house guest," she says. "But it's very temporary."

They had company for dinner the night before, people who were still there when Sophie went to bed. But why would the Newalls stay? And why just one of them?

"Did they have a fight?" she asks.

"Who?" Now her mother turns to look at her.

"The Newalls."

Her mother quickly makes the connection. "No, no," she says. "Not the Newalls." Another deep sigh. "Her name is Winnie, and she was staying next door."

Sophie has a good idea who Winnie is. The house next door turns a blind side to the road. Major windows face either a front or a back garden. But day before last, Sophie was coming home from Megan's, and it was quicker to go through the Nelsons' yard, and more fun as long as you avoided the cactus. She was running past the front window because it was already dusk and she didn't want to be grounded and she saw this—she couldn't tell if it was a teenage girl or someone slightly older—anyway, a slim blonde person kind of swooping around the living room. She was holding a glass of wine and wearing a pale blue bra and matching tap pants. There was music playing—Sophie could hear it even though the windows were closed. It was some of the old stuff her father liked. Some guy singer with a smoky voice.

Sophie's pretty sure the girl—Winnie—never saw her. And she isn't supposed to cut through other people's property, so she plays dumb. "She's Mrs. Nelson's niece," her mother continues. "She was house sitting."

"So why is she here?"

Her mother sighs, and looks up at the mountains again. "Where's your father?" she says. "Go see where he's gotten to." As Sophie starts to leave the room, she adds, "Stay away from the guest wing."

Unlike her mom, Sophie's dad is a morning person. Even though they have a gardener, he does a lot of puttering in the yard. He puts in cactus; he takes out cactus. He moves rocks. He especially likes to prune things. But today is different. She finally spots him out in front near the mailbox. He's just standing there.

When she reaches him, Sophie can see that he's looking down through the cactus at what you can see of the Nelsons' house next door. There's a sheriff's car parked across the end of the driveway and a deputy leaning against it smoking a cigarette. Yellow and black tape stretches across the porch from column to column. That means the place is a crime scene, just like on TV.

"Hi," her dad says and reaches out his right arm to let her slide in under it.

"Hi, yourself," she says. And waits. He is as distracted as her mom. And he doesn't seem about to explain anything. Does he think she can't see what's in front of her? Does he consider her a baby?

Finally, she asks. "What happened?"

Her dad shakes his head. He makes a noise between a sigh and a whistle. He turns toward the house. "C'mon, pumpkin. Your old man needs coffee." Then something seems to strike him. "Did your mom send you looking for me? Were you wandering around the yard?"

"Yeah. Of course."

He shakes his head again. "She wasn't thinking. No one's used to this. You can't go outside alone right now. You've got to stick close."

"Line of sight?"

Her dad nods. "Line of sight." It's an old joke, a term they used on vacations when she was eight or nine and impatient with long lunches at sidewalk cafes and needed to move around.

"Okay," she says. "But you gotta tell me."

Her dad takes a deep breath.

"I know there's been a crime," she says. "And I know some house sitter named Winnie is in the guest wing. So all you need to tell me is what kind of crime and who did it."

They've reached the front door. Her dad's hand is on the latch, but he stops and looks at her. "A man was killed," he says. "And as for who did it, I don't think anyone knows."

#

The Pergama clubhouse is buzzing. The homeowners' association president introduces Grady, who simply says that no one in this room has anything to be concerned about and turns the meeting over to Davis.

Andy clears his throat nervously. A public speaker he isn't. He does get the facts out, though, working from notes scrawled in his pocket notebook. Grady knows he gave a statement to the reporters—and is using the same careful words on the residents.

"At approximately 2:15 a.m. this morning, a person temporarily residing at 7701 Ocotillo Way discovered the dead body of an adult male in the living room of that home. She made her way to the house next door, where the residents called 9-1-1. Upon responding to the call, deputies discovered said dead male, and confirmed the death, which is an apparent homicide."

Grady knows that the residents will assume that Davis is withholding the identity of the victim pending notification of next of kin. Fresh bodies usually come with names. Not true here. The naked man with the slashed throat isn't just unknown to the house sitter, so far he's unknown to the world. "No ID?" Grady had asked Davis. "Shit, no," Andy grumbled. "No wallet, no crumpled pieces of paper, not even a used Kleenex."

Davis was continuing in the official monotone. "Our technicians have made an initial examination of the body and the crime scene, and the body has been removed to the morgue. We have searched the surrounding area. At this time, we have no one in custody, but we are following a number of leads." (Translation, thinks Grady, they haven't a clue.)

A man with the sleek look of a retired banker speaks up. "Are we in danger?"

Davis reassures him in his cop-speak way. "We believe the perpetrator has left the area, but we're continuing to patrol."

There is an audible sigh—somewhere between relief and

disappointment.

Jill isn't there. No one from her household has attended. And neither Grady nor Davis answers questions as to who the "temporary resident" is or where she is stashed by saying anything other than "she's safe" or "she's with friends." But their discretion is a joke. Everyone knows: the crowd's murmurs have her pegged from the start as "the house sitter." More up-to-date residents are filling in their neighbors on when the Nelsons bought the house, what they like in furniture and food, who they play bridge with, where they've gone and when they'll be back. As Grady says his goodbyes, they're still chattering over their coffee.

#

The guest wing is hardly ever used. You go down the stairs to the lower level, past the exercise area, the laundry, Sophie's room and her mom's study, and enter it through double doors that open into a hallway. There are two small bedrooms and a shared bath on the right, a larger bedroom and bath on the left and an open area at the end with a big TV set and a kind of mini-kitchen. Sophie has plans for the guest wing. She figures that when she becomes a teenager, especially once she can drive, it will make a great private suite, kind of like her own apartment. Now if you could only open the door right onto Disney World... Or a stable.

Sophie is campaigning for a horse. Lots—well, a couple—of her friends have one. In some parts of Tucson, people even live on "horse property." She doesn't see why her family can't. What's so great about dumb old Pergama, anyway?

She is musing about all this when she goes downstairs to brush her teeth. Her dad made pancakes, and her mom insists she scrub the syrup out of her mouth almost as soon as she finishes chewing. If she had a horse, it would stay outside (duh!), which would avoid the issue of pets and her dad's allergies. It would be a healthy interest that would keep her away from drugs and running wild (not that she would ever be that stupid anyway).

And if you get a girl horse, a filly, and she grows up and has babies, you can sell them and make money. She puts the toothpaste on the brush and pushes the little button. Not babies, dummy, foals. That's what they're called. And horses only have one at a time. But how often? And what are they worth? She can find out on the Internet.

The electric toothbrush stutters—it has a two-minute timer—and in the pause before the vibrations continue, Sophie hears something. Or thinks she does. Sophie's bathroom backs up on the one attached to the largest guest bedroom. Is that noisy pipes, a distant radio—or is the unseen guest, the mysterious Winnie, singing in the shower?

Sophie's mom worried, over breakfast, about Winnie. The girl is clearly in shock, she said. Here she was, this grad student, come to Tucson to what she thought was a safe place, and what did she get? A dead body! There was talk of sending Sophie to stay with her grandparents. (No! Sophie screamed inside. It would mean missing all the action. How could they send her away from a murder next door?) But, on the outside, she was mature about it and even persuasive. They have locks; they have an alarm system. They can get a gun. Sophie said the last part to watch her dad's reaction.

"Never!" he exploded (as always). "There are too many guns in this country already."

"Look, Charlie. Those guns aren't going to vanish. And we have a right to self-defense..." Sophie's mom was actually trying to convince him! Usually she argued like she was trying to get him to agree to something far-fetched, like vampires are real. This time was different, Sophie could tell. This time, she meant it.

Sophie's mom can shoot. Jill grew up on a ranch outside Tucson. Even though with her long streaky blonde hair she looks as good (Sophie thinks) as a model (and is just about as skinny) and spends most of her outdoors time playing tennis and golf, she knows the desert.

Finally, they decided that since Sophie will be going to sports camp during the day and since they have the alarm (that Sophie mentioned) and the locks (that Sophie mentioned) and if she promised not to open an outside door or leave the house alone... "Do you think whoever did this is hanging around here waiting to be caught?" her dad said at one point, either as an argument for not sending Sophie away or not buying a gun. Or maybe both. And her mom was forced to agree that living next door to where a murder just happened was probably, ironically, a really safe place to be. Anyway, they let her stay.

Sophie thinks it must be awfully hard work being an adult. It seems to take so long to figure out simple things.

She switches off her toothbrush. But all she hears through the wall is the rush of water.

.

4

Someone has torn a ragged hole in the tightly woven fabric of Jill's world, and she can feel the chaos outside threatening to rush in. Jill believes in flossing, daily workouts and a solid domestic love. Hers is a life formed by effort and underpinned by the comfort of the commonplace. She has no affection, or affinity, for mystery.

She begins cleaning up the breakfast things, making a cup of tea, trying to settle herself. As she moves about the kitchen, she can feel the heat of the day in spite of the A/C, even through the triple-paned windows, the blinds closed against the sun. (They can well afford the extra load on the air conditioners, but Jill grew up on the family ranch when it was a lot of dust and a few saguaros, long before her dad formed a partnership with a developer and began raising houses on most of the acreage. She is frugal.)

Just as Jill finishes putting things back in order, Winnie—hair wet and slicked back, eyes red, wrapped in Jill's second-best terry robe—creeps into the kitchen. Jill notices that the robe is hiked up under the belt so it won't drag on the floor. And the matching slippers are much too big.

"Hi," Winnie says in her soft, little girl voice. Just one word, but she sounds unsure of her welcome. She looks around uncertainly, searching perhaps for a coffeepot, a chair, a friend—a doorway to something beyond last night's events.

"You slept," Jill observes. "That's good."

"Yes...I guess I did. Thanks for the pill."

She sits down at the table (in Charlie's place, Jill notes, and then scolds herself for being both rigid and uncharitable). Partly to make up for it, she grabs a mug and pours coffee.

The girl nods her thanks and takes the cup but doesn't raise it to her lips. Her words seem reluctant, as if she doesn't really want to ask the question. "Is there any news?"

Jill has caught more than one local newscast. She knows that, although still nameless in the press, Winnie is suddenly notorious. The promotional visuals haven't been much—just stand-ups in front of Pergama's closed gates. But the voice-overs have been grabbers. "Houseguest stumbles over body in living room of foothills mansion." (We live in large houses up here, Jill thought, but hardly mansions.) "Claims not to know identity of murder victim. News at noon."

But she supposes that's not what Winnie means. "I haven't heard a thing," she says. "I can't see your aunt and uncle's driveway from here, but my husband tells me that people have been in and out all morning, and my daughter saw the forensics van leave about an hour ago." Feeling a need to explain, she adds, "Sophie—that's my daughter—likes detective shows."

"Oh." The girl's voice is almost inaudible. "Are the police still there?"

"I think so."

Knowing that the sheriff's people are still next door should reassure Winnie, Jill thinks. Instead, she seems even more upset. When she speaks, it's a painful whisper. "I have to go back there."

"It's a crime scene. You can't..."

The girl's body is rigid, but her voice shakes. "I have to."

As a dentist, Jill sees panic every day. And Winnie has all the signs. Her hands are clenched around her coffee cup. Her spine is curved protectively over her core. Jill is driven to say something, anything, to break the spell. "So..."

"What do we do?"

Jill doesn't know what the girl means. There isn't anything for them to do. "Nothing."

Winnie jumps to her feet and stands facing the window that would overlook the back corner of the Nelsons' if the blinds were open. "It's not that I want to...but...what else can I do? All my things are there. I don't have any money. Aunt Mary said I could... I needed to..." She visibly steadies herself. "I was going to live the whole summer out of their freezer."

Jill normally would rush to hug someone in such distress. But something about Winnie's back is implacable, as if only her self-reliance is holding her together. "It'll be okay," Jill finally says in the calming voice she uses with her patients. "You're all right."

Winnie doesn't reply.

Jill makes what she thinks is a sensible suggestion. "Why don't you call your parents?"

"I'm twenty-three years old!" The words are hoarse and edgy, a strangled shout.

"You're still a student. You're still their child."

"I can't."

"Sure you can. They'll want to know you're safe." Jill grabs the portable telephone from the kitchen desk, holds it out to Winnie. "Here."

Winnie turns, faces Jill. Her face is red, features distorted, tears starting in her eyes. "They're dead," she blurts. She pushes the phone away. The movement is abrupt, and takes Jill by surprise. The telephone crashes onto the travertine floor. Winnie collapses onto a kitchen chair and buries her face in her hands. Her shoulders shake with barely controlled sobs.

Jill recovers her own composure, hands the girl a tissue and lays her hand over Winnie's. She feels like an insensitive fool. And the wound seems so fresh. "It was recent?"

The girl nods. She speaks without looking up. "I...uh," she stammers, as if acknowledging the tragedy means reliving it. "I...uh...I don't...I can't...talk about it."

"But didn't they...don't you...have other family? Resources?"

Winnie shakes her head. "Aunt Mary and Uncle Ed are my only relatives. And we were never close." She lowers her sheltering hands, wipes her eyes. "The political thing, I guess."

Political thing?

The girl holds her head high, as if pained but proud. Tears roll down her face. "My parents were activists. They spent their whole lives living on nothing."

The Nelsons are to the right of Attila the Hun. Even in a conservative community like Pergama, their opinions are extreme. Jill can see how a rift would have been inevitable.

Winnie keeps talking, the words pouring out. "I've been going to school on loans and grants. I've worked full-time every summer since I was fifteen. So when Aunt Mary sent a card after Mom and Dad died and invited me to come visit any time... Well, I knew she didn't mean it... it's the kind of thing you say at a time like that, when you're being polite to a great-niece you've never met... But I wrote back and she answered and... it was so nice to have relatives no matter what my parents thought of them... And when she mentioned their trip, I offered to housesit." Winnie pauses, breathes, slows down. "So that was the plan. I'd watch the house all summer. And then I'd spend a week with them when they returned. Before going back to school."

She sighs, a sound somewhere between release and longing. "It's so beautiful here. It would have been so nice, with just my books and the pool."

It must be tough needing a rest at twenty-three, Jill thinks. She shudders inwardly as her imagination places Sophie's face on the young woman in front of her.

Winnie is visibly calmer, but Jill knows how she must be feeling. "You're safe here for now." It's all Jill can say and be honest, but it seems such a limited response to this bereft creature, like the flowery verse in a sympathy card—well-meant but of little real comfort.

"Thank you." Winnie reaches for a fresh tissue and brushes away a few last tears. She blows her nose. Then she picks up her coffee cup and finally takes her first sip. "You have a lovely home. But you know that, don't you?"

While Jill is still pondering how to respond to such an unexpected, if true, observation, Charlie wanders into the kitchen. Grabbing a diet soda out of the refrigerator, he smiles at the two women. Jill knows he sees her, and he sees her with love and in the way of long habit and years of late Sunday mornings at the same table, which means he seldom notices her appearance. She's all right with this. It allows her to wear her favorite ratty t-shirt, to stumble in for coffee with her hair uncombed and her facial muscles not yet in working order. It's what marriage is about.

At the same time, she can't help but realize that he *sees* Winnie. And she doesn't think he sees her as a crumpled, sniffling person to be pitied. Suddenly, Jill doesn't see Winnie that way either. Suddenly, Winnie's back seems straighter, her hair blonder, eyes no longer bloodshot but moist, semi-precious aquamarine. Her breasts are, for the first time, evident (and evidently perky) under the thick terry cloth. Her mouth is not anguished, but piquant. And one too-large slipper has fallen from a dainty foot that can't help but draw attention to a gorgeously formed leg that shows to mid-thigh (and great advantage) through the front opening of the robe.

All Charlie says to this fantastic being is, "Good morning." Then he stops seeing. Jill watches him do this. Charlie was unprepared when he entered the kitchen. He was merely a man, primeval and testosterone driven, for perhaps thirty seconds. Then he went back to viewing the world through the eyes of a husband.

#

The rest of Grady's Sunday is a blur of beer, bad old movies on TV and the occasional burst of gas from Bear. The Shepherd's digestive system produces aromas that make you sit up and take notice no matter how far into apathy you've fallen. And Grady has fallen pretty far. It doesn't help that his mind keeps tracking what they'll be doing now, his old buddies: the usual surveying of the usual suspects, the calls to the morgue, the discussion of the forensic evidence, the speculation about overtime. Pain in the ass, he tells himself. Anyone'd be better off in the private sector. Like me. That's where I am. Smack in the middle of the old private sector.

Which was never where he planned to be.

Finally, he pulls himself off the couch, locks the door to his tiny "guesthouse," in reality just a fancy name for a garage-sized house behind a larger one, makes his way out of his patch of dirt and through the general litter of the main yard and walks down the street to Safeway. He picks up kibble for Bear and a barbequed chicken for himself, biscuits for Bear and a fresh bottle of booze for himself.

It is still 95 degrees at ten o'clock at night, but when he gets back to his place, the swamp cooler is blowing away and Bear is all but shivering. A swamp cooler is the poor man's way of surviving the heat. It's cheap, and it works until the humidity rises—which means that it doesn't help at all during July and August. When the summer rains come, he and everyone else in this central-city neighborhood of cheap apartments, tiny stucco-covered shacks and the occasional semi-reputable single family house will baste, stewing in their own juices.

I'm too old for this, Grady thinks as he pours out chow for Bear and whiskey for himself. I should be cruising through life right now, on course for a pension and some land outside of town. I should be keeping cool all year long.

But he isn't. So he dozes off to an old Bogart movie and finds himself back in the snow field and his ice axe is gone and his left foot is gray and his hands are numb, until he wakes up enough to pull a blanket over himself. Then he falls asleep so soundly that he has to let Bogie solve his own problems and work out his own fate.

31

5

All emergency rooms look alike. Grady sits in a hard plastic chair behind curtain number six, watching his mother's chest go up and down.

For years, Virginia Grady has been in a holding pattern, breathing two liters per minute of oxygen 24/7, her lungs kept functioning by an assortment of inhalers and pills that eat up most of Grady's pay. That's the norm. Then there are the crises.

She was gray and listless when they brought her in. Two hours, one chest x-ray, a breathing treatment and some I.V. antibiotics later, she is unconscious, but it's sleep, not the fringes of coma. They're waiting for a bed. Grady knows the drill from this point. Several days in the hospital, then weeks of recuperation at home.

God, he needs a smoke. He makes his way to the exit, stands under the entrance canopy and lights up. The sun is still low, but it must be over 90 already. A lizard skitters across a patch of gravel. A bent old woman holds a red umbrella over her head as she inches toward a bus stop.

He takes a deep drag. He's baking, but he has half a Marlboro to go.

A blue Toyota pulls into a parking spot, and a woman gets out.

Something about her—maybe her walk, maybe her build, maybe just his need—reminds him of Frannie. Shit, he's pathetic today. Must be all this medical stuff.

But he sure could use a sibling right now. Forget the money, the work of caring for his mother. Just to have someone to share the pain with—what a thing that would be. To have Frannie back.

She was way too young to die, his kid sister. He wasn't there when it happened, but the mental picture is indelible. Frannie, a pony-tailed, vibrant thirty-four, off on a married woman's toot, sitting happily next to her husband, Jerry, in his new red Miata (top down, radio blaring)—as he swerved to miss a joyriding teenager in an old pickup. And slammed the car into an underpass. Grady was on a case, interviewing a rape witness down in Sierra Vista. His partner held Frannie's hand while they cut her out of the obscene mix of twisted guardrail and car, blocking her view of Jerry with his head caved in and his face turned to blood and bone.

By the time Grady got there, she was gone, leaving behind a daughter on the brink of adolescence. Now that brink was the edge of a chasm. Gina was a drunk by thirteen, an addict by fourteen, on the streets before her eighteenth birthday.

A decade without Frannie. Gina has tried all the programs, he has to give her that. She cleans up, comes home for a while—her grandma always takes her in. But it never works. The television disappears, or the microwave. Gina even stole her grandmother's wedding ring. And when Virginia said, "No. There is no more money," she slapped her grandmother across the face.

"Maybe it's in the genes," he thinks as he stubs out his cigarette. Most of the time, he can draw a line between his habits and Gina's. Other times... The sun is climbing higher in the sky, the mercury heading for triple digits. He turns away from the glare and goes back to his mother.

#

Six hours later, Grady is still running on cigarettes and vending machine coffee. When he stops at his office before going to the nearby taco joint for a very late lunch, he isn't expecting to do more than drop off his briefcase and maybe leaf through the mail.

But as he pushes open the door to the low-end executive suite, the receptionist flags him down. "Hey!" she yells, as he rushes by. She's waving a wad of small pieces of paper. They're phone messages. And they're his.

"Off the hook," she says, gesturing at the telephone. "All day. They say your voice mail is full. And when it's full, it bounces back here." The phone rings. She glares at it.

Grady flips through the slips of paper. Reporters. Board members from Pergama and every other community under his umbrella. Residents he's heard of and many he hasn't. Notes of repeat phone calls with "pissed" scrawled helpfully across a few. He can only imagine the backlog on his pager and cell phone—both of which are in his briefcase, turned off as they have been all morning. No. Longer than that. He dumped them in there after the Pergama meeting yesterday. Just hit the off switches and got on with his life.

Not that he'd have been much more reachable with the damn things on. Most people are stuck with the office number—and voicemail. He gives board members his pager info; presidents get the cell phone. But only his mom, Jill and a few others have his home number, which, in fact, is listed in the name of his dog (a move he made when the media was hounding him during what he now thinks of as the purge of Jack Grady). Mr. P. Bear (for Papa, not Pooh) has since built a credit history that attracts several offers for pre-approved credit cards each month.

Shit.

As far as Grady is concerned, there was a dead body, he was called, he saw the sheriff's department doing its thing, he reassured the residents. That should have been the end of it.

It never occurred to him that these people wouldn't get it. In law enforcement, there's a clear division of labor. You do your part, turn it over to the next guy, go home.

Grady's well aware that his former colleagues on the force think his job is a joke. And they're mostly right. It's a post-retirement gig that a newly retired detective, Roger Calthorpe, cobbled together out of the 9/11-fueled paranoia of the area's wealthy residents. Then, a few months after assuming his new position, Calthorpe came into unexpected money and took his inheritance down to Florida, gifting the job to Grady.

Common wisdom was that Grady was a drunk and a fuck-up. Calthorpe didn't care. Grady took a bullet for him once. (It got Grady in the shoulder, it would have gotten Calthorpe in the head.) And if the sacrifice was inadvertent (no secret), the job was a way of repaying the debt. Grady's stumble in a dark hallway saved Calthorpe's life, and Calthorpe's casual handoff of a position with an impressive title and four grand a month saved Grady. He climbed mostly out of the bottle, took his two sport coats to the cleaner and became respectable again.

For more than a year now, he's had an identity—Security Director for the Association of Catalina Foothills Communities—and a salary. The duties mostly involve hiring and managing gate guards, producing dull-as-dirt safety reports and attending homeowners' association meetings, where he tries to stay awake through nasty fights over growing trees that block views.

Occasional concerns, even a few outright complaints, about Grady's lack of accessibility have been the only dark clouds on the horizon of his new career. So he can't ignore the stack of messages. But a man has to eat (something the force understood). He has the cell. He'll return calls over lunch. And if people pick up the number through caller ID, he can always change it later, in the name of security.

#

Tito's is dark and cool. Grady sits in a back booth with combination #2 (carne asada with rice, beans and flour tortillas) spread out in front of him, two Coronas mid-table. The beer is getting warm; the food, cold. After 45 minutes, he's still on his first phone call. People are nearly hysterical with fear, Doris Asprey says. And while she thinks that is an over-reaction, as president of the Pergama homeowners' association she has a responsibility to take their concerns seriously, and since he is their head of security and this is a security issue...

"What about the sheriff's people?" Grady manages to ask. Not responsive, Doris tells him, not responsive at all. (Grady can imagine. He figures Andy Davis was friendly to the first few callers, terse to the next dozen and outright rude after that. Yup, unresponsive.)

He flips through the messages as Doris talks. Sure enough, there's one from Davis at 9:45 with big quotation marks drawn around Andy's words: "Get these x#& people off my back!"

The cell phone beeps to let him know it's dying, and Grady digs through his briefcase for his spare battery. He had one in there at some point—he's sure of it.

Which was why he doesn't see them walk in. In retrospect, he thinks that if he hadn't been distracted, he might have had time to make a break for the men's room. Which might have been a smart thing to do.

Jill is leading the way, with that girl from the Pergama crime scene, Winnie, dragging along behind her. Doris Asprey is still talking: "Jack, can you hear me? Are you there?"

"My battery's dying," Grady says. "I'll call you back."

Jill looks pointedly at the Coronas. "I suppose it's the cocktail hour somewhere in the world."

Grady glances at his watch. "Off the coast of New York," he says. "Out in the Atlantic. On a sailboat."

Jill snorts. "You've never been on a sailboat in your life."

"Nice image, though," Grady slings back. It's an exchange reminiscent of the last days of their marriage—although conducted at much lower volume. He gestures at the carne asada. "Want some food? Doesn't look like I'll get a chance to eat it."

Jill waves Winnie at the bench opposite Grady, and the girl slides in slowly and reluctantly, pressing all the way up against the wall. Jill sits down next to her.

Grady doesn't feel the need to begin a conversation. And the women across from him are silent—one clearly gathering her thoughts, the other... He recalls Winnie's adorable factor, but intellectually rather than in his gut. Today, she is less a helpless kitten than a shriveled, rabbity creature, nervous in a way that calls up dark places and skittering noises and...fear. That's what it is.

Finally, Jill takes a deep breath. She lays her hands flat on the table as if they're her cards. "Okay," she says. "I've only got a few minutes. I'm supposed to be prepping Marcy Dalton for a crown right now."

Grady picks up his fork, takes a bite of refried beans. "How'd you find me?"

"Your receptionist. She says you're very predictable."

Grady takes a bite of rice. Jill glares. Knowing she expects him to put the fork down, Grady keeps eating.

Finally, Jill caves and begins talking. "The police came to see us..."

"Sheriff's department." Grady interjects.

"Whatever. The police came to see us yesterday. Twice. The first time, they talked to all of us, except Sophie really—they only spoke to her long enough to confirm that she slept through the whole thing. The second time, they just wanted to see Winnie. They took her into Charlie's study and interviewed her..." Here she turns to Winnie for the first time since they sat down. "Is that what they called it?"

Winnie nods, and Jill continues. "They interviewed her for about an hour and a half."

"Two hours." Winnie's voice is faint, squeaky.

"And they hinted they might want her to come down to, whatever you call it, the department, their offices, today."

Grady has moved on to the shredded beef. He speaks with his mouth full. "The station."

"Yes," Jill says with more than a hint of tightly controlled sarcasm. "The station."

It seems to him that it's bad form to be so clearly annoyed by someone you evidently want something from. But, he guesses, Jill pretty much can't help it where he's concerned.

"I can't believe it. This poor girl, all she's been through, no family...a stranger in our community...and instead of doing what they're supposed to do, they're harassing her."

Grady just keeps eating. He notices Winnie eyeing his untouched glass of water and shoves it over at her. She grasps it in both hands with the uncertainty of a small child forced to deal with adult-sized objects and takes a sip.

"So," Jill finally says, "we need a few things." Grady watches her prepare to tick them off. Here is another Jill he knows: the organized Jill, the determined Jill, the Jill who was number one in her class at USC dental school. "First, we need to know what Winnie should do."

"About what?"

"About a lawyer. Should she get one?"

"I dunno. Does she have any money?"

Winnie shakes her head miserably. "No," Jill says.

"Well, then I guess she shouldn't." Winnie looks so limp that he relents. "Look, if she was a serious suspect at this point, they'd have hauled her in. Odds are they're fishing. They haven't got a clue, and unless the guy was killed somewhere else..."

"Was he? Killed somewhere else?"

"You know damn well I'm not in on the forensics."

"But? There is a but in your voice, isn't there?"

Grady concedes that there is. "It looked to me like he died where he fell and he fell where she found him. It was obvious from the blood. And it looked to me like it would have taken someone a hell of a lot bigger than Ms. Pearson here to take him down."

"So?"

"So they're looking at her because she was the only one there."

"Except the murderer."

Grady shrugs. Jill is clearly frustrated by this conversation. He gives her a moment to get over it before he speaks. "What else?"

Jill goes back to ticking off points. "Two, what about her stuff? Everything she has with her, which is practically everything she has in the world, is at the Nelsons'."

"And she needs it?"

Clearly, it's obvious to Jill. "Yes, she needs it."

"Then she should go over and get it."

"Can she do that?"

"Probably. A crime scene isn't sealed indefinitely. Only until the techs have done their thing. Given the income level of the neighborhood, I'd say they've focused a lot of energy on this one. They're probably done by now."

The third thing is a place to stay.

#

As Jill leaves her ex-husband and former house guest in the restaurant, she knows that Grady caught her on that one. She used her child as her excuse, saying, "This isn't good for Sophie." And she meant it. But she saw Grady's veiled disbelief and realized he knew that Sophie could cope handily with a little temporary excitement.

She's grateful that he kept his opinion to himself. He has no right to judge her, after all. Even if what she was really saying was that she wanted her family's life back. And that for some reason—maybe her discomfort with the events of Saturday night, maybe innate selfishness—getting Winnie out of the house seemed urgent. Jill sympathizes with the girl's predicament, but there are limits (in this case, somewhat unexpected ones that she has discovered within herself).

Tucson's June light blasts her as she walks the short distance to her car, and, perhaps as a small penance for her lack of charity, she delays putting on her dark glasses and takes the full force of the sun. June is her least favorite month. The local thermometers hit 117 one year. 105 is more normal, but 110 isn't unusual. There is never any rain. Even for a native, June is tough.

The inside of the Mercedes would fire clay. "Give yourself a break," she mutters aloud as she folds the silvery shield placed in the windshield to shelter the dashboard and cranks up the air conditioning. "You're only one person. You're not social services." Feeling a little better, she sets her mind to the afternoon's dental work and pulls into traffic.

6

Grady can't believe he let Jill get away with dumping the girl on him like that. But he's stuck, no doubt about it.

The first thing he does is pick up his dying cell phone and call Andy Davis, who isn't so sure that he wants to see Winnie again, at least not today. And he confirms he's done with the crime scene. "Sure, she can go in there," Davis says. "She might not wanna, but she can."

Winnie is huddled in the corner of the booth. She looks as if she's trying to disappear. Grady thinks he should probably ask if she's eaten: she seems too frail to be skipping meals. But subbing for a parent isn't the sort of thing he's good at. Look how Gina turned out. So he just shoves the half-empty basket of tortilla chips in her direction. After a moment, she picks out a chip and takes one slow, tiny bite, then another.

"I guess I have to go to Aunt Mary's." It's somewhere between a statement and a question. Her voice is low, shaky, almost a whisper.

"Yes," he says. "You do. But not alone."

He sees a blink of relief. He dumps the dead cell phone and message slips in his briefcase and thumps it shut. Winnie's problem overrides the rest of this mess. Jill saw to that. Doris Asprey will have to go screw herself for a while.

He's in desperate need of a smoke, has a cigarette already in his mouth as he pushes open the restaurant door. Puffing hard, he stews over his continued inability to stand up to Jill. Jeez, they give it up after less than three years of marriage, and almost fifteen years later she's still bossing him around. Jack and Jill, people used to joke. But in the end, just like the nursery rhyme, it didn't work out.

He motions Winnie along ahead of him. In the spotlight of a bright desert day, she is even less appealing. Pale hair fading into pale face, eyes squinting against the glare, small frame lost in a pair of Jill's jeans and a shirt that hangs like a tent. He wonders why Jill draped her in stuff so over-sized when the girl probably could have squeezed into something of Sophie's.

He waves Winnie toward his car. "The white one," he says.

She's off by two, stopping next to the passenger door of a late model BMW, 7 series.

He unlocks the door of his battered Ford Taurus. "I guess you think everyone in Tucson is rich," he says, pushing the hamburger wrappers and junk mail off the passenger seat onto the floor. Winnie climbs in and reaches around for her seat belt, which is stained by some prior owner's crud. Grady grinds out his cigarette in the overflowing ashtray and starts the engine. "Open your window for a minute," he says. "We gotta get some circulation going." He feels the A/C begin to struggle against the superheated air, lights another Marlboro and rolls out of the parking lot.

#

There's a Sheriff's car parked in the Nelsons' drive, nose over to the right, up against the bougainvillea. As Grady and Winnie approach, a long, lank deputy climbs out, drops his cigarette onto the cobblestones of the driveway and grinds it out with the toe of his boot. "Hi," he says. "Lieutenant Davis said I should give you this." He holds out a key to Winnie, who stares at it as if she doesn't recognize the object. Grady takes the key, and the deputy gets into his car and backs out quickly, taking a sprig of bougainvillea (caught in the bumper) with him.

The Nelsons' two-story Mediterranean demi-mansion looks violated. Torn crime scene tape dangles from the porch pillars. Cigarette butts litter the flagstones. A half-full styrofoam coffee cup keeps company in a ceramic urn with a low-spreading palm.

Grady opens the door. Smudged footprints dull the marble floor of the foyer. The house is cool, but the air is foul. Grady expected the stench. Blood. Soaking through the carpet, seeping along the subfloor. Dried by now, no matter how much of it, because this is Tucson after all, but still spreading its perfume of death.

"Wait here," he says to Winnie, and she sits down on one of the low steps leading in from the foyer.

The living room is ghastly. Fingerprint powder blackens sills, end tables, the ornate silver tray that sits on an elegant silk ottoman—any promising surface.

Worst of all is the floor: the thick, cream-colored wall-to-wall is trampled. The area near the main seating group is black with crusted blood. Blood blotches the skirt of the pale blue sofa and blurs the pattern of the Oriental rug that lies under the glass and cherry coffee table.

He goes and gets Winnie. "It's a pit," he says. "It always is when cops go through. Looking for evidence messes things up. Besides, it's just the way they are." He leads her into the living room, thinking that if she sees the worst first, the rest of the house may be bearable.

She stands in the middle of the vaulted space and turns slowly all the way around.

"No one can ever live here again." It's not a question but a pronouncement. Winnie Pearson, penniless grad student, has just condemned the Nelsons' multi-million dollar house.

"Well, actually," Grady says, "there are people who will take care of this."

Winnie looks her question at him.

"There're companies that come in and clean up messes like this."

"Ghouls," Winnie says.

"No," Grady replies. "Just a bunch of ordinary folks busting their butts so people like your aunt and uncle don't have to deal with the crap."

"Just like the rest of life."

"Pretty much."

They sit at the round table in the immense, granite-clad kitchen and drink ice water out of heavy octagonal glasses. Winnie taps one. It makes a solid, rounded "ping." "Crystal," she says. She takes another sip. "Now what?"

"You can have the place cleaned up and stay here just like you planned."

"No," she says, "I can't do that."

"Sure, you can." He'd asked Davis whether his people were in contact with the Nelsons. "No luck reaching them so far," Andy had said. "What a fuckin' complicated itinerary. We keep just missing them. But we've left messages everywhere, so eventually we'll catch up."

"The cleaning crew will be glad to bill your aunt and uncle," he reassures Winnie.

"It's not that," Winnie says. "It's well...what if he, they... What if whoever did it comes back?"

Grady shakes his head. How to explain to a civilian? "That doesn't happen," he says.

He's surprised by the intensity of her response. "Oh. You know that for sure? We don't even know who this...body...was and who did it and why, but you know they won't come back? I can't believe you said that." She puts down her glass and rushes out of the room.

Grady drinks his water and puzzles at the ways of women. God, it's hot. When he and Winnie came in, he opened several pairs of French doors to get cross-ventilation going and felt obliged to turn off the A/C rather than try to cool the whole outdoors (as his mother would say). But the June wind blowing through the house is bringing in the heat without making a dent in the smell.

He gets a little more ice water. Then he picks up the phone on the kitchen desk and calls his mother. He'll visit this evening, he promises, sorry she's there in the hospital all alone. Don't worry, she says. I'm fine. He hangs up and calls the nurses' station. She's doing better, they tell him, but won't be going home anytime soon.

He finds Doris Asprey's number in a Pergama directory sitting next to the phone and pushes the buttons. A recorded voice tells him the Aspreys aren't home right now, but if he'll just leave a message at the tone, they'll be delighted to... He hangs up.

He drinks some more water and decides the Nelsons won't mind a little smoking, given the covering aroma of decay. He waits through two cigarettes. Finally, he goes looking.

He finds her in a glassed-in room that juts off the front of the house. The room is full of potted trees, striped upholstery and (to Grady's eye) clashing, but obviously color-coordinated plaid and floral print throw pillows. A shiny baby grand piano occupies the far corner facing the windows. Winnie is sitting at it, her hands resting lightly, and silently, on the keys.

"You know," Grady begins, "I'm just a guy. I say what makes sense to me."

He watches the back of her head bob. A nod. He makes his way to the piano.

A Yamaha. He's heard they're hot. "Move over," he says. She scoots along the bench, and he sits down next to her. "Most of the time I mean well," he says.

She nods again. "Do you play?"

"A little." He tosses off a brief boogie beat with his left hand. "I was in a jazz band in high school. I have a crappy memory for music, though, and I can't improvise worth shit. I need to look at the notes. So no career there. But, jeez, it was fun."

"Jill said you used to be a cop."

"She never could keep a secret." He runs his fingers over the keys in a little arpeggio. Nice action. Very responsive. Bright but mellow tone. "This is some piano."

"Good?"

"Yeah. Very."

"Do more."

So Grady plays. He plays the only three tunes he knows by heart: *Bill Bailey*, *Kansas City Stomp* and *Moonlight in Vermont*. (When he hits the first few notes of that one, Winnie smiles, "So you're a romantic.") She keeps smiling and moving gently to the music, so he plays his few songs for her over and over as the hot breeze blows, the smell fades into the background and the sun goes down.

#

This is how Sophie sees them. She's cutting through from Megan's again, trying to beat dusk. She doesn't have any water with her, and that's against the rules even for a short distance, especially this time of year. "Remember, the desert kills," her mom always warns out-of-towners when they talk about hiking. But then she reassures them it normally only kills the stupid (Sophie's word, not her mom's—which is "foolish"). And it kills the helpless. Sophie knows what she means. Last year more than 130 illegal border crossers, including little kids, died in the desert south of Tucson.

And even if she had water, she's not supposed to be bopping around alone (even in their subdivision—*especially* in their subdivision) because a man was found dead (murdered!). She is supposed to be getting a ride. But Megan's mom is out of town, and the housekeeper can't leave until Megan's dad gets home, so no one was there to drive her. In short, Sophie lied. If she's late this time she'll definitely be grounded, and being grounded is a huge pain in the...ass... She thinks to herself, "I may not be allowed to say "ass," but I'm almost thirteen. I can think it."

She's running through her mental list of other words she's forbidden to say but feels she can give herself permission to think when she draws parallel with the Nelsons' music room. Is that Uncle Jack? He isn't her uncle, of course, but she's mostly allowed to call him that since her mother doesn't seem to care about him at all—

except for once in a while when she gets really annoyed. Then all of a sudden it's, "That's Mr. Grady to you."

Sophie stops behind a tall, multi-armed saguaro. She hears piano music, not classical, but the old-fashioned kind just the same. She makes a quick move to the back of a large rosemary bush. She has to crouch, but it's not as prickly as the saguaro, and she can peek around the edge.

Yup. It's Uncle Jack all right. And Winnie. Sophie is puzzled by Winnie. Around Sophie's mom, Winnie is small and thin. Her back curves like she has that disease where they make you wear a brace. Around her dad, Winnie is rounder; her arms and legs are longer, and her eyes aren't scrunched together. Alone, standing in the kitchen looking out the window when she doesn't know Sophie's in the doorway, Winnie is straight; she has square shoulders.

Now, Winnie is sitting on the piano bench next to Uncle Jack, moving to the music, smiling a little. And every once in a while, when Uncle Jack hits a wrong note (wrong enough so that Sophie can tell even though she doesn't know the songs), the smile has a little break in it.

Not that Uncle Jack notices. His eyes are on his hands except when he closes his eyes and sways (kind of like that old blind singer, Stevie something-or-other). He usually doesn't keep his eyes shut very long, though, maybe because that's when he hits more of the wrong notes. He has a cigarette hanging out of the corner of his mouth. The Nelsons won't like that, Sophie thinks. Nobody in Pergama allows smoking in the house. As she watches, Uncle Jack takes the cigarette out of his mouth and flicks the ash into what looks like a water glass. Yuck!

Okay, Sophie's thinking as she moves off toward home, there was a dead guy in there Saturday night. And now it's Monday and no one knows who killed him, and maybe the detectives know who he was and maybe they don't, and here's Uncle Jack and this girl sitting there and playing some dumb old music. And she swears to herself that when she grows up, whatever else she does, she'll try to always make at least some sense.

She figures she has only a couple of minutes before her mom will be calling Megan's to find out where she is, so she's moving quickly. You don't run through natural desert landscaping, Sophie discovered when she was very small and her mother had to pull more than fifty cactus spines out of her right palm with a pair of tweezers. But you can kind of lope, if you're very careful and ready to move sideways—or stop—at any time.

Because it is that funny time between day and night and because she is moving so quickly, she almost misses it. She only sees it because she's concentrating so hard on every detail of her surroundings—in order not to get poked. The prickly pear cactus and Texas ranger are thick. There are even a few cholla, known as "jumping cactus" because the needles seem to jump into your clothes, or your skin. As she moves carefully past a low-lying prickly pear, something glints. She bends, and uses a twig to push a lobe of the cactus aside. It's a key. She picks it up, shoves it into her pocket and covers the last couple of hundred feet to her front door.

"Hi!" she calls breathlessly, pushing the door open.

"There you are!" her mother calls from the kitchen. "I was about to send out the bloodhounds. Five minutes till dinner."

Sophie bops downstairs, dumps her backpack on her bed. She's grungy, and even though she was careful there are a few cactus spines in her jeans. When she pulls them off, the key falls out onto the floor. She picks it up and examines it. It's gold-colored, long and funny-looking. She stows it in her jewelry box and goes into her bathroom to wash up for supper.

It never occurs to her that she should mention her find to anyone. For one thing, it's just some stupid lost key. For another, that would mean admitting that she found it outside the (murder!) house when she was supposed to be sitting with Megan in the back seat of a Mercedes S500 gliding gently over Pergama's speed bumps toward her front door while Mrs. Kaplan told her (as always), "Say hello to your mother. I really should see her about whitening my teeth one of these days."

7

It's full dark outside when Grady stops playing. Winnie reached up sometime earlier and switched on the little lamp that illuminates the keyboard. He's run through every variation on his limited repertoire that he can think of and even tried a couple of pieces he only half knows. Those were less than successful, but Winnie didn't seem to mind.

"Well," he says, standing up. "Okay."

Winnie just sits there at the piano, her back to him, looking out at the night.

"So," he continues. "I guess I'll be going."

She nods without turning around.

"You'll be fine," he says. "Your nose gives up on the smell after a while. Just close the windows, crank up the air conditioning and use the alarm."

She turns, her pale face and hair ghostly in the small circle of light. "You're right," she says, her little chin tilted up bravely. "I'll be fine."

"Oh hell," he says. "Go get your stuff."

He knows she doesn't have money for a motel, and he sure can't afford it. So he does what anyone would do. He takes her home.

#

Grady pulls into the rutted area that serves as his driveway, in past the big house (bigger than his—but nothing to write home about, either), and parks near his front door. The guesthouse windows are cracked open because of the swamp cooling, and he can hear Bear greeting the car. Winnie has two large duffels and a backpack. Making his way around the joyful dog, he helps her bring in the bags

She stands in the space that serves as living room/dining room/kitchen and looks a question at him. "There's no guest room," he says. "Just the couch."

He introduces her to Bear, and she bends to pet him. He notices that she does it right for a big animal, with authority and strength, not like Bear is some sort of yappy lap dog or, even worse, a cat. They pile her stuff in the far corner, and she excuses herself to go change out of Jill's oversized garments into some of her own things.

While she's in the bathroom, Grady takes Bear outside to do his business. He picked up beer and Mexican take-out on the way home. So after he deals with the dog, he begins laying out dinner on the counter that divides the kitchen from the rest of the room.

He doesn't have placemats, but if he wipes off the surface it's reasonably clean. He owns two stools, that's good, and he turns one around to hide the place where the vinyl is torn.

He knows his place is crummy. There isn't really a yard, just some dusty earth with a few scraggly bushes. Not even a cactus. Inside, he has a mattress on box springs and a beat-up nightstand with a wall lamp hanging over it. That's the bedroom. The front room holds a sagging couch, a ratty chair left by a former tenant, his TV set (he doesn't even have a VCR, let alone a DVD player), his turntable and speakers and his boxes of records. The records go back to his early teens and are the only things in his life that are always in order. The mini-blinds are bent, the frig is dented and the bathtub doesn't want to drain.

He knows all this. But he never thinks about it in anything other than a general so-this-is-my-life sort of way. Seeing it through Winnie's eyes—even though, for all he knows, her grad student place back in Michigan is just as much of a rat hole—is different. It makes him embarrassed. And being embarrassed makes him angry. He pops the tops on a couple of Coronas and has slugged them both down before she returns from the bathroom.

"That's better," she says, and he suddenly remembers that he thought she was cute—well, beyond cute—the first time he saw her. She is wearing a pair of shorts that sit down on her hips and a little cut-off t-shirt that barely covers her breasts. She's barefoot.

"Warm in here," she says.

He nods. "Swamp cooling. When the humidity goes up a little, it kind of conks out."

"Humidity? In the desert?"

"We get summer rains, big thunderstorms. We call it 'the monsoon season.' It starts to get steamy in advance—sometimes weeks in advance. Every year, it feels like the rains will never come. But they always do. Eventually."

"So it's a leap of faith kind of thing."

"Yeah. Something like that." He gestures at the styrofoam containers on the counter. "Dinner," he says.

"Looks great." She kneels by the boxes that hold his records, crooks her neck to read the titles on the spines. "Do you think we could have a little music?" She picks Monk's *Round Midnight*, and he puts it on the turntable.

Then she scoots up onto a stool and digs into her food. "God, this is good," she says. "There are places in Ann Arbor that claim to be Mexican, but it's nothing like this."

He finishes his third beer and offers her one. She shakes her head. "I'm not really a beer drinker." She looks at him thoughtfully. "You know what would be great with this? Tequila."

As Grady is telling her he's sorry, he doesn't have any tequila, she climbs down off the stool, digs in one of her duffels and brings out two limes and a bottle of Sauza Conmemorativo. He recognizes the lush, aged liquid from weekends cavorting with Jill long ago in what Tucsonans call "Rocky Point" down in Sonora on the Gulf of Mexico. "I don't think Aunt Mary and Uncle Ed would mind," she explains, "given the circumstances."

At first, they drink the tequila out of two of Grady's mismatched glasses. Then Winnie says, "Do you know how this tastes really good?" And she pours a slug down her throat, squeezes in some lime and sucks salt off her fisted hand. "Okay," she says, "now you." And he pours tequila down his throat and throws in a squirt of lime and sucks salt off his hand.

"Let's try something," she says. And she throws back a gulp of tequila, squeezes the lime and softly places her mouth on his neck at the tender place just above the collarbone. "Umm," she says. "Just sweaty enough."

The phone rings just as Winnie applies her mouth to the other side of Grady's neck. She stretches a free hand behind him to where the thing sits on the counter and unplugs it. Grady reaches for her, but she moves away. By now, the music is Coltrane, the deeply sensuous *Ballads* album, and she moves to the playing as if she is the saxophone itself. "C'mon," she says. "Let's dance."

"I can't dance," Grady says.

She holds her arms out to him. "Sure you can," she says.

And, to Grady's surprise, she is right.

#

Later in the dark bedroom, she hovers over him, her small, round breasts almost glowing in the moonlight that streams in the windows. She smiles, bends down to him and kisses him. As she lowers herself onto him, Grady, gratefully, loses the world.

After, Grady sleeps. He sleeps like he never does any more, deeply and without dreams. If teenagers rev their motorcycles, he doesn't hear. If he needs to pee, his bladder waits. If Bear needs to go out, Grady doesn't know.

When he wakes, it is to bright sunlight glaring through the open windows—and hammering. He pulls the pillow over his head, but the hammering continues. Pound. Pound. Poundpoundpoundpound... A male voice is shouting his name. He swings his legs over the side of the bed, pulls on his jeans and stumbles groggily to the front door. Opens it.

And sees Andy Davis, red-faced and sweating, his unmarked car sitting behind Grady's heap in the yard, its motor running.

"Is she here?" Davis is still shouting.

"Who?"

"The goddamn house sitter." Davis pushes in past him.

"Yeah. I think so." Fog sloshes around in Grady's brain. He is asleep, doesn't want to wake up, staggers back into the house after Davis, with Bear bumping his legs, whimpering, needing to go out.

"Winnie?" he calls.

"Winnie, my ass." Davis is ahead of him, checking out the bedroom, the bathroom.

"Huh?"

"The real Winnie Pearson just turned up."

"Turned up?"

"Yeah. She turned up dead."

8

Grady looks at the color photographs Davis has spread across the desk. A small woman lies curled up in the open trunk of a large car, probably a Caddy. She wears a pink tank top and khaki shorts. The state of decomposition of the visible soft tissue says she is very dead.

Davis indicates one of the photographs, a tight head shot. Short blonde hair. Eyes filmed over and sunken by decay, but once an unlikely shade of blue. Nose swollen and pig-like, but once tiny and up-turned. Teeth jutting from discolored flesh, but once sheltered by full lips. Backdrop of gray felt trunk liner dressed up with a hint of blood.

Grady feels dizzy. For a wonderfully paranoid moment, he wonders if Andy, knowing about the lack of romance in Grady's life, has tricked this up as some sort of bad cop joke. Except Grady isn't a cop anymore, and Davis has better things to do than play games with computers and composite photos and doesn't like him or hate him enough to risk his job doing something so monumentally dumb.

"Found in a long-term parking structure at Metro airport. A favorite dumping spot for certain elements of Detroit's Italian community."

"You don't think this was?"

"Who knows? Every time they find a body out there, it's splashed all over the local news. You don't gotta be Mafia to play follow the leader."

They're in Davis's office. The place is the size of a closet, but since Andy is a lieutenant, at least he has a door he can shut. Grady sags against it now, mug of standard-issue, burned cop coffee clutched in his hands. He feels as if his hold on the cup is the only thing keeping him on his feet.

They rode to headquarters in Davis's unmarked Chevy. Grady is still groggy. He guesses Davis thinks he's hung over, but Grady is all too familiar with his own capacity and is surprised that a couple of beers and a few shots of tequila could put him in this condition. He knows what Jill would say: it's the emotional wallop.

"She'd been dead about a week." Davis keeps spewing out reality whether Grady wants to hear it or not.

"How?"

"Not gunshot. Haven't seen the final report, but the preliminary says closed head injury, probably due to blunt force trauma. A blow to the head."

"How'd they I.D. her?"

"Winnie Pearson—this one—really is a grad student at the University of Michigan. There was a receipt in her back pocket. Library fines. She paid in cash. $2.25. From there it was student records. You know the drill."

Grady nods. He does know the drill. Davis's people were in touch with Ann Arbor law enforcement, checking out the house sitter. She was coming up squeaky clean, Davis says. Then they found the body. Detroit Metropolitan airport is handy to Ann Arbor, less than 30 miles east on I-94.

Davis begins tossing other documents down on the desk, piling them up like stones on Grady's heart.

A student transcript. An apartment lease. A car registration.

A copy of a Michigan driver's license, complete with photo.

Winifred Jane Pearson.

Dead.

She—whoever she is—must have known, Grady thinks. Whatever the hell she's doing here, she must have known how little time she had.

Grady considers what he has. Winnie Pearson "A" (the real one): 61 inches tall, 101 pounds, blonde, blue, birth date April 10, twenty-three years ago. Winnie Pearson "B" (the imposter): to all appearances also 61 inches, 101 pounds, blonde, blue—but maybe a little older? Before she said she was twenty-three, he placed her at twenty-eight. Still young, but with thirty beginning to loom.

A sister? A cousin?

"Do you know who she is?"

"Our 'Winnie'? Not yet. But we will. There's a tight connection."

"Could be a close relative."

Davis shakes his head. "No. There's a mother spending the summer at a cottage in northern Michigan and a father in Oregon. Divorced. Two brothers. No sisters, no female cousins."

They go over it again. Winnie B (now a fugitive) has clothing. She took her backpack from Grady's living room, and the duffels were gone from his bedroom. Money? His wallet is empty. But other than the few bucks that were in there, who knows. Wheels? Her wreck of a car—which is, indeed, registered to the real Winnie—is still in the Nelson's garage with a dead battery and bald tires. That was one reason (Grady tells himself and Davis) that he took her home.

Is she an accomplice? To what? One murder—or two?

"And you slept with her." (Grady has skipped some of the more embarrassing details, but he's seen no point in denying the sexual outcome.) Davis shakes his head. "But whadda fuck did you know? Still, pretty dumb."

"I'm not a cop," Grady reminds him.

"Yeah...right," Davis agrees after thinking about it a moment. "No conflict of interest shit. You get to dip your stick wherever you please."

"One of the few advantages."

Davis shrugs.

Grady knows he doesn't have to justify his behavior but finds himself doing it anyway. "You told me she wasn't a suspect."

"I said I didn't think she killed him." For a moment, Grady thinks Davis is going to continue, but he lapses into silence.

"So where would she go?" The question is rhetorical. "You've checked the airport, the bus station."

Davis's look is dismissive. "Nuthin'."

It isn't usually all that hard to find a fugitive in Tucson. For a metropolitan area that stretches over more than 700 square miles and has no real center, the community is surprisingly tightly knit. The local joke is that there might be six degrees of separation in other parts of the world, but in Tucson there are only two. Everyone knows someone, who knows someone, who knows...

And when this web of connections doesn't turn up the person you're hunting, you check the standard exit routes (not forgetting the shuttles to Phoenix's Sky Harbor airport). You canvass the homeless shelters. You talk to the patrons of those shelters who hawk newspapers at major intersections or hold signs offering to work for food. You query the rental car outlets, the emergency rooms and urgent care centers. You investigate the registries of hotels, motels and bed and breakfasts. You check the campgrounds up on Mt. Lemmon. You put out the word that someone might stumble over something unpleasant in the desert.

All this is only true, of course, as long as you are talking about either your involuntarily missing person or your usual slow-witted slug of a criminal, some low-life with "roots in the community."

With a girl as smart, pretty—and, presumably, desperate—as this one, all bets are off.

Odds are, she just stood by the side of the road and picked up a quick ride out of town. Tucson only has one major highway, I-10, which runs north-south along the western edge of the city, then turns east-west just south of town. Going one way gets you to Phoenix and, ultimately, the West Coast. Going the other takes you through New Mexico to points east.

But there is also I-19, which starts south of the city and leads through the retirement village of Green Valley and the artist's colony of Tubac, winding up after 60 miles or so at the twin border communities of Nogales, Arizona and Nogales, Sonora—the local gateway to Mexico.

So 90% of Grady's brain says that she's gone. She left his bed sometime between midnight last night and the moment Davis pounded on his door this morning. By now, she could be zooming across the panhandle of Texas or sipping a frosty cerveza down on the Gulf of Mexico.

The other 10% says she'll turn up in a hidey-hole as stupid as the guy who shot up the Circle K a few years ago and fled to his girlfriend's, or the gangbanger who hid in the wrong backyard and was chewed by pit bulls.

None of Grady's thoughts would be news to Davis. He's put out the APB, he's doing everything else he can, but he doesn't seem particularly hopeful.

"Somebody'll find her," Davis says. "But the longer it takes and the farther away she is, the worse we'll look. I just hope to hell we get her before the press gets us."

#

The only coffee worse than the thick brown liquid poured from a detective squad pot is the crap that spews out of a hospital vending machine.

Grady suffers through a cup while Virginia eats her lunch. The stuff tastes vile, with chunks of undissolved material. But caffeine is caffeine.

"Jack, dear, can you help me with this?"

He pulls the plastic top off a small container of chocolate pudding. His mother repeats her usual mantra: "I'm so much better today."

Jack looks at the half-done crossword puzzle, the shaking hands, the I.V. taped into her arm, bruising the fragile skin, all the signs that she still has a long way to go.

His beeper goes off—again. He's been trying to ignore it, but this time it flashes the number of the guardhouse at Sungate.

Harry, Sungate's lead guard and Grady's go-to guy for logistics, is apologetic. "Sorry to bother you," he says. "When I couldn't get you earlier, I decided it could wait, but we're just too short-handed."

"Not a problem," Grady says. "Shoot."

"I had somebody quit. Just drove up yesterday morning and turned in his keys and uniform. Said he's moving to New Mexico."

Damn. With the vacation season coming up, he'll need to fill the slot ASAP. Until then, Harry will have to shuffle schedules like mad to cover the shifts for all five communities.

"Who was it?"

"Willis."

Without his willing (or wanting) it, Grady's mind does what it refused to do a little more than 48 hours before. Pulls up an image of a Pergama log sheet.

Shit.

He hangs up, pushes the buttons. Gets lucky: Davis on the first try.

"Willis is gone," he says.

"Who?

"The Pergama guard. Saturday four to midnight. He quit. Said he was leaving town."

"So?" Grady can almost hear the shrug.

"So they came through on his shift."

"Yeah. Maybe. But if they did, he didn't notice. You know how crappy your system is. Couple of guys drive up to the gate, say 'Hi,' guard calls whoever they say they're there to see, gets the okay, sends 'em on up. Saturday nights your people put that arm up and down so often they could do it in their sleep. Hell, I'll bet half the time they are doing it in their sleep.

"We leaned on Willis. We leaned on all your Saturday guys. Shit, you know we did. But either he doesn't remember, or he's too fuckin' embarrassed to tell us he does. And he checks out clean. So let him go. Guys quit you all the time."

The phone goes dead. Grady has to admit that Davis is right about turnover. Filling the guard jobs is no problem, but keeping them filled with people who are at least minimally qualified is. With the low pay and crummy hours, you can't expect a man with anything on the ball to stick around very long. Every guard who lasts has something wrong: lack of smarts, obesity, old age. Something.

"Looks like I'm going to have to go earn my pay," he says to his mother. "Do you need anything?"

Virginia considers. "Well," she says, "they take care of me very well here. But..." She plucks at the hospital gown. "I would like one of my own nighties, and maybe a robe."

Grady knows this about her, knows that she can tune out the constant hubbub, the beeping monitors, the interruptions for vital signs. She will accept with good humor the need to use a bed pan and make a friend out of the grumpiest roommate—but she feels better in her own things. He's ashamed. He missed visiting her last night—for the crappy reason that he was having sex with a young woman who, if not #1 on Tucson law enforcement's hit parade, has unquestionably gold-medaled in the perps-who've-pissed-us-off category. And he didn't even think about bringing a care package.

Par for the course, Grady, he scolds himself. Out loud he says, "Sure, Mom. Your best nightgown. You bet."

The only good news is that the fog has lifted. He's awake at last. But all the bad coffee has created an urgent need to pee.

He steps into the room's attached bath. The seat of the toilet is double-decker, built up for people whose weakened muscles make lowering and raising themselves hard work. A receptacle is positioned to catch—and measure—urine output. He could relocate the beaker, hold the thickened seat up with one hand and do his business with the other. But he is suddenly so sad that all he can think to do is flee.

Then, as he turns, he catches a glimpse of himself in the mirror over the sink. Whether it is the lighting, the events of the past twenty-four hours or simply an unposed, unguarded dose of reality, any illusions he has entertained about looking younger than his years are shattered. His eyes are bloodshot, his stubble gray, his scalp apparent through the faded brown of his overgrown crew cut. He's always had a big-boned kind of ruggedness. Women used to say he reminded them of Harrison Ford (a youthful version, he always hoped). Now all he sees is a wreck of a man.

He slinks back into the hospital room, trying to convince himself that nothing he saw on the other side of the bathroom door is real.

.

9

Jill only takes the call because she is so annoyed. She's mad at Grady for being just as inconsistent as he's always been. And at Doris Asprey, who keeps calling her, for assuming that just because Pergama's security director is her ex-husband she has some responsibility for the man. The way she feels right now, she's furious at the whole damn world.

"Owwagh!" groans Mrs. White, and Jill realizes she has probed that rotting molar just a bit too hard.

So when Wendy tiptoes into the room and whispers that she has a phone call from Mr. Grady and that he won't leave a message and insists on speaking with her, Jill breaks her own rule about the sanctity of a patient's time, grabs a magazine out of the nearby wall rack (an old issue of *Popular Mechanics*), plops it on Mrs. White's lap, gives her what is meant to be a reassuring pat on the shoulder and tells her she'll be back in a moment.

The next treatment room is empty so she picks up the phone there. "Yes, Jack," she snaps. "What is it? I have a patient." Give me half a chance, she thinks, a small excuse, and, by God, I'll castrate you through the phone line.

But when she hears why he's calling, she's stunned.

"They'll find her." She states it as if it's a fact. And then waits for reassurance.

"Probably."

"Her picture must be all over TV."

"Uh uh. The press doesn't have it."

"You're kidding."

"No. They're keeping it quiet."

"Why?"

"I dunno. At this point, they just want to talk to her."

"But they will arrest her." Reassure me, Jack. You've never been good at it, but try... Make me feel better.

"Sure. Plenty of charges they can use."

"So why..."

"This is how it works. You weigh the advantages of plastering someone's mug all over the place..."

"Finding her."

"Finding her more easily, maybe a little more quickly."

"Versus?"

"Versus just how red your face is—and how pissed off your boss is—that you let her get away in the first place."

"God! Talk about getting your priorities screwed up. Male ego. It's awful."

"No. Cop pride. That's even worse."

"And if I go to the media?"

No response. I can do it, she tells herself. I'm not a cop's wife anymore. I don't have to buy into this code of silence. But she won't squeal, and Grady knows she won't. Has known, she understands, since before he picked up the phone.

Odd kind of honor, she thinks, but what she says is, "I won't. Of course, I won't. But give me one good reason, beyond a bunch of embarrassed cops, why I shouldn't."

"Nobody thinks she's going around slitting throats. They don't even have a good guess about what she *has* done. If anything. And she doesn't belong in Tucson. Chances are she's long gone."

As she hangs up, Jill looks at the clock. She thinks about Sophie. Can she catch her at sports camp? Or is this a short day? Yes. So she'll already be at Megan's. Jill hates running late. A couple more minutes and she'll have to numb Mrs. White again. And she can see Wendy escorting another patient into Room 3. Should she have Wendy call Megan's house and check? No. Sophie is fine, and Jill is running the risk of becoming, well, more over-protective than she already is. A helicopter parent. Ugh. It's all too easy to smother an only child.

Still, she'll feel better when they're home with the blinds closed and the alarm on. Even though it's silly. Why does this girl...whoever she is...threaten her so? God knows Pergama is the last place she'll head at this point. And apparently she isn't dangerous anyway. But she wishes Charlie hadn't left on that damned business trip, and to some dot on the map in Maine, of all places.

Shake it off, she tells herself. He'll be back Friday. You'll be home in four hours. And Sophie will be chattering about her tennis serve and complaining about tonight's dinner menu. Right now, you need to get back to work. So she pulls herself together, the efficient lady dentist again, all set to return to Mrs. White. But, first, she goes into her office, opens the small wall safe, reaches into its depths and takes out her gun.

#

In spite of the speech Grady gave Jill about...Winnie? It's hard to stop thinking of her that way, as Winnie, who licked tequila off his skin, made him dance...and used him. Yup, he has to admit, he was used. But God, oh God, how he enjoyed it.

The blue of her eyes, the fur of her hair, like...like the girl curled up stiff and dead, rotting in the trunk of a big black car. Obscene. He's always thought of death—abandoned death like that—as obscene.

Anyway, he's feeling like the world's dumbest asshole.

He tries to give himself a pep talk.

Shit, Grady. So you've been used.

What are you going to do about it?

But he knows there's no point in asking the question because he knows the answer will be the same as it has been for years.

Survive. That's what he'll do about it. Survive.

Not to show her or to spite her, whoever she is. Just out of habit. Like most people. He is in the habit of waking up in the morning, putting one foot in front of the other, doing his job (mostly) and if not paying all of his own bills on time, at least paying his mother's.

He sits at his kitchen table and looks at the phone messages, the ones from his briefcase (yesterday's), the ones he jotted down from his voice mail (last night's and this morning's), the ones the pissed-off receptionist read to him over the phone (yesterday's and last night's and this morning's). Bear is sleeping at his feet. The ashtray is nearly full. The swamp cooler blows its dank air through the room, picking up fragments of ash and whirling them into dust.

He needs to return calls, lots of calls, starting with Doris Asprey. He needs to be a good son. First, he'll finish the calls, pulling his feet out of the fire. Then, he'll go over to his mother's house, pack a few of her things and make his way back to her bedside. No one ever said life would be fun. He rubs Bear's ears, feels the reality of his fur and, just for a moment, remembers how warm last night was and just how long it has been since he had a memory that could have been good to think about.

He decides to allow himself one whiskey, just a quick one, before getting on with business. Little sips at first, and then the rush of fire pouring down his gullet. After the glass is drained, he can't help but take five minutes to feel sorry for himself. And then five minutes more.

\#

Somehow, by parceling out whiskey and sorrow and alternating them with phone calls in which he eats lots of crow and reassures those who will never have enough security in spite of their money, he gets most of it done—the essential parts, at least.

But as he talks with Doris Asprey and agrees with her that, yes, he should be easier to reach, and, yes, the sheriff is absolutely right, this was an isolated incident and none of Pergama's residents are in any danger whatsoever, something keeps nagging at the very back of his mind, tickling him like a small pink tongue peeking out of very white teeth. He's done well on the telephone, reminding the officious Ms. Asprey (subtly, he hopes) that he has a certain amount of equity with the members of Pergama's board because of a burglary ring he broke up a few months after he was hired. It was actually just a bunch of dumb kids and a little luck. He ID'd one of the kids as a resident and called the cops. The kid caved, and then the others fell like a bunch of over-priced dominoes. Because of who they were and the parents they had, there was no jail, just some tastefully supervised probation. No matter. What he did still counted.

He rations the whiskey, speaks with the others he has to and convinces some of them to take on the job of talking with their neighbors. He earns his money (for once), and when it starts to get dark he takes Bear for a walk. He survives.

And all the while it nags.

He isn't used to things pulling at his brain this way. Hasn't done any real detecting in...how many years? Two? No, three. His skills are atrophied, his intuition rusty.

But this won't go away. And, after all, he has to go over there anyway.

#

Even before he comes within a block, he knows his gut is right. He turns off the lights, then the ignition, and coasts to a stop a hundred yards or so down the street.

The place looks the same as always: small, one-story stucco painted white, set well back from the road, shutters a faded teal, wire fence weighed down by time and bougainvillea, the yard not as neat as when Virginia could care for it herself, but the mesquite tree thriving (as mesquites do) and the plants still alive. Grady sees to that, breaks his back every spring repairing the drip system, spends several mornings every summer replacing clogged heads or finding leaks. It has been home to Grady's mother since his dad died, since she sold the bigger house and moved into this one with his sixteen-year-old sister. He was wild then, roaming the streets with his buds, sleeping on any empty couch or with any available girl, getting ready, as it turned out, to settle down and enter the army as so many wild young men did and then, after the army straightened him out, the police academy.

It's a thin line, they always say, between criminal and cop. He never thought they were right. Maybe he started that way, just staying on the right side of the law, but the line became a chasm over the years, to the point where he faced the sinners he arrested over a veritable Grand Canyon, with his righteousness on one rim and their evil on the other. But then Frannie died and Gina went bad, and he stumbled into that canyon, into it and down, to the very fucking bottom.

So he sits, looking at his past and his mother's house. When a light comes on in the living room.

He's surprised. He expected some illumination, anybody would need that, but he assumed that it would be faint, hidden by drawn blinds, perhaps visible only from the back yard.

This is bright, white and right up front.

As he opens his car door, he hears a crashing noise. Then voices, loud—and female. Shouts like: Bitch, and get the fuck back, and whaddya think you're, and who the hell and...

The yelling continues. He runs for the front door—and kicks it in.

10

Gina has her treed.

He sees them the instant he kicks open the door. The girl he still thinks of as Winnie is perched on the wing of his mother's high-backed sofa, way back in the corner, with nowhere to go except straight up the wall or forward into his niece's flailing arms.

Gina is doing the yelling. She's bouncing on the balls of her feet like a boxer. Her right hand holds a butcher knife. "Bitch!" she's screaming. "Whaddaya doing here? Whaddya after? Bitch! Whaddaya doing here..." Her shouts have rhythm, a drug-crazed loop of outrage. She's wearing a faded blue tank top, stained by something more than sweat, no bra, a pair of ragged shorts and flip-flops. Her hair is hacked off, pale roots a couple of inches long now, ends still tipped with the remnants of the dead-black dye job. She's skeletal from uppers and burned brown from too much time on the streets.

As Gina dances around her captive, she shakes, quivering head to toe. Her knife arm, however, is surprisingly steady.

Grady saw "Winnie" react with shock and surprise when he burst into the room. But Gina's focus didn't change. The splintering of the wood, the crash when the door slammed back against the wall didn't deflect her attention one iota. "Bitch! Whaddya doing here, whaddya after? Bitch!"

He calls out: "Gina."

No response.

He walks up behind her, giving her knife arm a lot of room. "Gina."

"Bitch! Whaddya doing here, whaddya after. Bitch!"

"Gina!" he shouts.

Startled, she whirls. He reaches up with his left arm, catches her right wrist, disabling her. She's frozen, but the knife doesn't fall. It remains tightly caught in her grasp. Jeez, she is really wired.

"Gina," he says, using the preternaturally calm voice he developed for use with prospective jumpers, husbands threatening to cut their wives, wives holding guns on their husbands. "Gina, give me the knife."

She shakes her head violently, her ruined hair whipping, her reddened eyes dilated, huge black pupils letting in way too much light, shutting out common sense and rational thought. "No, Uncle Jack. No. She shouldn't be here. She's not supposed to be here."

He keeps his grip tight on her wrist, holding it up over her head. Christ, her arm should be going numb by now. But the knife doesn't fall. There are ways to disable her, but, shit, even if what he's fighting is the dreadful strength of crystal meth, this is Frannie's daughter.

"I know, Gina," he says soothingly. "I know. I'll take care of it."

She shakes her head again, wildly, emphatically, but her grip is weakening. He wiggles the knife out of her fingers.

Still holding onto Gina, he pulls open the top drawer of the breakfront behind him, drops the knife in and slides the drawer closed. Then he eases her into the big corduroy recliner. The tubing that connects his mother to her oxygen concentrator is still sitting where the paramedics left it when they carried her out, and Gina's rear plops down right on the nose piece.

"Arrest her." Gina is still trying, but she sounds weary, defeated. Maybe she's coming down from whatever she's on, maybe it's just a lull. She could go off again at any moment.

"Gina," he says, "you know I'm not a cop."

Gina shrugs. She's becoming lost in her own misery. Not pleasant for her, but at least she's less of a threat.

He turns his attention to the other young woman in the room.

"You don't have to stay up there," he says.

He watches her clamber down. She's wearing the clothes she wore last night, the ones they discarded gradually as they moved toward the bedroom. They left the cropped t-shirt on the living room floor, the shorts on the couch, the lacy underpants...

"Grady..." she begins.

"They found her body," he says.

"Oh!" she says, either startled or giving a damned good imitation of it. "Grady, I..." He makes a dismissive gesture, meant to silence her, and it does. She shuts up. He picks up the portable phone from the small table next to the recliner. The doily that usually lies under it rests on the floor. He pushes "Talk," but there's no dial tone.

"The battery's dead," the girl who used to be Winnie says.

Grady can imagine his mother calling him, barely functioning, her mind slowed by hypoxia, the doily falling to the floor, her hands fumbling, returning the phone to its place on the table out of sheer force of will, never noticing the blinking light warning of the dying battery. He can see her leaning back, gasping for breath, the paramedics removing the oxygen cannula from her nose and replacing it with theirs, lifting her onto the gurney. But the young woman in front of him doesn't need to know this.

"Okay," he says to the girl, "you're going to walk in front of me into the kitchen. And you're going to keep your hands up and out from your body where I can see them." As if she could hide anything bigger than a dime in that outfit.

He can see her trying to stall.

"Look," she says.

He cuts her off. "Shut up. Maybe I'll let you talk after I call the cops. But probably not."

She moves ahead of him through the archway. He can see his

mother's gleaming stove, the table with her special cushion sitting on the chair at its head, the collection of salt and pepper shakers on the shelves he hung for her just after she moved in. He especially likes the two kittens, girl (salt) and boy (pepper), batting their paws at a small red ball of yarn that is forever attached to its ceramic base. He sees the magnets on the refrigerator, the toaster (a mere shape within its pink quilted cover), the coffee mug sitting by the sink... Shards of glass in the sink. He reaches out a hand and flicks back the ruffled curtain.

The girl in front of him shakes her head. "I didn't do it," she says.

He picks up the receiver of the wall phone.

"Uncle Jack!" Gina is standing in the archway. "Do you know her?" The words are an accusation.

"Shut up, Gina."

But his niece has regained some force. "No. I won't. She has no right to be here."

"Neither do you." He feels bad about it as soon as he says it, even though to his mind it's the truth.

Gina explodes. "This is my grandma's house. I can be here anytime I..."

"No, you can't."

"Where is she, anyway?" She looks around, then answers her own question. "The hospital again?"

"Yes."

"She okay?"

"She will be."

He turns his attention to the broken window.

"I didn't do it," the girl in front of him says again.

The window faces the backyard. An obvious way in.

The phone receiver in his hand lets out an obnoxious squeal, telling the world that it's been ignored too long. He reaches up and jiggles the hook, regains a dial tone.

"How did you get in?" he says to "Winnie."

"I used the front door. It was open."

Maybe. It wouldn't have been the first time the paramedics overlooked a detail of property preservation in their rush to save a life.

He looks at Gina.

"This is my own grandma's house," she defends herself. "I should have a key."

"But you don't."

"I'm family. I should," she whines.

Then her mood swings. She's as unpredictable as any other junkie—as any bad drunk, for that matter. She's shouting again. "She's in my grandma's home and she shouldn't be. The bitch has no business here. She's breaking the law and somebody needs to call the cops."

She snatches at the phone, surprising Grady, digging her nails into his forearm, drawing blood with a scratch across his face. Grady grabs her, locks his arms around her, immobilizing her. She gradually quiets. The phone dangles from its cord.

"Why are you here?" Grady challenges her. "What the fuck are you doing breaking your grandmother's window?" He can still see the frenzy in her eyes, but he knows she's hearing him. He pushes her away, back across the kitchen. She falls against the refrigerator, slides down it. "Like I don't know. Look at you! All you want is money! The only reason you ever come here is money!"

"It's not true," Gina wails. She's sobbing, mucus running down her face, a terrible lesson in the downside of junkie-dom. "I love grandma. You know I love grandma." Major amphetamines, he guesses. She has to be using heavy-duty crank. She's bawling now, crying with the abandon of a little girl—or an addict with no point of reference except herself. Her eyes search frantically for a way out.

Grady can't deal with it anymore. "Button it up, Gina," he snarls. Then he breaks one of his few rules. "How much do you need?"

The wailing stops. She snuffles. "Sixty dollars?"

He gives her forty.

She folds the money into her shorts pocket, wipes her face on her arm and makes for the front door.

Can't wait to get out of here, he thinks. Where's your concern for your grandma's property now? He goes after her, reaches out and grabs her arm just as she gets to the front stoop.

"I want you to know something, Gina," he says. "If you ever take anything—just one little thing—that's important to your grandma, I'll hunt you down. Whether she forgives you or not. And I may forget all about who you are."

Just as he regrets his words, just as he thinks about hugging her, she pulls away and is gone.

He pushes the damaged front door shut behind her, shoves a small but heavy chest in front of it.

He hears a sound in the kitchen, rushes through the archway and out the open door wall into the backyard.

The girl is halfway to the fence, backpack slung over her shoulder, running flat out. But the yard is dark. She catches her foot in a gopher hole, drops to her knees momentarily. She recovers quickly, is up and moving again, but her stumble gives Grady the seconds he needs.

He tackles her and she falls onto the grass.

11

He's got her around the legs, expects a fight—but she doesn't struggle. He starts to relax his grip to let them both sit up when he realizes that she's digging in the backpack. Shit!

He moves to stop her—too late. Her hand emerges, holding...a shape in the darkness.

A gun???

He grabs her arms, pushes her roughly face down in the dirt, slams his right hand over hers. "Give it up!" he demands. And she opens her hand. He feels paper...folded bills. No weapon.

"Sorry," she says.

He pulls her to her feet, drags her back into the house. He drops the backpack and the money on the kitchen counter. Looks like about $8, all he had left in his wallet the night before, minus a few bucks.

"Just let me talk to you," she keeps saying as he pushes her across the kitchen toward the side door. "Just let me tell you about it."

Well, there are things to do before he can leave anyway. He sits her at the kitchen table while he tapes a piece of cardboard over the broken window. His mother has to have air conditioning. Grady sees to that, and he doesn't want to pay for any more electricity than he has to. The cardboard will keep the cool air in, but it doesn't solve the security issue. And it might actually rain one of these days. He'll have a smoke and then cover the opening with something more substantial.

"Give me ten minutes," the girl pleads. So he digs in his mother's refrigerator and finds the only alcohol in the house, an open bottle of Gallo Hearty Burgundy that has been in there God knows how long. He pours two glasses and takes a swig. It's dreadful. He sets one drink in front of the girl, opens the door wall, lights a cigarette and stands in the opening, puffing away.

She looks at him.

"No one," he says, "smokes in my mother's house. Not even me."

She nods her understanding.

"Now talk," he says. "Who are you?"

She takes a sip of her wine, makes a face.

"This tastes awful," she says. But she takes another sip.

Grady waits. Finally, she begins.

"My name is Clare Lynn Dorsett. And I am a graduate student, but not at U of M. I go to Purdue. That's in Indiana."

"What's your major?"

"I'm working on a Ph.D. in art history."

"Impressionists, expressionists and all that?"

"Yes, all that."

"Surprised I knew that, aren't you?"

"No. Should I be?"

"Hmmfph." Grady stubs out his cigarette, lights another one. His wine is gone. "And you were in Ann Arbor because?"

"The art fair. They have a big one in July every year. I figured I'd have a great time and gather some material for my dissertation—which I will write eventually. I'm interested in how historical art trends are playing themselves out in these inexpensive commercial venues. I mean, can anyone really do impressionism in a valid way in the twenty-first century?"

"I have no idea."

"Sublets are cheap—another attraction. And, frankly, Ann Arbor is more interesting, even in the summer, than West Lafayette, Indiana."

"So there you were, gathering."

"And starving. I should have been working, but I got there too late. The jobs were gone."

"You were starving."

"I know what you're thinking. You're thinking, fancy grad student, she doesn't know what it's like to be down and out. Well, you're wrong. I do."

Grady knows his body language says, show me.

"I sold some platelets. They're worth more than whole blood. I was getting ready to hock my laptop."

"You're pretty resourceful for an art student."

"Art history."

"Still."

"I've been scrounging for years, Grady. I'm a survivor."

Grady backtracks. "How did you know Winnie?"

"I did my undergrad work at U of M. Her freshman year, I was a resident advisor in her dorm. She had boy problems, I was a good listener. We got to be friends."

"You stayed in touch?"

"On and off. And then we were both stuck in Ann Arbor for the summer. So we hung out."

"What was Winnie's major?"

"She was in business school. She figured someday she might have to actually earn a living."

"Someday?"

"She had parents."

"And you don't."

"No. That part was true."

"And she's dead."

"Yes."

"You knew that."

"Yeah. I... I was pretty sure."

"You saw her die?"

"I... Yes, I think so."

"You think so. You weren't involved in her death?"

"No! Of course not. How could you think that?"

Grady is silent, and she answers her own question.

"I guess it's pretty easy to see how you'd think that." She drains the rest of her wine, sets the glass on the table. "Can I have some more?"

He sits down at the table opposite her, hesitates a moment, then pulls out another cigarette and lights it. The door wall is still open. Most of the smoke will float out into the backyard. And he'll get a fan in here tomorrow, totally clear the air before his mom comes home. He divides the remaining wine between their two glasses.

"Thanks." Her voice is quiet, grateful. Her right hand holds the glass, brings it to her mouth. She takes a tiny sip. The fingers of her left hand are playing with the edges of the place mat that rests in the center of the table. It holds a small pot of violets flanked by a pair of blue candles. Grady cannot remember a time when the candles weren't there, nor can he remember them ever being lit.

"How'd you get here?" he says.

She looks puzzled.

"This place," he says, gesturing at the kitchen, the backyard, the house in general.

"Walked. It's not that far from your..."

"How'd you know where..."

"You told me she was in the hospital, that she lived alone. You were asleep. I looked around. Everybody has papers."

"And I pay her electric bill."

"I would have used your address book, but..."

"I don't have one."

"Right. Your stuff is really in a mess, you know. You don't seem

78

to have a filing system."

"I have a drawer."

"You seem to have parts of a number of drawers. And a few shoeboxes. That's not much of a system."

"It works for me."

They sip at their wine without speaking. Her—Clare's—eyes are roaming the room, maybe noticing how neat it is, how everything has a place, maybe wondering how someone as well organized as Virginia could have given birth to such a slob.

"How'd she die?" he asks harshly.

"I think she hit her head."

"She hit her head."

"They pushed her. She fell backward. There was a fake fireplace. It had a hearth, about a foot high, a tiled thing you could sit on. Or put plants on. She fell against it."

"Where was this?"

"Her apartment. The living room."

"Who pushed her?"

"Them. Some men. I don't know who they were."

"How many were there?"

"Three? Maybe four?"

"But you saw them."

"I saw pieces of them. The back of a head, an arm, a thigh."

"You saw pieces?"

"That's all I got from where I was hiding. Just glimpses."

"Where were you hiding?"

"In the next room. I was there first—before they all came in. I was returning her purse." She takes a deep breath and continues.

"She called me that morning and told me she'd left her purse somewhere the night before. She was frantic. But I had it, so she calmed down. I told her I'd drop it by later in the day. She was going to study, stay home, so that was okay.

"About three o'clock, I decided to take a break. I stuck her purse into my backpack and walked over. It was a hike—she was living in a prime area near campus. I was in the boonies."

"What time did you get there?"

"About four, I guess."

"Then what?"

"She lived in an old house that had been converted. I went in and walked down the hall. She lived in 1B."

"How many apartments in the building?"

"Only four. Two on each floor."

"Go on."

"I knocked on her door, but there wasn't any answer. I knocked again, but it was pretty clear she wasn't home. There was no music from inside, no noise at all. I figured she'd had to run out for a few minutes, and it occurred to me that I had her keys. I decided I should just leave her purse. So I unlocked the door and went in."

"Did you lock it behind you?"

"I don't know...I think so...maybe. I mean, the outer door to the building wasn't locked. It never is in these student places, and that's always made me nervous."

"Go on."

"I decided I'd leave her a note. I knew she kept a scratch pad in one of her kitchen drawers, so I went into the kitchen..."

"It was adjacent to the living room?"

She nods. "The apartment was nice, but it wasn't big. The kitchen was through an archway. With beads. She'd hung it with beads."

She takes another sip of her wine. "I was just starting to open the kitchen drawer when I heard voices outside the apartment—in the hallway. I thought I heard Winnie. And it sounded like there were several men. I started to go into the living room, but then I heard yelling. Like anger. A lot of anger. So I stopped and just stood there in the kitchen, waiting.

"The apartment door began to open, and I realized that something very weird was going on. There were a lot of four-letter words being thrown around, and it didn't sound like anyone was kidding. I was suddenly terrified. I remember my heart was beating so fast I thought I'd have a stroke."

She pauses, looks at Grady. "Fight or flight response," she says. "It's what happens."

When he doesn't react, she takes a deep breath and continues. "I just stood there, not knowing what to do. It sounds like this took a long time, but it all went through my mind in an instant. While I was standing there frozen on the outside and racing on the inside, I noticed that the pantry door was ajar. Well, Winnie called it her pantry, but it was really just a kind of low cupboard. I'm small. I knew I could fit. I crawled in and pulled the door closed—or as closed as I could. It wouldn't shut all the way. There was stuff in that cupboard with me, cans and boxes, something poking me, maybe a spatula.

"I stayed in there, not moving, afraid I'd sneeze or cough. Afraid they'd find me. But they were making so much noise, they'd never have noticed. I realize that now. I could have gotten out and done something. I wish I'd realized that. I wish I'd been thinking clearly."

Grady knows she wants to be reassured, wants to be told that she did all she could, all that anyone could—which, apparently, was nothing. But that kind of dishonesty, kind though it might be, has never come easily to him. When he and his partners ran their good cop/bad cop scenarios over the years, he was never the one to hand out the false comfort.

"You said there was a lot of yelling. What were they saying?"

"The men kept calling her names. Cunt. Bitch. Things like that. They kept saying she was holding out on them and they weren't going to take it."

"Do you know what they were talking about?"

"No. I had no idea then, and I still don't. But they went on and on. And they got louder and louder. I heard more yelling, grunts, groans. It was awful. I don't think I remember all of it. It was hot and cramped in the cupboard. I thought I'd pass out."

"Why didn't anybody hear it?"

"You've never been in Ann Arbor's student ghetto in the summer. It's empty. You can sublet an apartment for almost nothing. People will practically pay you to camp out there and watch their stuff while they go home or travel. Whatever. She was the only one living in the building."

"Did she scream?"

Clare doesn't answer.

"Did she scream?"

Clare nods. Her eyes are wet with tears.

Grady hears Davis's voice in his mind. Davis was laying out the photographs, covering the ugly metal desk with even uglier evidence of a brutal crime. "They found a lot of semen," Davis was saying. "In her vagina, her mouth, her anus. There were rectal tears, bruises. There were at least three of them, and it went on a long time." He picked up one of the photos, indicated the khaki shorts, the pink tank top. "They dressed her," he said, "after she was dead." He paused. "No underwear." He shook his head, put the photo back on the desk. "Yeah, I know. Some go without. But the medical examiner says."

Grady lights another cigarette, letting the act of flicking the lighter, holding the flame to the tobacco and drawing the first smoke into his lungs wipe the thoughts from his mind, praising, for once, the blessed nicotine racing through his bloodstream. Only two left in the pack, he notes. It won't do to run out.

He says to Clare: "You couldn't see what was going on."

"No. I told you. Just pieces."

"But you saw her fall."

"I could see part of the fireplace wall straight on. It was pretty clear, even through the beads. I saw Winnie move in front of the fireplace and two guys come after her. I could only see their backs."

"White? Black?"

"White."

"Short, tall?"

"Both big but not fat. One with dark hair. Curly. There was at

82

least one blond in the room, and I think he might have been taller. But he wasn't in front of the fireplace."

"Then?"

"Winnie was struggling with them, fighting them. She was... she was naked, and she looked awful, kind of banged up. She kept hitting at them."

Clare brings her glass to her mouth, but it's empty. She looks at it briefly, in surprise. Grady reaches over, takes the glass and sets it on the table. He looks steadily into her eyes, waits for her to continue.

"Then one of them—I'm not even sure which one it was, my view was so limited and there were so many arms—anyway, one of them pushed her. He pushed her really hard. She crashed back, down against the hearth. And just lay there.

"The hearth was that hard?"

Clare nods. "Marble. I think maybe it was original to the house, from before it was apartments. And the edge was sharp."

She stops, looks away, maybe at the broken window, maybe at the tempting promise of the door wall leading to the backyard. "You wouldn't have wanted to have a toddler in that apartment," she says. "Too dangerous."

Her eyes are brimming again.

"I knew she was dead."

12

Grady has a little wine left, the dregs. He hands her his glass.

She gestures at the far wall, at the shelves holding his mother's treasures. "I like the salt and pepper shakers," she says. "Very fifties."

He shouldn't let her change the subject. The worst time to let up during an interrogation is when the subject is near the breaking point. That's exactly when you put the pressure on.

He goes over and takes down the battling kittens. Fuck it, he thinks. I'm not a cop.

"She collects them," he says, handing her the kittens. "My sister used to give her a new set every Christmas, every birthday. She always knew what to do for Mom."

Clare holds up the two empty glasses. They're out of alcohol, Grady tells her. She asks for tea. He fills the kettle, sets it on the burner, turns on the gas.

"You can have Lipton or Lipton," he says. "My mother's a traditionalist."

She smiles. "That's fine. You get pretty tired of all this organic, college-town stuff after a while."

She takes her tea with a lot of sugar. He watches her drink two cups while they talk inconsequentials and, mostly, just sit quietly. Then even though he's not a cop, even though Davis will just do this all over again and would be pissed as hell if he knew Grady was interviewing his witness, he returns to the topic. He gets her back into that terrifying cupboard in a campus apartment on a hot summer afternoon. They start where they left off, with Winnie's still-warm body crumpled against the hearth and Clare peering through the crack in the cabinet door.

"They were talking about what they were going to do with her," she begins, "how to get rid of her body. They were talking about plastic garbage bags, wondering whether she had some in the kitchen. I was in the same cabinet as the garbage bags. I had to get out of there. I didn't think I could move, but I knew I had to.

"I was quiet crawling out of the cupboard. No one seemed to hear me. But then I had to get out of the building. There was a window, one of those double-hung ones that you push up. I knew that wouldn't work. It would slide open fine for the first few inches, but then it would stick. Like a bastard, Winnie used to say. All the windows in her place were basically painted shut except for one that she managed to force open in the bedroom to get her fan in. Winnie used to joke that it got hot as hell in there sometimes, but at least she was safe." Clare's voice breaks. Her shoulders shake. She's holding onto the tea cup so hard Grady almost expects it to shatter.

"There were only two ways out of that room: the archway into the living room or the window I couldn't open. The building was old. The windows were single-pane. And Winnie had heavy wooden kitchen chairs. I picked one up and smashed the glass."

"So you're out."

Clare doesn't seem to hear him. Her words are flat, almost mechanical. "I jumped out. Got scratched a little but not really cut. Then I ran. I could hear someone—at least one of them—coming, so I kept going. I looked over my shoulder once, just a glance. He was back there."

"He?"

"One of them. It was starting to get dark, so I'm not even sure which one. But they were after me. That's all I needed to know. So I just kept running." She visibly shudders.

"And you got away."

"I've been jogging for years. I'm in good shape."

Yeah, Grady thinks. Like I haven't noticed.

"I made it out the back gate, down the alley, through another yard. I knew the shortcuts. And then I got lucky. When I got out to State Street, there was a band playing on an outdoor stage and lots of people. I'm short. It was easy to blend into the crowd."

"So you're away. You're safe."

"No! I wasn't safe!" Why would you think I was safe? My friend's lying dead, and the men who killed her are after me! Safe!" The words come out rapidly, piling on top of each other. Clare's gulping, gasping for air.

"Sssh," Grady says in his best imitation of a soothing voice. "Easy there."

"I'm not used to this! I'm just a student," she protests. But she collects herself. He watches her settle down, land at something like normal. At last, she says quietly. "I didn't know what to do."

Didn't know what to do? Where does that come from? "Why didn't you go to the police?"

"What?"

"The police. You know, the good guys."

Clare gives him a look of disbelief. She shakes her head wordlessly. The tears start again, and she buries her face in her hands. Grady waits a moment, then reaches over to move her hands away from her face. At first, she resists, but then she gives in. Holding her hands, keeping them down, but not ungently, he asks again: "Why?"

"Why?" She still seems astonished by the question. "Don't you get it? I told you. Those guys saw me! And they thought I'd seen them. Even though I didn't. And there was nothing I could do for Winnie."

"Justice?"

"You weren't there! You don't know what it was like. I was so scared. And I really couldn't help the police at all. Then I realized I still had her purse in my backpack. I went to my apartment, stuffed some clothes into a couple of duffels and hiked to her car. It was parked about a mile away."

"A mile away from her place?"

A nod. "There was a party the night before. I didn't have wheels, so she picked me up. When I went to leave, Winnie's car was still there, but she was gone. Somebody came running after me with her purse. That's why I had it. She'd left it in the bathroom. I caught a ride home."

"But if you had her purse, you had her car keys."

"No one needs a DUI."

"How'd Winnie get home?"

A shrug. "Some guy, I guess."

"And in?"

Another shrug. "A hidden key, I guess." Clare looks away from him, down at the table, her hands, the ceramic kittens.

"Why did you decide to pose as Winnie?"

"It seemed like it was the only thing that could save me. I didn't have anybody to turn to. A few friends in Indiana. No one in Ann Arbor. No real family. I'm an orphan, remember? I was sure those men would try to find me. But they wouldn't be looking for her."

"And you thought you could get away with it."

"We're the same size, the same coloring. We both have little noses. People always asked if we were sisters. The haircut was easy. I bought some clippers in Toledo. Did it in a motel room."

"You're older."

She nods. "Four years. I took a break during undergrad. Bad idea. I don't advise it."

"I'll keep it in mind. Why run to Tucson?"

"Winnie mentioned she was planning a trip down here. And I found a letter from her aunt in her purse, even a little address book."

"They'll check all this, you know."

"Yes."

"You didn't think the police—or the people who killed her—would figure it out?"

"I pretty much knew somebody'd find dead Winnie in Michigan. Eventually. But who'd have a reason to question live Winnie in Arizona? Her aunt and uncle knew she might not arrive before they left town. And in a few days, they'd be up on a mountain.

"I guess it was some sort of weird illusion. But I thought I could use Arizona as a refuge until I could figure things out. Or until they'd give up. As long as I kept a low profile. Not much driving. No using her credit cards. I did use her ATM card twice, though. I had to. I ran out of money."

"Even cops have computers these days, you know."

"I'm not running from the police."

They sit there in silence. Grady can hear the air conditioner kick on, the faucet he tried to fix only a couple of weeks ago start its rhythmic drip again.

He makes his tone as unthreatening as he can, but it's still a statement, not a question. "You know this doesn't make sense."

"I thought it did. It seemed to... Maybe it was the shock, the trauma, I don't know. And once I was into it..." Clare's gaze has been all over the place, down at her hands, the teacup, the far corner. Now, she looks at him straight on for a quick moment before her eyes retreat again. "You're judging me, aren't you?"

It's a direct question—and an appeal, but he doesn't say anything. If she wants to feel guilty, let her.

"It really seemed like the only thing I could do. Do you think it was PTSD?"

He has no idea, is not sure he's ever understood human behavior except to observe that people can act squirrely when they're so far outside their comfort zone that they have no context. He remembers the young mother who woke up one morning to find her husband dead in bed at her side. She nursed her infant daughter, paid her bills, watered the flowers on her patio, and slept by her deceased husband's body each night until someone in the next apartment complained about the smell.

He brings Clare back to something useful.

"What about the dead guy in the Nelsons' living room? Was he one of them?"

She shakes her head helplessly. "I don't know," she says. "Could have been."

She pauses, picks up one of the kittens—pepper, looks at the little animal, puts it back down next to salt. "Somehow I knew they'd find me," she says, as limp as the tea bag sagging in her empty cup. "I just didn't think it would be so soon."

13

It's been dark outside for more than an hour. Grady and Clare have been sitting in an artificial twilight created by the florescent bulb on the stove. As Clare finishes her story, Grady reaches out and switches on the lamp that hangs over the kitchen table.

"So we'll be going to the police now," he says.

"No." She seems surprised, as if she thinks he understands and that understanding makes all the difference.

"Why the hell not? They're pretty unhappy with you already. Keep it up and they'll be really pissed. I know you're not stupid. What do you have, some sort of weird problem with the authority?"

He thinks he's being forceful, maybe even sounds outraged, but she laughs. "Pot and kettle, Mr. Grady. My 'problem' is a healthy suspicion of the police." My parents were creatures of the 60s. What was that t-shirt, 'Question Authority'?"

"I have to take you in," he says.

"No, you don't. You have no official role in this."

"There are still laws. I've probably broken ten or twelve already."

She smiles, and he remembers the taste of tequila on her skin, the warmth of her breath. "You're a real danger to society," she says.

He wants beer—or Scotch. But there's nothing, so he heats up some more water. Clare insists on reusing their tea bags. "Otherwise, it's such a waste."

He hands her a full mug. She adds sugar, stirs.

"Don't doubt me," he says. "I will do it."

She nods. "I know." She blows on her tea to cool it, picks up her mug and takes a first, tentative sip. Her free hand reaches out and squeezes his. "But we have to go this minute?"

She is so tired, she says, and filthy. She needs a shower or, better yet, a bath. She wants a good night's sleep.

"No dice," Grady says.

But she feels safe in his mother's house, safe with him. It seems like so long since she's felt that way.

Squad cars are safe. The station is secure.

She knows she has to go to the authorities, she says, admits that's what she should have done that night in Ann Arbor. But she's just a scared and foolish witness, not a criminal. What can a few hours hurt? Who will care? Who will know?

He needs to finish securing the place anyway. They walk around the house together, checking doors and windows, pulling shades and blinds. They find a couple of old boards in the garage, and Grady creates a makeshift barrier for the broken kitchen window.

Finished, he puts down the tools and washes his hands, turns out the kitchen light. They can't go out through the barricaded front door, but there's a side entrance off the kitchen through the small laundry area. He gestures toward it.

She looks at him wearily. "Now," he says.

She nods, seemingly resigned. "I need to get my things."

He follows her down the hall to the spare bedroom. "Look," she says, "I was not yanking your chain. I am truly exhausted. I have had, basically, no sleep. And, well, facing this is a big deal." Tears start in her eyes. "I need to pull myself together."

If not a nap, she begs as she stuffs clothing into her backpack, how about the bath? Can she at least have the bath?

Grady has to admit there's no emergency here. One hour won't make a damn bit of difference. But as soon as she's clean, he'll call Davis. If she's lucky, Davis will send a guy with some perspective. Otherwise... He's not sure how he'll feel watching them cuff her and put her in the back of a squad car.

Grady's mother uses the walk-in shower with handicapped bars in the bath located off her bedroom, so the tub in the hall bath is dusty. Clare rinses it out. Grady digs through the bottles under the sink and finds an ancient box of bath beads. Clare turns on the faucet, holds her hand under the stream to test the temperature.

"Careful," Grady says. "It's June in Tucson. There's no such thing as cold tap water. It's warm right out of the ground."

Clare regards the rising bubbles, adjusts the temperature. She looks around for towels. Grady points her at the linen closet down the hall. Instead, she comes back carrying the two faded blue candles that have sat on his mother's kitchen table for more than a decade. She positions them on the ledge of the tub and holds out her hand for his lighter.

The wick on the first one catches. She lights the second, then makes a quick trip to the hall.

She lays three rose-colored towels on the lid of the toilet. Grady looks at the stack.

"One for my body," she says, "one for my hair, and one for you."

He shakes his head. "I can't do that."

She smiles at him. "Of course you can."

"That's a one-person tub," he says. It is the truth: the powder blue tub is a short, shallow model dating from the '50s. But it wouldn't matter if they were looking at a tin washtub or a Jacuzzi. He's not getting in.

She pulls her tank top off over her head. He starts to turn away.

"Don't be silly," she says. "Nothing you haven't seen before."

As she slides out of her shorts and kicks off her lacy thong, he tells himself that her loveliness is remote, that she is simply an object that can't move him. He doesn't succeed.

As she lowers herself into the tub, he stands there dumbly, then sits, suddenly, on the toilet lid, hoping to hide his erection, pushing the towels onto the tile floor. He reaches down, picks them up, piles them on his lap.

He hears the phone ringing. The sound is faint: the bathroom door is closed. To keep the steam in, Clare has said. There are only two phones, the one on the wall in the kitchen and the portable, which is still sitting dead in the living room instead of in its usual nighttime home next to his mother's bed.

While he's still considering whether he can get to the kitchen in time, the ringing stops. His mother has no voice mail, no answering machine. Unless he hits *69 to return the call, he will never know whether the caller is an anonymous voice trying to sell Virginia a magazine subscription or a friend wanting to chat. It can't be Frannie, because she's dead. It can't be his mother, because she has no reason to call her own house. It can't be Gina, because she is undoubtedly high. Last time he checked, Bear still hadn't learned to dial a phone. And no one else, nothing else, really matters.

It has been a long time since he's been part of a web of meaningful social interaction. Eons since he had a fiance, and then a wife, planned for a home, maybe a couple of kids, went to dinner parties, hosted barbeques—and heard in the ringing of a phone the promise of possibilities.

He isn't a monk. There have been a few women since the divorce, including three or four that he thought of as girlfriends and two women that he moved in with. But even those more intense relationships were short-lived. One woman had already slept with most of the detective squad (he later discovered) before she and Grady hooked up, and within weeks after she invited him into her apartment she bedded one of his former partners.

The other simply had the bad luck to run into him shortly after Frannie died, at a time when all he was blurring the pain with work and drink. She quickly tired of the cop talk, the odd hours, the middle-of-the-night phone calls and his moods. Finally, he closed down the bars with his buddies once too often, and when he staggered up the driveway, he found his stuff on the lawn.

Clare splashes him, and he startles back to awareness. She laughs. "Where were you?" She splashes him again, a vigorous slosh that spatters his face and shirt.

"Now you have to get in," she says. "We can fit like spoons."

It doesn't matter, Grady tells himself. It doesn't matter at all.

He kicks off his shoes, tugs at a sock. Clare begins humming the old Henry Mancini tune *The Stripper*. Grady pulls off his soggy polo and does a bump. She laughs. He unzips his jeans and gives her a grind. She whistles. He tosses his boxers at the ceiling. They catch on the top edge of the medicine cabinet, hang there a moment, then fall to the floor, where they land in a puddle.

The water is warm, and Clare is wonderfully slippery. She sits between his legs, leaning back against him. He reaches around her and strokes her breasts, burying his face in her neck. She turns in the tub, settles with her body toward him, puts her hands on his shoulders. He feels her sex melt slowly onto his and gives himself up.

Later, they rest, Grady spreading suds across her belly, drawing a smiley face with her navel as the nose. The candles drip wax onto the porcelain.

An hour later, they've used up all the hot water and splashed the small bathroom from top to bottom. Together, they wipe up the spills with fresh towels and dump the sodden linens in the empty tub. Clare shakes her short hair like a wet dog, and Grady uses one of the last dry towels his mother owns to pat her down, enjoying every touch of the cloth to a curve or a softness, turning the procedure into a kind of lovemaking.

Then they carry their wet clothes into the laundry room and stick them in the drier. Grady manages to find an old bath sheet and wraps it around his waist. He goes through his mother's bureau and (guiltily) discovers her drawer of lingerie. Virginia will spend another night in the hospital gown, and it's his fault. At least he should phone her. He glances at the nightstand, eyes the portable phone—and sees the nearby clock. Shit, it's already too late.

He hands Clare a faded lilac polyester gown. She discovers an old necktie that must have been his father's and uses it as a belt, turning the nightie into a sort of mini-toga. He struggles to get his feet into his waterlogged shoes.

Clare laughs at his efforts. "You're wearing a pink flowered towel. Why do you want shoes?"

Grady tosses her a pair of his mother's stretchy, vinyl-soled slippers. "This is the desert," he says.

"Huh?"

"Scorpions. You mostly find them up in the foothills, but they can turn up anywhere. We've seen a few here."

"You're kidding." She pulls the slippers onto her feet. "How do you live with that?"

Grady shrugs. "Every place has some downside. Earthquakes. Icy roads. We have critters."

They cook scrambled eggs, using all the eggs in Virginia's refrigerator, a whole dozen. Grady brews coffee, and Clare makes a pile of toast. She has found his mother's portable cassette player and a vintage Frank Sinatra tape that Frannie compiled twenty years ago as a Christmas gift. The songs go back to what his mother calls her "courting days" and remind him of his childhood, of his parents and their two children, together, healthy and happy. As Clare lays out plates and silverware and he slathers his mother's low-cholesterol spread onto the hot bread, he suddenly realizes that it's after midnight, and he hasn't even noticed he is sober.

They eat in the semi-dark. Neither of them wants the glare of the overhead lamp. Grady brought the blue candles back to the kitchen table, but they, or what's left of them, have become his mother's again, so he's left them unlit.

Clare spreads strawberry jam on a piece of toast and refills Grady's cup. "Now what?" she asks.

Grady takes another bite of toast, a swig of coffee. It's late, he thinks. At one a.m., almost anything can wait. It's a no harm, no foul time of day.

"I guess you get that good night's sleep," he says. "We'll bother people in the morning."

They rinse the dishes, and Grady loads them in the dishwasher. Clare wipes the table. Grady turns out the light, and she walks out of the kitchen ahead of him. He watches her, small and graceful in his mother's borrowed nightgown, move down the hallway toward the spare bedroom. He follows her as if an invisible satin ribbon is pulling him along. But he feels he is dragging something behind him.

Guilt.

"Just a minute," he says, and he walks back into the kitchen, goes to the table, picks up the ceramic kittens and replaces them on the wall shelf.

Feeling as if he's restored a small piece of order to his mother's world (after having failed to fulfill her simple request for a nightgown, kicked in her door, bribed her granddaughter, desecrated her house with cigarette smoke, burned her candles and jeopardized what was left of his moral core by fucking a fugitive in her bathtub), he retraces his steps. He can't fool himself, hard as he tries. Even if he's no longer a cop, he should have taken Clare in. Immediately.

But he didn't do it then. And he understands that he isn't going to do it now.

Clare stands facing him in the doorway to the back bedroom. As he approaches, she loosens the tie belt and tosses it to him. He catches it and takes another step.

She drops one shoulder strap, then the other. The nightgown slips to the floor.

Grady's senses are focused on the girl who is waiting, beckoning, drawing him toward her. She smiles, runs her small tongue over her lips, holds out her arms.

He takes one step, another...

Her face changes. He hears movement behind him. But before he can react... Pain. Sudden and searing.

His mind tries to operate his body, but his limbs won't obey. He sees Clare—in slow motion, distorted like a sea creature glimpsed through fathoms of water. He watches her—a pale pink anemone swimming through the murk.

The pain crowds her out. He feels his legs give way, sees his mother's sculptured beige carpet rushing at him...

Then the pain is everything.

Utter blackness.

14

Jill has suffered through a rotten afternoon. A crown wouldn't seat. An impression needed to be redone—not once, but twice, which embarrassed Jill and upset an already nervous patient. Jill is a meticulous and caring dentist. She hates it when things go wrong.

So by the end of her day, she is running distressingly late. And even when she is on schedule, Jill is often the last person to leave her professional building. Hers isn't a crack-of-dawn office. In a town where many dentists begin work as early as seven a.m. and are on the golf course by two, Jill never schedules an appointment before nine. This is her way of preserving some illusion of balance in her life. She may not always be able to put her family first (starting later means working later if a practice has any kind of decent patient load, which Jill's does). But she can at least put them first in her day.

So by the time she updates patient files, checks her e-mail, looks over the next day's schedule, and makes her way out to her car, it's after 6:30.

She tosses her briefcase onto the passenger seat and settles her cell phone into its hands-free cradle. She turns the key in the ignition and hits speed-dial—the "Home" button. Backing out, she counts the rings. Three, four, five... Her own voice. "Hi. You've reached the

Whitehursts. Please leave a message and we'll call you as soon as we can. Bye." She pushes "End" without waiting for the beep.

Of course. Sophie will still be at Megan's. A lot longer and later than Jill prefers, and an embarrassing imposition on Megan's non-working mom. Evenings like this—when something has screwed up and Sophie remains at a friend's house, an extra child as the dinner hour looms—are rich fodder for the gossipy moms who drop off their progeny every morning at the school bus stop just outside Pergama and pick them up, faithfully, every afternoon. Sometimes Jill wishes that Tucson were the kind of town where the well-to-do are disengaged enough to send their maids. But Morgan's mother will understand this time, under the circumstances.

Turning off Ft. Lowell onto north-bound Swan, she notices clouds gathering over the mountains for the first time in months. They are few, and they are wispy white rather than water-laden gray, but they are definitely clouds. For Jill, a life-time Tucsonan, they are a harbinger. They mean hope: the prospect of continued life for the plants and animals with the guts to make their home in the desert. The scattered puffs are a fragile promise of rain, a promise that will be kept sometime in the days or weeks ahead. They signal the beginning of the southeasterly flow of moist air that will gradually raise the dew point and one day soon, always just when it seems impossible, bring the monsoons.

Jill's eyes seek lightning. It will be dry—just heat lightning, but it is another heavenly sign. Nothing. She passes through the intersection at River Road and considers dinner. She'll pick up Chinese, a treat for Sophie. Egg rolls, hot and sour soup, maybe some crispy duck. Not among Charlie's favorite meals, but he won't be home anyway. His business trip has been extended, and right about now he's hustling through JFK, checking in for a flight to London.

She's in luck. The Happy Dragon is almost empty. Take-out should be quick. While she waits, she scrolls through her mobile's phone book and finds Megan's number. Megan answers after two rings.

"Hi, Megan," Jill says. "This is Sophie's mom."

"Hi," a bored but polite Megan says.

"How are you?"

"Fine."

There's silence on the line.

"Megan, can I speak to Sophie?"

"She's not here, Mrs. Whitehurst. My mom took her home a long time ago."

Jill hears a beeping in her ear.

"Mrs. Whitehurst? We've got another call. I gotta go."

"Megan! Megan, wait!"

But Megan is gone. Don't be anal, Jill, she tells herself—not for the first time. Compulsiveness is good in a dentist but bad in a parent. Lighten up. She picks up a magazine, thumbs through it.

Finally, the food is ready.

Jill settles the cardboard tray of bagged cartons carefully on the floor of the car. Why doesn't Sophie listen? True, Jill hasn't fully disclosed recent events about "Winnie" and who she is or isn't. But she has stressed that a murder next door is no joke. She was careful to explain that she knows Sophie is responsible. And her parents do trust her. But these are unusual circumstances. And the situation is temporary. Sophie can understand that.

In return, she was the recipient of an exasperated groan and the words "I get it, Mom, I get it" uttered in a weary, long-suffering tone. The "duh" was definitely implied. Clearly, Jill's I.Q. is dropping rapidly as Sophie approaches her thirteenth birthday. But she assured her mother that she did, indeed, understand.

So why did Megan's mother take her home to an empty house? Sophie is perfectly capable of speaking up. Clearly, she didn't pass her mother's wishes on to Mrs. Kaplan. Jill should have talked to the woman herself instead of sending the message via Sophie. So what if she finds Janet Kaplan both cloying and passive-aggressive? That's no excuse. She was too casual. It's all her fault, really. Sophie is, after all, the child. She is the parent.

Sitting becalmed in the construction zone on Sunrise between Swan and Craycroft (a mile of orange cones, flag men and large equipment), she dials home again.

No answer. Her daughter must be taking advantage of the empty house to turn up the volume. This time, when she hears her own voice, she leaves a message. "Sophie, this is Mom. I'll be home in a few minutes, and I have Chinese. Make sure the doors are locked and the alarm is on. Yes, I know that you know. But double-check anyway, okay? And, Soph? Turn down the music!"

Within minutes, the system will ring the phones notifying anyone in the house that they have voice mail and will keep trying at intervals until someone picks up. At least she can reach Sophie second-hand.

As she finally turns into the driveway, she notices with concern that the place is nearly dark. She can see only a glimmer or two of light. This is unlike her daughter. Usually, Jill comes around the corner and beholds an electric palace, with lights on upstairs, downstairs—everywhere. And is instantly annoyed. But right now she'd be delighted.

She pulls into the garage and rushes from the car, leaving the driver's side open and dinging. Fumbling with her keys, she struggles with the deadbolt in the door leading from the garage into the lower level until she realizes that she's turning it the wrong way: it isn't locked. As she enters, her eyes seek out the alarm panel just inside the entrance. She watches for the blinking light, hopes for the warning screech. Nothing. The system is disarmed.

Damn. How many times does she have to say it? This is it, Sophie is grounded. There'll be a sitter for a while, no matter how insulting the arrangement is to her daughter. But, first, please be okay, please be safe...please...

"Soph?" she calls. "Sophie?"

No answer. But loud music pours down the hall from the direction of her daughter's room. A swathe of light illuminates the carpet in front of her doorway.

Relieved, Jill retrieves her things from the car and closes the garage door. Inside the house once again, she lets the briefcase drop to the floor, cradles the bags of food in her left arm, and sets the alarm. She thinks about setting the food on the nearby chest, walking down to Sophie's room, teasing her about the noise, scolding her about the alarm, giving her a hug... But oyster sauce is dripping down her arm.

Trotting upstairs, she groans at the music. Why does each generation have to embrace sounds—and lyrics—so offensive to the one before? Then she scolds herself for not being able to keep her priorities straight for more than thirty seconds. A moment ago, she would have traded almost anything to know that her daughter was all right. What is wrong with her?

She plops the bags of food down on the kitchen counter and washes the oyster sauce off her hands and her silk blouse. (It seems to be a natural law: take-out cartons leak, no matter how careful you are.) She grabs a mug, fills it from the instant hot water tap, adds a tea bag (organic mint, very calming) and sticks two of the take-out cartons into the microwave to reheat.

She lays place mats on the kitchen island, pulls out plates and silver. No, they'll use the chopsticks tonight, the real ones that Charlie brought back from a business trip to Beijing a few years ago. Sophie will want a soft drink, and Jill will let her have one—but sugar-free and decaffeinated.

She flips on the little TV in the corner. PBS. Time to catch up on the rest of the world. She can still see most of Jim Lehrer's take on the day's events. The picture comes up quickly, but the commentator might be miming the words for all the good it does her. Sophie's music pierces the dry wall and rumbles through the air vents. Jill can almost feel the joists vibrating. What happened to the soundproofing Charlie and she were so delighted about when they bought the house? This place is supposed to be well insulated. And we have how many years of adolescence to get through?

It's just about time for dinner anyway. Jill picks up the phone on the kitchen desk to call Sophie's room. The Whitehursts' phone system has an intercom button for calling from one extension to another, and one of its idiosyncrasies is auto-answer. This can be handy. It means, for example, that when Jill is busy in the kitchen, Charlie can call her from his study and they can talk without the need for her to stop chopping or stirring to pick up the handset. This feature could, of course, be used to secretly listen in; in essence, for domestic spying. But that's theoretical: theirs is a respectful family.

So when she pushes the intercom button and the code for Sophie's room, Jill calls out "Sophie?" into the handset. But all she hears is music. She tries speaking more loudly, being more forceful. Still just the music.

Resigning herself to making the trek downstairs, Jill puts down her tea cup and pops the last of the cartons into the microwave.

The lower level is just as she left it: dark except for the light flooding the area outside Sophie's room. Prepared to give Sophie a hard time about the decibel level, Jill switches on the overhead cans and makes her way down the hall.

At the doorway, she pauses and sticks her head in—not wanting to startle her daughter. "Soph..." she begins. But the room is empty.

Jill feels a jolt of adrenaline shoot through her. With shaking hands, she shuts off the music, picks up the handset of Sophie's phone and hits the button for what they call the "God voice"—a feature that pages through every extension in the house. "Sophie," she says firmly into the receiver, "call me in your room. Call me now, Sophie."

Nothing. She waits. Tries again. No response.

Telling herself she's being silly, telling herself to calm down, she flicks on the light in Sophie's adjoining bathroom. Empty. She flings open the closet doors. Only clothes, shoes and games.

Fighting a sense that something is dreadfully, desperately wrong, Jill runs down the hall and throws back the double doors to the guest wing, checks the bedrooms, the baths, the closets. Still no Sophie.

Jill runs back up the hall, up the stairs to the main level. No daughter in the living room, the den, the master suite, the powder room or Charlie's study. Not there. Not there...

Where?

Outside. That's where she has to be. Sophie must have gone out in the yard. She isn't supposed to swim alone, but who knows? Turning off the alarm, Jill throws on the outside floods and rushes out onto the deck that overlooks the backyard. The area is eerily but clearly illuminated. Oleanders, palms, cactus, Texas Ranger, pool and spa all look back at her. There is no sign of her child.

Slamming the French doors so hard the glass rattles, Jill speeds back to the stairs, races down them and grabs her abandoned briefcase. With shaking hands, she crouches, works the combination and reaches in. Her right hand finds the gun, and her childhood training takes over. She hears her pop's voice: "If you can't handle a firearm coolly and carefully, you shouldn't touch one at all. You're only a damn danger to yourself and everybody else." Smoothly, she rises, the gun held solidly in her now steady hands. Her brain is working again.

She came in through the garage, so searching it seems futile, but she has to be systematic. And, now that she thinks of it, there's the row of closets across the front, ahead of the cars. They are wonderful storage. And they would make a wonderful hiding place.

She slowly opens the door from the house to the garage and flicks on the overhead fluorescents. The area lights only dimly. One of the two banks is out. Why didn't she notice that earlier? Or is this new?

Jill moves stealthily across the space—empty except for her car and the family's three bicycles, which occupy the third bay. She is making her way around the area in front of her car toward the closet door when...

BRRRINNGGG!!

Startled, Jill nearly drops the gun—and curses herself for being a fool. She reaches for the phone that hangs on the garage wall.

"You have one new message," the computerized voice says. She hits the buttons to retrieve it: 1, 1.

Her own voice speaks to her: "Sophie, this is Mom..."

Her daughter hasn't retrieved the message... Couldn't retrieve the message?

Jill replaces the receiver.

What to do? Call 9-1-1? Drive the neighborhood? Both?

She slumps against the wall. And the lights go out.

Her heart pounds, she can't breathe... then she realizes that she's backed against the light switch—and in the darkness she sees...a strip of light under a door on the far wall...a door she never thinks about...a door leading to what was meant to be a maid's room, never used for that purpose because she and Charlie would never have a live-in maid...a room that Charlie (and only Charlie) uses, to store his books, on shelves, on the floor, in the hundreds (it seems) of boxes that hold every volume he ever opened from his junior high days through business school.

Jill approaches the door as if stalking a roaring, 500-pound grizzly. Holding her gun out in front of her—safety off—at chest height, in both hands, she momentarily disengages her right hand, reaches out, turns the knob—kicks open the door.

"Put your hands up!" she shouts.

There is a gasp...a scream—and it is hers.

A slender figure stands over an open box, iPod clipped to its shorts, buds blocking its ears, books piled around it on the floor.

"What are you doing?" an astonished voice says.

She is pointing the gun at her terrified daughter.

15

The foreground is beige, a tufted landscape. The wing of a long-dead moth rests in a valley between two mesas. A ridge of mud-brown molding forms the horizon.

Grady struggles to his hands and knees and vomits.

He crawls the few feet down the hall to the bedroom and collapses just outside the doorway. He forces his neck to raise the throbbing weight of his head and searches the darkness for the lighted clock on the nightstand. The numbers swim in and out of focus, finally resolve themselves.

3:02. He was only out a few minutes.

He manages to sit up, leans back against the wall.

The place is quiet.

He crawls through the doorway where Clare stood only moments ago. He drags himself across the carpet where the nightgown fell.

The doorway is empty, the carpet bare. The tie Clare used for a belt lies crumpled on the bed where she tossed it.

He calls out. No answer.

Again. Nothing.

Her backpack is gone. No sign of a struggle.

All his instincts say the house is empty. But Grady's brain tells his body it's time to stand up. His body ignores the order. He tries again, manages to roll onto his knees and pull himself up painfully, inch by inch, using the old fashioned bedpost for support. He wobbles; the room sways.

After the floor settles down, he holds tightly to the bedpost and picks up one foot. It works. He tries the other. Success. Holding onto the bed, then the doorframe, then the wall, he makes his way back out into the hall.

Slowly, moving from room to room using his mother's furniture as support, he checks the small house. No one. He takes a sponge mop from the broom closet near the back door and, using the mop as a prop, manages to lurch a few painful feet into the back yard. A fat, nearly round moon looks down on Bermuda grass, a metal table with a furled umbrella. A snake slithers across the tiny patio and disappears into the yard next door.

Back in the house, he crosses to the front room. He doesn't have the strength to push the chest away from the door, but he slides open the big front window and leans out. Nothing, living or dead.

Letting the mop drop to the floor, he falls heavily into his mother's recliner.

Clare is in great danger. If her story is true.

But is it?

On the face of it, this is an abduction. And the girl he fucked (no—admit it—made love to, cooked with, danced with, laughed with) is the victim of a big-time crime.

Only hours before, they sat at his mother's kitchen table, and he asked Clare why when she left his place she didn't just get the hell out of Tucson. She didn't know what to do, where to go, she stammered. She only knew that she didn't want anyone to find her, that she didn't have any money. And she couldn't seem to think more than an hour or two ahead.

He'd told her about his mom being in the hospital, mentioned that her house wasn't too far away. She knew the place was empty.

And she didn't have a plan. So she searched for (and found) the address and grabbed a map from his car.

She was right: it was no plan. And her logic was full of holes. But emotionally it made sense—for someone not used to being on the run, an innocent caught up in something she didn't fully comprehend.

Points for Clare's truthfulness.

But there are other things: like what she saw and didn't see from her hiding place in the cupboard in Ann Arbor. Suppose she saw more than she admitted. Suppose she could describe and potentially ID the men.

That would put her at almost infinite risk. The law does not always catch the bad guys. People know that. And a lot of them also realize that any kind of witness protection is iffy at best. Making it credible that the night Winnie died Clare simply panicked—and ran.

On the other hand, when confronted with the kind of violence they've seen only in the movies, most ordinary, law-abiding folks call 911 first and think about it later. Grady saw this over and over during his years on the force. People think that once they push those magic buttons and blurt out their crisis everything will be okay. They've unloaded their problems onto the big blue shoulders. Life can get back to normal.

Clare made her low opinion of law enforcement pretty clear. Is that why Davis and his boys seem as frightening as whoever else might be hunting her? Or is there something in her past? Something in her present?

Grady has no evidence one way or the other. So that round is a wash.

Clare is bright and educated. She's shown she can think on her feet. But she's not equipped to survive on the streets. What did she expect would eventually happen? Did she really believe that the perps would be caught without her help and she'd just slip back into her old life at Purdue? Could she—could anyone—be that naive?

Hard to answer that question. He reminds himself that people, even the brainy ones, seldom make sense.

But then there is the capper. He was hit; she was taken.

The body at the Nelsons has to be related to Winnie's death in Ann Arbor. What is that old saying? If you hear hooves, think horses—not zebras. This just about has to be an ordinary horse of a killing.

So these guys wanted Clare, found her where she was hiding out at the Nelsons'. Somebody—one of them or someone else—died. And Clare got away.

That happened early Sunday morning.

A few minutes ago, they found a way to get to Clare again. Either they followed her, or more likely, they followed him, guessing correctly that he'd lead them to her.

But why isn't Clare lying dead on the bedroom floor?

He can kind of understand why he is alive. Whoever's tracking Clare must have decided that anything Clare revealed to Grady couldn't be more dangerous than the info she'd already given the sheriff. Which means that she knows something they're sure she's not telling. Maybe.

Whatever the reason, they disabled him, but let him live. Or, more likely, they hit him hard enough to get him out of the way and didn't give a damn whether he lived or died.

In the movies, people are snatched all the time. In reality, it just doesn't happen. If perps who've killed before believe that you're a threat to their lives or even their freedom, they simply blow your head off.

You never have a chance to resort to any cute action hero tricks.

And the creeps don't transport you to another location before doing you in—not when the set-up is perfect just as it is.

Okay, there are exceptions. Organized crime likes isolated killing fields where a body can just disappear, but this doesn't smell like mob. And some serial killers abduct and torment their victims before murdering them. But nothing here points to a psycho.

Rape isn't the motive. A gang bang like the one Clare witnessed in Ann Arbor is a perverted form of male bonding. The victims are almost always targets of opportunity: women in the wrong place at the wrong time—with everybody drunk or drugged out of their minds. It's not a crime people travel thousands of miles to commit.

Nope. Clare should be dead.

It occurs to him that his thinking vis-`a-vis Clare is a lot like the old test he heard about in school. Centuries ago, if a woman was accused of consorting with the devil, she was tied, weighed down with stones and thrown into deep water. If she popped to the surface, she was a witch. If she drowned, she was innocent.

He should call Andy Davis. Wake him, confess to another screw-up. Get the posse on the road.

But all he has is Clare's story—almost nothing in the way of hard facts.

All he'll be able to say is that some person or persons unknown appear to have taken a blonde, blue-eyed young woman, 27 years old. That she might be wearing a too-big, faded polyester nightgown and a pair of stretchy slippers. And that, by the way, this is a young lady the authorities were already seeking (see prior APB), who happened to be under his immediate, even intimate, control for, oh, eight hours, during which time he didn't bother to let anyone know.

That'll go over big.

He thinks back to his last conversation with Davis—when Clare disappeared from his bed and Andy came pounding on the door. At one point, he asked Davis about whether they'd gotten her fingerprints. Davis simply snorted. "What do you think?"

Grady was pretty sure that they hadn't. The only rationale for printing her would have been to eliminate her whorls and ridges from whatever else they'd found at the Nelsons. With her aunt and uncle unavailable to contribute their prints and the girl terrorized (and not going any farther than next door), they'd probably decided it could wait.

Davis ruefully confirmed Grady's thinking. To make matters worse, the Nelsons had thrown themselves a going-away bash. More than thirty friends laid their hands on the door handles, the coffee table, the mantle, the bar, the bathroom fixtures. The caterers were all over the kitchen. The maid would be stopping by during the summer to do light cleaning, but she was only scheduled to show every two weeks and hadn't yet been there by the night of the murder.

Davis shook his head in disgust. "Get this. We found a half-empty glass of champagne in the under-sink cabinet in the powder room, a couple of coffee cups behind one of those big indoor trees. We dusted everything, of course. But, fuck, the prints are mostly a mess. They mean nothing."

Yup, Grady thinks. Unfortunately, most prints that aren't totally smeared are partials, fragments that require careful interpretation by an expert. And computers aren't magic. It's not like the movies. As a practical matter, you make damn few matches.

He can't put the puzzle together: he's missing too many pieces. But he has no choice but to reach a couple of unpleasant, ego-destroying conclusions. One: Clare's story is a lie in some, most, or all of its particulars. The doubts that he felt when he was listening, and decided to leave to the inquiries of Davis and his bunch, point to some of the murky areas. And if Clare is an intelligent person (which she is) and a determined liar (which she seems to be), she'll have created layers of untruths.

He knows this firsthand. He was fired not so much for what he did, the authorities said, but for a lie. This was crap! his buddies screamed. Bogus! Bullshit! The asshole suits were crucifying a good cop on a technicality, throwing a man to the wolves for nothing—after almost twenty years on the force. They raised their voices in his behalf; someone got up a petition. But they never had a chance. Dumping Grady publicly, dramatically—yanking his pension and cancelling his medical insurance—was actually win/win. It took the union off the hook and prevented them from having to defend his actions. It saved the department the embarrassment of a trial. And, as only Grady knew, it left the big lie undiscovered.

So. Either Clare is in cahoots with whoever hit him on the head.

Or they had a reason not to kill her, at least on the spot. That leads inevitably to conclusion two: she is only alive because of her own big lie, whatever it is.

If Clare was a body, bloodied, battered, lifeless, Grady would be mourning her, screaming in pain. He'd be a roaring fury, vowing revenge as he hasn't since he went after that lowlife a few years back and ruined his career in the process. He would already be missing her for the rest of his life.

Instead, he's righteously pissed that she played him for such an obvious sap.

He pulls himself out of the chair and goes to find his clothes.

16

The lights are on in the rear of Luis's small adobe. Grady has a feeling the lights are always on, that sleep happens during the day when prowling the Internet is a lot less fun.

Grady pushes the bell. The ibuprofen he found in his mother's medicine cabinet is starting to work, but if he moves his head too quickly he's at risk of being dropped to his knees by the pain.

Within seconds, a male voice comes at him through the speaker.

"Whatever you're selling," it says, in unaccented English but with the lilt of old Mexico, "I don't want any."

"It's Grady."

Luis buzzes him in.

"*Buenas noches*," the disembodied voice says. "Shut the door behind you."

Grady obliges. He hears the electronically operated deadbolt click into place.

"Now come on back."

As Grady emerges from the dark hallway into Luis's lair, the fragile figure in the wheelchair rotates to face him.

The damage done to Luis happened before birth. Cerebral palsy locks up his legs, cocks his head and twists his left hand into a claw.

But his brilliant mind is intact, and his right hand can work a keyboard with utter fluency. Luis likes to say that for a spaz he is lucky.

"Jack," he says. *"¿Qué pasa,* man? What's it been, two years?"

"More like three."

"Heard you were off the force. Sorry."

Grady makes a gesture intended to acknowledge the sympathy and dismiss the event as something long past or trivial or both. "Water under the bridge."

"Shit, man, you're right. Gotta move on."

The room is a techie's paradise. A u-shaped counter holds monitors large and small. CPUs rest on the floor at intervals that allow a wheelchair easy movement in and out. Shelves stacked with electronic components and mysterious black boxes with flashing lights line the walls. Cables snake along the baseboard.

Grady whistles. "Looks like you've kept moving on here."

"Every six months. That's how often I gotta update this stuff. What I got woulda run NORAD five years back."

Luis was one of Frannie's causes and dearest friends. He arrived in her third grade class one morning knowing only a few words of English. By the first recess, "spaz" was the nicest name he was called. Frannie defended him, then educated herself and her classmates on his disability. Luis quickly picked up English; she learned Spanish. Luis proved to be a math whiz and a natural tutor. He won over his peers by walking them, first, through long division and later through algebra, geometry, even trig. When personal computers came along, Luis's world became digital. He was an usher at Frannie's wedding and an honorary pallbearer at her funeral, unable to bear the weight of the coffin but fully able to share the load of grief.

Grady has occasionally had use for his services, which sometimes skirt but, he likes to think, seldom break any serious laws. He has no idea of Luis's immigration status and doesn't care.

Luis is careful to protect his clients' privacy. Screen savers shine from all the monitors. Grady notices scenes of Mexican courtyards,

Mayan ruins, Bart Simpson and R2D2.

"How's Gina?"

"Same old stuff."

Luis shakes his head. "*Que lástima.*" What a shame. "*Madre de dios.* Hard to believe she's Frannie's."

Grady nods in agreement.

"Whaddya need?"

Grady tells him.

This is an easy one, Luis says. Not like national defense or financial crap. The fire walls are generally off-the-shelf junk with aftermarket customization that's a joke. The setups are so pathetic that some suit at Princeton broke into Yale's computer—just to see which students Yale was admitting. What a dope. Left a trail a mile wide leading right back to his desk. So...give it about an hour. Tops.

Grady doesn't want to watch Luis and knows Luis doesn't want to be watched. He thinks about going home. Walking Bear. He considers finding a drink. But like many cops, he has had more experience than he likes with head injuries. The mental confusion, vomiting and visual disturbances (not to mention the headache) are par for the course. Still, adding alcohol to the mix is risky. He isn't always sure he really wants to live, but he does have responsibilities, and right now he has something to do.

So he gets into his car and drives up and down the narrow streets of Luis's neighborhood, which overlap into Grady's mother's neighborhood, which overlap into his own. This is an older part of town, laid out in a grid pattern instead of those fancy cul-de-sacs you find on the East side and out in the foothills. Grady goes up one street, turns right, drives down the next...

He isn't searching. His driving is pointless. He is simply "maiming time," as Jill used to say. "Let's not kill time, Jack. Let's just maim it."

He remembers a night, about five years before. He and his partner were called to the scene of a homicide. A woman had locked her new husband out of the house. While he frantically tried to get in, her teenage sons gunned him down.

The crime scene was in one of those new cookie-cutter developments on the Northwest side, one of those areas that had been cactus and coyotes only a few years before. He and his partner wandered, took one turn after another. They got lost.

They finally had to call dispatch and squirm in embarrassment while the amused female voice on the radio talked them in.

The next day, Grady found a map of Tucson taped to his locker, along with a crudely worded suggestion about getting a GPS. He threw the map in his pickup where it lived until the truck died. Then he relocated it along with all the other junk to the fucking Taurus, where it remained until Clare took it.

The car's faltering cooling system can't decide whether to blow hot air or cold, so he rolls down the windows. This will be one of those nights when the temperature never falls below eighty.

A coyote slinks across the pavement ahead of him. Hunting rabbits or the neighborhood cats—to a coyote, food is food.

Forty-five minutes later, Luis buzzes him back in.

Grady stands behind the wheelchair. Luis hits a button and the screen saver is replaced by data.

Clare Lynn Dorsett. Graduate student at Purdue. 27 years old. Ph.D. candidate in art history. Solid record. Good standing. Oral exams scheduled this fall.

Luis's right hand plays the keys.

A graphic pops on the screen. A file photo, the one used on her student I.D.

Grady stares at the hair, eyes, nose, mouth...

Clare Lynn Dorsett is black.

17

In the summer when the snowbirds are gone, traffic is light, and the days are long and hot, Jill takes Wednesdays off. Sometimes Sophie skips day camp and the two of them swim or shop. If Charlie is in town, the three of them may pack a picnic lunch and drive to the top of Mt. Lemmon where the pine trees are green and the temperature is in the 70s.

This particular Wednesday morning, mother and daughter are still suffering the aftermath of last night's scare. Jill didn't sleep well. She kept seeing the after-image of her daughter standing there, buds in her ears, iPod on her belt, her dad's books around her feet, her eyes staring in horror at the gun in her mother's hand. She felt her muscles clenched around the grip, her finger on the trigger, nerves taut, brain ready to send the message from frontal cortex to spinal column to arm, to hand...

She was a split second away from shooting her own daughter. Charlie would never forgive her. She would never forgive herself. And, although he doesn't know it yet, he's won their long-running argument. She's never told him she has the gun, and now she'll have to get rid of it. Soon. Until he's back in town, it can live in their safe.

So this morning she is veering wildly between normal parenting (drink your juice, take out the trash, make your bed, help me start some laundry) and guilty permissiveness (a morning spent playing video games, you bet; it's only sports camp, not algebra).

For the moment, the permissive side has won. The music is blasting up through the floor, and Sophie is deeply into SimCity. Today, she seems to be focusing on improving her city's transportation systems.

Jill makes herself a cup of mint tea and pulls out an old *New York Times* Sunday crossword. Doing puzzles often calms her. Like mother, like daughter, she observes as she raises her pencil and thinks of Sophie at her computer downstairs.

Just as she is settling, starting to get an idea of what the theme of the puzzle might be, the phone rings. It's her service, who's been speaking to a Ms. Walker, Christine Walker, who is here in Tucson on business and, who suddenly, for the past few hours, has found herself in excruciating pain. Someone at her hotel recommended Dr. Whitehurst.

Jill asks if the service has suggested an ER. Yes, but Ms. Walker is sure it's dental. The woman is on hold.

Jill asks to be conferenced in. She was prepped for a crown shortly before leaving home, Ms. Walker says. There's a temporary filling. Could that be the problem?

Jill gives up. She agrees to meet the woman at her office in an hour. She'll take Sophie with her. Then they'll get lunch.

Sophie is having problems with her airport. She can get plenty of people in, but she can't get them out again efficiently, nor can she match them with their luggage. One particularly troublesome group is clogging the terminal, depleting food supplies and getting really nasty. She fears a riot.

She isn't about to abandon the situation to go with her mom to the office, the novelty of which wore off by the time she was six. She isn't allowed to touch most of the equipment, and she is years too old to enjoy fooling with the reclining chairs.

Her mother resists. No way is Sophie staying home alone. The terror of the night before is fresh, Sophie knows, but she also intuits that her mother feels guilty about over-reacting—and is shaken by the fact that she panicked over what turned out to be nothing.

So Sophie promises. She wheedles. She points out that it's broad daylight, she'll be behind locked doors, it's only for a couple of hours.

And her mother caves.

"You have to set the alarm after me," her mom says, insisting that Sophie walk with her as far as the garage.

"Okay."

"I'm going to call to check," her mother threatens as she gives Sophie a goodbye smooch.

"No problem." Sophie's intelligence is insulted. Like she doesn't know the drill?

But she understands that she blew it the night before. Megan turned her onto a whole bunch of really hot new singles, and she'd done the download and was playing them on her computer. Loud.

She was working on her city's roads while she listened. She was trying to decide where to put a new freeway interchange when she remembered that her dad had some books on urban planning in the room behind the garage. She'd heard him talking to her mom about the problems with leapfrog development and how the more roads you built, the more you needed. Perhaps she should consider mass transit.

Her iPod held a lot of stuff. Not as new, but still cool. She clipped the iPod to the waistband of her shorts, stuck the buds in her ears and left her room. Behind her, the music blared on.

So this morning, Sophie is careful. And when her mom calls from just outside Pergama's gates, Sophie is able to tell her the truth: she set the alarm immediately, as soon as her mother closed the door. It is armed. She is safe.

But her airport is in deep trouble.

Moments later, just as Sophie is debating whether to add a helipad, the phone rings again. Her music is back at its normal volume, so she can't hear anything, but she can see the light flashing on the handset. She hits the "mute" button on the keyboard and picks up.

"Mrs. Whitehurst?" a voice says.

It's William at the gate. He has to know her mother isn't there, has to have seen her drive out only minutes before. Sometimes Sophie thinks William is really dumb.

"This is Sophie Whitehurst," she says.

"Oh. Okay." A pause. "There's a flower delivery."

Probably her dad again. He does that sometimes when he's away on business, wires flowers to her mom. She tells William to send them on up.

Sophie hasn't even gotten back to her helipad when the doorbell rings. She looks through the peephole and sees a short man in a baseball cap nearly obscured from the waist up by a giant bouquet of flowers. Dad must feel really bad about that detour to England. A white van idles in the driveway.

"Just a minute," Sophie calls out, and turns off the alarm.

As she opens the door, she suddenly has an armful—a faceful—of flowers. Grabbing the bouquet, trying not to drop it, she stumbles back against the wall. And notices that the short man has come in through the door with the flowers. And that the short man has aquamarine eyes and a small turned up nose.

"Hi, Sophie," says Winnie.

Everything stops. Just for an instant.

Sophie stands there holding the flowers. She is stunned, but she isn't stupid. Her mother didn't tell her much, but she did imply that this person of the dancing and the tap pants and the piano with Uncle Jack, this person who looked so much different from one moment from the next, might be up to no good. Specifically, she told Sophie that if she ever saw anything odd at the Nelsons' or having to do with the events of last Saturday night or Winnie Pearson, she was to call 9-1-1. Period. End of instructions.

Sophie tries. She throws the bouquet at Winnie and runs for the kitchen.

Winnie catches her halfway down the hall. She pulls at Sophie. Sophie hits her. And kicks, trying to remember which vital organs you're supposed to aim at. All the instructions are about men. No one has ever said what to do when the person attacking you is a woman.

Winnie and Sophie are about the same size, but Winnie is stronger. Or luckier. She gets Sophie down and sits on her chest and holds her arms like some kid in a schoolyard fight.

Sophie yells, as loud as she can.

"Quiet," Winnie orders.

Sophie spits at her.

Winnie reacts, moving a hand up to wipe off the spit, and Sophie tries to push out from under her, but Winnie recovers and holds her down again.

Sophie looks up at the young woman on top of her. "Your eyes," she says in wonder. "One of them is brown." Then she draws the logical conclusion. "You lost a contact."

The baseball cap has fallen off. Winnie's fur-like hair is ruffled. Sophie can see darkness creeping in at the base of each shaft.

"Look," Winnie says, "I know this isn't any fun. I know it's scary. But nothing bad will happen to you or your family. And you can make me go away. Really fast."

"How?"

"It's easy. Just give me the key."

Sophie has no idea what the woman is talking about. All she has is a house key and the key to her locker at the club. Why would Winnie want one of those?

"What key? I don't have a car or anything."

"Don't be a smartass."

Sophie decides the person sitting on her is crazy. Maybe she should try a trick. She's seen it work on television. "Mom!" She yells. "Mom!"

"We know she's not here." It's a male voice.

A tall man wearing a ski mask looms over Winnie. He sounds

like he has a horrible cold, or something stuck in his throat. Sophie can see a shorter man also wearing a ski mask a few feet behind him.

"Let her up," the tall man says. He's holding a rifle.

Winnie helps Sophie to her feet.

"Look, kid," the man says. "All we want is the key."

"I don't know what you're talking about! I don't have any key!" Sophie is desperate. They want something she doesn't have, and they're going to kill her. And if her mom comes home, they'll kill her too.

The man turns to Winnie.

"Listen, bitch," he says. "We're here on your say-so. And the kid doesn't seem to know what the fuck is going on. You said you threw the key in the yard and she got it."

"She has it. I told you. I saw her pick it up."

Pick it up...pick it up... They can't mean the key she found in the cactus in the Nelsons' yard. That's just a funny old key somebody lost.

"I picked it up?"

Winnie nods. "I was in the music room with Grady."

Sophie shakes her head, not in denial but in confusion.

Winnie becomes emphatic. "I know you saw us, don't lie. The sun was going down, but it glinted off something in your hand. I know it was the key. You picked it up and put it in your pocket."

Sophie is hugely relieved. Maybe everything will be okay after all. Maybe Winnie is telling the truth. She'll give them the key and they'll leave. And maybe she'll never even have to tell her mom. She can throw the flowers in the big trash bin outside...

"Oh. That key," is what she says.

And she leads them downstairs to her room. She leads two of them, that is, the tall man and Winnie. The second man, the short one who hasn't said anything, stays by the front door. He stands there with a cell phone to his ear looking out through the peephole.

Sophie walks in front. Winnie is a step or two behind Sophie. And the man who talks (the leader, Sophie thinks, he has to be the leader) brings up the rear.

When Sophie reaches the doorway to her room, the man reaches out and shoves her across the threshold so hard she almost falls.

"You didn't have to do that!" Winnie protests.

"I just want to make sure she gets the point," the man says. He's wearing a t-shirt with no sleeves, and his arms look like Popeye's after the spinach, but the raspy voice is like an old man's. It should be funny because it doesn't match his body. But somehow it's scarier that way.

Sophie quickly moves across the room to her dresser. She opens the lid of the jewelry box revealing the top compartment. Her good watch, the mustard seed pendant Aunt Julia gave her, her charm bracelet. No key.

She slides open the first small drawer: earrings, a heart-shaped pin, a small golden horse... Where did that come from? But no key. The next: an ankle bracelet, two rings. The third. The last.

No key.

"It's gone," she says.

Someone calls down from the head of the stairs. Sophie realizes she is hearing the second man's voice for the first time.

"You've got ten minutes," he says. "Tops."

#

Jill waits 30 minutes past the appointed time just in case the patient has gotten lost, but the phone never rings and Christine Walker never shows. At one point, she calls the Doubletree where the woman is staying but is told there's no guest by that name. Did she say she was checking out, getting ready to catch a flight? Jill doesn't think so, but who knows.

Giving up in disgust, she heads for home. Traffic is light, the air conditioning is keeping up with the heat, and the classical radio station is playing Bach. Her annoyance evaporates, which, she thinks, is probably what happened to Ms. Walker's toothache.

As she passes the eegee's at the corner of Swan and Sunrise, she decides to take Sophie one of those slushes she likes so much. While she waits at the drive-through window, she punches the speed-dial for home. Three rings, four, voice mail.

The music again. She'll have to talk to Sophie about that, find some way to get through.

Jill waves at William as she passes through the Pergama gate. Sometimes there can be a surprising amount of traffic on Pergama Drive. But as she heads up the hill toward her house this late June morning, the place is quiet. She sees a window washing truck parked at the Wilsons', a landscaper trimming bushes a few houses farther up the road. Musing on whether it's too hot to lure Sophie to the Desert Museum for the afternoon, she doesn't register the vehicle that passes her going down toward the gate. The white panel van is merely a fleeting image in the corner of her eye. Her thoughts are on the wonders of the hummingbird exhibit. Glad to be home, Jill turns into her driveway.

The alarm buzzes as she opens the door from the garage into the lower level. Yes! she thinks. Good girl, Sophie. To her surprise, though, there is no music.

Whatever. It makes a nice change. She punches in the code and the silence is complete.

Jill can see the light streaming out of Sophie's open doorway—major wattage in the daytime. Amused at her daughter's two-steps-forward, one-step-back progression toward adulthood, Jill calls out: "Soph? Sophie? I brought you a goodie."

No answer. The iPod, Jill thinks. She's wearing the ear buds again. Carrying the large lime eegee's (Sophie's favorite flavor), she walks down the hall toward Sophie's room.

She reaches the doorway, looks in—and screams. The icy green drink drops from her hand and splashes on her feet, the open door, the rug.

The room has been torn apart. Drawers pulled from the dresser, their contents littering the carpet. Mattress half off its frame. A lamp knocked over. Books and school papers scattered. Sophie's prized computer—her space-blue I-Mac—smashed on the floor.

Sophie's bulletin board still hangs on the wall. And right in the middle, right over Sophie's favorite picture of running wild horses— stuck to it with a red push pin—is a torn piece of notebook paper. Scrawled on the paper in black marker are ten horrible words:

WE GOT YOUR KID. CALL THE POLISE AND SHES DEAD.

18

Grady sits on a bench under a mesquite tree sucking on a Marlboro. Two inline skaters whir by. A jogger pounds past, his body liquid with sweat.

After he left Luis's, he drove around for a while. Then he stopped the car at a Circle K, and used a pay phone in the far shadows of its parking lot to call Davis.

"Shit, Grady!" Andy didn't even say hello. Just started talking. "Where the hell you been? I tried your place, that fuckin' beeper you never turn on—even your mother's. I'm talking out of school here, shouldn't tell you jack. But I thought you'd wanna know just how screwed up this is. Whatever you're mixed up in.

"I heard from the boys in Michigan. The little blonde was killed in her apartment in Ann Arbor. There's blood, hair all over the edge of a hearth. Looks like it coulda been an accident. Shit happens, huh? Especially in the middle of a gang bang.

"But fucks like that, they mostly got no brains. They think with their dicks. And except for the hearth, that place was wiped clean. Like they didn't give a shit about hiding the cause of death, but they didn't sure as hell weren't going to leave any prints. Looks like we got somebody slowin' them down, thinking things through. Weird."

Grady had to agree with him that the behavior didn't fit. It took cold nerve to stick around where somebody'd just died and play janitor.

"And," Davis said, "there's the Caddy. Belongs to some nice couple on vacation in Italy. The shits drove her to the airport, picked a big car in a quiet corner and stuffed her in the trunk." Andy slowed down enough so that Grady could make out a wet, rhythmic sound between the words. He was at the station, so no smoking. Gum.

"I gotta tell you," Davis smacked. "Just between us, I don't have a fuckin' clue what's going on."

Then it was Grady's turn. He got the easy parts out of the way first. He thanked Davis for the heads up. He reassured him that, as far as he knew, he wasn't mixed up in anything. He managed to ask (although he didn't want to) whether the man found dead at the Nelsons' had recently had sex. "Came, no," Davis replied. "Been excited, maybe." They both knew that meant nothing, that men's bodies were perverse, could produce an erection and pre-ejaculate fluid from the stimulus of terror, even imminent death.

Then he told Andy most of it: Clare, the forgotten purse, the cupboard, the men, the flight to Tucson, the disguise as Winnie.

He did edit a little. He omitted any mention of Gina. He implied that the time between the moment he located "Winnie" and the instant somebody knocked him out was not quite the leisurely span it had been. He left out his trip to Luis. It would be a snap for Davis to check out Clare Lynn Dorsett using police channels. Andy would learn soon enough that "Clare" was just another lie. There was no point in raising Luis's profile or trying to gloss over the backdoor nature of his methods.

The conversation was still ugly. He felt like a damn fool, like everything he said was a red neon sign flashing the word "asshole." Which is what Davis called him as he slammed down the phone in Grady's ear. He was a piece of shit who'd let down a friend.

That's what conscience can do to you, he thinks. Funny when the little voice gets its job done and when it doesn't. Except where his mother is concerned, he thought he was a stone.

Well, he isn't. Clare—whoever she is—proved that. He doesn't know whether or not he appreciates the information.

He draws on the cigarette and regards the early morning parade—young people, white hairs, couples, singles, even a few babies squalling or smiling up from their strollers—walking, jogging, or rushing by on wheels—all following the three-mile path that forms the perimeter of Reid Park. All out early to avoid the worst of the heat. They exercise. He smokes. It's part of the balance of nature.

He moves his head tentatively on his neck, bobs it gently up and down. Physically, he seems to be okay. Maybe it's time to get some sleep.

#

Jill races across the room, tears the note from the bulletin board, smashes it into a ball and throws it into a corner. Making the horror go away, disappear—except it doesn't. She retrieves the crumpled paper and spreads it out on Sophie's poor battered desk that shows a dent where someone threw a dresser drawer (the broken drawer lies near her feet).

She is reeling. She hasn't fainted since dental school when another student was practicing his injection technique on her and hit bone. But she recognizes the feeling, and she knows the symptoms of shock. She sits down on the part of Sophie's mattress that still rests on the bed frame, and lowers her head.

"We have your kid…"

We??? Who? And why? What do they want? Money?

Children aren't kidnapped anymore. Not like this. There was a story about it on NPR just a few weeks ago, about the virtual extinction of kidnapping for ransom. Children who disappear are usually taken by an estranged parent. Not an issue here. Occasionally, a baby or toddler is stolen by an unbalanced mother wannabe. Sophie's too old. Rarely, a child is snatched by a pedophile. Horrible, horrible, horrible…

Head down, Jill. Found dead with evidence of sexual abuse, torture... Breathe. In, out, in, out... Horrible, horrible...

But people like that don't leave notes.

So what should she do?

In the movies, people call the F.B.I. And the F.B.I. taps phones and traces calls and constructs an elaborate trap. The parents go through hell and gather the money, and the F.B.I. uses the money to lure the kidnappers. They return the child to the arms of its parents. There are hugs and kisses all round. Then the curtain comes down, and you trip over the empty popcorn buckets on your way out of the theater. Happy ending.

In reality, Jill isn't so sure. During her years with Grady she learned that the people filling the prisons to overflowing aren't criminal masterminds. They haven't been caught plotting and planning and executing capers. Instead, they're sad cases with low IQs and poor impulse control. Jack always said he was convinced that the most commonly used phrase in any prison is, "It seemed like a good idea at the time."

So, the odds are, especially given the ragged, disorganized appearance of the note, that her daughter, her beloved baby, her Sophie, is in the hands, and at the mercy of, stupid people who act first and think later. She isn't at all sure that technology and intelligence on one side can combat impulsiveness and brutality on the other.

Jack. Jack will know what to do. She needs to call Jack.

#

Forty minutes later, Grady sits in her kitchen.

He stopped at the Pergama gatehouse on his way up. Sophie's abductors couldn't have timed it better. William did his best to answer Mr. Grady's questions. Unfortunately, he's dim. Grady was struck, once again, by the irony of enclaves of rich people being guarded by low-wage employees. And, he has learned, any attempt to change this runs head-on into the concrete wall of "budgetary restraint." He supposes it's all a matter of priorities—pretty plantings and a heated community pool being more important than competent gatekeepers.

Grady has pushed for a visual monitoring system. (No dice. We're paying for a manned gate, the Board said, and, by God, that should do the job.) Or at least a written record of the license numbers of all non-resident vehicles passing through the gate. Not a dime of extra expanse there, but the guards object. Things get busy, they say. People will be kept waiting, and rich people kept waiting get mean. There has been a compromise: the guards are supposed to use their "best efforts." In practice, that means compliance is spotty at best.

So William can contribute only a vague recollection of the few unfamiliar vehicles that have been through that morning. There was a window washer he's seen before, a new maid service and a flower delivery for the Whitehursts.

"Who was the florist?"

William shrugs. He doesn't remember a logo, but there must have been one.

It was a truck, but not a pickup. Something with closed sides, he thinks. A van, that's it. A panel van.

Color?

Something light, maybe. He isn't sure.

Who was inside?

Some delivery guy. But William saw the flowers sitting on the passenger seat. They were real nice.

#

The flowers lie scattered over the polished marble of the entryway.

Jack, thank God, was home, answered the phone, and promised to rush up to the house. He told Jill not to touch anything else in Sophie's room and she hasn't. She made coffee. She picked up the phone to call Charlie in London, then put it down again, finally made herself dial. She longed for his voice, his comfort, even though she knew he'd have none to give, dreaded telling him their daughter is gone, could be dead... What word to use? Abducted? Kidnapped? Stolen? Was relieved, guiltily, to learn he is out. She left the routine, innocuous, four-word message: "Please call your wife."

Jack hugged her at the door, took her into his arms for the first time in years, and kept her close to him as she led him down the stairs, along the hall to Sophie's broken room. He looked at the destruction wordlessly for what seemed like a long time, then walked her back upstairs.

Where they are now.

"So," she asks, "what do we do?" She is standing at the kitchen island, pouring them each a cup of coffee just for something to do with her hands.

"I told you on the phone," he says, but his tone is gentle, not scolding. There isn't much to go on, Jack admits, but he wants to get the sheriff to put out an APB anyway. "We call the cops, and they bring in the F.B.I."

"And that works. You're sure that works."

"Oh, Jill," he says in a voice that she hears as mournful, "there are no guarantees."

"But that's what people do."

"It's standard procedure."

Jill can't believe what he's saying. Can't believe he's so detached. She still has the coffeepot in her hand, and she slams it down on the granite counter. The glass shatters, shards shoot across the counter, skid across the marble floor. Coffee spots the floor, spatters the cherry cabinets.

"And you think that's good enough for my baby? Standard procedure?"

She feels her legs give out. She collapses to the floor, sits in the wet and the glass, sobbing.

Her ex-husband comes over, squats down in front of her, puts his hands on her upper arms.

"You have to get up," he says.

She shakes her head. She can sit there as long as she likes. She can sit there until Sophie comes in the front door, until Sophie smiles, until she stands up for Sophie.

"You're bleeding," he says, and he helps her to her feet.

Lucky, Jack says. She's only been pierced by a few splinters.

She holds her left hand under running water at the kitchen sink, and he uses tweezers to pick out the glass. The blood runs down, swirls and drains. She can see the metal points of the instrument digging at her flesh, but she doesn't feel any pain.

Not any physical pain.

"The people who took Sophie are stupid," she says.

"They're probably not mental giants."

"And you saw her room. They're violent."

"Yes." As if he doesn't want to admit it, but has to.

"The F.B.I. will blow it."

"Hold still. There's one last piece."

"I'm right, aren't I? They will blow it."

Jack doesn't answer right away. Finally, he tells her what she knows is the truth. "Possibly."

He squirts antibiotic cream onto her hands. Jill uses the undamaged index finger of her right hand to spread it over the small cuts.

"So what do we do?" she says.

What they do is wait. They sit side by side on the couch in the den with the cordless phone on one side of them and the regular one on the other. Grady turns on the TV, finds reruns of old situation comedies.

He pours Jill a large brandy and hands it to her with the classic line: "Here. Drink this." She rarely drinks brandy anymore. She takes the glass anyway, as something to hold onto. She notices he's chosen Charlie's good stuff, the Armagnac he saves for special occasions, but she knows it's unintentional. What does Jack Grady know about French brandy? And she knows it doesn't matter.

They sit through *I Love Lucy*, *Bewitched*, *The Dick Van Dyke Show*. Jill finds the laugh tracks excruciating. The day drags on. The comedy continues. The giggles and chuckles and rolling har-de-hars mock her pain.

19

The voice on the phone is deep but hoarse, all gravel. The words are few.

"We have your kid. Don't call the cops."

"We haven't," Jill assures the voice. "We won't."

"Fuckin' right you won't."

Jill has the portable phone to her ear. Grady is listening on the extension. He raises a hand in warning. Jill waits.

"Give us what we want and you get her back."

"How much?" Jill says.

There's a brief silence on the other end of the line.

"We don't want money," the voice says.

Grady signals to Jill. She takes a deep breath and plunges.

"Let me talk to my daughter," she demands.

No reply.

"How do I know she's alive?"

"You have a key," the voice says. "Somewhere in your house."

"What key? What are you...?"

There are muffled sounds. Then...

"Mommy!"

Sophie! But sounding so young, so scared...

"Mommy?"

"I'm here, Soph. I'm here." Jill steadies herself. "Are you..."

The deep voice in the background. "Hurry up."

"Mommy? They won't let me talk long."

"Go ahead, sweetheart."

"There's a key. I found it in the Nelsons' yard. It's gold-colored and long and has a kind of round thing on the end. It has a funny little mark, like a crown, on it and a number. I put it in my jewelry box. But it's gone."

"Sophie, why do they..."

"Find it." The strangled voice is back, and Sophie is gone.

They start in Sophie's room. Grady knows they're destroying a crime scene, but he also knows Jill isn't interested in preserving evidence that will likely be used only to convict her daughter's killers. Not when they can do something to prevent her death. Or try to.

They are systematic. Operating on the assumption that Sophie moved the key and forgot where she'd put it (although she has an unusually good memory), they divide the room into quadrants and search one at a time. They lift the box spring to check the platform beneath, remove the sheets and blankets from the mattress, shake them, spread them out, pile them on the bed. They sort the clothes that have been spilled from the drawers, examine each garment and replace them one by one. They look in pockets and game boxes. They find a hoard of Halloween candy (contraband in the Whitehursts' house), an old Barbie diary written in a round childish hand (a discovery that makes Jill cry), and a St. Christopher medal given to Sophie by a former maid. They do not find a key.

Jill declares herself stumped. She doesn't believe that Sophie would hide anything in another part of the house, can't imagine where the key can be.

Jill, Grady knows, has all the qualities that make a good dentist, including compulsive organization. She is neat to a degree that he has often found extreme. It was one of the points of stress between them (although a minor one). She always kept a mental catalog of the contents of every drawer, every shelf, every closet. When she states that she has no junk drawers, no unsorted piles, no collection of mysterious unmarked keys, he believes her.

They search anyway. Nothing in the unused maid's room behind the garage, nothing in the guest quarters, nothing in the exercise room, the laundry, the downstairs bathrooms. They do find a key hanging on a hook in the garage, but it is small, silver and, Jill knows, a spare for the padlock on the back gate.

Grady suggests they try Charlie's study next. He has a feeling that anyone married to Jill would need pockets of chaos, a refuge for secret disorganization. And he's right. The contents of Charlie's desk speak of a mild pack rat tendency. Grady takes the big file drawer. He searches through papers, magazines, unlabeled flash drives and torn envelopes with notes scribbled on the back. Jill sorts through the dead pens, broken pencils, rubber bands, ancient pocket calculators and bits of hard candy in the middle drawer. She moves onto the top right drawer, begins digging in frustration through piles of miscellany. Suddenly, she stops, calls out.

"Look!" She's holding up a piece of paper about 5 1/2 by 8 1/2. "Conners' Jewelers" it says across the top in ornate script. It's a receipt dated a week before. Waving the paper, she runs from the room, down the stairs.

Grady finds her in Sophie's room tearing through the pile of small items they left in the far corner. He sees her hand close on an object. Triumphantly, she holds up a small gold horse—an elegant, expertly wrought charm that could be worn on a necklace or a bracelet. Perfect for a young girl.

"It was Charlie! He does that sometimes. Leaves Sophie a little surprise when he goes on a business trip. He would have put it in her jewelry box."

"So Charlie found the key. And he moved it."

But where?

Jill makes another call to Charlie's London hotel. Still out. No, the front desk has no idea where. She swears aloud to Grady. Why wouldn't the man break down and buy an international cell phone? She leaves a message: Call your wife. Urgent.

The phone rings.

Jill snatches it up. "Charlie?"

But it's the strange, hoarse voice.

"Do you have it?"

Soon. Another hour. Give us another...

A dial tone.

Jill drops the phone, bursts into tears. Grady puts his arms around her, settles her down. He mulls over what they know. The key is long. It has a round "thing" on the end. It has a marking. It bears a number. And Charlie thought its use and proper location were so obvious he didn't even mention it. He just put it away. Where it belonged.

"It's a safe deposit box key," Grady says. "It has to be a safe deposit box key."

Jill rushes from the room with Grady close behind. Together, they pull up the carpet in one corner of the closet in Charlie's office. Jill works the combination lock, right, left... Pulls at the handle. Nothing.

"Damn," she says. "You try."

She recites the combination as Grady turns the dial. The tumblers click into place. He opens the door. Jill reaches in, pulls out a small leather box, snaps open the lid. Where there should be two safe deposit box keys, there are three.

They've found the key.

#

The phone rings. Jill snatches it up, shouts into the receiver. "Yes! We've found it!"

A surprised voice on the other end of the line. "Jill?"

"Charlie."

"Jill, what on earth..."

"I have to get off the phone, Charlie. I can't tie up this line."

137

"What in hell is going on?"

"It'll be okay. I'll call you back on another line. But I have to get off this one."

"I'm in transit. What..."

A beep in her ear.

She hits "flash" to take the other call.

#

Sophie lies curled in a ball on the floor of the van, her back against the side wall. When he stopped tearing apart her room, the man she thinks of as the leader picked her up and carried her down the hall and into the garage where he threw her into the back of the van and slammed the doors behind her. Winnie, she noticed, set the alarm. For a person who seemed so out of it during the couple of days she stayed at their house, she sure hadn't missed a trick.

Sophie isn't tied, which surprises her since this isn't how things happen in the movies. She can't see what's in the front seat because there's a heavy wire partition behind it, but there isn't much in the back of the van, just a few duffel bags and some bottled water. They wanted the key, she knows, not her. So they weren't prepared. Maybe they don't have any rope.

The doors open again, and Winnie climbs in. She's followed by the second man in the ski mask, the short one, and he's pushing her. Sophie is pretty sure that both men are mad at Winnie. Winnie starts to sit down opposite Sophie, but the man gestures at her with his gun and she moves across and leans against the van wall next to Sophie. Sophie hears the driver's door open and close. That will be the first man, the one who's the boss.

The garage door rumbles open, and the van backs up.

The "leader" barks an order: "Put this on her. Have the girl do it." A ski mask appears at a small opening at the bottom of the wire partition where it doesn't quite meet the floor. Man #2 hands the mask to Winnie and says, "Do it."

"Sit up," Winnie says to Sophie. She turns the mask so that the openings for eyes, nose and mouth are in the back and pulls it over Sophie's hair and down over her face until it covers her chin.

The mask is scratchy and hot. Sophie can't see, and she feels as if she can't breathe. She begins to gasp. Megan's mother has panic attacks and Sophie has heard of hyperventilating. She knows it's bad. That you can pass out. But her lungs keep trying for a fresh breath. Her hands go to the mask.

"No." Winnie's voice again. "You have to keep it on." Sophie forces her hands to return to her lap. "Try to relax," she hears Winnie say. "It's knitted. You'll get plenty of air."

Sophie feels the first speed bump, the second. Three and four follow in rapid succession. Maybe they'll be stopped at the gate. William will wonder about this beat-up van, which, she now realizes, has no florist's sign. Why was it delivering flowers? He'll keep them there and call 9-1-1.

One more speed bump and then the circle around the fountain by the gate. Count the seconds. One-one thousand, two-one thousand, three-one thousand... There's the last speed bump. She feels the van begin to take the curve. Stop, she prays. Please stop.

Fourteen-one thousand, fifteen one-thousand, sixteen...

She feels the van accelerate. They are outside Pergama's gates. She won't be saved.

#

Jill is shaking. Grady places himself in front of her as she hangs up the phone, puts one hand on each of her shoulders in an attempt to ground her. Her eyes are wild, her right hand clamped solidly around the key.

"Ssssh," he says.

"We have to leave. We have to go to Sophie." It is a command.

Grady keeps his voice soft and slow. "We will," he says.

With his left hand over her right, he walks her into the kitchen.

He pulls the magnetized notepad and pen off the refrigerator and lays the pad on the counter.

Her fingers are a fist around the magic key, the totem that will unlock the door to Sophie. He pries them open, shushing her sounds of protest.

He takes the key from her open palm, places it on the notepad and traces the outline. He notes the number etched into the surface, the color (an odd bronze tone), the thickness. Then he turns to her. "I need a camera."

Jill looks at him as if she thinks he's insane. But she gets her digital camera, and watches as he takes several shots.

"We're going to have to give it up," he says, adding "if we're lucky" only to himself. "Now we need some putty."

In the utility closet that opens off the garage, they scan the shelves. Flashlight batteries, light bulbs, a can of pink paint (Sophie's walls when she was five), lubricating oil, a spare paper towel holder, plastic trash bags. No putty.

"How about modeling clay?" Grady asks.

Jill shakes her head. "I don't think so. Sophie's a little old for... Let me... Wait! The science project!"

In Sophie's shattered room, they root through the piles. They're looking for a partial box, a leftover that normally lives on the closet shelf.

Jill throws aside books, clothes—finally pulls it triumphantly from a stack of games.

Grady digs out a stick—bright red. Back in the kitchen, he flattens the clay, then presses the key into it, first one side down, then the other. "This needs a safe place," he says. Jill drops the drawing and the impressions into an envelope, seals it and tucks the envelope and the camera into the top right drawer of the kitchen desk, behind her mother's favorite recipes.

Grady cleans the clay from the key, holding it under a light to make sure no trace remains.

#

The desert south of Tucson doesn't resemble Utah, the Sahara,

Death Valley—or even Yuma. The yellows and browns of sand and rocks are gentled by the gray-green of bushes, even trees. Rolling hills dotted with scrub spread from the roads in graceful undulations. Stands of cottonwoods and eucalyptus line washes that fill with water during heavy rains. Mountains add drama in the distance. In the spring, there are wildflowers.

Tucson is the only real city in the region. The Tohono O'odam Nation lies to the Southwest. For a traveler headed due south, the only towns between Tucson and Mexico are the retirement village of Green Valley, 24 miles down the road, and the artists' colony of Tubac, another 18 miles along. Drive sixty-four miles total, and you reach the sister towns of Nogales, Arizona and Nogales, Sonora. The trip has been a gradual uphill climb, and the elevation at the border is nearly 3,900 feet. The air is five degrees cooler, the landscape visibly more lush. Cactus is the exception, rather than the rule.

But it's still a desert.

They stop at the airport just south of town, locate Charlie's Land Rover (which he always parks in the same section of the lot), and trade Grady's beat-up Taurus for the truck. Fifteen minutes later, Grady swings the silver SUV onto the entrance ramp for I-19.

They are as prepared as possible, but it feels like they are ready for nothing at all. Grady grabbed a cooler from Jill's garage and—over her objections that it would take too much time—stopped at a Circle K on Valencia. He gathered water and snacks. She picked up a first-aid kit, putting it on the check-out counter without a word. He added a map in spite of the truck's built-in GPS. And to Jill's obvious disgust, he bought a carton of Marlboros.

They both knew they might need protection from the desert, so Jill is wearing jeans, hiking boots and a t-shirt. Her hat and long-sleeved shirt are in the back seat. Grady was already in jeans and a polo, and Jill supplied a shirt and hat of Charlie's. His Nikes will have to do for footwear. Jill threw a pair of Charlie's cowboy boots into the truck, but Grady tried them on during their supply stop and discovered that Charlie has outsize feet for his height. The boots are much too big. Their arsenal consists of two weapons: Grady's gun, on his belt as usual, and Jill's, in the glove compartment.

They've been given only partial instructions: Head south on I-19 to exit 48, the voice said. Turn right and head southwest on Arivaca Road until they are well away from the highway. Then pull off and wait. They'll be contacted again, on Grady's cell phone. He hopes to God they don't lose the signal.

Whoever they are, they've been told Grady is coming. It would be a bad idea to surprise dumbfucks who are already stressed out by the biggest crime of their lives, so he convinced Jill she had to make his presence a condition for the meeting. In terror, she made her demand. She needed to bring a friend, she said, someone who could drive her. She was too upset. She'd wreck the car.

In terror, she waited for the voice to reply. She was certain that refusal—or silence—would be followed quickly by her daughter's death.

The hoarse voice didn't like it, she could tell. But it agreed.

Once they're past Tucson's southern fringes, it's amazing how quickly the city falls away. They see only the occasional car, a few trucks headed north, mostly "tomato men" bringing produce up from Mexico. Grady doesn't get down this way very often any more. When he was younger, it was a different story: trips to Nogales, scuba diving at Rocky Point on the Gulf of Mexico, camping near Patagonia. Since then, he's gotten used to Tucson's burgeoning "California-style" housing developments blotting out the desert. Now he is surprised at just how much open space remains. He finds himself remembering canyons, washes, ghost towns and the excitement of crossing the border as a teenager with his buddies for a night of carousing.

The signs along I-19 are in kilometers, rather than miles. Green Valley 32km, Tubac 61, Nogales 80. It adds to Grady's sense of unreality, as if they are already in another country.

20

Not long after the van passes through Pergama's gates, it stops. Sophie hears the passenger door open and another person get in. A male voice she hasn't heard before says, "Hot out there, dude." Then, "What the fuck? You snatched the kid?"

It's the short man's voice that answers. "Had to, man."

"Shut the fuck up, both of you," says the scary, hoarse voice. Then the door slams, and the van starts up again.

Music blares from the front. Pounding, loud, with the kind of lyrics her mother disapproves of. These aren't kids, she thinks, but maybe they're not really adults. They listen to old music, but it's not grown-up music. She feels her stomach tighten as if she's been kicked. She would not have believed she could be more scared, but for some reason, the realization that these big, powerful people might be as dumb as some of the losers who are always screwing up at school is terrifying.

They ride for a while. The two men in the front seat are talking, but the music is too loud. She can't hear what they're saying.

Then the van stops. The music pounds. It gets hot. The engine is running, which means the air conditioning should be working, but it doesn't feel as if any cool air is making it into the back. Sophie feels sick behind the scratchy knit of the mask. She starts to get sleepy, which seems weird when she is so scared. She lies down on the floor of the van, and wonders if she is passing out.

Later—she can't tell how much later—the music stops. Someone pulls her roughly into a sitting position, yanks the hood off, and sticks a cell phone in front of her mouth. The leader's voice, coming out of a head swathed in a ski mask, says, "Talk to your mother."

Her mom's voice! She wants to cry, but she doesn't. She isn't even half done talking when the phone is snatched away.

She fights when he forces the ski mask back on her head. She kicks and she bites, and he slaps her. She slumps to the floor, and he rolls her onto her stomach. He pulls her arms roughly behind her, wraps something around them again and again. This time, she does pass out.

When she comes to, the music is blasting and the van is moving. She feels a hand resting on her shoulder. Just sitting there lightly, as if, maybe, it's trying to keep her attached to the world. Winnie, it has to be Winnie.

#

Grady and Jill drive in silence. They get off at exit 48 and pass through the tiny town of Amado. Even with the GPS, it takes a couple of false turns and a look at the detail map to locate Arivaca Road. Southwest turns out to be the only direction it runs.

They bump along for about ten minutes. The route is rough and threatens to become little more than a path. Grady is grateful for the four-wheel drive. He reflects that it might be the one advantage they have over whoever is in the van.

Another mile or so along, he spots a decent-size level area next to the road and brings the SUV to a stop under a clump of mesquite trees. He sets the brake, lowers the windows and turns off the engine.

"Okay," he says. "We have shade. And we've got full signal on the phone. This is as good a place as any."

He reaches into the cooler, hands Jill a bottle of water and takes one for himself.

Jill accepts the bottle and twists the cap off. Settling the bottle between her thighs, she removes her sunglasses and wipes briefly at her eyes, puts the shades back on.

"She could have been ours," she says without looking at him.

Grady lights a cigarette. He doesn't reply. What is there to say? When they got married, Jill was a newly minted D.D.S., a debt-laden associate in a partnership with two set-in-their-ways men. Grady had just made detective. She worked days. He worked nights. They left each other loving notes, met joyfully between the sheets in the darkness of three a.m. and spent boozy weekends diving at Rocky Point, camping near Patagonia, or just in bed.

They fought hard and made up passionately. They disagreed over what car to buy, what to have for dinner, whether to buy a house. Jill spoke of building equity. Grady couldn't see himself giving up their time spent listening to music and drinking and making love, scuba diving and drinking and making love, hiking and drinking and making love, to do yard work. He'd never noticed that his buddies who'd rushed to save the down payment, buy the house, build the equity were doing all that well or seemed all that happy. That's what he'd thought. What he'd said (repeatedly) was: "What's wrong with the way we are, babe?"

She wanted him to finish the undergrad degree (he'd managed to accumulate two years of criminal justice credits at Pima, the local community college) and go to law school. He took one or two courses a semester, but his heart wasn't in it. He worked nights and when he was off during the day, he just wanted to sleep. And when he wasn't working and wasn't sleeping, he wanted to be with his wife. Truth was, in spite of the bickering and the yelling and the occasional small flying object, he was happy, absolutely delighted with his life. He also felt academically inadequate, overmatched by Jill. He'd never been what anyone would call a reader. Had merely endured high school except for his friends, football and the jazz band.

That was what he thought. What he said (to his wife's growing annoyance) was: "What's wrong with the way I am?"

Nothing, Jill would say. That's not the point.

But, over time, she proved relentlessly upbeat and consistently successful. She began her own practice, and it prospered. He plodded. A good detective. Not brilliant. But dependable. And well liked. He passed an exam, made Detective 2nd Grade, but there he plateaued (or stagnated, as Jill put it).

They kept fighting, but they no longer made up. At least not in bed.

Jill didn't get religion, but she got healthy. She gave up alcohol. At first, she didn't drink at all. Then she made rare exceptions—a glass of wine at a dinner party, a flute of champagne on a special occasion. She handed him articles on second-hand smoke, and one angry and rainy night she dumped every pack of cigarettes he owned on the patio. She began to spend her days off with her horses. Saturday evenings, they'd have dinner with another dentist and spouse or people Jill had met through her charitable activities. Whether they were hosting or at another couple's home or at a restaurant, it all seemed the same to Grady. He tired of arugula and wanted ribs. He refused to floss his teeth. At one point, he stopped brushing for an entire weekend.

In the end, they stayed together for six months after they'd given up because they couldn't even agree on who should leave.

Now, more than fifteen years later, sitting under a mesquite tree in the middle of nowhere with her daughter missing and her husband absent, Jill says, "We had fun, didn't we?"

Grady's silence hangs between them for a moment. Suddenly, I'm the white knight, he thinks. After years of being a bastard, a son-of-a-bitch, even a prick (in your less ladylike moments), I'm suddenly a prince. All because you hope I can save your daughter. But I haven't done it yet.

What he says is: "I would have been a lousy father. You got the right guy."

It isn't all of the truth, but it is enough of it. He toasts her with his bottle of water. "Drink up."

Jill forces the water down. She knows she has to stay hydrated. Okay, she thinks, he doesn't want to talk about it, to face the fact that Sophie could have been his daughter—talented, pretty, smart. A great kid, as Jack always says. Now taken, kidnapped... Don't think about it.

She and Grady married because of the sex, Jill decided long ago. She has a mind as well organized as her practice and her house, and she needed to file away her five years of Grady (two dating and three as his wife). To do this, she had to figure out how to label the mental compartment. "Mistake" was way too general.

"Anachronism," she told herself. "Throwback." Okay, so she and Grady enjoyed a strong sexual attraction. Nothing wrong with that. Opposites do attract. But in an age where people come together, fuck their brains out and then move on to form long-term relationships with more suitable partners, she and Jack attempted to base a marriage on lust. The consequences were pathetically predictable. Lust doesn't last, the advice columns always say. In this case, she suspected, lust might have lasted—that it tried to. They simply overwhelmed its force, wore it out.

He's right, though. Theirs was no life for a child.

Grady met Jill Thanksgiving weekend more than twenty years ago. He'd left the army only a year before, putting aside the black beret of a ranger, was a brand new cop, barely out of the academy and damn proud of what he'd accomplished. It was a party, and she was a partial figure on the other side of a crowded rec room. Dancing bodies, guys hitting on girls, girls flirting with guys, hands holding beer bottles or plastic tumblers of wine, a long table spread with chips, salsa and sandwich makings all blocked his view, but he would have sworn he saw her whole. Every other young woman in the room had a frizzy perm or streaky, layered wings flying back from her face. Not Jill. Her shoulder-length blonde hair was smooth. It shone in the light. She wore a long, flared black skirt and a white knit top with a scoop neck. He was standing with Sue something-or-other, a girl a buddy had just introduced him to, and he could tell this Sue was interested. He was strong and clear-eyed in those days, and because he believed he had a way with women a lot of them seemed to believe it too. Already, this one was laying a hand possessively on his forearm, sipping from his bottle of beer. She was probably the prettiest girl in the room. But then he saw the sleek blonde, and suddenly Sue's curves seemed excessive, her curly chestnut hair overdone.

He took a few steps to where the crowd was thinner, and Sue moved with him. He needed a better look at the blonde. His buddies would have said she was too scrawny, no meat on her bones. Grady thought she had more class—and sex appeal—than anyone he'd ever seen.

He took his time, planned his strategy, managed to disengage from Sue. No one seemed to know the girl. Someone said she went to school in California, that she'd come with a friend of a friend. He watched as one guy after another approached her and, as far as he could tell, was shot down.

Then around midnight when most of the crowd was either drunk or gyrating to Blondie (or both), he caught a flash of cool lemon in his peripheral vision. She was standing alone by the window holding a long-neck beer and looking not at the dance floor but at the night outside.

He walked up till he was standing a polite distance from her left elbow. Close enough to be heard, he calculated, but far enough away to be casual.

"Not your kind of music?" he began, thinking, God, I can't believe this is all I can come up with. C'mon, Grady, you usually do better than this.

But apparently he'd done all right. "It's not bad," a throaty voice said. "But I'm not nineteen anymore."

"Let me guess," Grady ventured. "You like jazz."

"Ummm. Yes. And classical even better."

"So if you're not nineteen, how old are you?"

She was twenty-four, it turned out, and midway through dental school. She was home for the holiday. And, it went without saying, she was bored.

"Could you use a little Gershwin?" he asked. "I have a major collection."

She sipped from the beer bottle, seemed to consider.

"Come see your etchings?" she challenged. "Is that what you mean?" But she sounded amused.

"I'm Grady," he said. "Jack Grady."

She offered him her hand and a stunning smile. "Hi, Jack," she said. "I'm Jill."

They were both native Tucsonans. Her background was almost as lower middle-class ordinary as his. Where he grew up able to get along in the barrio, she lived in the boonies and was always promising to shoe a horse, swearing she knew how. They both went to public schools, his in the south central, hers way out east. They both knew lots of kids who'd dropped out, or OD'd, or gave birth at sixteen, or spent their days behind the cash register at Circle K, or were still working on their GEDs. Grady knew more people who had gone to prison, but he was a guy. They figured that accounted for the discrepancy. She knew more who'd been verbally or physically beaten up by husbands or boyfriends. Some were still puzzled that being loved meant being hit. The rest had given up.

They both knew a few who'd done well—gone to the U of A or a technical school or (like Grady) into the military, and they congratulated themselves that they were among that group. They'd been lucky. Their parents hadn't been educated, but they'd both had solid homes, a caring upbringing. They'd both risen above their circumstances. Jill had achieved more, but on a relative basis Grady had come at least as far.

It should have worked. But it didn't.

He lights another cigarette. He watches bird crap plop onto the hood of the Land Rover. He hears Jill, his beloved, his till-death-do-us-part from whom he parted so long ago, sigh, and he knows it is just the least small expression of her agony, the tiniest involuntary vocalization of her pain.

21

Sophie drifts. To keep herself from panicking, she rebuilds her city in her head, making it bigger, stronger, better. Giving the children more parks, more places to ride their bicycles, more police protection. She manages to withdraw into a state that isn't sleeping but isn't full wakefulness either. When something pulls her back.

The van has parked—somewhere. The music has stopped, and she can hear the rustle of trees. It's hot, but air is moving. Sophie can feel it on her arms and legs even though nothing makes it through the mask. Winnie's hand still rests on her shoulder.

Sophie hears thumps, a shuffling noise. The rear doors of the van open, and the vehicle rocks as someone gets out. Then the doors close.

A whisper. Winnie's voice. "Sophie! Are you awake?" Urgency in her tone.

Sophie grunts. Yes. She is awake. For all that it matters.

She feels a tug. Winnie is working at the belt binding her wrists. She feels warm breath next to her ear. "Can you sit up?"

Sophie's hands come free. She hurts all over. The floor of the van is hard, bare metal. But with Winnie's help, she manages to sit up.

Winnie pulls off the ski mask. Sophie takes one deep, grateful breath. Then another. She looks around. They're alone in the rear of the van.

"Where..." she begins.

Winnie is stuffing a few bottles of water and a couple of old shirts into a backpack. Sophie notices Winnie's eyes are both blue again—she must have found her contact. But her cheek is bruised, she has a black eye and a cut lip. "Ssssh," she says. "We have to hurry. Two of them have walked off somewhere. To plan, I think. The little guy's supposed to be guarding us, but he's been bitching about the heat so he got out to cool off. He's half-drunk—had a bottle hidden, so the others don't know it. But even he's not dumb enough to still be out there when his buddies get back."

Crouching, she moves toward the van door, cracks it and peers out.

"C'mon," she says. "While his back is turned."

Sophie moves as quickly as she can. She's still stiff. Winnie eases the door open and jumps out. She helps Sophie down.

They're somewhere way out of Tucson. Sophie can tell they're south of the city because of the terrain, the bushes, the trees. The van is parked in a small clearing. Sophie can see their guard about twenty feet away under a cottonwood. He's peeing against the trunk. His rifle is lying on the ground near his feet.

Winnie moves away from the guard, toward the brush, motioning to Sophie to follow.

The guard zips up. He turns. He's short and thin, with reddish hair, pale, pimply skin and a big nose. He wears a t-shirt with a screaming head dripping blood. "Hey!" he yells.

"Run!" Winnie shouts.

Sophie tries. She gets her legs moving, but it feels as if she's in a dream, one of those horrible nightmares where she can only move in slow motion.

The guard could catch them easily. Instead, he scrambles for his gun.

Winnie stops, turns toward Sophie. "Run!" she shouts again.

This time Sophie's legs obey. She's catching up, is ten feet, eight, six, four from following Winnie into the brush. She can do it. They'll get away...

Then she sees the root. She orders her right foot to avoid it, skip over it, keep going...but... Her toe catches.

She crashes to the ground. A moment later, she feels the weight of a body on top of her, holding her down. She smells old sweat and new liquor.

She hears scrambling, breaking branches, swearing behind her. Then the leader's raspy voice.

"You dumb motherfucker," it croaks. "Can't you do anything right?"

She struggles to raise her head out of the dirt. She sees only bushes and trees. Winnie has disappeared. A pair of thick, denim-clad legs moves in the direction where Winnie entered the scrub forest. She hears a voice, the third man, she guesses. The one who was riding in the passenger seat. "Shit! The bitch is gone."

"She told us enough." The leader's voice again. "Let the snakes take care of her."

A hand grabs her hair, holds her head still. Then the man pulls the ski mask roughly down over her face, blinding her again. Sophie tastes dust. She sneezes violently. Somebody picks her up and throws her in the van. She hits the floor hard. Her ankle hurts. She's dizzy.

Before the doors slam, she hears the guard, the short man who screwed up. He sounds panicky. "Goddamnit, she saw me. The kid saw my face."

"Don't worry about it," the leader's voice says.

#

When the call comes, it is as brief as all the others. This worries Grady. To his experienced, if rusty, gut, it makes their foe less massively stupid—and more ruthless.

"You took the Arivaca Road?" the voice says. Grady confirms.

153

"Keep going southwest. To an intersection with a wooden marker. No writing on it. Just a drawing of a cow skull. Turn right. About three miles along, there's a road to the left. Take it two miles. When it opens out, stop."

"How will we know the place?"

"You'll know it."

Jill grabs the phone from Grady's hand. "Let me talk to Sophie... I have to talk to Sophie."

But the line is dead.

Grady is already starting the engine. The first call they received that afternoon showed up on Jill's caller I.D. Grady checked the area code—252. As he suspected, it was not helpful. "Where?" Jill asked.

"Somewhere in North Carolina. Probably a stolen phone. It's already in a trash can." This time, the number was local, with a 520 area code. Another stolen cell. Or a pre-paid throw-away. He notes it. But the information is useless. Without law enforcement's ability to triangulate the location of the phone... It was one of arguments he made to Jill, that the police can pinpoint exactly where a call was made. But could they have been there, set up, in time to do any good? This thing is moving fast. And now... Too late.

They are as ready as they're going to be. Earlier, he opened the glove compartment and took out Jill's gun. The weapon is a .38 with all the stopping power of that caliber, but small and light, made of aluminum alloy and titanium and sized to fit a woman's hand. It's still heavier than he would like. But it's the best he can do. He walked around to the back of the Land Rover, opened the tail gate and dug into the stash of snacks. Jill climbed out after him and watched as he pulled out a large box of cookies, opened it carefully and poured the contents into a paper bag. He tore a strip off a small utility towel that Charlie had left in the rear of the SUV, wrapped the gun in it and put it in the box. Then, he replaced some of the cookies on top of the gun and closed the flap. Finally, he walked away from the vehicle until he was well into the mesquite and creosote and tossed the paper bag even farther into the brush.

"Why..." she began.

He took off his Nikes and stuffed them under the driver's seat. Then he pulled on Charlie's cowboy boots, which gaped around his legs. Finally, he took his gun from his belt and shoved it way down inside the right boot. "We'll be searched," was all he said.

They almost miss the wooden marker. They lose the cell phone signal. And the dirt road is even worse than the one they were on, slow going even in the SUV. They follow ruts up one hill, down the other side and up the next. Grady concentrates on missing the worst of the rocks while Jill watches for their next turn. If they take out the undercarriage of the truck, Sophie is dead.

"There!" Jill exclaims at last.

Grady is doubtful. Something that at some point was cleared by humans does intersect with the cow path they're on, but it looks like little more than a trail. Is it passable? Have they missed the right road? Are they turning too soon?

"This has to be it," she says. "We've already come more than three miles, and the last real turn-off was more than two miles back."

Grady hesitates.

"Turn!" she says.

Creosote bushes scrape the sides of the Land Rover. Mesquite and Palo Verde branches screech along the top. They're in a scrub forest. The trail they follow is uneven and strewn with rocks. Even with four-wheel drive, they're crawling.

Just when Grady has decided this can't be right and is trying to figure out, first, how in hell he will tell Jill they're lost and, second, how he can turn around or back out, the trail curves sharply to the left around a rocky outcropping. Suddenly, the scrub thins—and the trail becomes a road—still unpaved, narrow, rutted, but undoubtedly a road.

Two hundred yards farther along, the road curves sharply once more to avoid another crag of stacked boulders. As they come out of the curve, they see the ruin of what was once a settlement. Ancient adobe buildings—roofs collapsed but a few walls intact—surround an open area that must once have been the village plaza.

They've arrived at a ghost town.

22

Grady drives slowly into the plaza. He notes the rotted remains of a corral at one side, rocks that were once part of walls scattered across the dirt of the main street, desert scrub restaking its claim.

He spots something interesting in the center. The remnant of the community well? Once the lifeblood of the town, it's covered loosely by boards that have warped over the decades, twisted by the rain and dried by the sun. Fragments of a crumbling stone wall run at a tangent nearby. He brings the SUV to a stop less than six feet away.

He lowers the windows and turns off the engine.

A raspy voice, recognizable as the one on the phone, shouts from the ruins straight ahead.

"Get out one at a time," the voice says. "I want your hands empty and up where I can see them."

"You first," Grady says to Jill. "Take it slow."

Jill opens the passenger door and climbs out. She holds her open hands over her head.

"Okay," the voice says. "Now the friend."

Grady pushes the driver's door open and steps down. The old ground-level structure a few feet to his left is definitely a well. And the cover is in bad shape. He can see wide spaces between the boards.

Two men holding rifles come out of the ruins. To Grady's surprise and relief, both wear ski masks. They may get out of this alive after all.

The men walk to within twenty feet of Jill and Grady and stop. One is short, maybe wiry, but with no weight to him. The other is tall, with the popped-out muscles of a serious body-builder. The tall one gestures at Jill with his rifle, and she moves to stand between Grady and the truck.

"Check her out." The oddly strangled voice belongs to the tall man, the leader. The shorter man puts down his rifle, walks over to Jill and begins to search her.

As the man's hands reach Jill's breasts, they threaten to linger. Grady sees Jill repress a shudder and damns his own helplessness. But the taller man takes care of it. "Speed it up, asshole."

Still leering at Jill, the small man shrugs. "All done," he says.

"Now him," the boss orders. And Grady stands very still as the man pats him down. He smells alcohol. The man isn't falling-down drunk, but his coordination is a little off.

"He's clean," the short man reports.

The tall man snorts derisively. "Try again."

The short man runs his hands over Grady again, checks the pockets of his jeans. He shakes his head at his boss. "Nuthin'."

"The boots, you idiot!" The tall man waves his rifle at Grady. "Take 'em off."

Grady complies, but carefully, knowing sudden movements could get them shot. He pulls off the left boot, hands it to shorty, who holds it upside down and shakes it, smiles at his boss as if to say, "See. Told you so."

Then Grady pulls off the right boot. Shorty goes through the same routine—and the gun falls to the ground. Shorty stares at as if it's a magic trick.

"Pick it up," orders his boss. And the small man retrieves the gun and tucks it into his waistband.

"Now look in the truck."

The smaller man gets into the SUV, pokes around inside. He pulls open the tail gate and checks the small tool chest Charlie keeps in the back (and which Grady knows is virtually empty). He digs through the food. He pulls out the box of cookies, opens it, stuffs a couple into his mouth, tucks the box under his arm... "Stop feeding your face," the boss barks, and the man lets the box fall to the floor. Grady mentally winces, waiting for the tell-tale "clunk," but the little man manages to simultaneously bang into the metal tool chest, and that and his explosive "Shit!" save them.

Rubbing his elbow, he climbs out of the truck. "Nuthin' there," he says.

"How about a phone? Don't they have a phone?" There is sarcasm in the tone.

The small man opens the passenger door of the Land Rover, reaches in, comes out with Jill's phone and tosses it to his boss.

The boss drops it to the ground, smashes it under his boot, picks it up and throws it into the brush. The short man walks away and picks up his rifle.

"Where's Sophie?" Grady warned Jill to be patient, to follow his cues, but clearly she's near her breaking point. "Where's my baby?"

"In a minute," the tall man says. He turns to Grady. "Where's the key?"

Over the past few minutes, Grady has been able to edge gradually sideways, away from the SUV, toward the well, and now he manages a good-sized step. Slowly, careful not to make any threatening motions, he reaches into his mouth, into the pocket between his teeth and his cheek and pulls out the key.

The boss looks in fury at the man whose search failed.

In that moment, Grady takes one last sideways step. Earlier, what now seems an age ago, while they were still sitting under the mesquites waiting for instructions, Jill asked him about his plan. "Trust me," he told her. "It's better if you don't know." Truth was, he didn't have a plan. As he learned in his years on the force, sometimes all you can do is improvise.

He's improvising now. And he is standing squarely in the center of the rotted cover of the well. What is underneath is either water or a big black hole.

He holds the key out in front of him, dangles it over an opening between the boards.

"Here," he says. "You get this when we get the little girl."

Raspy voice gestures to the short man. "Bring her out."

The man vanishes into the ruins. An instant later, Sophie appears, walking in front of the man, limping slightly, prodded by the rifle in her back. Then her face changes. "Mommy!" she cries and starts to run toward Jill.

The rifle cracks. Sophie stumbles and falls.

"No!" Jill screams, and starts to run toward her daughter.

But the gun was pointing at the sky.

Now the boss lowers the barrel, points it at Jill, and she freezes.

"She's okay," he says. But there's no reassurance in the tone.

To Sophie, he commands: "Get up."

Sophie struggles to her feet. "Mommy!" she sobs.

"Stand still, darling," Jill calls to Sophie. "Don't move."

Grady continues to hold the key out over the crack between the boards. His weight is almost too much for the battered cover. He can sense the shifting of the boards, the groaning of wood as it longs to give way, to let the ancient nails pull free...

The tall man walks over to Sophie, points his rifle at her head. "Go get the key," he orders.

Sophie takes one step toward Grady, two, three...

"No," Grady says. "Give the girl to her mother and I'll give you the key."

"Forget it," the tall man says.

Grady shifts his weight on the ancient boards, making them creak audibly.

"Look," Grady says. "You've got me. I've got the key. I'm unarmed. If you don't let them go, I'll drop the key down the hole. If you do, I'll give it to you. It's the only chance they have. It's also the only chance you have."

The tall man reconsiders. He gestures to shorty. "Go check it out."

The small man begins to walk toward the well. "Without the rifle!" the leader barks. And the short man leans the rifle against a rock.

He approaches Grady. "Not too close," the taller man cautions.

Again, Grady shifts his weight. More creaking—louder this time. "Careful," he says as the man edges toward him. "This won't hold us both."

The short man stops and scopes out the situation from a distance of at least ten feet. "Looks pretty bad," he reports.

Clearly relieved that his boss hasn't sent him all the way onto the well cover, he backs away and picks up his rifle.

"All right," the hoarse voice concedes, not happy about it. "Mom gets the kid." He points at Sophie. "Go." Disbelieving, Sophie doesn't move. She looks at the tall man and his rifle, then at her mother. "Go!" the man commands again.

This time the spell breaks. Sophie runs to her mother. Jill wraps her arms around her daughter, touches her lips to the top of Sophie's head, holds her tightly. Tears stream down her face.

Grady speaks carefully and calmly. "Get in the truck," he says.

"But..." Jill protests.

"Both of you. In the truck."

He watches Jill think.

"The keys are in the ignition," he says firmly. "Get in and get out of here. Now."

For once in her life, she obeys him. He watches her help Sophie into the truck and climb in herself. Their first meeting goes by when she puts her foot on the step, their dating years when she swings into the seat, their marriage begins when she starts the engine and is over by the time she turns the truck around and heads out of the plaza the way they came. For a moment, Grady is certain she's going to run down the short man. "No heroics," he silently wills, trying to decide what he'll do if she takes the little guy out. "You can't get them both, so if you hit one, we're all dead." But she apparently thinks better of it. The SUV drives away.

23

"Okay," he thinks, "so this is it." He tries to make peace with the prospect, to tell himself that whether it's water waiting at the bottom or a dry hole, this is as good a way to go as any. Jill will explain to his mother. They've always gotten along.

The short guy swings his rifle up, ready to take a shot at the retreating truck. "Put it down, asshole," says his boss.

Grady waits. His arm aching from holding out the key, he stands there until he can no longer hear the engine. Then he stands there some more. He considers what to do. He can simply drop the key between the boards, into the hole. He is as good as dead anyway, and he doesn't see why these assholes should profit. If the key goes "plunk," they'll never get it back. If it doesn't, they might—with enough time and rope and maybe a ladder.

He is still considering when the tall man makes the first move. "That's it," he says. "You're outta time."

He gestures at the short man. "Go get it, scuz."

"Them boards look like shit," the smaller man protests.

His boss makes a dismissive gesture. "He's bluffing. Just do it."

The short man lays his rifle on the ground and moves slowly toward Grady. With the tall man's weapon still aimed at him, Grady bends at the waist and lowers the key over the black opening between the boards. He has a feeling the little guy is expendable, and he's not sure if that's good or bad. "Shoot me," he says, "and it falls."

The short man creeps closer. Ten feet, eight, six, four... Just as the man comes within reach, just as he approaches the edge of the well cover, Grady holds out the key. The man can't quite reach it. Grady can see him think about it, watch him make the decision. As the man puts his foot onto the cover, Grady closes his fist over the key. Ignoring the shrieks from the rotten wood as the boards sag under the added weight, he swings his arm over the little man's shoulders, pulling his enemy toward him, kneeing him hard in the balls.

Then everything happens at once.

As the man collapses, Grady moves, rolling out from under him to the side—off the well cover. He hears the crack of the tall man's rifle, hits the dirt—and sees the short man land with force on the rotten cover, sees the boards give way. As he rolls behind a crumbling stone wall, he's aware of a shout, a scream descending, echoing as it drops, the sound of flesh and bone slamming into packed earth far below. Then silence. It is definitely a dry well.

They play hide and seek But it's uneven, with Grady doing all the hiding. He hoped to yank his gun out of the little guy's waistband before sending him down the well, but he wasn't quick enough. Maybe those skills are rusty. Or maybe it was impossible.

Whatever. The question is where the fuck do things go from here? His situation isn't much better than it was when he was standing on the rotted boards. There's damn little cover in the plaza. And he can't stay where he is forever.

A bullet sends chips flying from a nearby rock grazing his right shoulder, dinging his cheek. And he was turned away—didn't even see where the shot came from.

The man has Grady pinned down. And he knows it. He's being careful with his shots, not wasting ammunition. Clearly, the asshole doesn't want to get close, but unless he's a total idiot, he won't have to. All Grady's fighting, if you can call it that, is a holding action.

He considers his options. He's no desert rat, but he has to know more about the terrain than some greenhorn who made it to Arizona only a few days before. That has to be an advantage. What good will it do him? Hard to say.

Grady concludes that he has three choices. One: Die. Two: Hold out until nightfall. But full dark is still more than an hour away. And he's in his stocking feet, making silent movement through the desert in blackness impossible. Three: Try to take the man from behind.

Before the last stretch of the drive to the ghost town, Grady insisted that they prepare for the desert, and he put on Charlie's long-sleeved shirt over his polo. Now he takes it off. He crawls on his belly to a low growing shrub that sticks the tops of its prickly branches just above the sheltering rock wall. Carefully, he pulls the bush back and dresses it in the shirt. He finds a dead ocotillo rib lying on the ground, removes his polo and wraps it around the spiky wood to protect his hands. Then he scoots backwards on a diagonal from the shrub until he can just reach it with the pole-like stick and gooses it. The bush jumps, a fragment of Charlie's shirt rises briefly above the level of the wall. A shot ricochets off the rock. Grady releases the ocotillo, and the shrub falls back, the shirt hiding behind the wall once more.

Now he has a fix on his enemy's position. Stay where you are! he silently commands as he pulls the polo back on and ties Charlie's shirt around his waist. You know you can wait me out.

He was taught to crawl in his ranger days, and now the training comes back: his body remembers. He moves from wall to rock to boulder to ruin, trading speed when he has to for silence and invisibility. At last, he rounds the corner of a roofless adobe hut, and there is the man, less than fifty feet away, crouching with his back to Grady, ski mask discarded at his feet, the back of his thick neck already red. A water bottle's at his side, rifle across his lap.

The area between Grady and his prey is open ground. There's no cover, only low scrub. If the man turns, Grady is dead. But he was dead standing on the well cover. Why should he worry about dying now?

Grady inches his way across the clearing. At one point, a short, fuzzy cholla sends its needles through his jeans into his calf and he has to clamp his jaw to keep from crying out. Moments later, his foot nudges a rock just a little too hard, and Grady hears it bump against its neighbor. But the man is taking a swig from his water bottle. He doesn't react, doesn't turn or look around. Grady draws closer, twenty feet, fifteen, ten... He prepares to spring. Gets ready to overwhelm the man before he can reach his rifle. He takes a deep breath, moves closer still...

There's a sound behind him. Grady isn't relaxing, isn't drinking from a water bottle. He hears the noise and he knows it's bad. Before he can whirl, he feels an arm around his neck, cutting off his air.

Grady grabs the unseen man's arm, manages to pull it away from his throat. He gains some leverage with his left leg and hooks his foot behind the man's knee, putting him off-balance. A rifle cracks.

"Stop it, you asshole! You'll hit me!" The voice from behind his ear is rough. The body bulky. Grady wonders for an instant why he is bothering to fight this man he didn't know existed when the muscle-bound leader with the rifle can stand back and, if Grady is the winner, just pick him off.

But he struggles on. Instinct, maybe. The guy is big, but he's unskilled. Grady runs through his special forces' techniques and his repertoire of dirty tricks picked up over the years on the streets of Tucson. A thumb misses the right eye by an inch but slows his attacker down. A knee to the groin lands high, hitting abdominal muscles but doubling the bulky figure over. Protecting his throat, the man manages to dodge the edge of Grady's hand but loses his balance and topples backward. Grady follows his weight to the ground, punches him in the face once, twice, three times. You're out. Grady rolls off the unconscious man, planning to keep going, doing what he can to evade the rifle. But as his back hits the dirt, a boot slams down on his belly, knocking the breath out of him. He gasps, fighting to expand his lungs, to take in air. The boot moves up to his chest. He lies flat, pinned down, totally helpless. The tall man stands over him pointing the rifle down at Grady's head.

"You're done, asshole," the hoarse voice says. The man slides back the bolt.

Grady could swear he hears the zing of the bullet. But that would mean he's alive, and that can't be when clearly he is dead. There is an even heavier weight on his chest. He realizes that it's the tall man, collapsed on top of him. A small figure, backlit by the dying sun, stands over them holding the rifle the short man abandoned near the well.

"I know how to use this," Clare says. "Don't think I don't." She wears a hat and sunglasses. Grady can see a hint of a black eye below the bottom of the frame.

She waves the rifle at the burly man, still lying unconscious a few feet away. The guy's built like a refrigerator. Nothing else special about him, Brown, buzz-cut hair, a couple of junk tattoos on his forearms. One a badly done eagle clutching a writhing snake in its bloody talons, another that looks like it's supposed to be a demon, or a devil, or maybe his mother. It occurs to Grady that he's lucky the creep chose to fight conventionally, probably copying what he'd seen on TV. All he really had to do was run at Grady and slam into him at full speed. Game over.

"He was the lookout," Clare says. "His boss posted him back down the road a ways."

Grady realizes the figure on top of him is breathing. He pushes the unconscious man—the leader—off him and sits up. The guy is more conventionally attractive than his buddies, with chiseled features, blonde hair that might have been styled, a tan that Grady suspects came from a salon. Grady didn't think anybody wore muscle shirts anymore, but macho man is sporting one. And all the bulges steroids can buy. There is no blood.

"Shit," he says. "What'd you hit him with?"

Clare points to a hunk of wood, a two by four that has somehow managed to retain its integrity over the years.

"Tie them up," she commands. "Use their belts."

Grady trusses the unconscious men as well as he can, but it's nearly a joke. Binding people with leather belts only works well in the movies. And he can't tell how long either of them will be out. Already, the man mountain who attacked him from behind is moaning.

"This won't hold," he says as he finishes tying up the two men as best he can.

Clare shrugs. She doesn't seem concerned.

"Hand over the key," she orders.

Will she really hurt him? Maybe it's his ego talking, but he doesn't think so. Can't see the woman who kissed him, stroked him, slept with him, shooting him in cold blood. But what does he really know about her? Clearly, not much. And why take chances for the damn key? What does he really care?

He digs in his pocket for the key, pulls it out.

A smile crosses her face, a long slow one made up of satisfaction and joy.

"Toss it over here."

He obliges.

Carefully, keeping the gun on him, she bends and picks it up.

"Now what?" Grady asks.

She retrieves Charlie's boots from where they lie near the well, reaches behind a rock and pulls out a plastic jug of water. She throws him Charlie's boots and waits while he pulls them on. Then she tosses him the jug and gestures toward the road with the rifle.

"Run."

And Grady takes off. He's banged up, sore and beginning to stiffen, Charlie's boots are way too big, but he barely notices. He runs across the plaza to the road, to the route taken by Jill's truck. Once, he looks back over his shoulder. And sees Clare disappearing into the brush in the opposite direction. He thinks he hears the whinny of a horse.

24

Grady follows the road. The sun is going down, and the desert, which has been so silent in the heat of the day, is coming alive with bird calls. He wonders how long he has before the two men come after him, when he should abandon the rutted trail for the brush. He didn't see a vehicle back at the ghost town, but there must have been one. Sound carries in the dry desert air, he tells himself. He'll hear the engine before they can spot him.

He took a few measured sips of water as soon as he slowed from his initial sprint to a steady pace, and now he allows himself two more. He and Jill were careful to drink water all along their journey, so no matter what his dry mouth and parched throat are telling him, his body can afford to wait. Arizona natives like Grady are familiar with the dangers of dehydration. Even in the city where there seems to be a convenience store on every corner, most people keep bottled water in their vehicles as a standard safety precaution, like a spare tire. You never want to run out in the desert.

He thinks about the men he left tied up. Why didn't he kill—or disable—them when he had the chance? Clare? Would she have tried to stop him? Would she have even objected? The law? He respects it, but he also knows there are times when it has little to do with right and wrong.

He's a little surprised that as cynical, as disillusioned, as he is, he still stopped short of smashing a man's head, or even his legs, in cold blood. If there was anybody, or anything, up there watching, maybe his restraint earned him a nod of approval. He doesn't expect that celestial pat on the back to extend far enough to get him to help, or even back to the main road, but it isn't bad to think about.

And then there's the question of just who he would have been protecting. He isn't sure how long Jill and Sophie have been gone, but he figures they are well on their way to civilization. There's even a chance that the first vehicle he'll encounter will be a patrol, sent to find him.

It's almost full dark by now. The rising moon promises to be high and bright, although clouds are gathering. Grady judges he's come about a mile, maybe more. He passes through a narrow spot, a place where bush threatens to overwhelm the road, and climbs a slight rise. As he reaches the top of the hill, he sees it a hundred yards away.

The shiny silver Land Rover is upside down, wedged between rocks. The driver's side presses against a boulder. The front passenger door dangles at a sick angle, its hardware twisted. As he runs toward the wreck, he can see the windows are smashed. The only sounds are his running feet, his pounding heart and the song of birds.

The tailgate is open. The extra clothing is strewn across the ground. Most of the plastic bottles of water are gone, and the few that are left are empty, lids scattered. The cookie box lies against a rock. It's been torn apart, and a few broken pieces of cookie litter the ground. No gun. Grady pulls himself up onto the vehicle. He smells gasoline. The SUV rocks treacherously beneath him. In the moonlight, he can see the interior, the blackness of blood against the pale leather. But the truck is completely, blessedly, empty.

Where are they? He begins to walk the area systematically, in a spiral from the center out, his eyes searching for bodies. At one point a hummock of deer grass fools him. Adrenaline pouring into his veins, he bends to comfort it, perhaps to bury it. And is surprised when he touches its prickly blades to find tears running down his face.

He is at the very edge of the road, at the ill-defined border between rutted trail and bush when he hears the rustle.

"Don't move," a voice says. "Don't come any closer."

"Jill!" he cries out in relief.

"Jack? Ohmigod."

There's a scrambling in the brush a few feet away, and then Jill is next to him, her forehead bloody, her clothing disheveled, but unmistakably alive. The gun is clutched in her right hand.

"I was sure you were dead," she says.

"Sophie. Where's Sophie?"

She gestures toward the brush. "Back there." Grady is afraid to ask, so he waits for her to continue. "She's all right. We're both just a little banged up."

She looks around frantically, with a fear in her eyes that Grady has never seen. "We have to get off the road."

Grady follows her into the brush. We're prey, he thinks, and she knows it.

They huddle, hugging Sophie and each other. Grady feels wetness on Jill's face but never hears a sob. She's still Jill, he thinks. She'll never break down in front of her daughter.

They were driving, she tells him. She didn't want to leave Grady, but she understood why she had to.

As soon as they were out of sight of the ghost town, she told Sophie to find the cookies. Sophie thought she was crazy, of course. "Just do it!" Jill ordered. And Sophie wiggled around and found the box.

"Open it," Jill commanded. "Hand it to me." And Sophie's hands were shaking as she tore open the box and gave it to her mother.

Jill dumped the cookies and pulled out the gun. The ruts were awful, and the truck was lurching all over the place. There was no place she could stow the gun where she could reach it and be sure it would stay put, so she stuffed it into the pocket of her jeans.

Now she wanted to hurry, but she made herself keep the speed down. She's never been comfortable driving the Land Rover. It's too big. And she was nervous about the road, afraid to take it too fast, afraid of ripping out the bottom of the truck on a rock. So she forced herself to be deliberate. "Sing," she said to Sophie. And Sophie sang childhood songs, "The Wheels on the Bus," "I've Been Working on the Railroad," in a shaky, little girl voice.

They drove only a few minutes—Sophie was on the second chorus of "Yellow Bird"—Jill was watching the odometer and figured they still had two miles to go to the first junction. The road snaked. They were coming out of the curve—when a man appeared in the road. Jill hesitated, then hit the gas, and in that moment, the bulky figure swung a rifle up and she heard the boom of a shot. She sped up. She couldn't hit him, but with luck she could escape him...

The rifle boomed again. Jill swerved. A bullet slammed into the windshield, screaming between Jill and Sophie, missing Jill's right temple by inches. A hole appeared, and a volley-ball sized circle in the center of Jill's field of vision went in an instant from transparent glass to opaque web. Sophie screamed. Jill had to twist her body to see where they were going, didn't dare slow down, tried to steer straight. The undercarriage of the truck hit a rock, and the wheel became alive in her hands. She struggled to hold it steady, but the left wheels dropped off the edge of the road—and the SUV flipped. They rolled once, twice...came to a stop upside down, at an unnatural, creaking angle, dangling from their seat belts. Jill's forehead was wet with blood. "Play dead," she whispered to Sophie, not knowing whether Sophie could hear her.

Jill prayed that Sophie would be, could be, still. Prayed the man would decide it didn't matter whether they were dead or alive—that they were done for either way. She heard him clamber up onto the truck. Heard him swearing. Heard him rummaging through the food, the bottles of water. She thought he was throwing things out.

She heard him leave the truck. She had all she could do not to flinch as he smashed the windows. She heard more swearing. Then silence.

Sophie moaned.

"Sssh!" Jill hissed at her.

They hung there. Jill felt the blood pounding in her head, wondered if any was left in her arms, her legs, wondered if they would, could, move when she finally gave the command.

She decided she didn't dare wait any longer. She hooked her knees under the steering wheel, braced herself with one hand and fumbled with her seat belt. Finally, it gave way. She fell to the roof of the Land Rover, crawled along it and checked her child. Sophie seemed intact but was groggy, maybe in shock. Jill unbuckled her, lowering Sophie as gently as she could. She kicked the remaining glass out of the driver's side window, climbed out and pulled her daughter from the wreck.

Sophie lay on the ground, still bleary but beginning to recover. Jill searched among the debris. She found three intact sixteen-ounce bottles of water. For the first time since she'd seen the man in the road, she felt hope. They were alive. They had water. And Jill had the gun.

Then she and Sophie hid, while Jill tried to figure out what to do next.

That is the question, Grady agrees. From what Jill has told him, it was the walking refrigerator—the lookout—who shot at the truck. The man watched them drive by, heading into the ghost town for the meeting. Then he waited. He'd been told to get rid of anyone coming out, and that's what he did. Then he made his way into the ghost town to join his buddies—and caught Grady sneaking up on the leader.

So there are only two men that they need to worry about. But that is two too many. It means they can't retrace their route. Following the roads is too dangerous.

They can't go any appreciable distance cross country in the dark. The clouds are thickening, don't yet hold rain, but threaten to hide the moon. There are too many critters, spiky plants, unexpected holes that can trap a foot, break a leg.

And they can't walk to Arivaca once the sun rises and the air heats up. It's too far.

Grady concludes that they can't return the way they came at all.

He remembers the map, the one Jill pored over all the way down I-19 in the truck after he convinced her that there might come a point where they couldn't rely on the magic of the GPS. "What's out there?" he says to her. "What's in the other direction?"

Jill calls up the image of the area in her mind. "The wildlife refuge. A few settlements," she says. "Tiny ones."

Are they closer? Yes.

Grady's long-ago ranger training focused heavily on mountains and jungles. There was a brief nod to desert survival (and everyone assumed that he'd be a natural at it since he was from Tucson). As it turned out, he was just okay, but he learned some things. Now, he does some figuring in his head, the way he was taught, calculating distance, body weights, temperatures and available water.

They have three liters of water. Jill was concerned that Sophie was dehydrated and opened one of the sixteen-ounce bottles she found, making sure that her daughter drank most of it. Grady and Jill have shared the rest. There are two bottles left, and the half-gallon jug Clare tossed to Grady is almost full. Will it be enough? It's only one-fourth the amount any prudent person would carry. But if they keep to cover as much as possible, avoid the worst of the sun, make reasonable time... They can stretch it. Just.

He shares his decision with Jill. "That's the way we're going."

Jill is astonished.

"You mean we're going to cross the desert?"

"Well," Grady says. "It's more open than the way we came. But down here, it's all desert."

The wreck gleams in the moonlight. Grady searches the area and finds both hats, and he comes across a chamois in the back. He can turn that into a kind of bandanna. He discovers the map and folds it into his back pocket. He locates his Nikes and pulls them onto his grateful feet.

He finds the remnants of the first-aid kit. And he rescues Charlie's tube of Sport 50 sunblock from the glove compartment.

But the only food available is two power bars that their attacker apparently overlooked. Those calories won't last long. They'll have to travel on empty stomachs.

By the time he returns to their hiding place, the night is black, the sky scudded with clouds. Carefully, they move through the brush away from the road, 500 yards, 1,000. It's slow going. They travel to the chirping of crickets, the skitter of small animals. A pack of coyotes yelp in the distance. They're tired, bruised, and constantly wary of being speared by cactus, tripped by rocks or stumbling into the burrows of ground squirrels. Finally, they sink into a shallow wash. They find shelter under a copse of trees and do their best to sleep.

25

It's gray in the east by 4:30. By 4:45, it's light enough to see. Grady lays out the map and estimates the distance: about 15 miles if they stick to heavy cover, less if they skirt the hills and go due southwest. That route is more exposed, but will be faster.

By 5:00 a.m., they're moving, Jill in front, Sophie following, Grady bringing up the rear. Jill and Sophie wear the hats, Grady the chamois. The gun is tucked in his waistband. His long-sleeved shirt has become a knapsack that holds their bottles of water, and Sophie wears Jill's. It means he and Jill are more exposed to the sun, but there's no help for that.

They're slow, Grady knows. Jill used gauze and tape to wrap the ankle Sophie injured in her attempt to escape. Sophie can walk, but by ten minutes into their hike, she's limping. Under the best circumstances, avoiding the hills, they should be able to reach their destination before the full heat of the day and within a safety margin for water. At their current pace, it's going to take a lot longer.

They're rationing the water. And there's always the chance that they'll come across a ranch, complete with house, people—and a well. They'll be okay. Maybe.

By the time they take their first real break, they've been walking for nearly two hours. The map is of limited help since it shows only major landmarks and changes in terrain. They've been following dry creek beds whenever they can. The cottonwoods and eucalyptus that cluster along the banks provide more shelter from the sun—and possible pursuers—than the scrawny mesquites that grow farther away. But the walking is no easier, and their pace is already slowing.

Then they reach a point where the creek bed vanishes. They're forced to move into open terrain. Sophie's ankle has swollen, and she needs frequent pauses for rest. Grady is beginning to worry about the sun. It's still relatively cool, low 80s he guesses, but so dry that when he licks his lips he feels the skin crackle, and he knows that the temperature is heading for 100+. Sophie and Jill are sitting on a rock, and he's standing nearby doing the dreadful math of time and sun exposure and water in his head when they hear the shot.

A startled bird flies up from a nearby creosote bush. Grady pushes Jill and Sophie down, and they all scramble into the cover of the brush on the nearest hill while shots rattle the rocks around them.

"Stay here!" he commands. He takes off the improvised knapsack and pulls the gun from his waistband.

It's hide and seek again, but this time Grady is the hunter.

He crawls back onto the flats. The ground is dotted with jojoba bushes and hummocks of gray-green deer grass, some of which are four feet tall. He rolls from bush to bush, clump to clump with a certainty born of desperation, feeling small stones, cactus spines, now in his calf, now in his thigh. He tastes dirt, spits it out..

And when he's far enough away from Jill and Sophie's position, he chooses a spot where he can dive to cover behind a boulder. He'll be trusting to luck and reflexes to keep him alive, but there's no choice. He counts to five, takes a deep breath, gets ready—and shows himself, just for an instant.

A shot rings out. Grady is already moving. Another. He's behind the boulder, lying flat, panting with stress and exertion.

And now he knows where they are—in a hillside notch formed by two outcroppings of rock. Swiftly he moves from boulder to bush to rock to clump of grass to spindly tree, gradually climbing up into higher ground, circling around, triangulating on their position, praying that they'll still be there in two minutes, one, thirty seconds...

He reaches the rocks above the snipers' nest and looks down in relief and triumph—to see only one man. It's the guy built like a major home appliance, the one who tried to strangle Grady. The man squats there, his head swiveling from side to side as if he can take in the entire landscape by acting like a human periscope. He's wearing a hat, an inadequate ball cap, but he's got the bill pointing forward to shade his face, and he's tucked part of a torn-up t-shirt under the cap so that the fabric hangs down, protecting the back of his neck. Which means he isn't totally stupid about what the sun and the heat can do. His rifle rests steady in his hands. A liter bottle of water lies near his feet. He is only one of two. But one is a start.

Grady is still more than 50 very vertical feet away. He needs to get closer. He makes his way down the rocky face of the hill, careful to find solid footholds, crawling where he reaches a horizontal section. He prays that he won't dislodge a stone and give himself away with the noise of its fall. Sweat runs into his eyes. Twenty feet, eighteen, fifteen—still on the outside edge of the range of Jill's gun. And it's a weapon he's never fired, never sighted. If he misses, he'll lose the advantage of surprise. And he has no ammo to waste. The .38 holds only five bullets, and Jill keeps two of the chambers filled with snake shot—great for taking out rattlers if you're on horseback, but not much good for stopping human vipers. He's already checked to make sure that the solid rounds are in the next three chambers, but he checks again. They're playing for keeps. This can't be a wounding shot.

The man moves. He stands up, bends to pick up the water bottle. He's not a desert rat. Or like Grady he never planned to be out here this long. The rest of his arm is starting to blend in with the eagle's red talons. He stands once more.

Grady raises the gun. Takes careful aim. Fires. And watches with satisfaction as the bullet makes a neat hole between the man's shoulder blades. Birds squawk, taking the sky in a flurry of wings. The man collapses onto the rocks. The water bottle falls from his hand, tumbles down the face of the hill, comes to rest on a small ledge near the bottom.

Then all is silent. Grady listens, but the only sounds are those of nature. He knows without seeing it that the exit wound is the size of his fist.

Still one unaccounted for.

Forget retrieving the rifle. If he isn't shot trying to get to the weapon, he'll probably fall. The rifle's a luxury they'll have to do without.

But he has to get the water.

They have a chance of evading a human pursuer. They'll never escape the sun.

He works his way down through the rocks, heading for the ledge. Cover is even spottier than higher on the hill—and there'll be none at all for the last few yards. He passes the sniper's nest, the sprawled body, about 50 feet away to his right. Blood covers the rocks.

He reaches a flat spot, a natural platform ten or twelve feet above the ledge. The rock is shear; there is no sane way down. But the ledge below him projects several feet farther out from the face of the hill. Jumping would be quick, but he'd likely break a bone or two in the landing. Or miss the ledge and ricochet down the hillside into the rocks.

If he stays where he is, he might be shot. Even if he reaches the ledge safely, he might find the bottle punctured, empty.

It'll have to be a drop. He wants to get it over with, to know the outcome one way or the other, but he forces himself to slow down. He lies flat on his stomach, maneuvers his body around. He has to be careful to maintain control. There are no natural handholds, and wedging his fingers in the rocks won't work. No point making it to his goal if he breaks a finger—or leaves one behind. He gradually moves off the edge until he's hanging full out in the air, supporting his weight by the sheer force of his hands flat on the surface above him. No going back now. He says a small, involuntary prayer—and lets go.

He lands heavily, doesn't dare drop and roll because of the size of the ledge, but manages to flex his legs enough to absorb the worst of the impact. He's alive. No shots. No sound. And the water bottle is intact. He tucks it under his arm and crawls from boulder to boulder the rest of the way down the hill.

When he reaches the bottom, he moves as quickly as he dares. Jill can't know who is shot, who isn't. He told her to wait, but she's exhausted and in fear for her own life and, even worse, that of her daughter. He uses the same rolling, crawling strategy as before. Finally, he reaches the edge of the heavier brush, creeps into it.

They're still there, and the smile that covers Jill's face when she sees him says all he will ever need to know about relief and gratitude. He hands her the bottle of water.

"One down," he says. "But still one to go."

Then he tells her the bad news.

These assholes have been doing a better job of tracking than any greenhorn could manage. Somebody's got experience, probably military. He'd bet on it. If they're lucky, it was the guy he just shot. But it could be the other one. Or both of them. They're going to have to be more careful. They've got to keep to the hills.

If they moved slowly before, now they move with painful deliberation. As the sun rises higher in the sky and the temperature continues its uncaring climb, the wind begins to pick up. Grady knows they're sweating, have to be, but the moisture no more than leaves their pores before it's picked up and carried off into the superheated air. The terrain is flatter, but the vegetation sparse. It's increasingly difficult to stick to cover, and whenever they move into the open they expose themselves to the certainty of the searing sun and the possibility of bullets.

Just before noon, they reach a clump of small, twisted mesquites and Grady orders a rest in the broken shade. They'll wait until 1:30, he says, to miss the worst of the mid-day sun. Jill and Grady share a third of the remaining water and give a larger portion to Sophie. They sit wordlessly. In spite of the sunblock, everyone's skin is an unhealthy red. Sophie dozes. As the sun soars overhead, its rays piercing the spindly branches of the mesquite, she whimpers in her sleep. At 1:30, they wake her and begin walking again, making achingly slow progress in their disjointed trek toward the southwest.

By three o'clock, Grady is disheartened, all but despairing. They've entered another area of rolling hills and scrub forest, but the partial relief from the sun may be too little, too late. He's made a fatal mistake. They should have taken their chances on the road. The only possible sign of the remaining threat, the last of the three assholes who snatched Sophie, has been a movement in the far distance about 40 minutes back, a flash of color that Grady caught as he turned his head to scan the horizon, and a crack moments later that might have been a bullet, might have been a long-dead tree branch giving way in the hot wind, choosing that instant to crash to the desert floor.

A half hour later, they come over a rise, stumble into a small clearing—and see three figures under a tree. Jill gasps. Sophie lets out a squeal, all she has left in her of a scream. The figures recoil, the two smaller ones huddling together, the larger one waving a stick.

Border crossers, illegals. They look like a family: husband, wife, and a small boy.

The man waving the stick pokes at the air with it, aggressive as a cornered bear protecting his young. "*Buenos dias*," Grady calls. He holds his hands out and open.

The father and mother seem confused. Grady knows that he and Jill and Sophie don't look like border patrol. They look like what they are: a man, woman and child wandering in the desert, skittering along on the dangerous edge of dehydration. At the same time, they are Anglos. Maybe ranchers. And ranchers are threats. Some make it their mission to catch—and abuse—undocumented Mexicans heading North.

The man takes a few steps toward Grady, and Grady moves to

meet him. "*No inmigración,*" Grady says. He repeats it for emphasis: "*No inmigración.*"

The man nods.

Desperate Mexicans are usually smuggled across the border in groups, led by a "coyote," who is paid a lot of money—and usually armed. Grady doesn't see a sign of any other human presence, or recent activity. His guess is that the boy was too slow to keep up. The family has been left behind, on their own.

Grady knows how many illegal border crossers die in the desert south of Tucson each year. But there's no point in saying anything. It's too late for warnings.

He sees the woman looking at Sophie's reddened skin, her unfocused eyes. She must wonder what gringos are doing out here, Grady thinks. She must be shocked at the madness of Anglos who when they have money and cars and houses bring a young girl, unprovisioned, into the middle of the desert.

Her eyes find the two plastic bottles Jill is holding. He knows the woman has reached the correct conclusion: that this scanty three cups is all the water they have. She walks a few steps, takes a cloth bag from behind a nearby tree, and takes out a plastic gallon jug. Water.

She holds the jug out toward Grady, but her husband snatches it from her hands. Grady assumes this is the end of it. But the man takes off the cap, puts the jug up to his mouth, and takes a swallow. He wipes the opening on his shirt and holds the water out to Grady.

Grady takes the jug, holds it up to his own mouth, and takes a swallow.

He forces himself to stop and hands the jug to Jill, who laps at the water just as briefly and holds it to Sophie's lips. She lets her daughter drink what Grady judges is about a cup.

"*Muchas gracias,*" Jill says. She gives the jug back to Grady, who hands it back to the father.

"*En qué dirección vas?*" the father asks.

He's asking which way they're going. Grady points southwest.

The man begins talking more rapidly. Grady's Spanish isn't up to the speed, but Jill's got it. "He says there is a water station," she translates. More Spanish. "An hour away, maybe two if we're slow. He says we'll see a 'blue banner flying in the sky.'"

Grady knows about the water stations. They've been scattered across the desert by activists who believe that providing water is a minimal, humane step to help prevent unnecessary deaths. He also knows that there has been significant opposition, and that some believe that the water stations encourage border crossings, leading to even more deaths. He's never been sure where he stands on the issue. But he has no ambivalence now. He simply prays that they will reach the station in time.

"*Buena suerta,*" the father says. Grady understands that. Good luck. The family gathers its few belongings and disappears into the bush, heading north.

Grady considers the options. The scrub forest they're in is relatively gentle. But he can see the terrain ahead of them—sparsely vegetated hills and flats. With no shelter, the sun will dry a person in an hour, wring the last drop of moisture out of a man, woman or child in three or four, cause death in less than a morning, or an afternoon.

He wants to leave Jill and Sophie in the shelter of the trees, to go for help and come back and get them. But he doesn't dare. He doesn't know how far away help might be. Doesn't know where the last, and the most dangerous, of their pursuers might be. They have to move on.

Sophie can no longer walk. Grady picks her up and carries her piggyback. But he can do this for only brief periods. He's too weak from lack of sleep, food and water. They stumble along for five or ten minutes. Then he puts Sophie down and they rest. They repeat this over and over—four times, five, six... When Sophie can no longer hold on, Grady gives Jill the shirt-knapsack that carries their remaining water and picks the girl up in his arms.

The sun is relentless. The hands on Grady's watch move too

fast; and they are covering so little ground. Their periods of progress grow shorter and shorter, their rests longer.

Jill is in the lead. All day, Grady has marveled at her strength, wondered at how her will is fueling her physical stamina, worried about what it might be costing her body. Now, he has no mental energy to spare. He's simply an automaton, moving forward, ignoring heat, thirst, exhaustion. Pick up leg, step, pick up leg, step, pick up leg, step...

Then Jill falls. One moment she's a beacon of determination pulling him on. The next, she crumples, simply collapses to the ground—and lies sprawled on the baking dirt.

Grady puts Sophie down as gently as he can and, with a spurt of adrenaline, runs to Jill, stumbling, his movements as uncoordinated as a drunk's.

Jill is sobbing, but there are no tears. Her body can't spare the moisture.

"It'll be okay," Grady says, hoping his voice doesn't betray the lie.

There's a small copse of trees, five or six stragglers, a few hundred yards ahead. He picks up Sophie, carries her there, lays her down. Goes back for Jill.

He tries to help her up, but she doesn't have the strength to stand. He puts his arms under her, hoists her limp body and struggles to his feet. Staggering under her weight, he manages to get her to the minimal shelter of the trees.

He lays her next to her daughter and, panting with exertion and exhaustion, falls to the earth himself.

Jill murmurs something, but Grady can't make out the words. Sophie is quiet. Asleep? Or unconscious?

Another murmur from Jill. And this time Grady understands her.

"I'm staying here," she says.

The copse of trees looks so green in contrast to the brown surrounding it. So cool.

Such an illusion.

Grady shakes his head. Jill's skin is red. She is—all of them are—suffering from heat exhaustion. The next stage is heat stroke: high fever, delirium—and without medical attention—organ failure and death.

"Please. You can't carry us both. Take Sophie."

Grady doesn't—can't—reply.

"You'll come back for me." He can tell she's trying to state it as a simple fact, a predictable reality, but her voice trembles.

He doesn't know what to say. Other than no, I won't leave you. How could you think I would? He doesn't know what to do—other than sit and wait.

For?

Death.

And that makes no sense. Whatever his life has or hasn't become, Jill is a mother, and mothers protect their young.

Another murmur, with what is trying to be a smile. It's her turn to lie. "It will be fine." She doesn't do it much better than he did.

She doesn't want him to leave any of the water, but Grady insists on leaving one-third of what they have left, about four ounces. He puts the plastic bottle in her hand, won't leave until she agrees to take it.

And he insists she have the gun, wraps her fingers around the grip.

Then he picks up Sophie and sets out again.

He's told Jill that if he and Sophie are threatened, he will be able to get her child to cover. But he feels no such confidence.

The sun blazes. The afternoon wears on. Grady struggles ahead. He rests. At first, he's moving forward more than resting. But soon, he's stopping for five minutes, moving for two.

Sophie is silent, unresponsive, He manages to rouse her enough to give her the last of the water. But she has trouble swallowing it, and much of the precious liquid runs out the side of her mouth, down her neck, onto the ground.

Then Grady reaches a point where he doesn't know if he can get up again. Using every fiber of will, every scrap of belief that there is some chance for a future, he puts his arms under Sophie, hoists her limp body and struggles to his feet.

But his knees buckle. He sinks to the ground in despair. As he lifts his eyes to curse the heat, the sun—his arrogance in getting them into this—there it is!

A blue banner, the flag of the water station, flapping in the distance, welcoming them, waving them in.

Grady finds new strength. He shifts Sophie's weight, struggles to his feet and heads for the beacon.

As they're crossing a wash and at their most exposed, a shot sings off a rock to the right. He hits the ground, covering Sophie with his body.

Half-staggering, half creeping along the dirt, he manages to pull Sophie to the shelter of a clump of boulders. Now they're protected on three sides and totally vulnerable on the fourth. Grady positions himself looking that way, a sharp rock in his hand. All he can do is wait. The sun beats down.

A second shot hits the trunk of a mesquite thirty feet away. A third slams into a fallen log only inches from their hiding place.

Sophie moans, and Grady covers her mouth with his hand as gently as he can.

A figure staggers into the wash. It's the tall, muscle-bound blond, the leader, the moving force behind Sophie's abduction, the deaths of the short man at the well, the bulky man in the rocks. He's hatless, waving his rifle wildly in the air. His exposed face and arms are seared a violent red, a horror of burning blisters. Blood stains his t-shirt.

The man stumbles, falls to his knees, then collapses to the ground. He lies there for 10 seconds, 15, 20... Grady is getting ready to go after him with the rock, at least get the rifle, when the man rises again, first sitting, then struggling to his feet. He tears off his t-shirt. His torso gleams dead-fish white against the scarlet of his face and arms, except for a blood-black wound in his right side. The man drops the shirt in the sand, grabs the rifle and lurches up out of the wash in the other direction, away from them.

Grady waits one minute, two, three...until he doesn't dare wait anymore. The wash is empty. There's no sign of the tall man, no sound other than the wind rattling through the scrub. He picks up Sophie, makes his feet move, resumes his struggle toward the blue banner.

500 yards. Breathe, walk, count it down...

400 yards... 300... 250... 200...

Sophie seems heavier than ever, totally limp, motionless. He can't tell whether she's breathing. Is he carrying a dead child?

100 yards... 50... 25...

A tower of life in the desert, only feet away. Saved, Grady thinks, we're saved!

But as he moves closer, he can see they are lost. The station has been vandalized, the metal tank knocked from its stand, punctured, torn apart by a pick or an axe. The stand is in pieces, the water a dark stain on the ground.

He collapses to the ground, all but dropping Sophie.

They are about to die.

As he becomes resigned to the prospect, his head clears. The ground is still moist, and dampness doesn't last more than a few minutes in the desert. If whoever did this is still in the area, maybe he can get their attention. It's risky. There are groups fanatic about preventing illegal immigration—at any cost. But these vigilantes kill by proxy, letting the sun do their dirty work. He doubts they'll be up to face-to-face murder—and Sophie and he aren't their targets. No. Attracting their remaining pursuer, who might still have his rifle, might not have lost all of his wits, that's the real risk. But the chances of bringing help outweigh the danger. He has no choice.

The banner flies from a metal post 30 feet tall. Grady picks up a piece of the ruined metal stand and swings it with all his might against the hollow steel pole. The clanging resounds, ringing across the desert.

He draws back the hunk of metal and slams the post again.

Clang!

And again. Clang! Clang!

Nothing.

Grady rests. Gathering the last of his strength, he gets ready for one final effort.

As he sets his weary muscles to send the pipe crashing into the metal, he hears an engine. A white jeep roars over the rise and down into the clearing. Grady catches a flash of a uniform at the wheel, spots the crest on the door.

It's the border patrol.

26

Sound carries in high-desert air. Grady hears the whomp whomp a long moment before the helicopter appears in the bright blue sky.

Even before the chopper touches down, the doctor and nurse are pushing the gurney toward its open door.

Grady has insisted on waiting for the Medivac bird. Against medical advice. The docs wanted him in an ambulance, an I.V. in his arm, on his way to the same trauma center up in Tucson.

No way he's leaving the area.

First, he's seeing Sophie on her way. Then he's going back for Jill.

He stood his ground in the ER, signed himself out of the small Nogales hospital. He told the authorities that they need him, pushed his Ranger credentials, lied about the extent of his desert training, all but guaranteed them that he can help trace his path back across the wilds, find one copse of spindly trees out of many.

If he finds Jill—*when* he finds Jill—he won't be able to tell her that Sophie's okay. Even when their marriage was a chaos of anger and pain, he didn't lie to her, not about anything important. And she wouldn't want him to be less than straight with her now.

It's clear help might have come too late: Sophie is in the last stages of severe heat stroke. He doesn't know what the odds are. But least he can tell Jill that her child has a chance.

The chopper lifts off, and Grady climbs into the Jeep idling at the edge of the pad. The man behind the wheel is typical southern Arizona border patrol, mid-30s, a bit paunchy, outwardly affable—but Grady senses he is one tough motherfucker when it counts.

Others are already hunting. The border patrol has jeeps on the ground, planes flying a search pattern over the area. The grim looks on the men's faces say how hard it will be to locate Jill and what they expect to find, but they're giving it everything they've got.

"That's your ex-wife out there?" a guy with a face like desiccated cardboard asked, rhetorically, when Grady was making his pitch to be included in the search.

Grady nodded.

The asshole shook his head, almost grinned. "It were my ex, I'd..." He got it then, and shut up before Grady could deck him.

Grady feels like crap, knows his core temperature is way too high. And in spite of all the liquids he's consumed, the I.V. fluids he allowed the ER personnel to administer, his body is a long way from fully hydrated. But the chance is his to take.

The military had drugs you could use when you hadn't slept, hadn't eaten, were dying from the inside out. Drugs that would compensate, keep you going at top speed—at least for a while. All Grady has is will and adrenaline.

They gave him a hat, wouldn't give him a gun.

The driver—Bill—tromps on the gas and wheels the Jeep up hills and through gullies. Bill is chewing gum, says he's giving up smoking—which reminds Grady that he's been without a cigarette for more than 24 hours. And hasn't noticed. Funny how broiling like a piece of cheap meat shoves those urges right out of your mind.

Much sooner than Grady expects, he sees three other Jeeps in the distance.

"That them?"

Bill nods. "Told you we'd catch up."

Grady is relieved to see the search party. But he thought they'd be farther away, would have covered more ground.

Aren't the fuckers trying?

Bill picks up his radio, relays their position, and the three other vehicles stop, waiting.

They're men Grady has already met. The one in charge, Joe, a sharp-faced guy with a crew cut, is on the radio. Grady can hear the static.

"...circling Three Rock Wash..." the scratchy voice says through the speaker.

"You've covered all the area between there and Ruby?"

"Affirmative."

Ruby, Grady has learned, is the name of the ghost town where they had the meet with Sophie's abductors.

As Grady walks up to him, Joe shakes his head. The look on his face is grim.

"Nothing yet," he says.

The sun is beginning to lose some of its intensity, but it's still hours until dusk. Darkness will be good for Jill in one way: cooler. Infinitely more dangerous in another. Even with the border patrol's sophisticated instruments that can "see" body heat, she is a very small needle in a very large haystack.

"We're running out of time," Grady says.

Joe's sharp face tightens. The man shrugs. Then, perhaps realizing that Grady knows the score, he nods.

"You gotta get me up there."

The man makes all the arguments Grady has already heard back in Nogales. There's no time to land and take off again. Everything looks different from the air, and Grady isn't trained to translate from one visual point of view to the other. He doesn't know shit about the area. He'll just slow them down.

His arguments aren't getting him anywhere. Time to try another tack.

"Where are your maps?"

191

Maps he knows. Maps he's been trained on. He can read terrain.

They pull out a sheaf, and unroll them on the hood of the jeep.

He needs to narrow the search. If he can't focus them—and focus them on the right area—Jill is dead.

Grady traces arroyos with his fingers, walks with his hands over the hills, skirts the roughest, feels for the balance, the tipping points between rugged and passable terrain. He puts himself mentally on that ground and visualizes their route.

Finally, he takes a pen from Joe and draws a red circle on one of the maps.

"She's in there," he says.

"You're sure?"

Grady nods—hoping, praying, that he's right.

Joe takes the map. "Okay," he shouts. "Listen up."

The four vehicles divide the search area into quadrants. Joe lays out a pattern. It won't be perfect, can't be without roads, more accurate coordinates, more definitive landmarks. But it's the best they can do.

Grady chooses to stay with Bill. They have quadrant three.

Bill wrangles the vehicle down the middle of a wash. They jounce along the dry river bed.

As they pass an outcropping of rock, Grady spots a likely looking clump of trees, jumps from the jeep and runs to it. Thin trees, tall and barely leafed. A boulder...

A lizard looks back at him from a log. No Jill.

He sights another copse, a third, a fourth. But none of them are the exact vegetation, just the right arrangement of boulders.

The afternoon is passing too quickly, moving into evening. Shadows lengthen. When they pass through the darkness created by an overhanging rocky shelf, the air feels almost cold.

"We're going to run out of daylight," Bill says. Then, apparently, regretting the bluntness of his words, he adds, "But our pilots can do a hell of a lot with infrared."

The radio squawks. No one is having any luck, and the jeep

searching Quadrant 2 has stopped to scoop up a group of illegal immigrants. Grady doesn't get why they didn't just leave them the fuck alone and go on looking.

Bill wheels the jeep around a clump of boulders and pulls to a stop on a small rise. Grady brings the binoculars up to his eyes, looks, puts them down and shakes his head.

Bill clears his throat. "I hate to say this..."

"Yeah," Grady says. "I know. Give me ten more minutes."

They both know they have almost no visibility left. They are running up against the immutable deadline of night.

Bill puts the Jeep back in gear. They bump down into an arroyo and up the other side. They round a rocky hillock.

And Grady sees it in the distance.

"There!" he shouts.

Six spindly trees. A couple of boulders.

Bill steps on the gas and they careen across the desert.

Grady leaps from the Jeep. In the dying light, he glimpses colors that aren't found in nature. The coral of a shirt, the faded blue of denim, a shock of blonde hair.

They've found her.

She lies curled around herself in the nest of rocks. Blood has turned the right leg of her jeans a deep red-brown. Insects buzz. The water bottle is on the ground to her left. Astonishingly, it still holds an ounce of two or water. The gun lies near her right hand.

"Jill!" Grady calls her name. Nothing. He shouts.

Her eyes don't open. She doesn't move.

Bill radios for help. Grady rummages through the back of the Jeep, pulls out the medical kit.

"Let me," Bill says. He lifts Jill's eyelids, feels her neck for a pulse.

"Is she alive?"

Bill shakes his head, but Grady can tell it doesn't mean no. It means I don't know.

Grady grabs a knife. He slits the leg of Jill's jeans, pulls the pants

193

leg open. Her thigh is wet with fresh blood. Not pumping, but seeping. It's bad, he can tell. And it looks like a bullet wound. But if she's bleeding, she's alive.

He rips open a pack and applies a pressure bandage.

What happened? Was she so despairing, was her suffering so bad, that she shot herself? No way. It's not like Jill to give up. She'd never leave Sophie motherless. And unless her hand slipped, the target wouldn't have been her leg.

Where the hell is the chopper?

He holds his breath, clenching his teeth, willing the sky to stay light just a little longer.

"You got a flare?" he says to Bill.

"Sure. And if it gets dark, we'll use it."

Grady wonders if Jill has a chance in hell of surviving a ride in the jeep. He reaches for the flare...

At last, the desert echoes with the sound of chopper blades.

And here comes the beautiful bird.

27

Grady paces the waiting room outside the ICU. He sits. Stands. Paces some more. He isn't family, and he's not the law. So no information. Goddamn privacy rules. All he can do is watch the hands of the clock go around.

It's 3:00 a.m. when a nurse heading for her break takes pity on him. "They're still alive," she says as she steps into the elevator.

Grady sits down on one of the vinyl chairs. His head will no longer stay upright on his neck. He leans it against the wall, struggles against exhaustion. And loses.

It's full light when he opens his eyes. The waiting area is no longer empty. A couple sits in the far corner, their arms wrapped around each other, the woman quietly weeping. An older woman a few seats away from the couple stares into space. Three young men slump silently in their chairs, maybe regretting a night that has landed a buddy in deep trouble.

He feels like hell and probably looks worse, like a street person using the hospital as shelter. He borrowed a t-shirt from one of the guys helping the Border Patrol and washed his face, but his jeans are torn and filthy, he's scratched, battered and working on two days of stubble. The older woman momentarily catches his eye. Grady gives her a look right back and she turns away.

He sucks at bad coffee from an urn in the corner, manages to choke down a couple of candy bars from a vending machine. He thinks about trying to convince someone he's Jill's brother, curses himself for not having thought of it before. He tells himself Jill and Sophie have apparently survived so far. This has to be good. He tells himself he would have noticed if one shrouded gurney—or two— rolled by during the night. That something in the sound, a disturbance in the air, a void opening beneath his soul, would have awakened him.

Except. These are public elevators.

No. They have another route for the dead.

So Grady just sits, impotent, watching time go by. He's in a pained limbo where every hour is both forever and only a moment.

At 4:10 p.m., Charlie arrives.

He steps out of the elevator and rushes by without a word. Grady sees him pause outside the double doors labeled "ICU - North," grab the receiver of the wall phone that hangs there, and say a few words. The doors swing open. Charlie disappears.

Grady paces another few hundred laps. When he can't pace any more, he sits down. And though he wouldn't have thought it possible, he passes out again.

Then the waiting area is empty. Charlie is standing in front of him.

Grady comes fully awake. Behind Charlie, he sees the wall clock. 7:00.

"How are they?"

Charlie shakes his head.

Grady has always thought Jill's second husband looks young for his age, at least a decade less than his 45-or-so years. Now, his face is ravaged. The man is gray.

"I'm not sure," he says. "Sophie, well, Sophie's holding her own." He lets out a long, ragged breath. "The problem with heat stroke is that organs shut down. To protect the brain. Sometimes, they don't start back up again. Then you have organ failure. Multiple organ failure. But they think she'll be okay."

"Conscious?"

"No."

And Jill?

"Blood loss. Dehydration. Heat stroke. They won't even give me odds."

Grady doesn't know what to do, what to say. He wants to break something.

They're still breathing, he tells himself. They're still breathing. And Sophie. Sounds like good news.

But Jill...

She can't die.

"They wanted me out of there for a while. They have things to do." Charlie slumps into a chair, rests his arms on his thighs and sits staring at the floor.

Neither of them speaks for five minutes, ten, twenty.

Finally, Charlie looks up. But he isn't looking at Grady. Maybe he's watching the clock. Or the small dark crack where the ceiling meets the wall.

"I guess I'm supposed to thank you," he says. "But..." He shakes his head, letting his voice trail off.

Grady knows Charlie blames him. Can't argue with the guy for that. Shit. He blames himself.

Charlie stands up. "I'm going back in."

Grady nods. He knows he's been dismissed. He walks to the elevator bank, pushes the down button, finds a pay phone in the lobby, calls a cab. And goes home.

At first, Bear is one conflicted dog. He's been fed and watered by the kid in the front house, but apparently he's been inadequately walked. The shepherd's shame at the puddle by the front door and the pile next to the couch battle with his joy at seeing Grady. And

Grady has to reassure him for a good ten minutes before tackling the smelly mess.

A half-hour later, as he opens the door to return the Lysol he's borrowed from next door, Grady is confronted with the specter of the TV News 4 van parked in his driveway and two more rolling up out front. A reporter and a guy carrying a camera rush at him, the reporter shouting something about how it feels to be a hero and is it true he saved a woman and a little girl and tell us, Mr. Grady...

He slams the door in the man's face. He was News at 10 once before in his life, and he didn't enjoy it. He wants to sic Bear on them or tell them to go fuck themselves. Instead, he locks his door and pulls the shades. He's out of Scotch, but there's still half a bottle of Clare's tequila. He doesn't even need ice. An easy dinner.

He's never been a hero. In all his years as a cop, years when he did his job, arrested a lot of people, solved a few crimes, even saved a life or two, he never fooled himself about that. He wasn't a person deserving any special recognition. But he basically believed in what he did. He felt that way about his work on the force until the very end.

And now... When he thought it wasn't possible for him to fuck things up any more than he already had...

He turns out the lights and puts on some early Armstrong. Sits there staring into the darkness, letting Louis sing his blues.

\#

Sophie stirs. For a moment, she thinks she sees her father's face hanging over her like a balloon. Then she's gone again.

Jill floats. It's dark and cool in whatever space she is moving through. She is weightless, worryless, egoless. A mere fragment of Jill. Not even a memory.

II

28

Andy Davis slams his fist on the table—again. The one-way glass in the observation window rattles.

"I knew you were an asshole," Davis snarls at Grady. "But I never thought you were a fucking retard!"

They're in one of the two interrogation rooms in the foothills station. Davis picked up Grady at home and gave him the silent treatment all the way across town. At one point, Grady lit a cigarette, and Davis reached over, pulled it from his mouth, threw it out the window and stabbed with his index finger at the "No Smoking" symbol on the dashboard of the unmarked car.

Grady glanced at the overflowing ashtray but decided not to comment.

"Shithead," Davis muttered, and stepped on the gas.

Now Grady sits at the scarred wooden table facing the opaque observation glass, not much caring who or what is out there. He's already looked at mug shots. With no luck, which surprises no one. They all know these boys weren't local.

Davis paces. Every once in a while, he swears under his breath and kicks one of the empty metal chairs.

Grady's head is pounding. Davis pulled him out of bed at what felt like dawn. The only reward he's gotten for the agony of coming to consciousness, getting dressed and dragging his hangover out into the world has been Andy's periodic phone calls to the hospital. Law enforcement can get information that Grady can't.

Thanks to Davis, he knows that both Jill and Sophie are hanging on.

"Three bodies!" Davis yells.

Andy must have learned something on his last trip out of the room. This is a new, and higher, number.

There's the little guy down the well.

And the John Doe who had the bad taste to die indoors where the scavengers couldn't clean things up, in the wealthy enclave of Pergama.

But that's only two. Who's number three? The man he shot in the desert? The tall, sun-crisped leader? Clare?

"They found him 'cause of the birds," Davis is saying.

Him. It's a him. Not Clare.

Grady isn't updating Davis about what happened with Clare—or whoever she was. Hell, during the trek across the desert, he had lots of time to tell Jill about Clare's sudden appearance in the ghost town but never said a word. He isn't sure why. Maybe just natural caution. Maybe preserving his options.

The last anyone except Grady knows, Clare was disappearing into the bush while Sophie watched from outside the white van where she had fallen.

No one's quite admitting it, but Grady is pretty sure that the cops believe she's died in the desert.

Davis is still talking. "We got to him before he was too eaten up. And the description fits the guy you shot."

"Big bulky guy with a hole in his chest and an eagle on his arm?"

"Yup."

Davis kicks another chair, mutters a little more, finally sits down at the table across from Grady. "Gimme a cigarette."

Grady points at the non-smoking symbol on the door.

"Don't be a smartass," Davis says.

They smoke. Then Davis brings in another detective, and the three of them go through the events of the past five days all over again.

"What kind of key was it?"

Grady describes it once more.

"So something's in a bank somewhere."

Grady nods. He guesses so.

"And it's something valuable."

Grady can't argue with the logic of that.

And where did the key go?

It flew out of his hand, Grady tells them (again), during his fight with the two men in the ghost town.

"How'd you do that?" Davis asks (again). "How'd you k.o. two guys?"

Grady shrugs. "Beats the hell out of me. I think maybe one of them fell over his own feet and banged his head. Or when I ducked they hit each other."

Davis snorts. "What do you think this is? TV?"

A uniform brings in burgers and fries, sodas. Davis asks questions as he chews. Grady answers between bites.

And, just one more time, where did the key end up?

Somewhere in the dust of the ruined plaza, Grady says, trying to sound like a man weary of being made to repeat a truth. He thought the two men would find it when they came to and twisted their way out of his crappy bindings. But then they took the trouble to track him (and Jill and Sophie) down so he guesses that maybe they didn't.

Maybe?

"Could be they found the key but decided they didn't want witnesses."

More TV bullshit, Davis's face seems to say. But "these guys weren't Rambo" is his only comment.

"And they sure as hell weren't rocket scientists," the other detective adds.

Eventually, everybody runs out of questions, and Davis drives Grady up to Jill's to get his car.

Davis does most of the talking. He bitches about the long hours and the lack of overtime, the candyasses they're getting for rookies and the lowering of the department's standards, the difficulty of passing the annual physical and the budget-induced shortage of free donuts. He saves his strongest language for the "fuckin' sensitivity" policies. "I tella funny joke—but the wrong joke, if you get my drift—and some 'protected class' overhears me, and next thing I know I'm in fronta a goddamn board of inquiry. Or my ass is sued. Or both. You don't know how good you got it," he continues. "The private sector. That's the place to be. The goddamn private sector."

The rant is standard stuff. Nothing Grady hasn't heard before. Davis has twenty-eight years in, and he's going for at least thirty. He loves his job.

As they turn onto Sunrise, Davis returns to the topic of the kidnapping.

"You shoulda involved us," Davis grouses for what seems like the fortieth time. "No matter what the kid's mother said. Shit, Grady, you know better than that."

Grady thinks it is clear that, in fact, he doesn't know better than that, but he keeps his mouth shut.

"You nearly got that little girl killed. Not to mention losing your own ass. And her mother may still die." Davis rolls through a stop sign and swings left onto Pergama Drive.

"You were damn lucky," he declares, for the fifth or sixth or twentieth time.

Grady isn't so sure he agrees. But silence still seems the best policy.

Davis bums another cigarette. "I gotta empty this ashtray," he says. "Go to a car wash, rinse the crud off this thing and empty the ashtray. If they see these butts, it's my butt." He shakes his head, another comment on what the world has come to.

Finally, they pull into Jill's driveway behind Grady's car.

"Shit," Davis says as Grady opens the door and climbs out. "We go through alla this and we still got one asshole unaccounted for and that motherfuckin' John Doe hangin' around our necks like a...a... What's that damn bird?"

"An albatross."

"Yeah. One o' those."

Davis backs out of the driveway so fast he lays a little rubber. The neighborhood's so damn quiet the squeal echoes off the cactus.

Grady stands on the pebbled concrete of the Whitehursts' driveway. The house looks deserted, or maybe it only looks deserted because he knows Charlie is at the hospital watching over his wife and daughter.

The heat beats down on him, and his body remembers the hellhole outside Ruby, the goddamn sun cooking the life out of every bit of human flesh.

He pulls out his keys, turns to unlock his car.

His eyes scan the cactus and land on the Nelsons' house, sideways on its lot, looking at him. Mary and Ed Nelson are on their way home from Nepal, their trip of a lifetime aborted by the bloody mess in their living room. But they're not here yet.

If he's going to do it, it has to be now.

29

He looks around. No one in sight. The nearby houses on their acre lots are hunkered down, walled and landscaped, shuttered against the sun.

He walks casually up Jill's driveway to the street, along it for 50 yards, and down the Nelsons' drive.

As he nears the house, he hears gunshots and lurches into the shrubbery. Shit! Then he realizes. Just a few distant firecrackers. Kids getting an early start on the Fourth. He curses himself for his nerves.

He pulls himself out of the damn bushes, climbs the broad steps to the front portico. The day he took "Winnie" to the Nelsons' planning to leave her there, he stuck the house key on his ring for safekeeping. And it's still there. Should he have turned it over to Davis? But maybe he forgot, or maybe he remembered...

He's betting no one has thought to turn the alarm back on—he knows neither he nor "Winnie" did. And since the niece was going to be housesitting, no neighbor was watching over the place. So unless the Nelsons have contracted via long distance to get the cleanup started...

He inserts the key in the lock, turns it, clicks the latch, pushes— and mentally crosses his fingers. He is "Security," but getting away with this might be pushing it.

No buzz. No blatt. He's seen the alarm panel more than once and it could be set to send a silent signal, but not likely. Most homeowners want a loud noise to warn them and scare off an intruder. He is golden.

He steps into the foyer and gags. The air is cool but stinking, pungent with the stench of decay. Even in the desert, there are plenty of bacteria eager to digest the leavings of death.

He needs to open a window, get some air moving. But he doesn't dare. He struggles not to vomit. He'll get used to it, he tells himself. Don't think about the smell. Focus.

He moves in.

The living room is just as he last saw it—furniture shifted by the cops and never put back, fingerprint powder covering all promising surfaces, the blood now a black crust on the sofa, carpet, nearby chairs.

He scans the music room, trying not to think about playing the piano for "Winnie." At least he doesn't need to go in there. It's a fishbowl.

The house is large. So it takes him a while to do the complete tour, insides of closets and all. He's not sure he really thought there was any chance she might be (or had been) hiding there, but if he did, he was clearly wrong.

Now it's time for his real work.

He checks out the kitchen, where his glass and Winnie's still sit in the dishwasher, the nod they made to cleaning up after themselves before getting the hell out. He remembers that she insisted on adding soap, starting the wash cycle. So no fingerprints there. Not that it matters. Davis's boys dusted the hell out of Grady's place. Whoever she is, they haven't found her prints on record anywhere.

He gazes at the knife block sitting next to what appears to be an auxiliary sink. (He has no accurate vocabulary for some features of the dwellings of the rich.) The knife block was the home of the murder weapon, and he remembers Andy Davis's odd reference to the extra empty slot, the missing small knife, probably gone for months, even years, accidentally thrown out with the garbage... He pulls one knife out of the knife block and examines the markings. Draws out the rest one by one. They're a set, all with the same markings, the same brand: Messermeister.

He opens a cupboard. Glasses are lined up, cups hang from evenly spaced hooks. Stacks are uniform. Everything matches. He begins counting. Then he opens other cupboards, drawers.

There are two sets of china, one for 16 and one for 24. Both are complete.

Also two sets of flatware. Again, one for 16 and one for 24. Also complete.

The place is almost military in its degree of organization.

Every pan is the same brand. Every pan has its lid. All spatulas, cooking forks and spoons are made of the same shiny stainless steel in the same style except for a few that must be some sort of fancy acrylic (and all those are the same color and shape, every one akin).

He pulls open drawer after drawer, finds one built specifically for knife storage. Maybe these are the cutting implements of lesser quality, or less frequently used—or simply not for show. These knives are Henckel. Like everything else, they match. And every space is filled.

By the time he reaches the family room, it's dusk, and two lamps plugged into timers have come on. The box of Kleenex still sits on the coffee table in front of the pink linen sofa. A crumpled tissue is caught in a crack between two cushions. Dried mucus. Which means DNA.

He doesn't have access to a lab, but what the hell. Waste not, want not. DNA for a rainy day. He pulls another tissue from the box, uses that to cover his hand and collects the specimen. He goes back to the kitchen, finds a small plastic ziplock bag, drops the tissue into it.

In the garage, he takes a flashlight from a drawer and a small crowbar from a pegboard.

He carries the crowbar with him into the guest bedroom "Winnie" occupied, the bedroom entered from the hall that comes off the living room.

He unlocks the French doors leading to the adjoining patio and locates the nearest outside light. Then he checks along the back wall of the house until he finds a low metal box. Padlocked. Using the small crowbar and making a mental apology to the Nelsons and whatever gods are offended by petty, if necessary, vandalism, he breaks the metal hasp.

The timer inside the box is set to turn the back outside lights on at 1:00 a.m. Set wrong originally? Or fouled up by a power surge? Happens all the time in this land of thunderstorms.

He fiddles with the control. The light blinks on. It shines on the little patio, angling its beam into the guest room.

So... if you were sleeping and it came on...

He thinks back to the night of the murder. Winds picking up late in the day, not calming with sundown, but continuing to blow. He remembers leaving his place after being awakened by Jill's phone call. The heat. The unquiet air.

He puts the control back to its original 1:00 a.m. setting. The light goes off. He closes the metal box and decides he'd better take the broken hasp and the padlock with him. The gardener will notice their absence eventually, and they'll be replaced. In the meantime, it's not exactly a big security risk.

He reenters the guest room from the patio and turns the lock on the French doors. Then he shakes them, does his best to imitate the effects of a wind. The doors are loose, imperfectly fitted. They move against the jamb.

Clare's rattling. And her light...

A genuine source of her terror? Or useful material for an elaborate lie?

He lies down on the bed, imagining himself a young woman (impossible), imagining himself naked, vulnerable, running from some unknown...

Did he ever really buy her story?

Or did he just want to fuck her again?

Someone, maybe Woody Allen, once observed that anyone could make it through a day without food, water or sex. But no one ever got through a day without a good rationalization.

Back in the living room, he stands in the bearded man's footprints, the ones that are deepest, that contained the most blood. He feels the presence behind him, the knife drawn across his throat, even lets himself collapse onto the filthy floor.

He stands. And this time he is the killer. Behind the footprints, subduing the big bearded man.

He's holding the man as his victim fights first the blade, then the horror of seeing his own blood spraying the room, holding him as he weakens, until he is, literally, dead weight.

And where is Winnie/Clare?

She ran. Talked her way into Jill's house. (And was awfully damn creative about it.) Seduced Grady (okay, so it wasn't much of a challenge). Hid. Told either some version of the truth or a wild tale to keep him from turning her in. Lied about her identity not once but twice. Was up to her neck in shit after she helped snatch Sophie. Escaped. Showed an impressive flair for violence in the ghost town. And got away again...

Not asleep. Not an innocent. He'd bet on it.

He gives in to the emotion roaring through his veins and curses the room, the blood, the stupidity of men, his own brainless dick and her goddamn lithe little body.

Then he stops, forces himself to be still and silent for a moment.

He replaces the flashlight and the crowbar. Walks to the front door. Lets himself out.

The next step has to be done in daylight.

30

Don't be scared, Sophie tells herself. Nothing to be afraid of.

But she is.

She doesn't want to open her eyes, doesn't want to look, but she has to.

And she's alone.

There was a policeman outside her door. But now the door is open, and there's no one there. His chair is gone. He won't be back.

Where's her dad? Why isn't someone watching out for her?

Don't be scared. Don't be scared.

She's safe. The nurses keep saying that. "You're safe now." They say it every time they come in to take her temperature, or bring her the bed pan, or draw blood. Like if they say it enough, she'll believe it.

Like if they say it enough, *they'll* believe it.

They know she's not safe.

She's not safe.

The three men will get her. They can walk right into the room.

No. Uncle Jack shot one of them out in the desert. And another one fell down a well.

But there's still the tall man, the one with the big muscles and the awful voice. He was the boss. And nothing Sophie ever saw or heard hinted that there was anything good or kind about him. Born mean, her grandpa would say.

She's seen his face. Way out in the desert, a crazy man stumbling around firing a rifle up in the air, the image all woozy—as if she wasn't really there. But she feels like she was. And that's why they kill the people they kidnap. Everybody knows that. You see the kidnapper's face, you die. And he has a gun.

No. Someone will spot him. He won't get in.

But even if he can't sneak in on his own, maybe he can get help. A lookout or something.

No one will help him. All his friends are dead...

Except...

Winnie. Or whoever she is.

But Winnie isn't bad. Winnie tried to help Sophie escape from the van.

Wait. Winnie caused all the trouble, from the beginning. Sophie doesn't know how, but somehow she knows this is true.

Without Winnie, she would never have been kidnapped. The men were stupid. They could never have thought up a way to get Sophie to open the door.

Winnie did that.

And Winnie could sneak in anywhere. She's pretty. And she's good at fooling people. She fooled Sophie's mom. Even Uncle Jack. And he used to be a policeman.

So Winnie can sneak the tall man in here.

And if she sneaks the tall men in here, he will kill her.

He'll drag Sophie out of her bed, and out of the hospital, and kill her.

Where can she hide? The closet's no good, or the bathroom.

How can she escape? She's hooked up to wires. There are tubes running out of her.

"I want my mom," Sophie cries. "Where's my mom?"

She twists and kicks. Pulls at the wires. Tugs at the tubes sticking into her arm.

"Mommy!" she screams. "Mommy! Mommy!
"MOMMY!!!"

#

Now that Grady's ready to leave Pergama, he discovers that his car is dead. The damn thing won't even crank. Typical sudden death for a battery in Tucson's extreme climate: alive and well one day and a hunk of useless metal the next.

He rifles through his wallet, locates his AAA card. Expired two years ago.

He could call one of his guards to give him a jump. But the last person he wants to see is one of his guys. Too many questions.

He doesn't have the energy to put on an act, so he calls someone who already knows the worst of him. Andy Davis.

They try jumper cables with no luck. It's either tow the car to a garage or bring a new battery to the car. And whichever it is, Grady can't make it happen tonight.

So Davis drives him home.

Grady wants to stop at the store on the way. He can say he's out of food. Which is okay. something Davis can understand.

But then he'll see the shape of the bag in Grady's hand, the outline of the bottle.

And Grady doesn't need that. He doesn't need anyone—even Davis—thinking about him being a loser right now. The shit storm inside his own head is bad enough.

And it's only a few blocks. Bear will enjoy the walk.

#

He wakes the next morning foggy and aching. He phones Davis, gets him to check the hospital again.

He makes coffee, doubling the number of scoops so he won't just crawl back to bed.

Somehow, he forces himself to concentrate. The night before, just before the alcohol shut down his brain, it occurred to him that he could rent a metal detector. Not that he has the budget, especially after he deals with that piece of shit car. But it would make the search easier, boost his chances of success. Assuming that what he's looking for is there at all. That his deduction bears any resemblance to reality.

But then he calls up a mental image of the terrain. Desert landscaping, which means native plants artistically placed, vegetation much denser than it would ever occur in nature, and every cactus, tree and bush ready to defend itself with spines, thorns or needles.

He'll have a hard enough time maneuvering through the area even without a mechanical appendage. So no metal detector. He'll have to depend on his own eyes.

By noon he's bought a battery and cabbed it up to Jill's (not daring to call Andy again). He's installed the thing in his car, successfully started up the beater and backed it out onto the street, where he parks it in violation of Pergama's homeowners' association rules.

He forces himself to drink a good twelve ounces of water from one of the bottles he bought at the convenience store next to the auto parts outlet and pulls a baseball cap with a large brim onto his head. He's wearing a long-sleeved shirt made of tightly woven denim, jeans, socks and hiking boots to protect himself from the worst of the spines, but this still won't be fun.

He starts at the Nelsons'. There's no clear evidence of the exact path Clare took from the Nelsons' portico to Jill's front door, but he can estimate the probable boundaries—how far she could go toward the road, how far toward the walls that surround both back yards. He pretends he's a short woman who doesn't dare stand up straight, who's hiding, crouching in dense, thorny brush and adds on the maximum distance that her arm could throw a small, awkward object.

He's defined the area he has to cover.

He walks it slowly, head bent, examining the ground—while trying to avoid being poked, stabbed or scraped by thorns, spines, cactus needles and small branches.

213

He's looking for something partly shiny. Something too big to be carried away by a packrat. Which is good.

But maybe not too big to be scooped up by a crow. Shit. You just can't control nature.

He finds an empty beer can, an ancient People magazine with nearly all the print washed away, the feathers and tiny bones of a dead bird. His spine aches from its stooped position, the back of his neck is sunburned, tight and painful.

He allows himself to pause every 30 minutes to straighten up, stretch, chug some more water. He's overheated, dehydrated and developing cramped muscles radiating from his spine into his lower back, even his shoulders.

He spends the rest of the afternoon searching the area between the Nelsons' and Jill's, the "yard" where Clare told him she hid from the men who invaded the Nelsons.

But there's no sign of the paring knife. Either he hasn't spotted it. Or that hypothetical crow got it. Or—more likely—there's nothing to find. It was never there.

#

Jill surfaces, coming up from a darkness so deep it has been simply an absence. She's in a bed. A hospital. Her eyes don't want to stay open, her mouth doesn't work.

She tells her right hand to move. She draws in the air with her finger.

"S"

"She's alive," Charlie says.

"?"

"She's alive."

The next time she's awake, she can tell it's hours later. There's a tray in front of her. Little tubes full of some red liquid. Somebody is fooling with her arm.

"S" She draws in the air.

The young woman holding the syringe frowns. "I don't understand."

"S"

"I'm sorry."

"S" "S" "S" ...

She pushes the tray away, hears the tubes clatter to the floor.

31

Grady goes back to doing what he has to do. He spends a few hours at his mother's house, installing new glass in the broken window, replacing the stumps of the blue candles that sit in the middle of the kitchen table with new ones, repairing the front door. Then he retrieves Virginia from the hospital, gets her settled.

Each evening after work, his car wanders over to the hospital. He gets as far as the double doors leading into the ICU, but never into the area, let alone the room. He isn't on the list—could bluff his way in, but doesn't. Charlie clearly doesn't want him there, and Grady can't blame him.

Ten days after the narrow escape in the desert, Grady's driving away from the hospital when his cell phone rings. He's been leaving it on, even charging the battery, not wanting to miss any of Davis's updates on Jill's condition.

This time, Davis has another agenda.

They meet at Goodtime Charlie's. The joint isn't a cop bar. Hanging out with a disgraced former member of the force requires discretion, even for someone with Andy's credentials. Like a cop bar, though, the place is cheap.

By the time Grady settles down at the booth in the far back

corner, Davis has one dead soldier in front of him and is working on number two. And to Grady's surprise, all Davis does for a while is shoot the shit. Just when Grady's starting to think Andy simply wanted company, he gets down to business.

They've found another body. "Damn good thing vultures don't collect teeth," Davis says, taking another swig. "Otherwise, between them and the coyotes, we'd never ID the creep. As it is, it'll give the forensic people fits. But he was only a few miles from Ruby, and the medical boys tell me he's the right size and age."

"You find the rifle?"

Davis shakes his head. "No. Prob'ly never will."

He waves the waitress over, and they order another round. "By the time they found the asshole he didn't have a whole lot of flesh left. Even so, the docs are pretty sure he died of exposure. The desert got him. So that's that.

"One thing, though. Looks like he was shot. Not a bad wound. Not that they can tell, anyway. And nobody's lookin' to blame anybody but the asshole himself. But a bullet hole all the same. And you say you didn't do it."

"Never had the chance."

Grady knocks another cigarette out of the pack he's laid on the table. Davis reaches for the pack, takes one.

He shakes his head at Grady. "Don't say it. I have a wife. Don't need you raggin' on me, too." He lights up, inhales and blows out the smoke in a long, gray stream. "Anyway, like you know, we found a gun lying next to Ms. Whitehurst. And it had her fingerprints all over it."

Grady shrugs, both acknowledging the fact and signaling that it's inconsequential. It's her gun. It's registered to her. And Grady left it with her. Doesn't mean she used it—or even could have used it.

All of which Davis already knows. And all of which Grady points out.

"Yeah," Andy says. "You're preachin' to the choir. And your wild west shoot-out blew away one shithead. We all know that. But, just out of curiosity, how many bullets were left in the gun when you took the little girl and left her mother?"

Grady knows how many bullets. He knows the answer is two. And that it doesn't matter whether the gun was discovered with two bullets or one or none. Jill was shot. If she shot back, good for her. It was self-defense. She's a heroine.

But she doesn't need the questions. Whether she recovers next week, next month or next year, this needs to be over. He can't spare her much, but he can spare her this.

"Only one," he says, guessing that, being grievously wounded, she had time and strength to get off only one shot. He's also inferring that the shell casing hasn't been found, maybe carried off by a pack rat, or a crow.

"You're sure."

He fed Davis the right answer, sees it in Andy's face. "Yup. Definitely one."

"And she was in bad shape when you left her."

Grady exaggerates just a little. "Unconscious," he says. "In and out at best. How she got shot?" He shrugs and signals for another round.

Davis picks up the thread. "We'll never know." He can tell Davis thinks he's lying, but is happy to let it go. Grady's response allows him to clear up one small part of the hot mess he's been drowning in, and that's what matters. Between them, he and Andy have settled on what will become an official truth: Ms. Whitehurst was left unconscious with a gun that had one bullet, and found still unconscious, though wounded, with a gun that still held that bullet. "Civilians think you can always wrap everything up. Like a package. With a fuckin' bow. Doesn't always work out that way."

Davis isn't home free, of course. He still has a big problem: the murder that started everything. That case is getting cold. But now he has material to work with: three more male bodies, all definite perps. Not that anyone has put names to a single corpse at this point. The naked guy didn't have any papers, and the other three carried false

I.D. But two of them—the muscle-bound leader and the walking refrigerator—were definitely big enough to have done the cutting that hot Saturday night.

Grady knows that Andy is figuring how he can pin the body in the Nelsons' living room on one of those deceased perps. End of questions in the media, end of agitation by the rich and all-too-energetic residents of Pergama, end of paperwork. Shitstorm over. Grady wishes him imagination and luck.

Three nights later, Grady's cell phone rings again. It's Davis, with another summons.

The crowd is still as low-rent as the decor, but the beer is cold and the jukebox is good.

This time, Davis starts crowing as soon as Grady sits down. He waves over a waitress and puts a beer for Grady on his tab. He's even smoking his own cigarettes from a pack sitting in plain sight on the table. "Celebrating!" he says. "Fuck!"

His people identified the little guy who went down the well, and the other ID's have fallen into place from there. They have names, even a couple of street monikers: Walt "The Shrimp" Simon, Harold Taylor. The tall blond man, the leader with the hoarse, gravelly voice, was William "Billy Oz" Ostrowski. The dead body at the Nelsons' belonged to Victor Vassallo.

All were born and bred in the Midwest (the Detroit area to be precise) except for Taylor (whom Grady still thinks of as the human tank), who began his life in Queens and migrated to Michigan in his early 20s. They were wanted, variously, for armed robbery, assault, breaking and entering—even a stack of unpaid parking tickets.

"Billy was the boss," Davis says. "Only one with any smarts. Even squeaked by a GED."

"Huh. Just smart enough to make plans and just dumb enough to try to carry them out."

"Yup. Pro'bly thought he was some sort of criminal mastermind." Davis stabs out his cigarette like he's attacking the ashtray. "I fuckin' hate Hollywood."

"What was with the voice?"

"Some other lug almost took him out a few years back. Fractured his larynx. Shithead nearly suffocated."

Davis lights up a fresh cigarette, Grady takes a good long swig of his beer. He knows they're both thinking how much better off the world would have been if whoever beat on Billy Oz's neck had managed to finish the job.

Grady breaks the silence. "Any military background?" Grady asks, remembering the surprising way the assholes followed the trail in the desert.

"Taylor. The guy you shot. Did part of one tour in Afghanistan. Dishonorable discharge."

Over the next few days, grieving mothers and angry fathers and a sister ashamed to be related to the deceased Billy claim the remains, except for those of The Shrimp, whose battered body nobody wants and who is eventually placed in an unmarked grave. Winnie/Clare—whoever she was—is assumed to have died in the desert. The mystery is not really solved, but everybody seems to accept that whatever happened, it's over.

Not that everything goes smoothly for Grady. In spite of his friendship with Andy Davis, the powers that be in the Sheriff's office aren't inclined to cut him any slack. They're still pissed at him. There is even talk of charges (on what basis he isn't sure).

And often, when he is falling asleep or just waking up, Grady can feel something tugging at the back of his mind. But no matter how he tries, he can't get it to surface. Eventually, he gives up.

There is some good news: Sophie is recovering, and Jill is out of danger. In fact, Jill is now strong enough to talk. He knows this because she's taken to calling him from the hospital every couple of days just to make sure, she says, that he's okay. And to thank him again. If Grady has grave doubts about his actions, she clearly doesn't. So when he lets slip that he might be in legal hot water, he gets a phone call from Doris Asprey. The Pergama Homeowners' Association president insists on (quietly) hiring him the best criminal lawyer in town—who quickly, and even more quietly, makes the threat go away.

He starts to drift. He has his job, which takes less and less energy, his dog, his jazz collection and his bottle, although he does manage to cut down some on the drinking. At one point, he takes up vodka martinis, but they seem fussy so he goes back to whiskey. He checks on his mom nearly every day. From time to time, Gina stops by while he's there, but he contrives to mostly miss her visits and to protect her grandmother from the worst of her messes. At one point, Davis apparently overcomes his fear of being tainted by association and invites Grady to join his pool league. But almost all the players are with the department, and Grady declines.

Within a few weeks, things are mostly back to the way they were. The newspaper coverage takes a little longer to die down than the electronic media. Toward the end, there are even a couple of letters to the editor urging Grady's reinstatement on the force. But that exceedingly minor grass roots movement doesn't come to anything. Which is just as Grady expects. The debacle that resulted in his expulsion was too public. It's been years, but it was yesterday. The personnel running the department are the same. To them, he is still an embarrassment. So rehabilitation isn't in the cards. He'll never be a cop again. And, to Grady's surprise, he isn't so sure he's sorry. It's taken a long time, but he doesn't feel like a cop anymore.

Then Jill is released from the hospital. And this time the summons comes from her.

32

No one has lived in the old ranch house in more than a decade.

When Jill's parents sold the land, they kept the house and five acres. The property is on the far east side, backed up against the Rincon Mountains, and used to be miles outside Tucson. Now it's an island surrounded by subdivisions.

The family seldom visits. The place is too close to be a weekend getaway, and the land isn't high enough to be much cooler than their more modern (and air conditioned) residences. Grady hasn't been near the place in years.

The building itself is an odd combination of faded brick and adobe. Cats Claw vines dotted with yellow flowers cover the walls. An ancient multi-trunk mesquite shades the entryway. Grady lifts his hand to ring the bell, but Jill opens the door before his finger can reach the button.

"Sssh," Jill whispers. "She's sleeping."

Grady understands that Jill is referring to Sophie, but he doesn't understand why Sophie would already be asleep for the night since it's barely 7:00. Maybe her recovery isn't complete. He can only guess why Jill and Sophie are here. And doesn't have a clue why she wants to see him.

Jill walks ahead of him down the hall that leads to the core of the house. Like all true Arizona dwellings, this house turns its back to the street. Its important rooms face a walled rear yard. The place is swamp-cooled, but even though they're deep into monsoon season, it's been a dry couple of days. The old-fashioned "refrigeration" method is doing its job, and the air feels crisp, almost cold.

Jill is wearing faded jeans and a pale blue knit top. Her blonde hair is long and loose. Her feet are bare. Grady can't believe how wonderful she looks. Part of it may be that it's so amazing to see her intact: walking, talking. If he were a spiritual man, he might describe her appearance as miraculous.

They enter the main space, a combination family/dining room, with an adjoining farmhouse kitchen. With its low ceiling, honey-colored adobe walls, red Mexican tile floor and dark, rough woodwork, this big room never pretended to be anything but the heart of a working ranch. It was always the gathering place, furnished with comfortable couches flanking a stone fireplace, built-in shelves lined with books, a long table and oddly assorted chairs. Grady always liked it.

Now, the room is sparsely furnished, but somehow manages to retain its warmth.

Jill leads the way to a Sonoran-style sideboard so old it's almost antique. She pushes her hair behind one ear, picks up a tall bottle and reaches for a short glass sitting next to an ice bucket. The bottle is Sauza Extra Gold, a premium tequila he and Jill used to treat themselves to once in a while, long ago, when they were hanging out in Rocky Point, down on the Sonoran Gulf coast.

"Drink?"

Grady shakes his head. He doesn't want her to think she has to pour him alcohol the moment he walks in a door. "Just water."

She sets the bottle and glass on top of the sideboard, goes through the wide archway into the kitchen, takes a tumbler from a cupboard and fills the glass from a pitcher in the refrigerator. "Lots of dry air out there," she says.

"Feels like it will never rain again."

"Just a lull, they say. The monsoons will be back any day now."

"Any day."

Grady takes the water from Jill's outstretched hand. "Please," she says, "sit down." She gestures toward a floral print sofa set perpendicular to the large casement windows, which are open to the backyard.

Grady seats himself at one end of the sofa. Jill perches at the other, leaning tensely forward. She motions at the open windows. "If she wakes up," she says, "I'll have to close them."

Why, Grady wonders. One of the good things about swamp cooling is that it creates positive pressure. Cooled air is drawn into and through the house and then flows to the outside. Leaving windows open even helps the system work more efficiently.

"It scares her," Jill says.

The open windows frame a view of a mesquite bosque. The grove of gnarled trees with black trunks and bright green foliage is as lush as Arizona desert gets without a lot of extra water. Long shadows fall across the pebbled yard. The Rincon Mountains rise above the trees, their rounded outlines purple in the fading light. Grady enjoys the illusion of cool, and of being far from civilization. The stucco houses parked in their neat rows on the surrounding streets might be a thousand miles away.

He wishes he'd taken the drink.

"I know you're wondering why you're here," Jill says. "But you'll see. I have to show you." She glances at her watch. "Excuse me."

She stands and walks into the kitchen. After a moment, Grady follows.

Jill is pulling items out of the refrigerator, assembling a plate of cheese and fruit. "This should hold you for a little while," she says.

"Sure," Grady says. He hopes she doesn't think she has to feed him dinner.

Jill opens the pantry cabinet. "I have some nice crackers."

She takes out a box of Bremner Wafers and adds crackers to the cheese platter.

Then she reaches into the pantry cabinet again and pulls out a can of chicken soup and a small jar of applesauce.

She places them on the counter. "For Sophie," she says. She takes a can of 7UP from the refrigerator.

"It's all she'll eat. And I have to open them in front of her."

Grady looks a question at her.

"Poison," she says.

Grady carries the cheese plate into the room, sets it on the coffee table.

Jill sits next to Grady on the sofa. She motions at the food. "Please," she says. "Eat."

He waits.

Jill's eyes are on Grady's, and her look is steady, but Grady has the sense that the eye contact is a conscious act of will, that without firm control, her gaze would slide away to the windows, the landscape outside, anything that isn't this.

He waits some more.

Jill cuts a small slice of cheese, picks up a cracker, places the cheese on it, looks at it—and puts it down on the table.

Grady's not sure what to say. It needs to be something that will help, or comfort, or at least not make things worse. Jill is sitting quietly, very straight, her face composed.

When she finally speaks, it's as if she's starting in the middle of a paragraph. Unlike Jill, with her organized mind and orderly way of expressing herself.

"This place is pretty primitive, almost empty, only one bedroom furnished. But it's secure. So is our house, of course. But I'm hoping...that, well... maybe Sophie will believe that here she's safe."

Grady sees tears well up in her eyes. He begins to reach out, begins to speak, "Jill, I..." A scream cuts through his clumsy speech.

" Mommy! Mommy!" Another scream, the words incoherent, distorted by terror.

Jill runs out of the room, down the hall. The cries continue, diminishing slowly. Then quiet.

Grady waits. The room grows dark. He thinks about pouring himself a drink, but some equation of basic fairness in his head says that if Jill can't escape, he shouldn't either.

The hall light blinks on. Jill is coming back. A child is huddled against her. Grady knows the girl is Sophie, but if he saw her on the street, anywhere out of context, he's not sure he would recognize her. She's dressed like Sophie—shorts, a t-shirt and moccasins. But she's clinging to her mother, her face turned in, all but hidden in the crook of Jill's arm. The mother and daughter walk like a four-legged creature.

Jill's head is bent toward Sophie's, and as they approach, Grady can hear her crooning, repeating over and over: "It's just Uncle Jack. You know Uncle Jack."

The Jill-Sophie creature hobbles into the room and moves without pause toward the kitchen. Jill gives Grady a look that seems made of equal parts apology and despair. With one hand, she motions toward the open windows. Grady closes them, and draws the drapes.

Grady watches from the darkened living room while Jill fixes Sophie's supper. Seen through the archway, the lighted kitchen is a stage for a tragic play. Sophie's eyes don't leave Jill as she opens the soup, heats and serves it, pulls the tab on the 7UP and pours it into a glass, spoons the applesauce into a small bowl. Sophie feeds herself slowly, examining every bite, and pushing the food away before she's eaten even a third.

"How about just a little more, Soph?"

Without looking up at her mother, Sophie shakes her head.

"You know you need to eat to get well. You need to be strong to play videogames and ride horses and do all the things you like to do."

Sophie shakes her head again, harder this time, and Jill visibly gives up. She draws Sophie gently to her feet, places her arm around the child and walks her into the living room. Grady realizes she's heading for an overstuffed chair that sits at a right angle to the sofa.

It's dark in the room, but he's afraid that if he moves he'll disturb the delicate balance of Sophie's fears.

Jill manages to reach out with one arm and switch on a lamp. She lowers Sophie into the chair.

Sophie tries to pull her mother down with her, but Jill shakes her head. "It's just Uncle Jack," she says. "It's okay." But she sits at the end of the sofa that's only inches away from her daughter.

"Hello, Sophie," Grady says.

Sophie looks down at her hands, twisted in her lap.

"Sophie," Jill says. "Say hello."

"Hello," Sophie says, without looking up. Her voice is flat.

"I'm glad to see you," Grady says.

Sophie nods. She's quiet for a moment, then says, in the same, flat voice: "Did you bring your gun?"

"No."

Jill strokes her daughter's hair. "He's not a policeman any more. You know that." She stands up, gives her child a kiss on the top of her head and moves over to the sideboard.

"You should always carry your gun," Sophie says. She's speaking to Grady, but her eyes track her mother's movements.

"I'm not going anywhere," Jill says. "I'm just getting your medicine." She opens a drawer and takes out two pill bottles. Then she turns and moves into the kitchen.

Sophie's sharp intake of breath as her mother turns her back long enough to grab the can of 7UP from the kitchen counter is the sound of panic.

"It's okay," Jill says, her voice calm but her movements quick. She sits down on the sofa again. Sophie's eyes return to the hands writhing in her lap.

Grady says the only thing he can think of to say. "I don't need a gun here."

Jill nods approval at him. "That's right. Nothing bad is going to happen."

"We're safe?" Sophie actually looks up for a moment, places her

227

eyes on her mother's face.

"Yes," Jill says softly. "We're safe." She hands Sophie two pills and the can of 7UP. "Time to go to sleep now, sweetie."

Sophie places one pill in her mouth and takes a swallow of the soda. Then she stops.

"This is the same can as before?"

Jill nods. "Yes. We left it on the kitchen counter. You saw me pick it up."

Sophie places the second pill in her mouth and takes a second swallow of 7UP.

"The men who took me are dead?"

"Yes." She strokes her daughter's hair again.

"All of them?"

"Yes."

Sophie shakes her head. Her face twists into something that is almost a smile, but on someone older would be a grimace. She looks back down at her hands. "I don't believe you."

This time, after Jill has guided, almost carried Sophie down the hall toward the only furnished bedroom, Grady pours himself the drink. He refills the ice bucket, drops two cubes into the short glass and sloshes in a generous portion of tequila. Sophie sounded like a much younger child. Grady doesn't know much about kids and developmental stages, all that crap, but he felt like he was watching a frightened three-year-old. What the hell is going on?

Jill bathes Sophie in the old-fashioned claw foot tub, soaping her daughter's arms and shoulders, shampooing her hair just as she did when Sophie was a small child. Then she wraps Sophie in a towel and helps her back to their shared room. She dresses Sophie in a soft, pale green nightgown, pulls back the sheet and folds her into bed. Sophie's eyes close almost before Jill can pull the cover back up over her. Jill knows that the sleep comes from the drugs, but she is grateful for any relief granted to her daughter, no matter what the mechanism.

She watches Sophie's sweet, steady breathing for a moment, then turns to go—and catches an inadvertent glimpse herself in the bedroom mirror. She looks tired, but that she is physically coherent at all is still a shock to her. She continues to assume that her pain is far more visible.

She turns out the lamp, turns on a nightlight, opens the door and steps through.

Still standing by the sideboard, Grady watches her walk down the hall and into the living room. She stops in front of him and folds her arms around herself, her head bowed; then, with an obvious effort of will, looks up and directly at him with something like her old force.

"She's not the same child," Jill begins. "Charlie thinks she can be. That it's just temporary. He doesn't want to face it."

Her gaze breaks loose, and her eyes dart around the room, landing here, there, moving on. "So when he left yesterday on a business trip, I packed us up and brought us out here. Our house just...well, reminds her."

The bottle of tequila still sits on the sideboard. Grady takes out a second glass, scoops a couple of cubes into it and covers them with a good-sized pour of tequila. He holds the glass out to Jill. It is a gesture of comfort—and a question. They both know that she hasn't tasted hard liquor in more than fifteen years.

I deserve a drink, she thinks. We deserve a drink. And then she thinks, we always deserved a drink, or it had been a shit day and we needed a drink, or something went right and we were celebrating with a drink, or something went wrong and we were comforting ourselves with a bottle. There was always a reason—at least one—to have a drink and never any reason not to. Neither of us ever said, "I've had a great day. I think I'll enjoy iced tea with my meal." Neither of us ever suggested, "For our anniversary this year, let's open a bottle of cranberry juice."

She thinks all this in the instant in which her ex-husband offers her the glass. Then she reaches out her hand and takes it.

Swallowing the tequila is like coming home. It burns the back of her throat in a way that grabs her attention, pulling her back to herself. She knows it has to be a psychological effect, but she can swear she feels her arms loosen, her legs stretch, her spine relax.

She thinks she hears Sophie stir, but when she goes in to check, her daughter is sleeping gently, her right hand tucked under her cheek, her hair still damp from the bath. Jill bends and kisses her forehead.

She closes the bedroom door. When she re-enters the main room, she sees that Jack has turned out the lights, pulled back the curtains and reopened the casement windows. He's standing in front of them, looking out at the mesquite bosque. Jill pours another couple of fingers of tequila into her glass and stands beside him. She sees only moonlit landscape: twisted limbs, brush, a few clouds over the mountains, silent lightning in the distance. The ranch house has become a universe so small that it is all center—and all edge. Jack puts an arm around her shoulders. Another gesture of comfort. Another question? She suspends thought and lets herself lean into him.

Jack pulls the drape back over the window and turns on the small lamp that sits on a nearby table. He turns toward her, awkwardly, as if uncertain what is next. His hair is ruffled, just there on his left temple. She reaches up to smooth it back and touches his ear, then has to stroke his cheek, his neck.

Then his arms are around her, and his lips are on hers. The length of his body presses against hers.

She hasn't felt this sweetly piercing sensation, this swimming of desire in years. Too many years, her body says. She needs it. She wants it. She deserves it...

Suddenly, Jack freezes. "Stay very still," he says.

She follows his gaze. There, sand bright on the red Saltillo tile floor just inches from her right foot, is a night creature come out to hunt when Jack turned off the lights and now beached, stranded mid-room. Its tail is up in armed, venomous threat.

Jill regards the intruder carefully. Then she raises her bare foot—
and brings it down on the scorpion.

33

Jill lives. She knew she would. The effects range from mild pain and swelling to convulsions, but no one has died from a scorpion sting in Arizona since the state began keeping records. Jill proves to be moderately sensitive. She has five hours of agony. She swallows Benadryl and ibuprofen, accepts an ice pack, tries to drown out the howling pain by counting the cracks in the adobe wall. It is a fair trade: she is no good at all during those five hours to her damaged, infinitely precious daughter. But she is satisfied that by making this relatively small sacrifice, enduring this minimal mortification of the flesh, she has protected her daughter, her husband, her future, her life.

Grady sees Jill misstep, sees her thin, naked foot reach the scorpion's tail just before his large shod one. He is appalled at her injury, wrecked by her pain.

And he knows instantly that whatever was about to happen—whether it would have been a temporary return to intimacy or the beginning of a second chapter in their lives—will never be. He puts Jill to bed in the other twin in Sophie's room.

He doesn't allow himself to wonder about the why of Jill's accident, although he is surprised that she, who is so graceful and athletic, could be so clumsy. The sighting of a scorpion might, he thinks, shock an Easterner into irrational action, but not someone who grew up in the desert. He attributes the incident to the stress of caring for her daughter, her few unaccustomed sips of tequila and his own stupidity.

He reruns those few moments in his head, trying to change the outcome. In each revision, he is silent about the spiked tail rising from the floor. Sometimes, he simply brings his shoe down quickly, unquestionably putting an end to the creature. Sometimes, he sweeps Jill up in his arms, lays her carefully on the sofa and lets the scorpion go about its business.

He wants to take the last version further, but he finds he can't. The prospect of it is too wonderful, and his inability to make it real too painful.

He feels as if hope, which for years has been an unaccustomed feeling, sprang up and quickly died. Jill killed it as instantly and certainly as she did the scorpion. He will suffer its memory and mourn its loss long after Jill is fully recovered and back in the arms of her husband.

And yet...and yet... He's dragged a chair into the bedroom, where he watches over Jill as she lies, stoic in her pain (as always, he recalls), her leg propped on a pillow, her head turned so she can look constantly, every moment, at Sophie sleeping undisturbed just a few feet away.

Jill didn't scream. She collapsed to the floor, turned pale. But she never made a sound.

Grady knows she didn't want to wake her daughter.

He skips over the physical act of love and runs other scenarios. Jack and Jill together again. But too close to middle-age to party gracefully, and with no other real way to relate. Sophie confused by joint custody, never sure where to find her homework or favorite pair of jeans. He runs other scenarios, but some of them end with Sophie permanently held captive by her trauma, others with her careening into the first stages of juvenile delinquency, still others with her living full-time with Charlie—and Jill broken-hearted. None of them is any good.

Grady takes a long drag on his cigarette, filling the empty places inside him with smoke. He changes the ice in Jill's ice bag and pours himself another tequila.

#

At 4:00 a.m., he jerks awake in his chair with a cold stab of panic. But the small lamp still burns on the nightstand between the two beds. Jill is asleep at last. And the belly-thrust of fear is accounted for, at least in part, by the dregs of his drink. He's knocked it over, and the melted ice has drenched his crotch. He finds a cloth and mops at the dampness, reflecting that as a guardian angel he has always been a bust. Watching over people doesn't seem to be his thing. By 4:15, he is descending into the pit. By 4:30, he has a full-fledged case of the middle-of-the-night dooms. And he knows from experience that when the dragons are this fierce they won't be driven away by alcohol.

The fire-breather that visits him tonight is the worst: the demon that cleaved his life in two. The one that taught him once you cross the line you can never get back.

It all started over Gina (he's always thought), but sometimes he suspects it was really about Frannie. Six or seven years back, Jimmy Q. was a lowlife who'd blown in from L.A., running from someone or something. He quickly made himself known as trouble, but he was nothing special. He was just another punk.

But then Jimmy sold Gina crack, gave her heroin. Grady was certain he was the one who turned her out, pimped her when she was still a teenager and heartbreakingly pretty in spite of all the drugs.

It was one of those situations where all the cliches about the revolving jailhouse door seemed true. The law was ineffective. Jimmy was arrested a few times—hell, more than a few times, but he always beat it. They said he had a way with a knife; there were rumors about acid. No one who had anything on him would talk.

Then Gina turned up pregnant. Scrawny, scabby, puffing cigarettes, shooting smack. Not a mother. Not even a decent incubator. Anyone could see that.

She came to Grady for money. She'd talked with a counselor, she said, and the counselor had convinced her she couldn't have the baby. She had been thinking of adoption, of finding some nice couple who'd pay all her expenses and maybe kick in a few thousand bucks under the table and give the kid a sweet life. But the social worker had talked about low birth weight and prematurity and learning disabilities and deformities and... The nice couple would never want her kid. That was the truth, and she needed the money for an abortion. The state wouldn't pay.

Grady knew she was right about the potential problems—they started with fetal alcohol syndrome and went from there. The baby could be born addicted. Gina might even be HIV-positive. He didn't know and doubted if she did.

But this was Frannie's grandchild. A piece of his sister. How could he let that go?

The counselor had taken Gina to a clinic. She was nearly twenty weeks along. That's why it would cost so much. She needed more than $2,000.

Grady asked Gina to slow down. They could deal with the problems, he said. There were programs that would help her get off the drugs and minimize any harm to the baby. He'd find a way to get her medical care, the very best. He'd find the baby a home. He secretly thought that maybe he could raise the child himself (his mom would help), that in caring for Frannie's grandson or granddaughter, he could restore a small piece of the world.

Gina threatened to go to Virginia. "Grandma loves me," she screamed, "even if you don't!" She wouldn't want Gina to go through all this. She'd come up with the money.

Grady calmed her down. He reasoned with her. He begged. He manipulated. He promised. And he convinced her (he thought) to wait. He told her he'd pay for the abortion if that was what she wanted, but he didn't have the cash. He had to get the money. And he would have, borrowed from buddies, leaned on Artie, his current partner, called in all his chits, then held out the cash in one hand, and slammed her still-pregnant butt in a rehab program with the other. The child was not yet at viability, but close, so close.

But Gina disappeared. She didn't turn up for one week, two. Grady asked around, put the word out. Got nothing.

He took to spending his off hours looking for her, cajoling where he could, threatening where he had to.

He convinced Artie to spend part of each shift driving the south side. They broke up a minor drug ring. They prevented two rapes and inadvertently picked up a killer wanted in three states. But they didn't find his niece.

Then Grady saw her, on the corner of 36th St. and 2nd Ave., outside a Circle K. She was leaning against the building, her head resting on the shoulder of a skinny guy with scraggly long hair and a backwards baseball cap who was holding up the piece of wall next to her. Her face was turned to the January sun. She was blissfully whacked out on something.

Artie hit the brakes, and Grady was out of the car before it stopped rolling, across the parking lot in a blink and in Gina's face before she had time to react.

"Where the hell were you?" he demanded.

She shrugged. "I went to Phoenix."

And the baby?

"The baby's gone."

Grady grabbed her. His eyes filled with tears. He began to shake her. "You fucking slut!" he screamed.

"Hey, man," the guy next to her protested, "this ain't your business."

Grady held Gina back against the wall with one arm and pulled out his shield with the other hand. Flipping it open, he held it under the creep's nose.

"Start running," he said. "I'll give you ten seconds."

The punk wasted time protesting, but Grady kept counting down, and finally the little shit took off.

At "zero," Grady was after him, across the parking lot, over a fence, through a back yard owned by a furious Doberman that strained frantically at its chain, along an alley, around the corner. Grady caught him on the other side of the block in front of a laundromat. He slammed him against the wall and pummeled his mid-section. The kid tried to fight back, then collapsed to the ground. But Grady yanked him to his feet, held him up and kept punching.

People had come out of the laundromat to watch. Two guys working on a motorcycle across the street stopped to stare. Artie swooped around the corner and brought the car to a halt up on the sidewalk.

"You got him," he said to Grady. Grady hit the creep again. "That's enough," Artie urged. Finally, Artie wrapped his arms around Grady, restrained his own partner.

The perp was charged with assaulting a police officer and resisting arrest. There was a little trouble with probable cause, even though Artie did his best to back Grady's story. But the eyewitnesses didn't mean much, mostly didn't have any accurate idea what they saw.

So everything would have been okay except for the video. Juan Gonzalez was getting ready to go to Los Angeles for a cousin's wedding and needed clean clothes. He'd bought a camcorder to capture the ceremony as a favor to his aunt and decided he'd try it out while his jeans were in the drier. He caught the whole thing.

Grady looked vicious, he had to admit when he saw himself on the six o'clock news. The video showed him holding the creep in place in order to keep hitting him. And you could tell Artie was trying to get him to stop. The review board said that it was the lie that mattered. That if he'd just acknowledged a loss of control, which (although always regrettable) could be understandable in a street-worn veteran, they might have been able to refer him for counseling, park him at a desk for a while and save his job. But Grady knew better. He was an example, a bad one. All the anger management classes in the world weren't going to change that. So he blew them off. He knew his career was over.

Stupid. That's how he felt. Taking out after that punk had been a stupid and—it turned out—useless thing to do.

The paperwork and negotiating took a while. It helped that the "victim," as the media called him, had a few warrants outstanding. Probably saved Grady from a criminal trial. And, to everyone's amazement, no one sued. But it didn't matter. Before his administrative leave became termination, he had already solved the real problem.

Her Uncle Jack was an ass, Gina'd been saying all over town. Not only wasn't Eddie (the punk who'd been unfortunate enough to have his arm around her that day) the father, she barely knew him. Had only met him when they scored together that morning. The father, she thought, was probably Jimmy Q. Grady knew that whether or not Jimmy was biologically at fault, he was morally responsible. Although Gina probably would have gotten there anyway, Jimmy was the one who had put his niece on her back.

Still roaring with the pain of his loss, Grady made certain arrangements. Through an informer, a snitch he'd turned years ago, he lured Jimmy to a spot under a railroad bridge about ten miles outside of town. He had some idea of giving Jimmy an ultimatum: get out of town.

But it quickly became clear that if Grady was selling, Jimmy wasn't buying. He liked Tucson, he said. It was now, he said with a swagger, his fuckin' hometown. He owned it, or enough of it to have a good thing going. Why the fuck should he leave? He wasn't afraid of the cops. And he sure wasn't afraid of Grady. He spit on the ground. "Fuck off, old man." He turned to go.

"Fight me for it," Grady demanded. He pulled out his service weapon. "You got a piece? Show me."

"You wanna fight a duel, man?" Jimmy laughed sarcastically. "I don' think so."

Grady pointedly released the safety on his .45. "I said, get out your gun. Slowly. And make sure it's aiming at your feet."

Jimmy reluctantly bent over, pulled up his pants leg and withdrew a .38 automatic from its holster.

"I'm going to count to three," Grady said, "and throw my weapon on the ground. And you're going to do the same thing."

Jimmy shook his head. "I throw mine, you don' throw yours. You think I'm crazy?"

"C'mon, you coward, you fag, you cocksucking little girl. Show me you have some balls."

Grady knew he was taking a real chance goading the punk. He put the safety back on. Then he counted to three...and threw his weapon into the dirt at the side of the clearing.

Jimmy was still holding the .38. He sneered. He waved the piece at Grady. Grady waited for the shot. But the asshole took the bait, chose to defend his turf—and his manhood. He mouthed the word "Pow!" and tossed the gun to the ground.

Then Jimmy whipped out a knife and rushed him. Grady should have been prepared with his own blade, but wasn't. He figured he was dead. But he was in the habit of surviving. He dodged Jimmy. They grappled. Grady pitted his aging, overweight, alcohol-soaked body against Jimmy's young, skinny, drug-laced one. Jimmy hurt him, even cut him, but fate or maybe some underlying force of justice was on Grady's side for once. He called up a kick he hadn't used in nearly twenty years and knocked the blade from Jimmy's grasp. It skittered across the ground. Grady dove for it, grabbed—and suddenly found, almost discovered, the knife in his own hand. And he cut Jimmy worse. A lot worse. He stood over him as the ground turned red. He knew he should help him—pick him up, throw him over his shoulder, dump him in the back seat, drive him to the Kino ER. After the little shit recovered, he might even have the sense to leave Tucson.

But he'd just spread his brand of poison somewhere else. Destroy someone else's daughter. Fuck up a lot of other lives. And he was hurt pretty bad. Why not let God, or fate, decide?

Grady watched Jimmy bleed for a while, and then he rolled him into the weeds where, with luck, the only creatures that would find him for days or weeks would be the scavengers. Jimmy would be more useful as dinner, anyway. Grady hoped his tainted meat wouldn't poison the coyotes.

Grady kicked some dirt over the bloodied sand. He pushed Jimmy's Harley into the ravine, watching it crash down through the tree branches, hearing a satisfying crunch when it hit bottom. He could have used a few stitches, but he did without and the cuts eventually healed, leaving only a few scars that didn't matter. He watched the TV news every night for weeks, kept an eye on the newspapers, listened to the street gossip. No one seemed to know where Jimmy Q. had gone. And few seemed to care. There were rumors of a move to Miami.

Grady kept his own counsel, and he'd never shared with anyone the extent of his rage or his plans. But he knew he'd been pretty nuts and probably hadn't covered his tracks all that well. He expected to be caught any moment, maybe even wanted to be caught. But although the paperwork that would separate him from the force proceeded inexorably, his one-on-one face-off with everything that symbolized evil to him—and to most of the cops he knew—never came to light.

Unfortunately, over time his reaction to it changed.

At first, he was sorry that he'd given Jimmy such a gentle way to go. Bleeding to death, he'd always understood, was kind of like falling asleep. And Jimmy was already unconscious when Grady stowed him in the brush. But as the days and weeks went by, he began to feel queasy about the whole thing. He told himself that he shouldn't let it bother him, that it was wrong to let a worthless shit like Jimmy Q. find a form of immortality by haunting his nights. That he should feel glad about what he'd done. But he didn't. And Jimmy's body never turned up.

In the several years since, Grady has decided he doesn't know what is worse. Knowing that you have killed a man. Or not being quite sure.

34

He never does get back to sleep. He watches the crack around the edge of the shutters change from purple to deep blue to a bright yellow-gray. He's still slumped in the chair, trying to achieve mental blankness, when Sophie opens her eyes.

For an instant, she looks just like the Sophie he knows, just like any normal 12-year-old waking up on a summer morning. Then her face changes, and she lets out a small cry. He's sorry that her remembering happens so quickly. And surprised. Even he is usually granted a little longer than that.

He moves to help her, but she's already out of bed and shaking her mother. Her looks at him are filled with alarm. His presence is worse than useless.

He goes down the hall to pee. His joints creak from the night sitting up in the chair, and he feels like he's been wearing his clothes for days. His normal emotional state isn't anything to boast about. If pushed, he'd have to admit that most days he fluctuates between mild depression and gloom, with occasional moments of pleasure. But his outlook this morning can only be described as bleak. His anger and confusion are strong enough to tip the emotional balance of the entire valley.

Jill hobbles around the kitchen making breakfast. Grady urges her to sit down, to let him take over, but she refuses. He's surprised to see that Sophie doesn't seem to notice Jill's disability. She's as clinging and silently demanding as she was the night before. He does what he can to help, making coffee, pouring juice. But he's allowed to handle only food for himself and Jill. And when he accidentally touches the unopened oatmeal packet intended for Sophie, she erupts in cries that verge on hysteria. Jill waves Grady off, and spends the next ten minutes calming her child.

As Sophie becomes quiet, Jill looks up and catches Grady's eye. "Not your fault," she mouths. He retreats to the living room with his coffee and collapses on the sofa.

When he opens his eyes, the sun has shifted. The mesquite bosque to the east of the house is in shadow; it's clearly well past noon.

Jill is dozing in a nearby chair. Her feet are drawn up. Her head rests on her chest.

He needs to pee, moves as quietly as he can, makes it to the bathroom and nearly all the way back before Jill stirs.

"You're awake," she says. Grady looks at his watch. Almost 3:00.

"Where's Sophie?"

"Sleeping. She takes a nap around this time."

Grady looks his question at her.

"She gets very tired."

Jill looks exhausted. Grady figures some of her fatigue is from the scorpion toxin, the pain and the lack of sleep. But from what he can see, her everyday life has become a physical hell and an emotional torment.

He has always managed to know as little as possible about what he considers the minimally effective science of psychiatry, but he has to admit to himself that Sophie isn't pretending, that she's not throwing some sort of weird, prolonged temper tantrum. She's unimaginably far from the bright, happy 12-year-old he knew only weeks before.

He understands the cause, whether or not he knows what fancy label the doctors have put on her condition, but he hasn't a guess as to the cure.

"PTSD," Jill says as if she's been reading his mind. "Post-traumatic stress disorder. You've heard of it. It became the acronym everybody used after Vietnam. All those soldiers who came back to the States but left their minds in the war."

Grady remembers. Some of them became street people, some conspiracy nuts. There were even men who woke to an innocent sound in the middle of the night, found themselves back in the jungle, and slaughtered their families, convinced they were Viet Cong.

"It can happen to anybody," Jill continues, "given the right kind of stress. And terror. Prolonged terror seems to have a lot to do with it. Some doctors think children are particularly vulnerable. Others think children are particularly resilient."

"Nobody knows nothing."

Jill actually manages a slight smile. "Kind of."

"She's on medication?"

Jill nods. "Not to cure her. Just enough to let her sleep and to keep her from screaming—or totally retreating—the entire time she's awake. And even at the minimum dosages... well, she has a good brain, and it's still developing and everybody wants to give her a chance of becoming herself again."

"A chance?"

Tears fill Jill's eyes. "Hard to believe, isn't it? That's the way they talk about it. A chance."

Grady tries to keep his face composed, to prevent the shock he feels from communicating itself to Jill. Shit! What Jill is saying without saying is that Sophie could be like this the rest of her life.

Goddamn motherfuckers! Taking a great kid and screwing her up so much that... "Is there anything I can do?"

"Maybe."

Jill stands and walks over to the sideboard. There is still half a bottle of tequila. "Drink?"

He nods.

"Can you stay a little longer?"

He can.

She pours, but only for him. He gives her the sofa, and she stretches out and is asleep within moments. He gets some ice from the kitchen, adds another inch of tequila to his glass and sits looking out at the wild and the mountains. Heat lightning flashes over the Rincons. The sky is bright blue to the South. To the North, dark clouds are gathering The air in the ranch house feels clammy, as it approaches its saturation point and the cooler loses effectiveness. It's twilight at only 5:00 in the afternoon.

He waits.

At one point he dozes off and finds himself on a stakeout on some city street. Everything is gray: the pavement, the sidewalk, the buildings, the sky. He's been assigned to stand outside a doorway, forbidden to move, forbidden to go in. When he looks down, he sees that his trousers and his shoes are gray. He knows that the only color he is capable of seeing is red. And he knows he is waiting for something terrible to happen.

Then he's being nudged awake. He's aware that both Jill and Sophie are in the room. And that Sophie is sitting at a table in the corner and, apparently, playing solitaire.

"Hey!" he begins, thinking how wonderful it is that Sophie's doing something normal.

"Sssh!" Jill hushes him. She beckons him over. As soon as he stands up, he can see that the rectangles Sophie is shuffling, laying out, turning over, picking up and shuffling again aren't cards at all. They're photographs. And there are only a few.

As he approaches the table...

"What in hell?!?" The words burst from him. Sophie drops the photographs and reaches for her mother in panic. Jill bends, picks up the photos and hands them to Sophie.

Sophie straightens them, shuffles, begins laying them out carefully, taking time to straighten them, to make sure the spacing between them is exactly the same.

Grady draws Jill aside. She can't move more than a few feet away from Sophie, so he keeps his voice low.

"Holy shit, Jill."

Jill nods slightly, as if to say, "I know."

"Are those what I think they are?"

Jill nods again.

"Where in hell did you get them?"

"I can't say."

'Cause somebody would be in a shitload of trouble, Grady thinks. It was one of the doctors, had to be, wouldn't have been a detective, certainly not Davis. Nope. With Jill's connections in the medical community, it was one of the doctors.

Grady takes a few steps closer to the table. Jill's keeping pace with him, but at the same time holding tightly to his arm, restraining him. "Don't go too close," she says.

Sophie is shuffling. She lays down one photograph, straightens it, lays down the second...

There are four.

Vassallo, gash in his throat purple, face gray-green. The Shrimp with his neck attached to his head at an angle that can only mean he broke it in the fall down the well. Harold Taylor, open eyes rolled back in his head, staring at nothing. And a chewed, rotted thing that might once have been the face of Billy Oz.

Grady is gaping, can't help it. "They're autopsy photos."

Jill pulls him back, away from the table. "Keep your voice down."

"What the fuck are you doing with them?"

"She needed closure, her doctors said. She needed to know that they couldn't come back and get her. That they didn't have power over her anymore." Jill's using her authoritative voice, the one that says, I'm a medical professional, something of a scientist. And you're not is always implied. Grady knows this trick from countless old arguments. It won't work.

But Jill can't keep it up anyway. As she talks, she sounds more and more like what she is: a desperate mother. "We told her and told her and told her that they were dead. We showed her the newspaper articles—in print, not just online. Nothing helped. 'What if?' she'd say. 'What if they were pretending? What if they were fooling the police the way Winnie fooled everybody before?'

"She couldn't sleep. She wouldn't eat. It didn't seem there was enough medication in the world to help her—and least not drugs that wouldn't cause their own damage." Jill takes a visible breath, bigger and longer than she could possibly need, as if the she's trying to recharge more than her lungs. "So I talked to somebody I know.

"I know it's not healthy. I know it's ghoulish, that it's not good. But she's my daughter."

Her voice breaks. Grady watches her catch herself, pull herself up straight. Then her shoulders collapse. She moves him a few feet farther away. "This is Sophie, Jack! What the fuck was I supposed to do?"

Sophie looks up in alarm. Silent tears run down Jill's face, and she wipes then away before turning her body to face her daughter straight on. "It's okay, Sophie. It's okay. I'm not going anywhere." Sophie returns to her "cards."

Jill's voice drops again, her words only for Grady's ears. "The photos—the proof—is helping. It's holding her together—just barely—until therapy can work. Until time can help her heal. It's helping.

"But it isn't enough. She keeps asking, 'What about Winnie? Where's Winnie?' And I keep telling her, 'Winnie ran away. She's gone. She's not coming back.'

"She doesn't believe me. No reason she should. The logical part of her brain is working fine. It's the part that puts everything in context, that takes all her experience into account when she decides what something means, that isn't. So from her point of view, if Winnie survived to run away, Winnie survived to return. And if Winnie betrayed her to killers once, Winnie can betray her to killers again."

"Fuck." It is all Grady can think of to say.

"Yes," Jill says. "Fuck. Good goddamn fuck."

And suddenly Grady knows. He knows why he is here. And he knows what she wants. And he hopes he is wrong.

"You want me to find Winnie."

"Yes."

"Jesus, Jill, you know enough about how all this works to know that this is a job for the police, not some freelancing has-been."

"You're right. I do know how all this works. And I know they think she died in the desert because they want to think she died in the desert.

"But I don't think she did. I think that sneaky little blonde—and she isn't even blonde. She has brown eyes and dark hair. Sophie told us about that. I think that Winnie or Clare or whatever the fuck her name is got away with it. Got clean away. And goddamn Andy Davis and his people aren't going to do shit about it!"

Grady is silent. Jill has intuited the truth. That whatever her name is, the sneaky little blonde has indeed gotten away with it. He isn't quite sure what "it" is, but she sure has gotten away with something.

But, damn, this is not his job anymore. If it ever was. And what if he did take it on? "Say I do this. Say I find her."

He can see hope in Jill's face, see her waiting for his next sentence.

"All I can do then is call the cops."

Jill shakes her head emphatically.

"I'd have to! Especially if she's crossed at least one state line—which is a pretty safe bet. I wouldn't be able to drag her back. Not without authority. There's no warrant out for her. She hasn't even jumped bail. But with enough evidence, I can get her arrested. Then we can get her extradited, tried, locked up..."

Jill shakes her head again—violently this time. Her voice is quiet but has the intensity of a scream. "No!"

"No??"

"It won't work. Sophie will think she'll get out. Every hour, every day, Sophie will be remembering how smart she was, how conniving. Sophie will expect her every minute, here in Tucson, on our doorstep."

Grady can't believe what she's saying. He must be hearing her wrong, misunderstanding her. "So you want me to..."

Jill draws closer to Grady. She speaks softly, calmly and with unmistakable clarity. "I want you to kill her."

Grady can't believe this is Jill, his law-abiding, strong but always gentle Jill. His mind recoils. But he flashes on something that Davis said as they sat over beers at Goodtime Charlie's, something that has haunted him, something he hasn't wanted to acknowledge.

"It was the throat that killed him," Davis said. "No question. A slice like someone was opening a side of beef. Deep and determined. No sign of hesitation. But on his back there were other wounds. Small. Shallow. Made by some sort of short blade. Doc thinks they were 'contemporaneous.' Big word for at the same time."

It made no sense.

"Somebody stabbed him while he was dying?"

Davis just nodded. Clearly even to a hardened cop, it was ghoulish.

Some sort of short blade. Like a jackknife. Or a paring knife.

The knife Grady was searching for without really knowing why. The knife he didn't find.

And he loves Jill. In spite of the fact that they can't live together, can't even have a relationship, he has never questioned how much he cares.

It's full dark by the time Grady pulls away from the ranch house. Lightning flashes as he backs out of the driveway. Dust skitters along the pavement, trees whip in the wind. He hears the boom of thunder.

As he turns onto the main road, the first drops of monsoon rain hit the windshield. By the time he crosses the city limits, the rain pours down. It bubbles in the gutters and forms sudden, rapidly flowing rivers across intersections. Lightning shoots white heat across the sky. The pavement glistens. He and his car travel up a long hill. Dark sheets of water stream down at him from the road ahead.

The sky is black to the west. He's driving into the storm.

35

The photo of the key, the tracing and the clay impression lie on Grady's kitchen counter. Jill put the envelope containing them in her mailbox as arranged, and he picked it up a few minutes later, barely pausing at the end of her driveway. Charlie's home, and Jill is leaving him out of this.

Good idea.

They're working with the key because they've come up dry so far. With Jill footing the bill, Grady found an independent lab to do a DNA analysis on the dried material on the tissue he pulled out of the sofa cushion at the Nelsons'. Then he dug up an old connection, a forensics guy with questionable ethics—too shady for him to hang with in the old days—and was happy to find that the man's hunger for an under-the-table payday still ran deep and constant. For a good-sized stack of bills, the tech ran a comparison with the available databases, inside and outside law enforcement. The hope was a cold hit. The results were just what Grady expected: nothing.

There are 36 full-service locksmiths in Tucson. Locksmith one looks at the photo in Grady's hand, doesn't even touch it and, basically, blows Grady off.

"You can't tell what it's for?"

The man shakes his head. Not worth my time, his body language says. And even if I thought it might be...

Grady pushes a little, gives him a hint. "Not a safety deposit key?"

A shrug. Grady gets it. The guy may or may not know, and given he's a counter clerk in a cookie-cutter franchise operation, Grady's guess is he doesn't. For the police, he might take a couple of minutes, go get somebody who has some meaningful experience in the field. Hell, at least pay attention. But without a badge, Grady's questions aren't worth the effort. Even worse, the glaring absence of the key itself makes them downright suspicious.

He tries two more locksmiths—and the results only validate his conclusion. He needs something better.

So he makes a late-night visit to Luis, who knows a guy. And the guy turns the clay impression into the real thing. Under Grady's direction and thanks to the photograph, the key is properly colored and suitably aged.

He makes dots on a city map and spends Saturdays and as much of his working hours as he dares visiting locksmiths. He starts with the ones near his office in the northeast foothills and works his way west and south toward center city. He gets used to shrugs and disclaimers.

Sometimes, the conversations seem promising: "Yeah. I guess it could be a safe deposit box key. Not sure what else it'd be used for." But then they hit the wall: "Nope, never seen one like this before."

Ten days in, he's on locksmith 28. This one is way across town, south almost to the barrio.

It's a Spanish-speaking neighborhood. *Casa Cambios*, *Telefonica Llama Gratis*, Shell Oil, Food City, *Carnecita*, Circle K, *Ropas para Damas y Ninos*....

It's a good thing he doesn't punch a clock, because it's taken him 40-plus minutes to get here, and locksmiths 29 through 36 are even farther away.

The place is two storefronts in from the corner. Juan Izaguirre &

Sons. Serving Tucson Since 1956.

A bell tinkles as Grady pushes open the heavy, wood-framed door. The store has, indeed, been around a while. The walls are painted slump block, the display cases vintage wood and plate glass. But everything is spotless, even polished. And the machinery looks as up-to-date as anything he's seen.

"What can I do for you?" The man behind the counter is Hispanic, in his 30s, and sounds as American as Grady.

Grady reaches into his pocket and pulls out the plastic bag containing the key. By this point, he's developed a back story.

"Mr. Izaguirre?"

"Yes."

"My aunt died recently, and we found this in her things. We don't know what it's for." He knows his story would be more compelling if the dead woman were his mother, but he can't bear to do that to Virginia, to bury her even as a fiction. He opens the plastic bag, takes out the key and lays it on the counter. "We were hoping you could help."

The man picks up the key, turns it over in his hand.

"Hmmm. Looks old." He turns toward a doorway that leads to a back room. "Dad!"

Mr. Izaguirre, Sr., is several inches shorter than his son and thin as a pipe, with skin the color of molé. His hair and moustache are black, his eyes clear. Only the lines in his face betray his age.

"*Que pasa,*" he says to his son, and continues in Spanish. Grady gets the gist, which is—who is the gringo and what does he want?

"*Muy tia es meurte,*" Grady says, hoping his limited Spanish will suffice, but the son jumps in, finishing the story.

Juan Izaguirre holds out his hand, and his son places the key in his palm. The old man jiggles the key in his hand as if weighing it, holds it up to the light.

He carries it to a nearby bench and examines it with a jeweler's loupe.

At last, the old man walks back behind the counter, and speaks in Spanish to his son, who translates.

"My father says he hasn't seen one like this in a long time."

Another exchange in Spanish.

"It's for a safe deposit box, clearly. But old-style. Real old. Like they used in Europe, pre-war."

Grady turns the key over in his hand. Europe is not what he's been thinking.

More Spanish. Then: "You're hoping it's an antique? Trying to find out if it's worth something?"

"Is it?"

"My father says no. He says this is a repro. Just made."

And wonders what your aunt was doing with it, say Izaguirre Sr.'s eyes. And whether there is an aunt at all.

Grady has nothing to lose. He pushes. "Is anyone still using keys like this?"

Quick Spanish. The elder Izaguirre shaking his head, waving Grady away, out of the store.

"We thought maybe she had a safety deposit box somewhere that no one knew about. She was old. Maybe she told her daughter, but her daughter died."

Anyone can understand family. And anyone can understand greed. Grady lets his urgency show. He knows they'll assume he's not seeking family keepsakes. He's seeking hidden wealth.

"You are her heir?" The father speaks. His English is heavily accented but clear.

"Yes."

"No one would use a key like this today. Not in *los Estados Unidos*."

"In Europe?"

"No."

It was no coincidence that four petty criminals from the Detroit area and a blonde imposter who (Grady was sure) spent at least one June night in Ann Arbor all made the trek to Tucson at just about the same moment. They weren't coming for the golf. So if the key is the means of entry to a safety deposit box holding something worth lying, kidnapping and killing for, that box must be somewhere south of the border.

"Mexico?"

Bingo.

The old man nods. "*Si*. But not in a big city. A little one." He slips into Spanish.

The son translates. "It would have to be a small place, some bank that is local, that hasn't updated in a long time."

"Do you have a directory? Some sort of list I could look at?"

The old man laughs, but Grady can tell he's not amused. "No, no, senor."

He places the key on the counter. There is the sharp click of metal contacting glass. Then he spits brief, rapid Spanish to his son.

Grady has pushed too far.

"My father says, if you need help, try the Federales."

It's time for Grady to make a graceful exit.

But now he knows for sure.

A small bank, in a small town, somewhere in Mexico.

The next step is going to take money.

#

He hasn't been seeing much of Jill. Which is odd in a way. You'd think asking someone to kill someone else for you would guarantee a certain continuing intimacy. It's a pretty big favor. But he tells himself that the silences mean she trusts him. Or that denial isn't just a river in Egypt.

And when he calls her to say they need to meet, she suggests a parking lot behind an empty store. At night. He could almost laugh, would if everything weren't so sad. She's seen too many movies.

"Let's have coffee," he says. "Or lunch. Or a drink. We've known each other for 20 years. We don't need to hide."

They sit at a corner table in the bar in one of those upscale foothills places that calls itself a bistro so people will think it's drop-in-for-a-bite casual even though the prices are sky high. Everything is black granite and stainless steel, purple-red paint and soft-focus, faux industrial lighting. Not Grady's kind of place. Or maybe it just makes him keenly aware of his relative poverty.

What the fuck, he thinks, and orders Glenlivet, rocks. Jill asks for iced tea.

He's updated her on the key and is trying to avoid being pushed into a field trip south of the border when she changes the topic.

"I want to tell you something. I can't keep it inside anymore, and you're the only one I can tell." She looks around. To see if anyone's listening? "I shot that man, Billy Oz."

Grady nods. "Yeah. I know."

"How? Nobody else was there. And he's dead."

"The autopsy. Davis told me he'd been shot. But the body was so chewed up they didn't find the bullet. And it wasn't what killed him."

"Good."

"Good? The man kidnapped your daughter. He tried to kill all of us, left Sophie a mental case—and you're happy you didn't do him in? For fuck's sake, Jill, There couldn't be a clearer case of self-defense."

"It wasn't."

"Wasn't what?"

"Self-defense."

Bullshit, Grady thinks. "What the hell do you mean?" he says under his breath.

"I didn't shoot him to save myself."

"Shit, Jill!" His voice is a low growl. If it wasn't a public place, he'd be yelling. "You're glad he's dead. You're glad they're all dead. In fact, you've asked me..."

She cuts him off. "Sssh! That's for Sophie. It's different."

"Different *how?*" In the same sotto voce yell. What kind of weird crisis of conscience is this?

"I was lying there, propped up on the rock like you left me, trying to tell myself that it would be okay, that you'd get help and come back for me, and even if you didn't you'd save Sophie. I was thinking about my life and my marriage and my child..." She's having trouble going on.

"He just appeared. One moment it was just the trees and the birds and the goddamn sun, and the next there he was about 30 feet away.

"I screamed. I couldn't help it. And he shot me. My leg hurt like hell. I didn't know if I was bleeding out or not. But it felt like it. I thought he'd hit my femoral artery.

"He came closer. I thought he was going to shoot me again. I didn't care. I was a goner anyway.

"But then I realized what he was going for. My water. The goddamn two ounces of water you made me keep. The couple of swallows I was hanging onto, saving for when I couldn't stand it anymore.

"So I picked up the gun and I shot him. I was weak, and my aim was off. I hit him in the chest, but the bullet just caught the left side of his ribs, not a place that would kill him even though I wanted to. But he was surprised. He dropped the rifle. And I still had the gun pointed at him. He knew I'd shoot again. He grabbed his rifle and got out of there as fast as he could.

"So you see what I mean. It wasn't for my life. I understood that I was going to die."

Grady still doesn't get what the fuck she's talking about. And she's looking at him like she's baring her soul, about to present some searing revelation. He can tell it's taking all the self-control she has—and Jill has a lot—not to break down. But they're surrounded by people, and whatever this weirdness is about what she did to Billy Oz, she's still a mom on a mission, determined not to attract any attention.

Her voice is low but harsh as a rasp. "I shot him for two ounces of water. God help me, I didn't want to die thirsty."

And she's torturing herself over that, Grady thinks. Shit,

countries have gone to war for less. But telling her this won't do any good. She believes what she believes.

And she never did drink the water, something she probably doesn't remember. She passed out instead. It occurs to him not for the first time that day, or even that hour, that life is a bitch. All he can do is order her another iced tea.

36

He caved on the field trip to Mexico. Jill waved away his arguments about futility and risk. He's not convinced she even heard the words. So he gets to enjoy a nice long drive south of the border. It's Labor Day in the U.S. but just another Monday down here. Grady's worked Saturday and Sunday, then taken comp time and tacked on two vacation days. He has a whole week to play gringo detective. Lucky him.

At least he's fortunate in one regard. As he pointed out to Jill, Mexico is becoming an increasingly dangerous place. But the areas he's focused on happen to be relatively safe. His biggest problem is boredom. By 8:00 am Tuesday morning, he's driving through the outskirts of Puerta Vallerta, heading into the boonies.

He figures the right tiny town with the right bank has to be in an area that is at least reasonably accessible from a region popular with tourists—off the beaten path, but not totally off an adventurous tourist's radar. It won't be Cabo San Lucas, but it might be near Cabo. It won't be Puerto Vallarta, but it might be within 20 miles. It won't be Cancun or Cozumel or Acapulco, but it might be an easy drive, or bus ride.

He's decided to start with Puerto Vallarta. After an 18-hour drive from Nogales the day before, he settled on a mid-range hotel. That's his base, the hub for his search.

He has the list of small towns that Luis compiled—places below a certain size but big enough (maybe) to have a bank of some sort. He has maps, bottled water, granola bars, a hat to ward off the sun and some extra pesos to mollify any over-zealous authorities. No gun. It's a foreign country, with some nasty laws regarding trial and imprisonment.

He's aware of the charm in the first small town, the second, even the third and fourth.

After that, they begin to blur.

Las Palmas, Palmillas de Cacao, Santiago de Pinos, Los Reyes, las Juntas, Las Desembocada...

Plazas, fountains, cafes. Small shops, dark-eyed women with shining hair.

Pitallal, San Sebastián del Oeste, San Ario, Juanacatlan, Río de la Plata, Embocadero, Los Cabos, Mascota, Yetapa, Chimo, Cuate, Talpa de Allende ...

Cars without fenders, without tires or engines, scrawny dogs, goats tethered to posts, children picking through piles of garbage...

Aranjuez, El Tuite, Llano grande de Pala, Ipala, Piloto, Cabrel, San Rafael de los Moreno, El Mapache, santa Gertrudis, El Mapache...

At least his car doesn't make him a target—for either crime or envy. No danger of being mistaken for a rich gringo in this junk heap.

El Tequezquite, Llano Grande, La Cruz de Loret, El Tule, Ma. Pino Suárez, San Cayetano, Vicente Guerrero, La Gloria, Nuevo Nahuapa...

Banks with imposing facades, banks in trailers, banks cum post offices cum general stores.

Zacalongo, Llano Grande, Amatlan de Cañas, La Puerta del Coche, Santa Rosalía, San Marcos, Antonio Escobedo, Santiaguito, Arenal, Pie de la Cuesta, Etzatlan...

Clerks who barely glance at the key before shaking their heads, clerks who call the bank manager, who barely glances at the key before shaking his head, clerks who speak only Spanish, clerks who practice their English, clerks who only shake their heads and don't speak at all.

La Estancita, Huaxtla, La Ciénega, Jesús Maria, Lucio Blanco, Teuchitlan, El Refugio, La Quebrada, Santa Cruz de Barcenas, El Carmen, Panico, Zacalongo...

Each evening, he drags himself back to that night's hotel, takes a long shower, avails himself of the local Tequila.

Each day, he trudges in and out of banks, using his broken Spanish and the few specific phrases Luis has suggested.

Llano Grande, Amatlan de Cañas, La Puerta del Coche, Santa Rosalía, San Marcos, Antonio Escobedo, Santiaguito, Pie de la Cuesta...

By the end of the day Friday, he's convinced that if he had one more day to spend driving from bank to bank in Mexico, he probably still wouldn't find the right town—and he would definitely lose his mind.

Saturday morning, he checks out of his current hotel, and points the car north, toward the far-away border. He treats himself, stops halfway to Nogales in a town that's too big to be a target of his search, at a hotel that he could never afford without Jill's bucks.

He takes a long soak in the tiled tub. He dines on elegant, Mexico City-style food.

And the towns run through his dreams...

Etzatlan, La Estancita Zacalongo, Llano Grande, Amatlan de Cañas, La Puerta del Coche, Santa Rosalía, San Marcos, Antonio Escobedo...

Back in Tucson at last, he meets with Jill, tries to impress upon her (again) the near-impossibility of the task. Recommends (again) that they hire somebody, or more than one somebody. Mexicans, people on the spot, people who know their area...

No. She won't hear of it. This has to be kept between them. Jill insists Grady continue the hunt himself.

Luis has cousins, and Luis will know who can be trusted. But Grady hasn't told Jill about Luis, and, in fact, hasn't told Luis about Jill. And if Luis wonders why Grady cares so much about a case that the cops consider closed, he's too discreet to ask. Grady can't break the silence now.

So he tries another tack, determined to, somehow, make Jill see reason.

There are other areas that need to be searched: Guerrero, the Mexican state that contains Acapulco, Quintana Roo (with Cancun and Cozumel). As a practical matter, Grady can't drive to those regions. There are time issues, difficulties with roads, bandits, gangs...

And he can't fly.

Jill is one of the few people who know that fact. Grady quakes, he sweats, he all but holds his breath from the time an aircraft begins its roll down the runway until the wheels touch down on his return. He's apprehensive before a flight and exhausted after.

He can't fly.

"No problem," Jill says. And writes him a scrip for Xanax.

So Grady works Saturdays and Sundays and takes his days off on Mondays and Tuesdays, claiming he's needed on the weekends when security issues are more likely to arise. Each Sunday evening, he drives into Mexico, just a single guy wandering on his own, and he flies, discreetly, from there. And as he boards each flight—sometimes a reasonable-size plane, sometimes a puddle jumper, he swallows the Xanax, which allows him (mostly) to swallow his fear.

Santiaguito, Arenal, Pie de la Cuesta, Etzatlan, La Estancita, Huaxtla, La Ciénega, Jesús Maria, Lucio Blanco, Teuchitlan, El Refugio, La Quebrada...

Three "weekends" of this, and even Jill agrees it's time to come at the problem from another direction: the North.

37

He's been searching for the proverbial needle in a very large haystack. There are thousands of small towns in Mexico. And thousands of small banks in those small towns. Maybe Grady's logic made no sense; maybe Luis's search criteria missed something critical. Whatever. It was way too many long days of wild goose chase. Complete with language barrier.

But dry. Hot, sure. But not humid.

Ann Arbor, on the other hand, has him dripping. The temperature is in the 90s, and the air is too super-saturated to accept any more moisture, even his sweat. Unbelievable. It's goddamn fall, almost October. Even Tucson is cooling down by now.

By the time he finds a parking place and climbs out of the generic white sedan he's rented in Detroit as his new alter ego, Nebraska resident James R. Bailey, he's a puddle, wet and geeky, in his white short-sleeved shirt, too-wide tie complete with clip, lined bifocal glasses and wedding band. He hopes to hell the stuff he used to temporarily turn his hair reddish-brown is waterproof. Otherwise, the color will sweat its way down his forehead.

The rest of his disguise is a small wooden chest, about the size of a shoebox, maybe something you'd use to store keepsakes. A taped-on label, written in a feminine hand, says "For Winnie."

He flew into Chicago, a jumping-off place for any number of destinations. After that?

Jill's money makes obfuscation easy. Right now, the Chicago rental car is parked in a garage at a rented vacation cabin on a lake in Wisconsin. From there to Detroit, it was Greyhound all the way. A shitty way to travel, but anonymous. Cash for the ticket. No trail.

1014 Briggs is an old house carved up into student apartments. The place looks like it was built no later than the 1920s and hasn't enjoyed any maintenance since. A stairway tacked onto the outside at the right rear leads to a second floor apartment.

The main entrance front door—an old-fashioned wooden thing with a glass upper half—is ajar. The entryway holds a couple of bicycles chained to the staircase and a pair of snowshoes. Given the heat, some tenant is a roaring optimist.

1B is first floor back at the left. Before Grady can knock, a young man comes bounding down the stairs. "John's not home," he calls out, grabbing one of the bicycles and working at the combination lock.

"John?" Grady expresses surprise. "I'm looking for Winnie."

The kid is aghast. He should never play poker. The look on his face says he has no clue what to do.

"Winnie Pearson. I'm her uncle."

"Jeez," the kid says. "I hate to tell you this, man, but she died."

"Died?" Grady does his best to look shocked.

"Yeah." The kid succumbs to the drama of sharing bad news. "In there." He points at the door to 1B. "She was killed."

"When?"

"June." It seems to dawn on him that Grady is Winnie's family and might be expected to have the facts. "You're her uncle?"

Grady nods. "My wife—Winnie's aunt, she and her sister— Winnie's mother—didn't get along. Hadn't spoken for years. And when Karen—my wife—died..." Here, he lets himself become suitably choked up, gestures at the box. "There were photos and letters. Things she wanted Winnie to have."

"That's tough, man."

"Did you know my niece?"

"Nope. I'm new. Just starting grad school."

"Is there anybody in the building who lived here last year?"

"Hmm. It's only five apartments. I know John wasn't here. He's new like me. The people in 1A didn't. It's their first year out of the dorms. And upstairs... The couple in 2A, he just started med school, came from Iowa. 2B is me. But Molly... Yeah, Molly. She's got the studio, the one with the outside entrance. She's lived here a couple of years."

"Do you know if she was here in June?"

The kid shakes his head as he rolls the bike out the door. "Doubt it. Nobody's here in the summer."

Grady goes outside, walks around to the side of the building and sees that he's in luck. A tall, big-boned young woman in a t-shirt and a part of running shorts is watering a collection of plants that occupies most of the landing at the top of the stairs leading to the upstairs apartment.

The landing looks too small for two people—and hardly strong enough for one—so Grady stands at the bottom and calls up.

"Molly?"

A nod.

"Can I ask you a couple of questions?"

"About what?"

"Winnie Pearson."

"Who's asking?" Molly begins pulling wilted blossoms off a small rose bush.

"Just me. Nothing official."

"Family?"

"I'm her uncle."

Molly picks up her watering can and positions it above the rose bush, but apparently thinks better of it and walks partway down the stairs.

"Family. When you go there they have to take you in, and when you die they have to bury you—and I guess even if the police give up on finding out why you died, they need to do what they can. So how can I help you, Mr. ..."

"Jim Bailey. From Nebraska. The kid downstairs told me your name, said you lived here last year when Winnie was...alive." Grady looks up at her with what he hopes is his most bereaved face. "You're going to tell me you've already told the police everything, but I'd like to hear it anyway."

Molly descends the rest of the staircase. "Actually, I haven't said squat to the police. Except that I wasn't here. They phoned me about that."

She sits down on the steps and sets the watering can beside her. "So go ahead with the questions," she says, "But you'll be disappointed. I don't know much."

"Okay. You said you weren't here."

"Right. I'm an ichthyologist. Fish. I spend my summer at the U's biological station in Northern Michigan. If you're a grad student, you gotta do it no matter how much it fucks up your finances. So I was long gone. And, like I told the police, my place was empty. I tried to sublet, but this building is a dump, and I just have a studio. Real apartments all over town go for nothing during the summer... I didn't have any luck."

"Was anyone else here?"

"In the building? Uh uh. Only Winnie. Except for her, the place was empty. And I was the only tenant coming back this fall. Everybody else packed up their stuff in May and went home or wherever until September, or graduated, transferred, left town forever. You know."

"So you've lived here a while."

"This is my third year. I'm A.B.D."

"A.B.D.?"

"All but dissertation."

Her look at him is challenging, as if there's a right response to

266

this definition—and a wrong one. He takes a guess. "You'll get it done."

A small smile. "You're right. I will." Evidently, he has said the correct, expected thing. But she turns to go back up the stairs anyway. He stops her with a question.

"How well did you know Winnie?"

"I didn't. Some houses are friendly, have parties and so on. This one never has, don't know why. I knew who she was. And once in a while I'd see her going in or out. But I have my own entrance, so I didn't even see much of that." She's still looking at him, but her tone says the conversation is over.

He attempts to direct her attention to the small chest he's holding by awkwardly readjusting so it's resting in both hands. It works, she's looking. "For Winnie," he says.

"Oh." There's sympathy in her tone, and maybe a little curiosity.

"Keepsakes," he explains. "Photos, letters. It was supposed to be a legacy for her. But now..." He goes into his uncle routine again, complete with long-standing family feud. He thinks he does it well, with a convincing crack in his voice when he speaks of Karen's "death." But he's barely laid out the basics when Molly stands and picks up her watering can.

"I wish I could help you, but I have to be somewhere in about 10 minutes. And I don't know anything. I know she lived here for a few months. I know she died. That's it."

Grady's surprised by the succinct, almost brutal, statement, especially to a bereaved uncle. Why? The police didn't badger the woman. Barely spoke with her, she says. There's more here if he can just find a way to dig it out. But that's not happening. He watches as Molly climbs the stairs, dumps the contents of the watering can on an unsuspecting rose bush, goes into her apartment, and closes the door.

The building in which Winnie Pearson lived and died sits in the middle of its block with converted houses to each side. Across the street is another chopped-up house, next to a slightly larger brick apartment building.

Grady figures five to six apartments per house and maybe 10 in the brick building. And not a glass of ice water in sight.

He's picked a time on a Saturday morning when most student types are likely to be home because they're asleep. He knocks. And people answer the door in boxers, kimonos, hastily pulled on jeans. He gets one offer of coffee from a guy who looks desperately hung over and another to punch his lights out. And a few people just don't seem to be around. Information? Nada.

It's nearing 11:00 when he gets his first hit.

She opens the door in response to his knock and just stands there.

She's early 20s, wearing polka-dot boxers and a tank top. Her feet are bare, hair uncombed. Her eyes are barely open.

"Shit!" she says. "You're not Angela."

Grady decides there's nothing much he can say on that topic.

"She was supposed to bring coffee and bagels. I dragged myself out of bed for..."

"Jim Bailey. I'm asking about Winnie Pearson."

The girl is suddenly wide awake. "Ohmigod. She died! I mean, right across the street. And nobody knows how it happened."

"The police don't know?"

"You're not the police?"

"Private."

"Huh. Well, c'mon in. I gotta have coffee. And seems if I want it, I have to make it."

She doesn't want to see a badge? Just invites a middle-aged male stranger into her home? Unless she has a hidden, silent Rottweiler or training in some obscure martial art, this girl is fond of living dangerously. Or, more likely, is still only half-awake.

She puts a kettle on to boil. "The police haven't arrested anybody, so I figure they don't have a clue. At least, I haven't heard they've arrested anybody." She spoons coffee into a Melitta filter. "So you're investigating?"

Grady shakes his head. "Not really. I'm her uncle. Well, her aunt's husband. We didn't know about the...the...her death. One of those estranged family things. And then when my wife died..."

The girl clucks sympathetically. "That's so sad."

"So I thought at least I should know what happened. Being family and all."

They sit at a small table tucked into a window alcove that overlooks the street.

"Sugar?"

"Just black, thanks."

The girl reaches into a drawer and pulls out a pack of cigarettes. "Mind?"

Grady shakes his head, gratefully takes out one of his own and lights up.

The girl blows on her coffee to cool it, then sips. "I actually didn't live in this house last year. I lived in the building next door." A shrug. "Same difference to you, huh?"

Grady acknowledges that it is. "How well did you know Winnie?"

She shakes her head. "I didn't. And I don't know anybody who did. Except that I remember when she moved in a month or so after school started. It's the kind of thing you notice in a college town— when somebody does stuff out of sync with the academic year. But I never talked to her. Never, like, even waved."

And he was thinking his luck had turned. Well, at least he got coffee.

But then the girl says: "Maybe I shouldn't tell you this, since you're her uncle."

Grady gives her a look that says, go ahead. Please.

"I did run into her once, at Bruno's."

"Bruno's?"

"Yeah. It's a dive near campus."

"When was this?"

"I dunno. Late winter, I guess. Some snow still hanging on in shady spots, but most of it melted. I'd had the mid-term from hell and a bunch of us decided to get plastered. So we went to Bruno's."

"Did you see who she was with? Talking to?"

"Sorry, no."

Maybe he looks surprised, or disbelieving, or maybe she just feels she needs to spell it out for him. "Look, Bruno's isn't a place you go to drink a pitcher of beer with your friends and hang out. You go there to get drunk."

"I know how students are."

The girl gives him a look that says: You were young once? Yeah, right.

"Cheap booze?"

The girl nods. "I was doing tequila shooters. Barely knew my name."

38

Bruno's is a few beat-up tables, a lot of standing room and canned music Grady doesn't recognize. He figures he's just way too old.

If pressed, he's still Jim Bailey, but this time Jim is a P.I. based in Detroit. Grady's lost the glasses, kept the hair color but done his best to spike it. He's added a temporary tattoo (a snake curled around a rose)—considered tasty in some circles. At least the clothes (black t-shirt, black jeans and ankle-height boots) are reasonably comfortable.

At 8 p.m., the place is almost empty. A couple of guys sit at the bar, one at one end, one at the other. A few people who don't look old enough to be allowed to chew gum are hanging out near a ratty dartboard. Everyone's drinking; almost everyone is smoking; no one's tossing darts.

The bartender looks wrinkled enough to have been here last summer, last decade—hell, he's grizzled enough to be original equipment.

Grady sits, lights up, orders Scotch, water back. Doesn't bother with rocks, doesn't bother calling his brand. No point in this dump.

The barkeep pours. "Two bucks."

Cheap booze is right.

Grady slaps a twenty on the bar. When the bartender lays down the $18 change, Grady pushes a one at him and leaves the rest lying there.

The barkeep gives him a nod, acknowledging that Grady plans to be there a while.

The "Scotch" doesn't even smell good. Grady knocks it back, sucks at the cigarette to drown out the taste. He needs to get things moving before business picks up, and he figures that will happen within the next 30 minutes.

He taps the bar to get the guy's attention, then points at his empty glass.

"Quiet tonight," he says as the barkeep pours.

The man shrugs. "It'll get busy later. Always does."

"Saturday night, huh?"

"Saturday night."

"You get a college crowd?"

"Yeah."

"Business is good?"

A nod. "Can't complain."

"And no one would listen if you did, right?"

The barkeep acknowledges the tired attempt at a quip with a weary grimace.

"You the owner?"

"You selling insurance or glassware or something?"

"Nah."

"Then I'm the owner. Looking for action?"

"Girls? Is that what happens here?"

"Sometimes."

"I'm a little old for the ones in this place."

"You'd be surprised."

"Another time. But I could use a little information."

"You're a cop. You look it. Or like a cop who's trying to hide it."

"I'm not a cop."

Shrug. "Even if you are, fuck it. I'm not talking about hookers.

Nobody pays for it in here. They all just screw like bunnies. For fun. No money involved."

"I was born too soon."

"Tell me about it."

Grady lights another cigarette from the butt of the first and takes a deep drag, wonders how the hell anybody does a decent investigation without nicotine.

Time to get down to business. "There was a girl killed last June. Grad student named Winnie Pearson. Her folks want to know how she got to be dead. And they're willing to pay." Grady pulls out a copy of the photo that appeared in the local paper and shoves it front of the guy. Luis cleaned it up, so it looks like a formal portrait, something a bereaved family might have provided.

"Money talks, but I don't. Didn't know the chick."

"I heard she came in here. Picture doesn't do her justice. Little blonde, short thick hair, big blue eyes. All-American girl, small size."

"Good things come in small packages."

"So they say."

"But I still don't know her."

Grady unfolds a twenty, lays the bill on the bar.

"She's starting to seem a little more familiar."

Grady adds another twenty.

"Keep talking."

"Not until I get some answers."

The barkeep shrugs. "Okay, maybe I did know her. Well, didn't really know her. Just poured her drinks, watched her wiggle her way 'round the guys."

Grady lays down two more twenties. "Did the police make it here? Talk to you?"

The bartender shakes his head. His hand rests on the polished wood, inches from the dough. "I was off a few weeks. Things are slow here in the summer, so I closed the place and got the hell out of Dodge."

"What about after you got back?"

"Nope. I figured if the cops wanted to talk to me they'd show up. Never did." His fingers creep toward the money. Grady glares at the fingers, and they move away.

"So she hung out here."

"Kind of."

"Kind of" doesn't mean shit, and the guy knows it. Grady sips at his drink, enjoys the quiet.

The man has no staying power. After only 30, 40 seconds, he fills the silence. "She'd come in sometimes."

"Often."

"Yeah. Not every day, or even every week, but pretty often. But she never really hung out, not that I saw."

"What would she do?"

"Come in alone. Hook up."

Grady pretends he's never heard the term. "Hook up?"

"Find some guy to buy her drinks. Have a few. Leave with the dude."

"Always?"

"Yeah. Think so. Can't remember a time she didn't." The hand covers the bills. Grady doesn't challenge it.

"And she always came in alone."

"Yup."

"She ever leave with the same guy more than once?"

A shake of the head.

"Never?"

Another shake of the head. "Not that I remember. I did notice that she made people uncomfortable. Maybe that's one reason she stuck to picking up guys. I don't think girls wanted to hang with her."

So Winnie was a good-time girl with notches on her belt—or her headboard. In the parlance of his adolescence, a slut. Exciting word when you're sixteen. Grady didn't hold it against any girl then, and it's way too late for him to start getting picky about sexual behavior now. Still, it's interesting.

The bartender's hand scoops up the bills, slides them into a pocket.

#

Another morning in Ann Arbor, another steam bath. Grady is back on Winnie's block, back in his geeky look and sick of both James R. Bailey and knocking on doors. He's rousted all of Saturday's missing tenants and annoyed the hell out of a couple of them, but he's come up dry.

He's unlocking his rental car, wondering how to stake out Molly's place without drawing unwanted attention, when he hears a voice that saves him the trouble. It's Molly, out on her porch again. "Hey," she calls down, and the next moment she's standing in front of him.

"You're not her uncle, are you?"

Grady thinks about blustering, try to bluff it through, finally shakes his head.

"Didn't think so. But whoever you are, you do seem to be interested in what happened. And given that a woman who lived alone was killed in my building, that seems to be a good thing. Maybe you'd like to see the apartment."

Grady would.

"John's gone for a few days," Molly says, turning the key in the deadbolt of 1B. "I'm feeding his cat."

The contents don't tell Grady a thing. He doesn't even try to subtract the sports magazines and Budweiser mug and visualize an overlay of youthful femininity. He didn't know the real Winnie. He has no idea whether she liked blue, red or yellow; whether she, like Molly, had a forest of plants; whether she was a slob—one of those women who step out of a bedroom all painted and polished leaving a wreckage of discarded clothing, makeup brushes, wet towels and damp footprints behind them—or a neatnik.

But whatever else "Clare" lied about, she told the truth about the layout of 1B. He confirms that the hearth is marble with sharp edges, that there is a cupboard in the kitchen that would hold a small, fine-boned woman, that there is an archway between the two rooms and that the archway would allow a glimpse from the cupboard of the area in front of the hearth.

The kitchen window is on the same wall as the cupboard, but with no line of sight to or from the living room. The drop to the ground is doable. There's a gate in the back fence, and behind that an alley.

Grady visits the bedroom and the bathroom. Both rooms are unremarkable and clearly belong to a young adult male, careful with his books and electronics, careless about making his bed.

They're back in the living room near the hearth that somehow did Winnie in. The cat—a skinny, gray-striped creature—brushes against their legs, and Molly stoops to pick it up. "I'll bet you're surprised it's rented," Molly says, stroking the cat. "Scene of an unsolved murder. A lot of places it wouldn't be. But an affordable one-bedroom this close to campus, they could rent it with the body still in it." She sets the cat down on the floor, and it protests with a brief meow. "You like cats?" she says.

Grady shakes his head.

"Me neither."

He figures maybe they're done, but Molly isn't heading for the door. The young woman turns to face a window that opens onto the small side yard that separates this house from the one twenty feet away. Not much out there to look at, but Grady figures she isn't thinking about the view. He senses that she has something to say and is fighting some sort of internal battle with herself about saying it.

20 seconds go by, 30. Then, without making eye contact, Molly speaks. "She was a bitch."

Don't speak ill of the dead while looking someone in the eye, is her rule, he figures. He waits, knowing she's just getting started.

"I hate to say it, but she was. She had a ghastly old car, this huge wreck of a thing that was always taking up more than one space. You can see all we have is street parking. It was rude. She'd park like she didn't even see the lines. Or they didn't apply to her."

"Did you talk to her about it?"

"Nah. I didn't have a car then myself, so most of the time I didn't care. But some of the other people in the building did, and she blew them off. One time, a friend of mine who was living across the street asked her nicely to repark the thing. My friend had an old Beetle and could have squeezed it in. Winnie told her where she could shove her car.

"Once—I believe she went away for a while—she left the clunker in the same spot too long. You can't park on this side on Wednesday. It was towed away. I don't think anybody was sorry."

Now that she's begun telling her truth, she allows herself to look at Grady.

"Do you know where she went?"

A shake of the head.

"Or when?"

"I'm not sure. Must have been during some break."

"What else?"

A blank look, so Grady prompts. "Tell me about her."

"Short. Small..."

Grady just looks at her.

"Oh. You know all that."

He waits.

"What's the word for her? Perky. She was always perky, like some sort of eternal cheerleader. Always up, even a little hyper. With a frantic undertone to her energy. I didn't run into her often, but when I did—at the mailbox or coming up the walk—she was always so loud. Kind of pushy. Sometimes I wondered if she was a touch manic."

"Friends? Lovers?"

Molly shakes her head. "Not that I ever saw. She seemed kind of alone. And I lied yesterday, just a little. We did have one house-wide party last year. Everybody who lived here and everybody they invited. It was a flop, never repeated. Bad mix, I guess."

"Bad mix?"

"Some heavy drinkers. Some heavy talkers."

"Winnie?"

"She was a drinker."

"Somebody told me she slept around. A lot."

Molly shrugs. "Couldn't prove it by me. But I remember hearing something about it. And guys will fuck mud. Not that Winnie was mud. She was cute."

Grady holds the door for her. They're in the hall outside the apartment when Molly says, "I'm sorry she's dead, because I'd be sorry anybody is dead. Especially at 22 or 23 or whatever she was. But cute is as cute does. The woman in 2A, who transferred to Stanford, told me once that Winnie complained to everyone about everything. Nothing was good enough for her, Gloria said. She thought maybe Winnie was born with a silver spoon up her ass."

Molly turns the key in the deadbolt and tugs at the door, checking the lock.

"Damn, she was a bitch."

39

Grady doesn't know about woman, but he's convinced that man isn't meant to fly. Flying in general is unnatural and, by definition, terrifying. And flying in and out of Tucson, with its mountains, thermals, and seasonal thunderstorms is even worse—way too much like an out-of-control amusement park ride. When he is forced to travel by air, he never unbuckles. His heart pounds; his hands sweat. Babies, someone told him once, are born with an instinctive fear of falling. He figures some people outgrow it, others don't. And the ones that don't should probably stay on the ground. To make things even worse, there's no in-flight entertainment anymore, no food. Which would be no big deal if they'd just let a man smoke. And he took his last Xanax on the outbound leg. That bumpy flight required four tablets instead of two, leaving him without pharmacological help on the return. Hence, the tiny bottles of Scotch that litter his tray table.

Within a few hours after landing in Tucson, he's hung over, jet-lagged. The fact that he's returned empty-handed (again) is the topper. So now he knows some titillating details about Winnie Pearson's character. Big fucking deal. How it fits, if at all—and how it helps him find the woman he's seeking is, at best, a question mark.

He's feeling about as prickly as the cactus that lines the road leading into town from the airport, but he forces himself to check in with Luis anyway.

And Luis has something for him. Winnie's transcript, her graduate student record.

She did her undergrad work at Boston University, a fact gleaned from her obituary. So Luis emailed the University of Michigan Records people disguised as their counterpart at BU. Grady doesn't ask whether Luis had the proper electronic ID or something so close it was undetectable or where he got it. Given the situation, a little hacking is not exactly a major concern.

U of M Records didn't get it at first. The student was deceased. As in dead. What did BU want with her transcript? Had to do with student loans, BU replied, all I do is what they tell me. Maybe something with the insurance?, U of M opined. BU (electronically) shrugged.

U of M caved, and sent the info.

So Grady's looking at what is essentially Winnie's detailed report card. Which is lousy.

She was on the brink of being kicked out, was supposed to be making up incompletes the summer she died.

So. Sexually promiscuous, loud, rude. And a good enough student to make it into a leading graduate program, but not talented—or, more likely, dedicated enough to stay.

Interesting. If he were writing a goddamn profile of the victim. But otherwise a big fat zero.

He thanks Luis, expresses what enthusiasm he can and gets the hell home to his dog.

And after that? Time goes by. Hours of it, days of it—even weeks. Whether Grady wants it to or not.

He does what he can, traveling to Mexico as often as he can make the time. The trips are frequent enough that he feels the need for cover, so he lets it get around that he's thinking of someday retiring south of the border, where the living is easy and the booze is cheap.

He's leaning on Luis's skills more than he'd like—and counting on his discretion. But the waiting, the inaction, and those fucking futile days south of the border are making him nuts.

And he still can't get his mind around the puzzle. He keeps worrying the pieces, trying to fit them into place. But either he doesn't have enough of them, or his brain stopped being a detective at the same time that his body did. He's not getting anywhere.

Throughout that fall, there are times Grady can't numb himself enough, can't turn off his mind, tries to listen to his music, sip his Scotch, but can't hear Bird, or even Billie Holiday. Instead, he hears Winnie's voice as she holds out her arms and urges him to dance, Clare's laugh as she splashes him with sudsy water from his mother's tub, the thwack of the 2x4 as it slams into Billy Oz's head—and the rustling of the desert as Clare disappears into the brush. He sees Sophie clinging to her "cards," shuffling and laying out the pictures of the body with its throat slashed and the three rotting corpses over and over until they become so worn that before they fall apart entirely Jill brings them to him—sneaking them out while Sophie is sleeping. He takes them to Luis, who digitizes the photos and prints duplicates—which, in turn, become ragged and need to be replaced.

He seldom sees Jill. Someone has to stay with Sophie, and the only people Sophie trusts are her parents. Jill has suspended her dental practice. She's bone thin, haggard. Her eyes are sinking into her face.

An old, bad joke keeps running through his head. Something like: If you love something, let it go. If it doesn't come back to you, hunt it down and kill it. If he didn't already drink, he'd take it up.

Night after night, his car finds its way to Goodtime Charlie's. Sometimes he meets up with Andy Davis. Grady never mentions June's events. But he listens, and in among the gossip, the talk about Andy's family and the sagas of other cases past and present, Davis drops the occasional relevant nugget. Grady stores each one away, like nuts—or ammunition he can use to convince himself that what he's doing is what he has to do.

More often, he sits alone over his drink, pulling on his cigarette, feeding the juke box when he's feeling flush and enduring some other joker's bad taste in music when he isn't. After enough alcohol, he puts in the mental clutch and lets his mind roam.

He's decided long ago that whatever he does (or doesn't) believe about what "Clare" told him, there are a few apparent truths. One, she saw Winnie die. And, two, she was hiding out in Pergama.

But the appearance—the materialization—of Billy Oz, The Shrimp and Vassallo at the Nelsons' that hot June night is still a big hole.

How in hell did they get there? To what might be called the right place at just about the right time?

Maybe she left a trail from Michigan to Arizona, but he doesn't think that's the answer. The guys looking for her weren't going to be tracing charge slips or other subtle spoor. No, it has to be something simple.

There has to be a Tucson connection. It makes sense that Winnie (the real Winnie) had the safe-deposit box key before any of the other bad actors in this mess went after it. That means she was some sort of meal ticket for Billy Oz and his boys. And Tucson was a jumping off point to Mexico. So Winnie was supposed to go to Tucson, and Billy knew it.

But once Winnie was dead, why in hell would Billy look there for "Clare"?

Start at A, he tells himself. And maybe you'll get to B.

For him, "A" is the murder at the Nelsons'.

And "A" is where his brain is stuck.

Until one chilly Monday when the bar's virtually empty and the jukebox is moaning through a Johnny Cash ballad. He's started at "A" yet again. Going over what he thinks he knows.

Who knew Winnie arrived? Who saw her in Tucson? The guards on the gate in Pergama.

So. Billy and his boys come through the gate on the 4:00 to

midnight shift that Saturday night. Willis—the man on duty—lifts the traffic arm and lets them in. Grady pictures—again—the log sheet and...

He puts down his Scotch, pays his tab, gets in his car and drives up to Sungate.

Harry is surprised to see him that time of night, and if the senior guard smells the liquor on Grady's breath, he ignores it.

Grady asks for the schedule, and Harry reaches for his briefcase.

"Not the current one," Grady says. "Year-to-date."

Harry is 70-plus, doesn't know from computers. The notebooks are on a shelf in the small inner office—one per community.

Grady pulls out the records for Pergama, flips through the pages. And there it is. Saturday, June 25.

It's gratifying to see it in black and white: Willis was officially off that night. The guard who let Billy Oz and his boys through the gate at Pergama the Saturday night that someone slit Vassallo's throat was not slated to work at all.

So it wasn't some quick green slipped in his hand on the spot that induced Willis to raise the gate. Or a mistake.

He has to be the Tucson connection.

Schedule changes are supposed to be done formally through Harry. But guys have been known to just swap shifts, figuring no one will notice, or, frankly, care.

So Willis traded. Made up a plausible excuse and offered to cover the unpopular four-to-midnight Saturday shift at Pergama. And Erwin, arriving just before the witching hour, wouldn't have tripped to it. Would have just taken over.

Grady knows how Davis missed it. The lieutenant's people moved quickly through that aspect of the investigation, did it by rote. Used the shift change sign-in/sign-out sheets to identify and interview everyone who was on the gate at Pergama during the 24 hours prior to the incident. The sheets sent them straight to Willis, of course. And they asked all the right questions—except whether he was supposed to have been there.

They never checked the sheets against the schedule that lived in the old guard's briefcase up at Sungate.

Grady thanks Harry, compliments him on the job he does, leaves him puzzled but smiling.

But no matter how hard Luis works his computer, nothing ties Willis to Billy Oz or any of his boys. Finally, Grady asks him to try it the other way around. Forget Willis. Start with Billy and the others and see if he can make his way to Tucson.

It turns out to be the lowlife son of Billy's mother's younger sister.

Grady pays him a visit. First, the punk accuses Grady of killing his cousin. "Nah," Grady says. "It was the sun." Then the scum squirms and denies and offers to prove that he was in jail up in Phoenix during the time period in question. Finally, Grady gets tired of the game and offers to turn him in to the cops (for what Grady isn't sure, but he's confident there's at least one warrant out there and he knows from his years on the street just how to make his threat credible). The guy caves.

He don't know nuthin', the punk whines. Just some college girl doin' business with Billy that his cuz needed someone to keep an eye on. She was going to be, like, locked in this fancy place with one way in. One way out. So he hung out at a few bars, played some pool, asked around, put out feelers like he was looking to get a security job up in the foothills and wondering what it took, what it paid. And found a hungry guard. Simple. Didn't even cost much. Those suckers don't make shit.

The asshole is right. Willis's file was squeaky clean. He was younger and brighter than most of the guards. He had a future in the real world outside this low-wage gig. But he was only human. The lousy hours, crummy pay and lack of benefits made for a low threshold of financial pain. Maybe he had a pushy girlfriend, a hidden gambling problem, or just a yen for a newer truck. And the guards' constant exposure to the conspicuous wealth all around them tends to produce a high level of cynicism. Maybe Willis didn't see the harm

40

A couple of days later, Grady is making one of his rare efforts to straighten up his place when it finally hits him. The loose end, the unformed thought that has been nagging at him, breaks through to consciousness. The duffels. When Davis asked about "Winnie's" stuff on the morning that she disappeared from his bed, Grady said it was gone. And, as far as he knew, that was the truth. His place is small, her bags weren't visible anywhere; ergo, she took them with her.

Now it occurs to him that all he saw when he found her at his mother's was the backpack. Maybe she dragged the duffels there, somehow lugging them all those blocks (or hitching a ride, catching one of Tucson's few cabs)...

Maybe she stuck them neatly in a closet, maybe Billy Oz and his boys gathered up all her luggage and carted it off after knocking him over the head... But probably not.

And the bags certainly aren't at his mother's now. His mother can't do much herself, recruits Grady two or three times a year to help her with any major cleaning. The last time he suffered through this was just before Thanksgiving. He would have found them.

Sophie described the van, what she saw before she was blinded by the backwards ski mask. There were duffels. Clare's?

No. It doesn't make sense. When she left his bed, she was running. She was strong, but small. She needed to travel light.

So, say she couldn't take the duffels with her when she vanished from Grady's place. But she didn't want them easily found either.

That means they're here, somewhere, in his few rooms. Or on the property.

Even though it's futile bordering on obsessive, he looks under the bed, moves and tips up the couch and checks his two closets. He's about to give up when the attic pops into his head.

It's a small attic, which he knows only theoretically, having never actually laid eyes on it. He borrows a ladder and a heavy-duty flashlight from the people in the main house, climbs up, knocks his head on the ceiling light, pushes aside the lid that covers the opening, stands unsteadily on a step not authorized by OSHA and sticks his head in. He shines the beam into every corner of the dusty space. But except for a couple of old cardboard boxes that once held someone else's stereo gear, the attic is empty.

It's time to look outside.

There are new tenants in the main house, and the derelict VW bug that sat on blocks in the backyard for years is gone. If they were hidden in the junker, so are the bags.

He prevails upon his new neighbors to check their ramshackle storage shed, without luck. He borrows work gloves and inspects the collapsing barbeque pit. Nothing but ancient ashes and the beginnings of a pack rat's nest.

Then his mother has a crisis, another hospitalization. And he has a relapse himself, backsliding from reasonable quantities of civilized Scotch into oceans of cheap whiskey. Maybe it's his mother's illness, maybe it's what he finds.

He's over at her place while she's in the hospital, sees she's been letting her paperwork go, unlike her. Wanting to put things right, he's sorting through the magazines that have been piling up on the lower shelf of the table next to her big recliner. Why isn't he better at this organizing crap? He's just about to toss the whole stack in the recycling bin when a name stares up at him from a church bulletin that's months old. Clare Lynn Dorsett, graduate student at Purdue—Clare Lynn Dorsett, who has just received an award—is visiting her aunt.

Shit!

An alias of convenience. His "Clare" just lifted the name and academic career right off the fucking page. He has to give her credit for thinking on her feet.

Goddamnit! It might be smart to shrug it off, but he's thoroughly pissed. No man likes being played for a fool.

When his mother recovers a week or so later, so does he. He borrows the work gloves from the neighbors again and goes back to his search.

First, he has to clean up the mess he left: the ashes and the pack rat nest (or what is left of it after birds and other creatures have scattered the debris across the yard and the winds have carried most of it away).

He uses the borrowed shovel, dumping the detritus into a trash can he drags over from the driveway.

There's lots of miscellaneous crap mixed in with the ashes and the pack rat droppings. Not surprising. Anybody growing up in Tucson knows about pack rats. Archaeologists love their middens. Like human hoarders, the creatures collect anything and everything. Grady himself has seen pack rat nests containing playing cards, scraps of cloth, even a set of false teeth.

He's scooping up the debris, lifting the shovel, turning it over to dump the contents into the plastic bin, working like an automaton, almost without thinking, lifting, moving, dumping, over and over—when he sees it—something shiny in among the ashes and rodent droppings.

His arms are so accustomed to the routine of their motion that he almost loses the shovelful into the trash can—catches himself just in time. He lowers the shovel to the ground, bends and picks through its load.

The shiny object is a barrette, a large silver one intended for clasping long, thick hair at the back of a neck. It is anonymous, untraceable. Could have belonged to almost anyone. But the sight of it convinces him that he may be on the right track.

Pack rats chew everything, have to in order to keep their constantly growing teeth under control. He remembers a high school pal who bought his first car, parked it in front of his house and went out the next morning to find that the little shits had eaten the wiring. Even the heaviest canvas would have been no challenge to jaw power like that—no challenge at all.

So if the barrette belongs to his little imposter, if pack rats dragged it out through a hole they chewed in a canvas bag, where's the bag?

There's only one place left to look: a pile of old boards, yard waste, junk, broken bits of toys and furniture, a coffee table missing two legs, a broken bicycle. This small, unofficial, very unsanitary landfill about 10 feet wide by five feet high occupies the far corner along the back fence. The heap started as a woodpile, but the guesthouse has no fireplace, and the one in the main house has been inoperative for years. So the logs have just sat, gradually evolving into a kind of informal compost heap of small tree limbs and other yard waste scorned by the trash man. Then the last tenants of the main house used this substrate for their own private dump as they moved out. He realizes that the jumble is double the size it was last June.

He begins pulling debris off the heap, making himself work systematically and deliberately. The mound is big but loose, the stuff carelessly thrown on. It takes him only moments to open a hole several feet wide that exposes the cache of mesquite logs that serve as the foundation. He goes into his kitchen and finds the borrowed flashlight, brings it back and shines it in but sees only termite-eaten wood. He moves to the left, throwing junk aside with abandon now, getting caught on a nail and ripping a glove but quickly creating a second hole in the heap. Finally, he climbs the teetering pile and looks down in. He uses the shovel to push aside ancient oleander stalks and mesquite trimmings.

And there they are, under a small mountain of yard debris that was hastily pulled over them, settled among the rotting vegetation: "Winnie's" two duffels. Hidden in the woodpile when she left him sleeping in a cloud of tequila and sexual satisfaction and vanished with only her backpack (and the few bucks he had in his wallet, he reminds himself).

He carries the bags into the house, dumps them on his bed and rummages through them, violating all the techniques he's ever been taught. Then, after that first, cursory look done in the full heat of discovery, he unpacks them carefully, one item at a time.

Just clothes. No books, papers or trinkets. If she arrived with grooming items, she took them with her.

Not a lot of help. In fact, no help at all.

He puts the duffels back where he found them, reconstructs the pile to give the illusion of a fresh find. He goes back in the house to call Davis, is reaching for the phone...

When he gets to thinking...

He pours himself a Scotch, paces, walks back and forth across his cramped living space with Bear dogging his heels, giving what's he's seen a chance to rumble around his brain.

He visualizes the clothing spread out on the bed. Takes a mental inventory of the contents. Something is odd. The girl is so tiny she was able to pack a relatively large wardrobe in a small space. And it was summer, so most things have little bulk.

But there seem to be a few too many little black slinky numbers, a lot of strappy high heels. The clothing mix is out of sync, and not just for the grad student she claimed to be. He knows she isn't Clare Lynn Dorsett. And he has no idea whether she is a grad student at all, whether she has ever even seen the inside of a college classroom. But this isn't the wardrobe of a business person or a nurse... What is she? A hostess in some fancy restaurant? A high-class hooker?

The abandoned clothing carries a hint at truth. And where there is one intimation of truth, there are perhaps others.

He waits until dark, retrieves the bags again, does a more thorough search.

He finds the snapshot underneath the cardboard stiffening in the bottom of one of the duffels. There is a slit in the lining, a deliberate cut, close enough to a seam to be all but invisible.

So the photograph was hidden by someone who wanted to make sure it stayed that way. Which makes it a secret. And, somehow, important.

But the content is all but useless. The picture is dark. It's so blurry the images seem smeared.

He calls Andy Davis, and turns the duffels over to the cops.

But he keeps the photo.

It's nothing but some abstract shapes at first. There do seem to be two people, though. Maybe one face, a body and the corner of another. Angles, jutting limbs, roundness. Pale flesh, but no clothing.

And one person seems to be female. And that person has short blonde hair.

Computers can do a lot these days, Luis tells him as they peer together at the muddled image on the screen. Something about software working with algorithms. Patience, man, he says, patience.

The Tuesday before Christmas, the mercury drops, and The Weather Channel predicts a hard frost all the way down to the valley floor before morning. Natives chuckle at the shivering busloads of tourists who think Arizona never gets cold. Grady stops by a Christmas tree lot on the way back from making the rounds of his communities, picks out a small spruce and carts it over to his mother's. They sit together over hot chocolate while she reminisces about Christmases past and he does his best to ignore Christmas present. Finally, he makes his way to the garage and shuttles in the boxes that he brings out every December and re-stows every January. Virginia digs out the hand knitted stockings—one with his name, one with Frannie's, one with Gina's, and he hangs them along the mantel for her as he has ever since his father's death. Then he has to leave.

He simply can't take the weight of the years any more that evening, although he doesn't tell his mother that. He makes an excuse about what a busy day he's had and how early he has to get up in the morning. He'll come back tomorrow and do the lights. Keep her company while she hangs the icicles, the ancient ornaments and hand painted globes, settles the faux gingerbread village on its sparkly white cloth.

He goes home to a can of chili, the comforting presence of Bear and *Miracle on 34th Street* on TV. After a while, he turns off the tube and puts on Thelonius, sips his whiskey (only an inch over ice) to the odd evocations of Monk's long, flat fingers that turn each piano key into its own clear statement that isn't a question but demands an answer. About midnight, he slips on a warm jacket and, as he's been doing every few weeks, goes to see Luis.

Nothing ever changes with Luis except the equipment. Every time Grady sees the place, the configuration of monitors and blinking lights is slightly different, the cables more tangled, or less. Lately, there's been a move toward wireless.

Luis reassures him—again. He's making progress, although it's slow. "Don't rush it, man," he says. "We'll get there. Give it time."

So Grady does. It isn't easy, but he gives it time.

And whenever he can find two days in a row, he's in Mexico.

The months crawl by.

Isla Mujeres, Playa Azul, Vicario, El Tucan, Joaquín cetina Gasca, Astillero, Punta Caracol, Puerto Morelos, Tres Marias...

Chiquila, Solferino, San Angel, San Hipólito, Santa Rosa Concepción, Kantunilkin, Popolmah, El Cedral, Vicente Guerrero, Valladolid Nuevo...

San Silvento, Yalchen, Tepic, Tihosuco, X- Cabil, X- Querol Xculumpich, San Ramón, Sacalaca, Huay Max, Trapich, Saban, Santa Rosa II...

January, February, March, April, May...

He's about to break faith with Jill, to hire someone in Mexico without telling her, when —at last—Luis calls.

They've caught a break.

#

Luis insists he pour himself a cup of coffee first, get comfortable. Grady's antsy, pacing, couldn't possibly achieve any state approaching comfortable, but Luis seems to need the ritual. So Grady sips at a mug of hot black stuff and pretends to be calm. It's a ceremony of sorts, an unveiling. At last, he stands behind the wheelchair as Luis plays the keys.

The screensaver vanishes. In its place, a driver's license, complete with photo.

"Just one catch, man," Luis says. "I know who she is—legally. And this is it. But I can't pivot off this data to anything else."

"Nothing?"

"Nada. I keep digging, but it's not there."

"How far back have you gone?"

"So far? Almost ten years."

41

Lonesome Lake.

Seems an apt name for a part of the country that has never heard of spring.

Even though it's nearly Memorial Day, Grady can see his breath.

Snow still sits in shady spots, under trees, on the north side of hills. And Lonesome Lake is apparently just the name of the area; where he is there's no sign of water.

He parks the rental car on the narrow shoulder between the dirt road and the ditch and stands looking down the long driveway—a quarter-mile of icy mud.

The sky is gray, a featureless bowl in a state famed for its dramatic "big skies." Grady can't tell if the slabs of clouds hold rain or snow, and he's so cold he doesn't care.

The house, a narrow two-story, its once-white paint now faded and peeling, stands among empty fields. In front of the house, a single tree stretches its bare branches. There is no other landscaping.

Grady stubs out his cigarette and starts the trudge up the driveway. The mud sucks at his shoes, and he's glad he decided not to chance it with the car.

What if she's here?

Follow the plan.

What if she's not alone?

Shit, Grady, you're chewing yourself up over something that's not going to happen. If he were the girl and he had any other fucking place in the world to go, he'd be there, not here. She's young, pretty and resourceful. The nearest town is two deserted stores and a bar. Not even a stoplight. He'd bet that this farm saw the back of her years ago.

The front door isn't graced by a porch, just a utilitarian concrete stoop.

The windows are curtained, and the curtains are open, but the panes are dark and blank. No sign of life.

He decides to try the back.

The rear of the house faces two ramshackle outbuildings, their roofs caved in. A rusted cultivator sits in the mud. Three scrawny chickens peck at the earth.

The kitchen door is no more welcoming than the front, but Grady sees faint light through a nearby window. He opens his briefcase and pulls out a leather folio.

There is no doorbell. He knocks. Waits. Knocks again, more insistently.

A woman opens the door.

She's at least late-50s, maybe 60s or even 70s, as gray and spare as the house and the sky, with a stern face that shows no fear, no welcome, no curiosity. She doesn't greet him, doesn't speak at all, simply stands there.

As Grady opens his mouth to talk, it occurs to him that the odds of getting much out of this tough old bird aren't good. All he'll likely accomplish with this trip is something of questionable value: seeing for himself.

He has several prepared covers to choose from. He goes with the census bureau. His gut says that this hard-bitten woman won't respond to anything less than government authority, and maybe not even to that.

296

"Hello," he says, whipping out his "official" identification. "I'm Wilson Moreland with the U.S. Census Bureau. I'm conducting in-depth interviews with randomly selected citizens. Are you Ruth Mary Lindstrom?"

"Yes." The word is clipped, the tone flat.

"And you reside here, on Lonesome Lake Road?"

A nod.

His basic questions—name, confirmation of address, including county, and phone number are designed to disarm her. She answers in monosyllables or clipped phrases. She doesn't expand on any of her answers.

He digresses for a moment, mentions the weather, refers to unseasonable cold. Lets himself shiver. But try as he might, he can't talk his way into the house. He's freezing, his nose dripping, his toes numb. She must see that he's miserable. He'd understand if he thought she was the least bit afraid of the stranger who appeared from nowhere. But apparently she is simply uncaring.

She's clearly wary by nature, and if he doesn't get on with his "interview," that ingrained distrust could become a real problem. So, next question, and this time a meaningful one: "How many people live here?"

She asks to see his ID again. Examines it carefully. Grady blesses Luis for his peculiar skills.

She answers. Only herself.

He moves on to questions about number of bathrooms, ethnicity, everything he and Luis could glean from census questionnaires or reasonably come up with themselves. He plays clerk, checking boxes, taking notes.

Then he returns to the number of occupants.

"You said you live here alone?"

"Yes."

"Way out here?"

"Yes."

"Have you always lived alone?"

She shakes her head. No.

"I ask because we need to cover a period of time. We use this data to compile statistics about changes over the last decade."

She doesn't acknowledge his statement.

"Did you live alone ten years ago?"

A nod.

Can he go back farther? Is she lying? Would she lie to the government? He can't believe she'd care enough about the government to bother making up a story. Try it another way.

"We also need data on family size, to calculate trends. Do you have children?"

"No."

"Sisters or brothers?"

"Dead."

"Nephews? Nieces?"

"Niece."

"And her name?"

Suddenly she's suspicious. "You're the government. You have it. Shouldn't need to ask me."

He pretends to check his papers. "Katherine."

She gives him a sharp look.

He drives it home. "With a 'K'."

She grants him a nod. She's allowing him, grudgingly, to continue.

"Her occupation?"

"She's a whore."

"What?"

"A whore."

Grady stares at her.

"Aren't you going to write that down? Occupation: whore. Didn't matter that I raised her right. Never asked for her, never wanted her, but I did my duty. Fed her, put clothes on her back, saw she did her studies, read her bible. Too late. She turned out just like her mother." She makes a noise that seems almost involuntary, a sound of disgust.

Now that she's started talking, she doesn't stop. The torrent spews from her. "I did my duty, tried to drive it out of her. Spared not the rod, but Satan spoiled the child. Filthy girl. Filthy."

Grady can almost see her calling down damnation there in the icy fields, over the years, hurling hard words at a young girl who has had no choice. Using the belt.

"I raised her right, but she laughed at me, she lied to me, she deceived me." Ruth Mary Lindstrom shakes her head in tight-lipped righteousness. "She took her sinful body to town."

Grady thinks he sees a way to get what he needs.

"She dishonored her name." He says it as a fact.

The woman snorts. "She dishonored *my* name."

"Did she by any chance change it?"

"Change what?" It's almost as if Grady has shaken her, shocked her out of a fit.

"Did she change her name?"

A nod.

"And what is her name?"

"Now?"

Yes, now. Please.

She speaks. Grady covers his excitement. At last, information he can use.

"It makes no mind. Just another lie. She can't hide. God knows, He sees. The devil will claim his own. Hell's torments await..." Suddenly, the torrent stops.

"You're not writing."

Grady positions his pen, begins to move it across the paper.

Too late.

She slams the door in his face.

III

42

Grady settles back in the cab and watches the buildings go by. It's hard to believe he's in a foreign country. When you drive down to Mexico, the language on billboards and buildings begins to change before you reach the border, and once you cross the line all the shifting pieces come together in an entirely alien world. Here, even though he went through customs at the airport, even though all the signs are in French as well as English, the overwhelming impression is one of familiarity. The freeway ramps and skyscrapers of Toronto look pretty much like those of Phoenix.

The sun is weak in comparison to Arizona and the temperature about 30 degrees cooler—low-70s, Grady guesses.

He has the driver drop him at the Four Seasons, slings his carryon over his shoulder, enters through the front doors, walks through the lobby and leaves through a side exit.

For one thing, he's not staying at this ritzy hotel. For another, before he finds some fleabag and pays cash for a bed for the night, he has shopping to do.

#

Bébé Blues is a cellar club in the great tradition of cellar clubs.

The neon over the blue-enameled door hints at a jazz lover's late night paradise. Framed posters tout the featured artists. He focuses on the headliner. "Exclusive Engagement!" "The Sultry Stylings..."

Her hair is sleek, deep brown, nearly shoulder length. Her eyes are shiny pieces of coal. Her skin is pale, her nose tiny and upturned, her smile coolly provocative.

He stands there for a few moments, just looking. Then he makes his way down the stairs.

The club is pleasantly retro, dark, with used brick walls and a mirrored bar down the length of the room. Not smoky. Apparently, nothing in Toronto is anymore. Instead, there's a door to an outside patio. The piano is in the center, surrounded by a few stools. Small round tables pack the rest of the space. The place is about half full, but it's early for a Saturday night—only 9:00 p.m.

The tune is "Body and Soul." She's singing to her own accompaniment, and her voice is deeper than he expected, a smooth alto with just a touch of breathiness, a feathering that relieves its perfection and makes it distinctive. She plays without sheet music, without charts of any kind. He watches, and listens, from the doorway as she expertly modulates from key to key, tossing off a nice, tinkly little riff on the uppermost reaches of the keyboard.

He picks a spot where he can see well enough but is himself in shadow, orders a Scotch rocks.

At the piano, she segues into "Stardust."

The drink arrives, and he sits there sipping it while watching her, listening to her music. Then he wanders over, takes a stool at the piano. She looks up, but her expression doesn't change. A slight widening of her eyes is the only sign of surprise.

"Do you take requests?"

She smiles as if greatly amused to see him.

"Sure."

She's waiting, winding up the tune. And after all the thinking, the planning, the rehearsing, Grady's mind goes blank.

She doesn't allow any dead air. "How about this?" She doodles the first few notes of "Moonlight in Vermont." Into the mike, she says: "Here's something for an old friend."

She sings it dreamily, very '40s late-night supper club, with just the right hint of melancholy, then follows the chorus with a deconstructed improv on the keyboard. "You look different," she says sotto voce, her fingers still stroking the keys. He supposes she's referring to his dark hair, the gray hidden, and the tortoise-shell glasses. His Toronto persona.

"You too."

She shrugs. "I like the hair. The glasses, I dunno."

She picks up the melody again, after the bridge, crooning the words into the microphone. The last chord dies away. She's just gone through one-third of Grady's entire repertoire. He doesn't think he can bear it if she moves on to "Bill Bailey" or "Kansas City Stomp." So he makes a suggestion. "How about some Monk?"

She plays the first bars of "Round Midnight." "This crowd is pretty mainstream," she apologizes. "Nice tune, though." And keeps going, transforming Thelonius's most accessible piece into something even less avant-garde, almost pop. "What'd you think of the arrangement?" she asks as she fiddles with a long, drawn-out coda.

Grady considers. He's noticed an unnecessary arpeggio, a few too many broken chords. "Not bad. A little flashy. I'm a purist."

"You're a snob."

"And you're Morgan York."

"Ummm. Well, part of it's a stage name."

"From your ex-boyfriend."

No response.

"The saxophone player. And the rest you just chose."

She nods. The notes travel up, down and around the melody, occasionally land there as a brief reminder, move off again. A couple in late middle age, verging on their golden years, takes two of the remaining three stools at the piano. Morgan smiles a hello. "Hey, sweetheart," says the man, "can you play 'Misty' for me?" He pats his companion's hand, grins at his own feeble joke.

Morgan shifts into the tune without interruption, segueing neatly from classic jazz to mushy standard. Her voice purrs. Her phrasing of the lyrics is unusually subtle for someone performing in what is essentially a piano bar, even as the headliner. She has it all, Grady thinks, all the talent he ever longed for. And it wasn't enough for her.

She looks up as she reaches the bridge winds up the tune and then moves into a jazz improvisation on "Ruby" without vocal, takes a swallow of water from a highball glass. "I suppose you'll still be here when I get off?"

Grady takes it as a statement, not a question. He signals for another drink.

He keeps an eye out during her breaks, as she circulates among the patrons, patting a shoulder here, sitting down for a brief chat there, sipping a mineral water at the bar. At one point he goes so far as to hang out near the ladies' room. "Go in and take a look," she says before she enters. "There's no window. It's a total dead end."

It's nearly 2:30 a.m. when she gets her things from behind the bar and walks to his table, stands over him. "Hungry?" she asks.

They go to a late night hole-in-the-wall down the street. "Last call in Toronto is 2:00 a.m.," she says. "But if you really need a drink, I can probably fix it." Grady declines. He wants his head clear—or at least not any fuzzier than it already is.

"Okay," she says after they order, "how'd you find me?"

Grady pulls out his cigarettes, looks around. No ashtrays. "You can't smoke in restaurants here," she says, "not even in bars." He forgot for a moment that he's a modern leper. Must be the jet lag. He thinks about popping a piece of the nicotine gum he bought for the plane but decides to tough it out.

"It wasn't easy," he says. "But you finally renewed your driver's license. Katherine."

He watches for a wince, but there isn't one. She gives a rueful little chuckle. "Actually, I lost it and had to go in and get a replacement. I don't drive much, but I need it for ID."

"I have a friend," he says. "Face recognition software has gotten pretty good. We used your friend Winnie's photo as a basis. Tweaked it. Did a pretty accurate job."

"Yeah, well. You did see me up close and personal."

"Then we started looking for a match. We searched the databases of all the states that keep digitized photos on file. It wasn't as simple as it sounds. Access is easy. But even though everyone's switching to digital photos, a lot of the work isn't done. And some states have issued driver's licenses good for ten years, or even more. Until those people renew and have their picture taken again, their faces are not in the computers. States could scan them in, but some still haven't because of the cost."

Their order arrives. Grady's is coffee black. His stomach's been telling him it can't handle food right now. Morgan—he still isn't used to that, wants to call her Winnie or Clare, anything but her real name—is eating chicken noodle soup with a side of fries.

"Now what?" she says as she finishes.

"We talk."

Her hotel is only a few blocks away. He lights up as soon as they leave the restaurant, and they walk slowly. Even though it's late June, there's a chill in the air, and Grady's grateful for his leather jacket. "Go on," she urges. "After you found my license. That's under..."

"Your real name. And you use a relative's address."

"My aunt's. I really am an orphan." She did have it shitty, Grady knows. She only had her mom, the old biddy's much younger sister. Things weren't easy. Dad was unidentified, never in the picture. But her mother had pulled it together after a rebellious, hell-raising adolescence and got and kept a housekeeping/cooking gig on a ranch. It was a pretty idyllic life for a kid, growing up on a spread in Montana, complete with livestock. Then her mom died, taken out by a resurgent drug habit everyone thought she'd kicked, and ten-year-old Katherine was shipped to her only living relative, that ranting, fire-and-brimstone aunt.

He takes a deep drag, blows the smoke out slowly. "You have a very nice Web site."

"But it uses the stage name..."

"York."

"Where did you... My aunt would never tell you. She hates me, but she hates nosy strangers even more."

Grady shrugs. Let her wonder. "People know you. Musicians. Booking agents. You're a talent. Dependable. Although you sell yourself short musically. You make all kinds of compromises you shouldn't."

"That's what they say?"

"That's what they say."

They stop for a moment under a streetlamp. Grady stubs out one cigarette, lights another—making up for five hours of airplane and a night of deprivation in the bar and diner.

"About the music," she says. "I like to eat. And let's face it, there are the big names and there are the rest of us. Jazz is not a growth industry these days. I'm a throwback, born too late. But it's what I know how to do. So I'm a journeyman musician, plain and simple."

"And you're 33."

She stops. He lights another cigarette directly from the burning butt of the last. "Give me one of those things," she demands, sounding stressed for the first time.

"You don't smoke."

She laughs. "This is a special occasion." He hands her the freshly lit Marlboro, shakes out another for himself. She takes it and inhales deeply. "Yeah, I'm 33. So sue me. It's a good age. Still two years younger than Mozart when he died. Same age as Jesus when the Romans got him." The gray smoke billows from her lungs and floats up toward the streetlight.

Her hotel is low-end, but the room has charm: a seating area with a small sofa, coffee table and side chair, a double bed with plaid coverlet, a rag rug, prints of old Toronto on the walls. There's a small refrigerator, though no mini-bar.

"I travel cheap," she says. "I have to."

"This isn't bad," he says. "I've stayed in worse."

She grimaces. "So have I. Actually, I'm looking for an efficiency. Seems I may have this gig all summer. Three months of security. Imagine. I'm not sure my psyche can handle it. I've been on the road way too long. If I wake up in the same place two weekends in a row, my body goes into shock."

She pulls a bottle of gin out of a bureau drawer, reaches in again and holds up a plastic jewel case with her picture on the cover. "Would you like to buy a CD?" Grady shakes his head. "Oh, that's right," she says. "You're one of those guys. Still with the turntable. You should give yourself a Christmas present one of these years. Me, I'm moving on to an iPod as soon as I have the dough." She tosses him the CD. "Here, take it anyway." Grady sticks it in the pocket of his jacket.

She lifts two glasses off the top of the bureau, pours a couple of fingers of liquor into each, reaches into the tiny refrigerator, takes out a jar of olives and plops three into each drink. "If you want ice, it's down the hall."

Grady shakes his head. He wonders where all the money is. She doesn't seem like a big spender, or someone who'd blow it at a blackjack table. and she certainly isn't lavishing it on her only relative—that nasty aunt.

Luis doesn't like to reach into the financial world. Those people, he made clear to Grady, have good security and no sense of humor about hacking. No sense of humor at all. But because it was Grady, he pushed the limits. And didn't find any brokerage accounts, or a trace of more than a few hundred in any bank.

Is it gone? Hidden away in overseas accounts? Is she that sharp? Or that paranoid? Has all this been her perverse form of retirement planning? He supposes that picturing yourself going from town to town playing piano bar as you hit your '60s or '70s might not look like all that much fun. Not to mention that most of your audience—who are a good thirty years older than you—will be dead.

No matter. He's not here about the money.

She settles into the corner of the sofa. Grady sits in the chair, at right angles to her. "So," she says, "I suppose I have to tell you all about it?"

Grady nods.

"Hmmm. Well... For that, I need another olive." She drops one into her glass, pours in a touch of the juice and sits back down on the sofa. "I've always enjoyed a dirty martini."

43

"Where do I start?"

"You pick. But I've always favored the beginning"

She gives him a look as if his sarcasm is affecting her. Which he thoroughly doubts.

"I'd been playing at a resort on Mackinac Island..." She holds up her right hand, palm out and touches her middle finger. "Here. At the top of the lower peninsula." The state of Michigan becomes a hand again. "And I had a gig coming up in Atlanta."

She picks up her glass, takes another sip of gin. "I'd given up on my old BMW. It broke down one too many times, and I didn't want to get stranded on the way south.

"So I was taking the bus. Which went through Ann Arbor. I wanted to break up the trip by staying over a night. And I was hoping to do it for free.

"The summer before, I'd played in a bar in Traverse City, up in Northwest Michigan, right on the lake. Winnie's mother was spending a few months at a cottage, and Winnie came to stay with her. She'd come into the bar sometimes—I think she was bored out of her mind—and we'd chat a little, though she was mostly interested in picking up guys. At one point, she gave me her phone number in

Ann Arbor."

Well, nice fiction... Sounds like she may be going for the innocent bystander approach—again. Does she really expect him to swallow this?

"So I called her. I remember I was standing at a pay phone on a dock not too far from where I worked. It was about seven o'clock. I needed to walk to the crummy b'n'b where I was staying and get ready for my show. I was feeling crappy, like life was passing me by. It was my thirty-second birthday. I think that's why I reacted when you mentioned my age. I'd celebrated it eating overcooked lake trout with a woman who had a gig at another resort. She was forty-five and dragging. I could see gray roots when she'd brush her hair back with her hand. She used to be a really fine singer. Now she was hoarse from all the second-hand smoke, not to mention her own cigarettes. She kept joking about Prozac. I paid for my own dinner and bought her a drink. We toasted."

Grady buys this part. Life on the road is glamorous only in the movies.

Morgan picks one of the olives out of her drink, regards it seriously and takes a bite, a careful half. "I was on a pay phone because my cell was disconnected. Money was even tighter than usual. I'd poured what I had into that piece of shit car."

She shakes her head, apparently remembering the offending BMW. "Where was I?"

"You're on a dock near Lake Michigan, bummed out of your mind, calling someone you barely know."

"Oh. Right." She drops the remaining half of the olive back in her drink, takes a sip.

"Winnie answered. I told her I had a gig south of her..." Morgan takes a deep breath, lets it out slowly. "I don't think I mentioned Atlanta. Just my normal caution, I guess, as a little girl alone in a big world. Or maybe gut instinct. Anyway, she insisted, just as I'd hoped, that I stop in Ann Arbor." Morgan shakes her head ruefully. "'You have to spend the night with me,' she said. 'We'll have a blast.'"

Grady's glass is nearly empty. Morgan points to the bottle of gin in a "help yourself" gesture. But martinis aren't Grady's drink. The hangovers are nasty. He shakes his head, goes into the bathroom and turns on the water, letting it run to get really cold. He fills his glass from the faucet, returns to the room, sits back down in his chair and lights another cigarette. "Keep talking," he orders.

"It was late when my bus got in. A Friday night."

"June 17."

"Right. I'd dragged all my stuff along, no real choice, so I strapped the duffels on a cart I always use and went to call Winnie. But the station there is tiny. There were only two public phones. One was out of order—the receiver was actually gone—and some jerk was arguing with his girlfriend on the other. Finally, I gave up and started walking. I knew it couldn't be all that far. Turns out Ann Arbor is full of hills, though. Not flat like the other parts of Michigan I'd seen. So part way to her place I gave up and found a pay phone."

"Still no cell?"

"Still no money."

Morgan is on a roll, and he lets her go on. "She was waiting for my call. 'Don't move,' she said. 'I'll be right there.' Ten minutes later, she pulled up. She had a big old car—you saw it. Maybe she thought it was cool. Maybe her parents had tightened up on the allowance. I dunno. We threw all my stuff in the trunk. By this time, it's after 11:00, and Winnie announces we are going out. 'We need to party!' she says.

"God! All I wanted to do was sleep. I spend enough time in bars. But what choice did I have?

"First she was hungry, though. We went to some crummy Greek restaurant. Not a college hangout. Way off campus, in fact. Apparently, Winnie liked their prices on ouzo.

"But even though she said she was hungry and we both ordered the gyros platter, I was the only one who ate. She picked at her food, but mostly she drank. And the more she drank, the more she talked.

"She was sick of graduate school, she said. Sick of silly

undergrads, sick of tweedy professors with scraggly beards and their hands always on her ass, sick of academic politics. The whole thing was beyond boring."

Morgan stops, sips at her drink.

"So she was dropping out," Grady finally prompts, recalling that whether or not Winnie was fed up with graduate school, it was just about fed up with her.

Morgan's eyes betray surprise at his knowledge, but she nods. "She was trying to. It was a waste of time, she said. And it was especially a waste of time when there were things to do that weren't boring."

Morgan takes an audible breath, looks away. "The thing that makes a martini is the olives. At least I've always thought so." Grady knows she isn't thinking about olives at all. They are about to come to some hard truth.

He sees her eyes refocus. She takes another sip of her drink, goes on. "Winnie started talking about spring break. She'd spent two weeks in Mexico with her father and his latest girlfriend, in a quaint little village way down on the Gulf coast.

"Where?"

He's broken the flow of her tale, and Morgan seems startled by the question. "Umm. I don't know... Somewhere near Veracruz..."

Grady tells himself it isn't the time to push, but he has all he can do to keep his mouth shut, to give her space to talk.

But Morgan has already returned to her story. "Anyway, she'd met this guy. Miguel. Gorgeous. Like a Goya painting, she said. The darkest hair, finest profile and smoothest skin you ever saw. He was from an old aristocratic family, one that opposed the current government. He told her stories of corruption, details about the manipulation of the judicial system. Appalling stuff. The worst thing was, the government had recently found ways to confiscate most of his family's assets. At this point, they were reduced to a crumbling hacienda, he told her, run by a few faithful family retainers. Real Gabriel Garcia Marquez material."

More like *Gone with the Wind*, Grady thinks but doesn't say. He lets her continue.

"There was wining. Well, drinking margaritas. There was dining. There was lovemaking." There's an edge in Morgan's voice. "You get the picture."

He does. He takes another swallow of the watered gin, puffs on his Marlboro. There was Winnie, cute, sexy—but about as popular as herpes, and this Latin lover actually wants to do more than fuck her. She's having a romance.

"I wish smoking was good for you," Morgan finally says. She raises a hand in warning. "Don't offer me another one." She plucks the remaining olive from her glass and takes one tiny bite, a second, a third. When the olive is gone, she continues.

"One night Miguel broke down—actually cried—and confessed that he was in terrible trouble. The family was basically under house arrest. They still had valuable paintings, sculptures, relics. But they were starved for cash. They needed to be able to sell their remaining assets—and eventually leave the country. It was a catch 22. Without money to create 'goodwill' with officials, they couldn't raise money, so without money they couldn't get money..."

She looks at Grady, apparently expecting a response.

"Winnie was sympathetic," he prompts.

Morgan nods. "She was all over it, holding him as he cried, frantic to make it better. How could she help? There had to be something she could do."

"And there was."

"Yes. He had an idea. The family possessed a very fine piece. It was small: a tiny statuette. Easily portable. Worth a lot of money. It could easily be sold for $500,000 American, maybe a lot more. But it was considered an antiquity. And the house was guarded by Federales. Everybody was searched entering and leaving. It was a form of harassment, he said. Very unpleasant. So he had a double problem. First, he had to get the statuette out of the house. Then he had to get it out of the country."

"Let me guess. He needed seed money."

Morgan gives him look that says: How did you know? "Yes. If he had $10,000, he could bribe an official to get the statuette off the estate. Winnie and he could store it in a safe deposit box. They'd wait a few days to make sure no one had caught on. Then she'd retrieve the piece, and he'd help her sneak it across the border. There were dealers in New York who'd be happy to take it, no questions asked. His family would use the proceeds to bribe higher levels of the bureaucracy. Then they'd be able to get the rest of their valuables out of Mexico."

"Sounds like a happy ending."

Morgan shrugs. "I guess."

He sums up for her. "So. Problems solved, cash in hand, Miguel and Winnie would start a new life. Together."

Morgan nods. "That was the idea."

Then she's quiet again. Grady is patient. He's starting to have a pretty good idea of why Morgan is living as cheaply as she is. No matter what path this part of her story takes from this point, it's going to end in the same place. He knows what happened to the money.

"Winnie did her homework," Morgan finally says. "She was in love, but, as she put it to me, her brain wasn't totally disconnected. Miguel gave her a set of photographs. They showed the object from different angles, including marks that supposedly proved its authenticity.

"She took the pictures to an appraiser in Veracruz. He confirmed that the statuette was rare, and almost priceless. But he told her that if anyone took it out of the country, they'd be breaking the law. And he charged her an arm and a leg for his 'discretion.'

"So Winnie did it. She gave Miguel half: a down payment for the official. Balance upon delivery."

"Where'd she get the cash?" Grady's research on Winnie had turned up some family money, a trust fund that she would have come into at twenty-five. But Mom and Dad had kept her broke and dependent in the meantime. Lots of parents didn't trust their children with money. And others just didn't seem to like their own blood. Grady has no idea what motive was operative here, and isn't sure it matters.

"She had some traveler's checks. She begged some bucks for shopping. She 'borrowed' her father's credit card and took an advance on it. She knew he'd be pissed but wouldn't do anything.

"The next afternoon, she met Miguel in a small cafe. He brought the statuette. She examined it. It was the one in the photographs. The real thing.

"They went to the bank together. He watched from outside. She made the arrangements for the safe deposit box—she'd worried it might be a hassle, was pleased that it wasn't much trouble at all. She tucked away the object, met him across the street and gave him the key for safekeeping."

"That way, each would need the other to retrieve the item," Grady says. "His key, her ID and signature."

"Right."

"But that's not what happened, is it?"

Morgan shakes her head. "No. The next morning, she went to the bank as soon as it opened. She was in tears. She'd lost the key to her new box. She had the papers, the proper ID. The bank charged her a small fee."

"They drilled the lock."

"Yup. The guy who did it even felt sorry for her."

"So she's got the statuette."

"Uh huh."

"And?"

"She stowed it in another bank across town, met Miguel for lunch and kissed him good-bye. She even managed to cry."

"And she left the statuette behind in that second bank."

Morgan nods.

"Why didn't she just take it with her?"

Morgan shrugs. "I can only tell you what she told me. She was flying, she was with her father, customs is always trickier than when you walk across. And I got the feeling that way down deep she wasn't so sure about Miguel's intentions. If she had tried to smuggle the item out on the itinerary she'd shown Miguel, who knew what might have happened?"

Grady can imagine Winnie's thinking. Maybe Miguel loved her, maybe not. She was cheating him, after all. Or at least giving herself the option. Why wouldn't he do the same? People project their own motives onto others, and Winnie's motives were shit.

Grady didn't admire the assorted lowlifes, punks and creeps he'd bumped heads with over the years. But he understood that they were have-nots who wanted to be haves and didn't possess the intelligence, character or drive to do it the right way. So they took shortcuts. And usually stumbled on their own stupidity. But Winnie had—or would have had—a lot of money. It was only two years away.

Grady supposes it's like the old story of the scorpion and the frog. The scorpion needs a ride across the river. The frog declines. "You'll sting me!" "Look," the scorpion points out, "I'm not stupid. If I sting you, we both drown." So the frog lets the scorpion climb onto his back, and they start across the river. Halfway across, the frog feels the sting. "Why did you do that?" he manages to ask as the poison spreads through his body. "I couldn't help it," the scorpion answers as he sinks into the water. "It's just my nature."

Greed. Amorality. From what Grady's learned, it was just Winnie's nature.

Apparently, Morgan is having similar thoughts. She looks down at the glass in her hands. "Maybe some people don't know how to love," she says, her voice quiet.

Some truth at last. But Morgan's gaze is drifting. Grady brings her back. "Last June. Ann Arbor."

Morgan gets up, walks across the room, dumps another couple of olives into the dregs of her drink. After a moment, she goes on.

"Anyway, that night in Ann Arbor Winnie said she thought that not doing the whole thing at once—not taking the statuette with her—had been a mistake. She was ashamed of herself. She didn't usually chicken out that way.

"But that was then, this was now, she said. It was time to go to Mexico and get it. She was pretty sloshed by then. I got her to eat a few more bites of her gyros. And I dumped a couple of ice cubes from my Diet Coke into her glass to dilute the ouzo.

"And that's when she made her pitch. She pulled out the safe deposit key, dangled it in my face. She had it right on her key ring! I should come along. We'd have a ball. We'd split the money, 70/30. Only one problem, all the contacts in New York had been Miguel's. Did I know anyone who could sell the thing for her? I said I didn't. I couldn't imagine why she'd think I did."

Morgan gives Grady what he's come to think of as her "little girl alone in the world" look. When he doesn't bite, she continues her story.

"It was okay if I wasn't interested, Winnie said. She knew a guy who was hot to do it. Only problem was he wanted to use the proceeds as a stake to buy drugs, then resell them, build up to some real money. She wasn't cool about that, but they could probably work together long enough to turn the statuette into cash. Then who cared what he did? She'd just split. In the meantime, she wasn't telling him any of the details—not the name of the town, not the bank, nuthin'—until she knew she had no other way to go.

"Then Winnie upped her offer. I could tell she thought I was lying. That I could take care of selling the piece if I wanted to. 'How about 60/40?' she said.

"I'm not naive. But in spite of what you might think, I've always been a pretty good girl. I don't pay much attention to the dumb laws, like pot or speeding on the interstate out in the middle of nowhere, but I watch out for the big ones and for the little ones that have wacko penalties. I was broke, but I wasn't so dumb that I wanted to be mixed up with some crazy grad student I hardly knew. I wouldn't turn her in, but I didn't want to get involved. So I just said thanks, but no thanks, I'm not interested.

"And that should have been the end of it. With any sane person it would have been. But she wouldn't give up. She kept nagging. Finally, I told her I'd sleep on it. Just to shut her up. I was leaving in the morning.

"We moved on to a crowded bar near campus. Winnie complained that she didn't know anyone, that they were all summer faces. Everyone worth seeing had left town by this time in June. They had internships, or families they liked, and only poor old Winnie was stuck here in sweaty A2. But that didn't stop her from drinking, or dancing up a storm. I was pretty sick of her by now, so I found myself a corner and just endured.

"It got late. The crowd had thinned. I heard last call. Even my new roomie would have to go home now.

"But I'd lost track of her.

"I looked around, checked the ladies' room. Nothing.

"I went outside. The place was locking up. Still no Winnie.

"Then I realized I had her backpack. She'd tossed it at me when she first went off to dance, saying, 'Here, watch this.' I opened it and looked inside. I always keep my wallet and keys on my bod when I'm traveling. But clearly Winnie didn't. Her keys were sitting on top of books, a sweater, a make-up kit and a bunch of other junk. I left the bar and found her car parked down the street where we'd left it. I thought I'd do us both a favor and drive the wreck to her place."

44

"I had the address and some vague directions. The car and I wandered for a while. That part of Ann Arbor has a lot of dinky one-way streets and not a lot of parking. Finally, I found a spot I thought was close, then realized I'd read the numbers wrong and was still a couple of blocks away. I was so tired I just grabbed both backpacks—hers and mine—out of the front seat, left the rest of my stuff locked in the trunk and hoofed it to her apartment.

"Tell me what her building was like."

"I did."

"You told me a lot of things." Grady knows that her description of the physical surroundings was generally accurate, but it's time for some FUD—fear, uncertainty and doubt.

"You think I lied about it."

Grady doesn't reply.

"I didn't," she insists. "I had no reason to make any of that up."

She stops, gives a little smile, as if she's letting him in on a secret. Maybe the alcohol is getting to her, maybe she just wants to show how smart she is. "If you've ever told a lie, a really important one," she almost whispers, "you know that the closer you stick to the truth, the easier it is. It helps keep things straight."

"Okay," Grady says. "You described the place to a T. But I'm getting old. My memory isn't what it used to be. Remind me."

"It was exactly like I said. An old house that had been converted. Four apartments, all but hers empty for the summer. The outer door unlocked because it always is in places like that. She lived in 1B, first floor back.

"As soon as I opened the door from the street, I could hear the music. Loud, all bass. Metallica or some such trash. I don't know what she was doing hanging out at my piano in Traverse City if that's the kind of crap she liked.

"There was shouting. I couldn't make out any words. It just sounded like people trying to talk to each other while getting their ears blasted.

"For a second, I wondered how she'd gotten in. Then I figured she must keep a key hidden somewhere. I hoped that she'd remembered she left her stuff with a virtual stranger and was freaking out royally. But then I heard a male voice yell 'Slut!'. And the response was this outrageous giggle. I knew it had to be her laugh. Like nothing was funny, but she could care less and was telling him so. I regretted not just staying on the bus, riding through the night all the way south. The backache from sleeping in the damn seat would have been easier to deal with than this.

"I knocked. Nothing. I knocked again, harder. Then I thought, hey, I've got her keys. I pulled out the ring, found the right one and opened the door.

"I expected to be greeted with a boy and a beer. I could just hear her saying, 'Morgan! Come on in, babe. Didn't I promise you we'd party?'

"But that's not what happened at all. Somebody'd been partying all right, but I didn't think it was Winnie.

"There were three guys. One short and skinny, a redhead. One bigger with a beard and a lot of dark curly hair. And one that wasn't fat but big and kind of thick, like a wrestler. They were naked. Except the short guy was wearing socks.

"Winnie was naked too.

"And there was a fourth guy, tall, blond, with the kind of muscles you see in ads for protein supplements, leaning against the wall. He was fully clothed.

"The three naked guys were all yelling at her. And she was yelling back. She looked kind of banged up, but she was on her feet, moving around. It was bizarre. And the bodybuilder wearing clothes was just watching, and kind of smiling as if the whole thing was really funny."

"What were they saying?"

"I told you before."

Grady doesn't belabor the obvious. He lets his silence make the point. She gives an exasperated sigh, then continues.

"The guys, especially, the hairy one, were calling Winnie names. Cunt. Bitch. You know the things that kind of men say when they're really pissed at a woman. The short one shouted, 'Stop holding out on us, bitch.'" Morgan shudders. Her gaze is distant again.

"And what were you doing?"

"Just standing there."

"Where?"

"In the doorway—the hall really."

"They didn't notice you?"

Morgan shakes her head. "God knows they couldn't have heard me open the door. They were all focused on each other, and Winnie at least was roaring drunk.

"The apartment was just like I said. You know, the fireplace, the hearth, the beaded curtain leading into the kitchen. I could see the cupboard through the opening, and it looked the way I described. But I don't know if I could have fit into it or not. I made that part up."

Grady isn't sure himself where he wants her to go from here. She may or may not be about to speak the truth, and to his surprise, he doesn't know whether he's ready to hear it.

"I was never in the apartment."

Lie.

But Morgan is still talking, placing herself in the open doorway of that Ann Arbor apartment, unseen and unheard.

"Winnie was telling them to fuck off. She called them assholes, shouted something about them being useless. I felt like I was watching some ghastly performance piece. You know the saying, 'This is not my movie?'"

Grady doesn't.

"Well, it wasn't. The shouting continued. It must have been only a moment that I stood there. But it felt like a long time."

Morgan looks into her glass, moves it to her mouth and tosses down the last of the gin in one shot.

"Then their argument got physical. Winnie was struggling with the hairy guy. She was pushing and he was pushing, and suddenly she lost her balance and fell. She hit her head."

Morgan clutches her empty glass like a life preserver. Her eyes fill with tears. She looks at Grady, as if for mercy.

In his own mind, Grady has been alternating between good cop and bad cop, giving her a lot of rope and then reeling her back in, keeping her off balance. He tells himself he is only playing her because it's an effective questioning technique. But he has to admit that on some level he's a man divided—still unexpectedly vulnerable, but also out to get some of his own back. He does his best to appear impassive.

Morgan takes a deep, ragged breath. "Anyway, she hit her head on the edge of the hearth. Her eyes stayed open, but she didn't blink. I was pretty sure she was dead."

She steadies herself and continues. "Somehow I managed not to scream. I would have snuck out of there. Called 9-1-1..."

"But?"

"But the guy who pushed her looked up. He saw me. I turned and ran."

There is a note of finality in her voice, as if she's said it all, told him all. She seems to think she has somehow brought things to closure.

She hasn't.

"How'd you get away?"

"It took them a moment to react. And three of them were naked. They ran after me down the hall, but to go outside they at least needed shoes. And they sort of fell all over each other at the outer door of the building, blocking the tall blonde guy, the one who was dressed, who'd been leaning against the wall. It was kind of like the Three Stooges.

"After that it wasn't so hard. I used to run track, I told you. I'm little and fast and I can hide under hedges and behind things. It took a while, but I went through backyards and alleys. Eventually, I made my way to where I'd left Winnie's car and took off."

Morgan seems too shaken to go on. She sits there on the sofa, a small, forlorn figure, still clutching the glass, looking into space.

Grady waits. Is she expecting him to sympathize? To do something to comfort her? He seldom has a clue in these situations, even when he isn't dealing with a woman who has more skins than a snake.

While he's thinking about it, he goes into the bathroom and pees, leaving the door ajar even though he doesn't think she'll try to rabbit. He zips up, runs his hands under the faucet, then goes back into the room and takes the empty glass from her hands. He carries it to the bureau, plops in a couple of olives and a splash of gin, hands it to her. It's the best he can do.

"Go on," he says, taking his place on the chair.

"At first, all I could think about was getting away, not being followed, maybe lying low somewhere for a day or two and then heading straight to Atlanta, pretending the whole mess never happened. Do not pass go, do not collect $200, do not get a bullet in your brain. Then I remembered the odd little key on the ring—the safety deposit box.

"There was a little notebook in Winnie's backpack. The notes in it were cryptic, but I knew enough of the story to decipher them. So I knew the town. I knew the bank. The box number was stamped on the key. I had her ID. And I knew I looked enough like Winnie to pass if I cut and dyed my hair and popped in a pair of blue contacts.

"I'd never noticed the resemblance between us, I guess because our coloring was so different, but there'd been one night in Traverse City when another customer had picked up on it, assumed we were sisters and that Winnie's hair was a bleach job. I figured it would be less than no problem in a Latin country. All the locals would see would be the blonde hair, little nose and blue eyes."

In spite of the refinements he and Luis made, Grady has been thinking of Morgan as Winnie's darker twin. They focused on eye and hair color, based their guesses on what Sophie glimpsed when Morgan lost a contact lens. Now, looking at her in the lamplight of the crummy hotel room and comparing what he sees with Davis's photos of the dead Winnie, the ones he pinned to his mental bulletin board almost a year before, he notices that Morgan's chin is slightly more pointed, the face just a tad less round and a little more oval. If it was a contest, he's not sure how he'd vote. He liked the blonde, furry hair, the aquamarine eyes. But this look isn't bad either. And he has to give her credit: she was thorough with her disguise. She was blonde all over.

Morgan is still talking, the words coming faster now that she's into this part of her story. "I decided I might as well go get the statuette myself. It wasn't doing anyone any good in the vault. I couldn't return it or share the proceeds with Miguel and his family because all I had was a first name. I didn't know who they were. And it didn't seem smart to try to find out."

One thing hasn't changed since Morgan's first "confession" that night at Grady's mother's: the other big plus of becoming Winnie. And Morgan articulates it now.

"There really were letters from Winnie's Aunt Mary, rubber-banded together in the bottom of her backpack. And the guys who killed her might be looking for a dark-haired girl who'd been an eyewitness, but they sure wouldn't be looking for Winnie. She was dead. So, just like I told you before, her Aunt Mary's house seemed the perfect place to hide.

"Things were still pretty scary, but now I had a plan. I always function better with a plan.

"By the time I got to Tucson, I was feeling safe. Safe at 'Aunt Mary's.' And safe about going to Mexico. The creeps knew nothing about all that. It was a complication of Winnie's life that had nothing to do with her death. It was too bad she died, but maybe I'd been given a chance at a new life."

"You never considered calling the police?"

"I told you. I was too scared."

"You could have described them."

"Yes."

"You lied to me about that."

A nod. "But I'd have been in danger. Don't even try to tell me otherwise." She's playing with the last olive, chasing it around the glass with her right index finger. "And what good would it have done? Winnie was gone. Nothing could change that." She brings the glass to her lips and tips the olive into her mouth. "I didn't want to end up dead too."

Grady's impressed by her ability to keep the twists and turns of her stories straight. In his experience, it's the rare bird who can do this, see a scenario and its implications so clearly that they never take a wrong turn toward the truth. "You didn't think that your plan was pretty risky?"

"Maybe.. But you dug into my life. You know my childhood ended when I was ten years old. Things have happened to me that, well...don't happen to other people. This could have been just a weird next step."

Grady reflects that there's never been any sign Morgan lacks nerve.

Her glass is empty again. She sets it down on the coffee table and goes over to the bureau. Grady figures she's going for another martini of pure gin and multiple olives. He wonders at her capacity.

But she opens a bureau drawer, pulls out an electric kettle, a box of tea bags, and two mugs. "Voila!" she says, suddenly cheerful. "Behold the well-equipped musician." She sounds as if she's just unloaded a burden. Her manner says she's cleared everything up and all is now fine and straight between the two of them.

She fills the kettle in the bathroom and plugs it in, tosses some packets of sugar onto the coffee table.

She hands him a cup of tea, takes one for herself, settles back down on the sofa.

Grady notices she's taking it black. The sweetening is apparently for him.

"No sugar?" he says. "I thought you liked lots of sugar."

Morgan shakes her head. "Not me," she says with a little smile. "That was Clare."

If it's meant as a joke, it doesn't work. If it's not, it's the first real slip he's seen. He wonders if she'd wishes she could take it back.

As if what she's just said makes absolute sense, she selects a CD from a stack that sits on the coffee table and pops it into a boom box. The strains of a saxophone float into the air. It's one of Grady's favorite albums, Coltrane at his most mellow. The same music she put on at his place, the first night they made love.

"I have to keep it down," she says. "But we have a right to music. It's after 5:00. Technically, it's morning."

"Tell me," Grady says, marveling again at her resilience. "What happened at the Nelsons?"

Another little smile, but shaky this time, not so sure. "Ah," she says softly, "The night we met."

45

"I went to bed just the way I said. But I knew the alarm wasn't on. The code was in one of the letters, along with information about getting a visitor's pass into Pergama and all that stuff. And I managed to disarm the thing when I arrived. But I'm not very mechanical. I didn't really understand how it worked. And I didn't want it going off just because I screwed up. So I decided not to use it.

"I was sleeping. But I was in one of those classic nightmare scenarios, dreaming that the men who murdered Winnie were chasing me on an interstate. I was driving Winnie's car, and they were in a Humvee, a black one with a grille that looked like teeth. The windows were tinted, too dark for me to see in, but I knew it was them. And Winnie's car was even more beat up than in real life. Parts kept falling off—a fender, the front passenger door. The steering wheel kept trying to jump out of my hands like it was alive and hated me. The Humvee was gaining. I was pushing as hard as I could on the gas pedal, putting all my weight on it, every ounce of force. But the damn car just kept slowing down. It was creeping to a stop. Then the Humvee rammed my rear bumper.

"I jerked awake. Three men were standing over me. They were just silhouettes, backlit by the light from the hall, but I knew who they were.

"They pulled me out of bed, dragged me into the living room. I was screaming bloody murder, but it didn't do any good. You've seen the Nelsons' house, that neighborhood. The houses are huge, the windows are closed, the walls are thick. Nobody was going to hear me, and these guys knew it.

"They pushed me down on a couch. It was the little guy..."

"Walter Simon," interjects Grady. "Known as 'The Shrimp.' He fell down a well."

"...the tall guy—the blond one who had his clothes on at Winnie's when everybody else was naked..."

"Billy Oz. Also known on the street as the Wizard."

Morgan stares at him. "You're kidding."

"I get the impression he was his own publicist on that one. A Wizard only in his own eyes. Given name William Ostrowski. Died of exposure."

"...and the hairy one."

"Victor Vassallo." Grady waits for her to fill in Vassallo's fate.

Finally Morgan speaks. "He was the body at the Nelsons'."

Grady nods.

"The fourth man, the one that was thick like a wrestler...he wasn't there. Maybe he was guarding the house, or waiting somewhere else. Who cares. God knows he turned up later."

"Harold Taylor. I shot him in the desert."

"You're making sure I understand they're all dead, aren't you? That I realize they can't hurt me." She takes a sip of tea.

Grady flashes on Sophie shuffling her "cards"—and her absolute belief that "they," a they that includes Morgan, not only can hurt her, but will. He shoves the image aside. "I just like to get the facts straight."

"Oh."

"You're in the Nelsons' living room, on the couch. Are you wearing a nightgown?"

"No one my age wears a nightgown. We wear t-shirts and

boxers, or tank tops. Stuff like that. But I was telling the truth before, that first night I talked to you. I like to sleep raw."

"And they didn't let you put anything on."

"No. Not a thing. You can imagine how vulnerable I felt. I was terrified. Absolutely scared shitless. I figured that if they'd gone to the trouble of tracking me down—somehow—they were going to kill me. Because of what I'd seen. Although, since then, when I've thought about it, I realize that all I saw was a sad accident. Maybe manslaughter. Do three men follow someone 2,000 miles for that?

"But the subtleties didn't occur to me at the time.

"I tried to be brave. My life didn't pass before my eyes. Maybe that happens to other people. I don't know. But it did seem important to make my peace with the universe. And I realized that there wasn't anyone I wanted to say goodbye to. Not a soul. Which made me very sad. So I focused on that, on my solitary life and the freedom it gave me to leave the world at 32 without opening much of a hole, and not on what was going to happen. Oddly enough, it helped. I felt a little calmer.

"Then they started asking questions. The tall bodybuilder guy—Billy?"

"Billy Oz."

"Yes. He seemed to be the boss. He did almost all the talking. He had a weird voice, deep but really hoarse. And he kept it so quiet it was almost spooky. I realized later that he almost always spoke softly. I guess he thought it was scary. Probably got it from a movie.

"And to my absolute amazement, he wanted to know where the key was.

"I played dumb. For one thing, the more they thought that I had something they wanted, the less likely they'd kill me right away. But why did they think I had it? How did they even know it existed? So I just kept saying, 'What key? I don't know what you're talking about.'

"I gradually realized that it was Billy that Winnie had been talking about. The guy she was going to work with and then dump. He told me that he'd demanded—the night Winnie died—that she

330

fork over the key. As security. That way, she'd have the 4-11 and he'd have the key, and they'd need each other. It was the smart way to do things, he said. But she'd told him, 'I couldn't do it even if I wanted to. I gave it to my girlfriend.' She began boasting about me, about how her BFF had come to town, how her BFF had connections, how she didn't need Billy anymore. She'd told this friend everything, she said.

"I doubt Winnie had any idea that her 'BFF' really did have the key courtesy of the abandoned backpack. She should have known. She'd had to dig her front door key out from under the mat or the flower pot or wherever she kept it. But she was too whacked out to make the connection. Didn't realize that she was missing her magic ticket to paradise. And her lie almost got me killed. Because it turned out to be the truth.

"I said it like a mantra, over and over: 'Key? What key?' But it didn't work. I should have known it wouldn't. They, well, Billy, started to threaten me. He asked me if I'd ever thought about being raped. If I'd ever had a nightmare about what it would be like. More than one man, he said, more than one time, in more than one hole. Over and over and over.

"Had I ever imagined, he whispered, what it would be like to be cut. The knife slicing through my skin. Slowly. Small cuts, then deeper. Blood everywhere. First disfigured, then dismembered. Begging to be allowed to die.

"I had to give them something. So I told Billy that Winnie had accidentally left her backpack with me. That I had noticed an odd key on her ring. That I'd taken it off the ring because I didn't need it. Had no idea what it was for. They could have it. It was with my things in the room where I'd been sleeping.

"The little guy walked me in there. He watched while I rifled through my stuff. He held out his hand. I gave him the key. He pushed me ahead of him back into the living room and tossed it to Billy. He was posturing like a fool, sort of proud, macho. One of those strutting little roosters. But it was a bad throw. The key fell short, onto the carpet. His boss had to bend over to pick it up. 'Asshole,' he muttered at the little guy.

"Billy looked at the key in his hand and smiled at me. 'We're making progress,' he said. 'Now we need the name of the town and the bank.'

"All I had to keep me alive was information, facts that would go to Valhalla or hell or wherever I was headed if they killed me. They'd never get what they wanted then. I had to hang onto my few assets, sell them dearly.

"'She didn't tell me anything about a town or a bank,' I said. "I didn't need the key. That's the only reason I took it off the ring. I would have thrown it out when I got around to it. I don't know anything.'

"The Shrimp sort of snorted at me, in disbelief.

"The boss, Billy, shut him up. Then he turned to the hairy guy with the beard...'"

"Vassallo."

"Vassallo. 'Take off your clothes,' he said. 'You're first.' Vassallo kicked off his shoes, unzipped his jeans, yanked them down and threw them on a chair. He was going commando, no underwear. He stood there in his t-shirt. 'All your clothes,' his boss said. 'You'll be needing a shower after.'

"The t-shirt was black and just said 'Bud' on the front, meaning the beer, I guess. I don't know why I even noticed, but I did. He yanked it off over his head.

"Now he was naked. He had long dark hair that needed washing. And not just on his head. On his legs, his chest, even his back. Ugh. And he had a major hard-on.

"'What a pervert,' I thought. 'I'm terrified and he knows it, and it's making him hot.'

"'Bring her here,' Billy said to the shrimpy guy. And he made me stand in front of Vassallo, just a couple of feet away. Vassallo was raring to go. 'Not yet,' Billy said. He turned to The Shrimp again. 'Go in the kitchen and bring back the biggest, sharpest knife you can find,' he ordered.

"I'd made myself dinner in that kitchen. There was a huge block full of knives. The one I'd used to slice tomatoes had been razor-sharp.

"I was so scared I was shaking. I was sure I would fall apart, become this raving, sobbing thing.

"The little guy came back, way too soon. He held out a knife to his boss, for approval I guess. The blade was long—six, eight inches. Billy laid the key down on the coffee table and took the knife. He walked over to me and ran the knife vertically, very lightly, down my breastbone. I watched as a trail of blood followed the blade. I felt pain—not severe, fragile, but somehow more terrifying because it was so butterfly-light. 'Are you going to tell me now?' he asked, almost gently.

"I made one last attempt to hold out. 'I don't know anything,' I stammered.

"'Okay,' he said, and he moved away from me. 'I think you need to understand your situation,' he said. 'So I'm going to show you just how serious we are.'

"He took a step or two, until he was standing directly behind the naked hairy man. I don't think anyone but Billy himself had any idea what was going on. In what seemed like one motion, he grabbed Vassallo's hair with one hand and pulled his head back. With the other he slashed the guy's throat. Blood spurted, gushed, sprayed all over me. Billy tossed the knife to the floor and held Vassallo while he struggled. The blood was pumping out of his neck.

"The little guy seemed amazed, appalled.

"'What did you do that for?' he yelled. 'Why in hell did you do that?'

"He picked up the bloody knife, waved it at his boss, maybe in defiance, maybe in self-defense, I don't know.

"Vassallo was already starting to go limp. 'Don't be an idiot,' Billy said, letting Vassallo's body slump to the carpet, dropping him down on his back. 'He got us into this mess. If he hadn't pushed that little cunt, our meal ticket would still be alive.'

"The short guy went nuts. I knew that Billy could fight him off in an instant, but for just that moment, they were both busy.

"I saw my chance, my one desperate chance, and I took it.

"I grabbed the key—my bargaining power—from the coffee table and ran to the front door, flung it open and ran down the front steps, into the driveway.

"I was trying to stick to the pavement, but it was pitch dark out there once I got beyond the light that spilled from the entryway onto the porch. The driveway seemed miles long.

"At one point, my right foot landed on a stone and I twisted my ankle. I was in front of the Nelsons' music room by that time, and I could hear them coming. I was naked, couldn't hide the key, or anything else, from anybody.

"I threw the key as hard as I could into the cactus and bushes. I had no idea exactly where it landed. But I knew it was so dark that they couldn't have seen me throw it.

"Then I ran down the driveway. I was heading for the house next door, but I knew I'd never make it in time.

"So I headed off into the shrubbery. I found a bush that wasn't too scratchy—everything seems to have thorns in that part of the world—and I curled up beneath it trying not to make a sound, telling myself that no matter what crawled over me or stuck into me it was better than the alternative.

"They looked for a while. I could tell they didn't dare make a lot of noise, and I had the idea they were even more scared of the cactus and snakes than I was. They tromped around and muttered. But eventually they gave up.

"I waited, made myself count to a thousand. Then I crawled out from under the bush and ran screaming to the Whitehursts' front door.

"I was scratched, bloody, out of breath, exhausted, terrified. I leaned on the bell. Finally, Jill opened the door."

46

Morgan has been staring straight ahead, as if she's seeing Tucson that night and not the crappy hotel room in Toronto. Now she stands up, walks into the bathroom and closes the door. Grady hears running water. She returns a moment later, looking calmer, more composed.

The CD is repeating itself. Track one has played for the second time, and they're into track two, "You Don't Know What Love Is." The saxophone keens. The melody mourns.

They listen to a few bars, a few more. When Grady figures she's had all the respite she deserves (and then some), he takes her cup and his and refills them both with hot water from the still-steaming kettle. He dunks the tea bags a few times, tosses them in the wastebasket, hands Morgan her mug and waits for her to go on.

Jill and Charlie rescued her—from a lot more than they knew. She was safe, at least temporarily. She couldn't stay at their house forever, though—or even for very long. She didn't dare go back to the Nelsons'. Or to her old life.

She shudders. "I thought if I found the key maybe I could find a way to trade it for my safety. I knew it was somewhere in the cactus between the two houses. Why do people want to live with all those spiky plants, anyway?"

Grady shrugs. He's never been clear on the appeal of 'natural desert landscaping.'

"But people never left me alone at the Whitehursts', and the police were all over the Nelsons'. I had no way to hunt for the damn key. Then, when you and I were sitting at the piano that day—you have a nice touch by the way, light but expressive..."

Grady makes a dismissive grunt, skeptical but pleased. He brings her back to the topic. "You were still trying to figure out how to go about the search when you saw Sophie cutting across the property."

Morgan nods. "She stopped, and I could tell she was watching us, although I was careful to keep most of my attention on you."

"You saw her pick up something."

"Yes. The sun was setting, but there was still some light, and the object in her hand glinted. I knew it had to be the key."

"And you couldn't leave town until you retrieved it."

"Right. I needed to be in Tucson. And I didn't have any money. I was so relieved when you took me in. I can't imagine... But I didn't dare stay with you, nice as that would have been. You were too connected to what happened. It would have put us both in danger. Plus I didn't want the cops to find me."

"So you went to my mother's."

"Yup. And you know most of the rest. They found me, they grabbed me."

Grady doesn't doubt that part. Following Morgan's trail wouldn't have been all that hard. And if Billy and his bunch were tracking him to find her, well, even if they weren't the smartest gangstas on the block, he wasn't exactly looking over his shoulder at that point. He knows hindsight is a trap. It's always 20/20. But none of them were as alert as they should have been. Except Morgan, and what did she know about being tailed?

He can see it.

The night Vassallo died, Billy and his boys waited quietly for their quarry to reappear—she couldn't stay in the brush, naked, forever.

They couldn't get to her as she ran up that walkway, but they saw her disappear into Jill's arms.

After that, all it took was a stake-out. Ironically, the protected environment, the gated community, made it easy.

Pergama's entrance has only two lanes in—one for residents and guests, one for larger trucks—and two out, in the same configuration. They could have parked just down the street outside the gates and followed Morgan anytime she left the development, no matter who she was riding with. If they left the van doors ajar, threw a little brush in the back, occasionally moved a clod of dirt or two, their crappy vehicle wouldn't have drawn any attention. They'd simply be yard men, part of the everyday landscape.

They probably would have snatched her from Grady's if she'd stayed there longer. Then, even though she'd given them the slip temporarily, they could count on Grady's anger, embarrassment and experience in tracking down perps to lead them right to her.

Coltrane's sax is moaning, whispering, ironically, how easy it is to remember—and goddamn impossible to forget.

To Grady's surprise, Morgan begins humming along. He realizes she's doing it unconsciously. The sounds are sadness rising wordlessly, with a roundness of tone that hints at the extent of her musical gifts.

"You've been playing all your life?" Grady asks.

"Pretty much. My mom—back when I had a mom—always said that I picked out 'Chattanooga Choo Choo' on my toy piano when I was three." She takes Coltrane's *Abstract Blue* from the stack on the coffee table and switches it with the CD in the player. "I thought we'd stick with a good thing."

He lights another cigarette and refocuses his attention on Morgan, sitting in this grade C hotel room, sipping her lukewarm tea. He's ready—has been ready for a year—to hear her version of what happened after the low-lifes knocked him over the head and took her from his mother's.

"So they've got you," he prompts. "Then what?"

"I told them where the key was. I had to. I even helped them plan how to get it back. They weren't all that bright. Their only tactics were brute force and sadism. Ugh." She makes a face, as if she smells something foul.

"I thought I could get into the Whitehursts' house and get the key without anything bad happening to Sophie or her parents. Yes, she'd see my face—but only as 'Winnie.'

"We were only able to get Jill out of the house for a little while. And we were lucky to do that. She was keeping a close eye on her daughter. Maybe a mother's gut instinct.

"When I delivered the flowers, those jerks were supposed to let me go in alone. But I guess they didn't trust me. Or they couldn't resist the heavy-handed stuff. Or both. They had to make a big show. Then, when Sophie couldn't find the key, Billy snatched her. I couldn't believe it. What the fuck were they doing? He said they were covering their bets: they'd make this whole thing pay off one way or the other."

Morgan tips her mug to her mouth. "I need more," she says. "Just a second." She rummages in the bureau, holds up the empty tea bag box. "Shit," she says. She pulls their used tea bags out of the waste basket, plops them in her cup, pours in the remaining hot water and takes her place on the sofa.

"After that phone call—when they learned that you and Jill had found the key, they gave up the idea of ransom. Too complicated for their pea brains, I think. Their focus shifted back to the safe deposit box in Mexico.

"And there I was with the missing pieces: the information. It took two unpleasant sessions—threats, knocking me around—before I gave it up. But within a couple of hours, I'd told them everything I knew. I couldn't hold out.

"So there we were, down in the desert south of Tucson, out in the middle of nowhere. And they had no further reason to keep me alive.

"I kept telling them they'd need me to go into the bank in Mexico. But I was pretty sure they were too stupid to believe me.

"I knew I had to try to get away, no matter how risky it was. And I got lucky. I had an opening, and I grabbed it."

"Sophie told us what happened."

"I tried to take her with me."

Grady nods, acknowledging the truth of that statement. "And you came back."

She nods. He waits. She doesn't explain.

Finally, he asks. "Why?"

She shrugs. "I couldn't just..." She looks at him. "I was going to help you, believe it or not. I grew up around animals. At least when I was little. Bareback's not easy but it can be done. I borrowed a horse from a field.

"But when I got there, to the ghost town... I saw Sophie and Jill drive out, saw you send the little guy down the well. Watched you sneak up on Billy. I almost missed the big guy, the one that got you from behind..."

"Taylor."

"Yeah. He came at the plaza from an unexpected angle. Could have caught me. But he was really only looking at you. I saw you fight with him, knock him out. And I realized Billy was going to shoot you. So I picked up the two by four and whomped him. Then I grabbed the rifle. And that's when I realized that I could get the key without hurting you. And without those creeps knowing I had it."

She takes a swallow of her tea, sets the cup down. "That's it. End of story."

She gets up from the sofa, goes to the informal bar that she has set up on the bureau. "The sun's coming up," she says. She screws the lid back on the olives and sticks it in the frig, recaps the gin and stows it in a drawer.

Finally, he asks her. "Where's the money?"

Morgan gives him an odd little smile.

"You went to Mexico, didn't you."

339

"Sure."

"And you had the key. And Winnie's ID."

"Yup."

"Where?" He has to know.

She looks puzzled.

"The name of the town," he insists.

"Oh. Tlacotalpan."

"Near Veracruz?"

"30, 40 miles."

Shit, Grady thinks. So close. Two more trips, maybe three. He tells himself it doesn't matter now.

"Go on," he says, trying to control his tone.

"I needed a grubstake. I talked a couple of old boyfriends into wiring me money. Then I snuck into the town. Wore sunglasses and a hat. I didn't want Miguel spotting me. Had a nice dinner in my hotel, drank a little tequila—very little—read a book. Had some trouble sleeping. Nervous, I guess. I got to the bank an hour after it opened the next morning. I didn't want to be conspicuous by being the first customer in or anything like that. I knew I'd stand out enough just by being blonde and American. I pulled off the hat and sunglasses once I was inside the door, presented the ID, signed the book—I'd practiced Winnie's signature. I was worried about that, but I got it close enough. I was escorted into the vault. The banker inserted his key. I inserted mine. He withdrew the box. I murmured 'Gracias' and he left me alone with it. I opened it."

She stops. Coltrane's playing "I Want to Talk About You," a Billy Eckstein piece. She hums along with the sax as it goes in directions no human voice should be able to follow.

"And?"

She turns it back on him. "What do you think?"

"It was empty."

She nods. "Bingo."

Grady sets his mug down on the coffee table. He stands up and walks across the room to the window, draws back the curtain, peers out. The sky is gray in the east, brightening with the first hint of morning.

Is she lying about Mexico? Grady is sure the answer is no. For one thing, he doesn't think she'd still be grinding out gigs with a pile of money stashed away somewhere. But more than that, his experience as a Southern Arizona cop tells him that if she opened that box—and even if she didn't—it was, as he's deduced and she's confirmed, empty.

He turns from the sleeping city than to the young woman in the room. It would be funny if it weren't so sad. "Five dead," he says. "A young girl traumatized. Her mother almost killed. And it was a con."

Morgan actually seems surprised. "Was it? It wasn't all that big a town. Really just a classy sort of village. Maybe Miguel's story was true. Maybe everybody knows everybody there, including the bank managers. Maybe he discovered what Winnie had done and was heartbroken. Maybe there were more people on his side than he thought."

"So he found a way to reclaim his property."

"Yes."

Maybe. But more likely Winnie Pearson was just one in a long string of gringas who fell for a slick Latin line. Grady doesn't bother to say it out loud. Let Morgan think what she wants. Let her have her little romance with the idea of Mexico. His gut says that more than a family heirloom, the statuette was a dependable source of recurring revenue.

He's tired of tea. He wants to go back to gin, wants some ice, thinks about going down the hall for it, decides against it.

"Now what?" Morgan asks.

Grady doesn't answer. He's still looking out at the skyline. The gray is shading into pale yellow. Morgan comes over and stands beside him. She puts her hand on his back, lightly. In other circumstances, the touch might be casual.

Now she's running her hand gently, up and down, caressing his shoulder blade. He lets her think she's in control, maybe even home free.

She's very good. She's been spinning her stories like Scheherazade. Telling tales. To save her life?

It's time.

He walks across the room to where his jacket is draped over the back of the desk chair. He removes the envelope from the pocket, and slides the photograph out of the envelope.

She is still turned toward the window, facing Toronto's newly minted day. He holds the photo in front of her, in her line of sight, where she has to see it whether she wants to or not.

There's a slight gasp. She shudders like a building that has been wired with explosives and has just felt the first shocks of demolition. He puts a hand out, steadies her.

When she finally speaks, all the melody has been driven from her voice. The words sound as if they're coming from a cold, distant moon. "Where'd you get that?"

47

It's the picture he found in the duffel, the snapshot hidden under the cardboard stiffening in the bottom of one of the bags. The photo that, by definition, carries a secret.

The photo he kept when he turned the duffels and the rest of their contents over to the law, in the person of Andy Davis.

The photo that seemed all but useless at first—the picture dark, so blurry the images looked smeared.

At first glance, it was nothing but abstract shapes. Maybe two people? One person female? With short blonde hair.

Luis worked on it and worked on it some more. And when the image finally came together, it was the key—or *a key* to the whole thing. It didn't help him find her. But it told him a hell of a lot about the why of what happened.

Morgan's voice interrupts his thoughts. "Where'd you get it?" she asks again. And he realizes he hasn't answered her.

"You left it."

Luis did all he could: scanned it, enhanced it here, lightened it there, zoomed in and fiddled around with the pixels. It was still crummy. But it was enough. Luis printed it out for him, 5 x 7, on photographic paper, and Grady carried it all the way to Toronto, flat in a large white envelope in a big inside pocket of his leather jacket.

He clears his throat. He's finding this harder than he expected. "When people set the timer on a camera so they can be in the shot, the results are usually pretty lousy. This one was underexposed, fuzzy. And the person who triggered the shutter wasn't quick enough, didn't make it all the way back into the frame."

He takes a breath and continues. "It's you and Winnie."

It isn't a question. In spite of the lack of clarity, in spite of the fragmentary quality of the image of Morgan in the lower right, in spite of the fact that all that was captured by the lens was a lock of dark hair, the left-most expanse of a forehead, a bare arm, the outside curve of a breast, the snapshot tells a story. It says that Morgan was rushing back to the bed to share the frame with the naked, lasciviously posing Winnie. Grady is making a statement of fact. And they both know it.

Morgan reaches for the picture, to take it from him, and he lets her. Tears are starting in her eyes. "I don't know what to do," she says. "I don't know whether to rip it up or frame it." She turns to him, as if the answer is written on his face.

"I'm not a lesbian," she says. "I'd never done anything like that before."

"But Winnie was experienced."

Morgan nods. "Yes," she whispers.

"She seduced you."

Now the tears are running down her face. She hands Grady the photo—shoves it into his hands—reaches up and brushes the moisture away.

"And you fell in love."

The dam breaks. The sobs pour out. Morgan is bending, staggering, collapsing under their weight.

He helps her over to the couch, hands her a box of tissues from the nightstand, sits her down and stands over her trying to decide what to do with his own body.

"Nobody liked her," Morgan sobs. "Not really." Something

Grady already knew. "But I thought they just didn't appreciate her. That she was unique. That they were too shallow. Or not adventurous enough. Or jealous because she was so cute and so smart and so...lively.

"We met just like I said. Two years ago. The summer before...before everything. In Traverse City, right near the end of my gig. Winnie was a revelation to me. I was so used to being alone, to being lonely. And now...

"We were like light and dark. The same size, the same shape. But different. Like those kittens of your mother's."

"Salt and pepper."

Morgan nods. "In some odd way, I thought we fit."

Grady knows that as he interviews her he should position himself opposite her. At least at a right angle. But fuck it, he isn't really her interrogator. Or is he? Isn't he here as both interrogator and judge? Oh hell, he isn't even in his own country. And he's already breaking a shitload of rules. What's one more? So he sits down next to her.

She doesn't notice his presence. Now that she is talking, really talking, the words pour out of her, tumbling one on top of the other, as different from her earlier, measured responses as a fast-flowing stream from a stagnant pond.

"My job on the island came to an end. It was time to go. But I was determined to stay. I couldn't leave her. I went all over town looking for work that would keep me in the area until her vacation was over. It didn't happen. No one needed me.

"And Winnie couldn't help. She had no money. Not of her own. She was still dependent on her parents.

"So I had to move on. Pack up my stuff, shove it in my car. I still had the BMW at that point. I hit the road." The tissue in Morgan's hand is soggy, shredded. She stars at it as if bewildered, puzzled by how it got that way and absolutely stymied by what to do about it.

Grady pulls another tissue from the box, replaces the one in her hand. "But you stayed in touch." he says.

"Ummm. Yes. Seems I always called her, though. She never called me. Or rarely. Initiated a call, I mean. Though sometimes she would call me back."

Grady knows this is why the Michigan police never guessed at an absent lover, never picked up a pattern from Winnie's phone bills. "You were all over the country," he says.

Morgan nods. "Two weeks here. Three weeks there. And I didn't phone her that much. Not nearly as often as I wanted to. I was always afraid of coming on too strong. I don't know why. So at first it was every few days, then once a week, then once a month. From wherever I happened to be. I kept trying to get gigs in Ann Arbor, but everybody loves to play there. And they have a lot of local talent. It's a hard market to break into."

She blows her nose, takes another tissue.

"I was so lonely. And I had no one to talk to. I couldn't tell anybody I was nuts about a woman." The sobs return. Her shoulders shake.

"Why not?"

"You mean nobody cares about that stuff anymore? Mostly never did in my line of work. In some states we could even have gotten married. Maybe it's the way I was raised. Everything was evil. Anything light or good or fun was a perversion. And pleasure! A greased slide right down to hell. Anyway, I just wasn't that brave.

"What was I looking for anyway? The house with the little white picket fence? But I was insane about her." Morgan buries her face in her hands.

Grady knows she's remembering. And he knows that trap. Memories don't have flaws. They're perfect—which makes them hurt even more. He needs to bring her back.

He puts a hand on her arm. "Last June," he says. "Tell me what happened then."

Morgan lets out a ragged breath, raises her head, doesn't look at Grady but at some fixed point across the room. Her voice is flat, as if she is reciting facts, describing a series of events that happened to someone else.

"I had a gig on Mackinac Island, just like I said. I tried like hell to get her to come up there, join me. She said she couldn't. Incompletes to make up. Studying to do. She had to get it together academically, or her money would be cut off.

"But I kept wondering. I knew she had the incompletes. It made sense that her parents would be pissed. But couldn't she have studied on Mackinac? Didn't she want to see me?

"By the time I called her from that pay phone on the dock I was miserable. And it was my birthday, just like I told you. I was scared, depressed, whatever you want to call it.

"My hands were shaking as I dialed the phone. The last few times I'd called Winnie, she'd been cold. So I was afraid she wouldn't even want to talk to me.

"But this time, she was warm. She had a wonderful surprise for me, she said. I had to come to Ann Arbor right away. And not to worry about the money. She'd take care of it.

"I quit my job. Actually walked out before the end of the gig. I'd never done that before. My car was in the shop, but it was a piece of crap anyway, so I just left it.

"She was supposed to pick me up at the bus station that Friday evening, but she wasn't there. So I did call her from a pay phone partway to her place, just like I told you. She came to get me. And when I saw her pull up in that monster of a car..." Morgan blushes. "Let's just say I couldn't wait to get her into bed."

"But Winnie insisted we go to that damn Greek restaurant outside of town. I wasn't hungry, but if we had to eat, why drag all the way out there? 'How about something closer?' I said, but she wouldn't hear it. Almost like she didn't want to be seen with me. At least by anyone who knew her.

"That's when she told me about Mexico, about Miguel. I never knew where she'd gone for Spring break, never understood why she didn't come to me.

"She saw my reaction. 'Don't get all weird,' she said. 'I had to go with my dad. Do you think he gave me a choice? And you know I was just playing with Miguel. At first. But then when I found out what I could get out of him... Whoo-eee!' She whistled.

"She told me this was our chance. 'I'm sick of grad school,' she said. "And I don't want to hit my head against some corporate wall for 30 years. This will be our grubstake. We'll go away together, somewhere warm, buy a little bar. You'll play and sing. I'll run the place.'

"She was drinking just as much as I said. I thought she was crazy, that she was spinning some wild fantasy. And that it was too dangerous.

"But she kept talking, and I began coming around. It might have been a dream, but it was a good dream. I didn't want to wake up.

"We'd drive to Arizona, she said. She'd drop me in Phoenix where I could get a cheap motel, maybe even work a little. She'd go on to Tucson, establish herself there as the good little grad student taking a break in her Aunt Mary's gorgeous house. Then I'd meet her, a couple of weeks later, on the Mexican side of the border. She had a little notebook in her purse, with all the details written down.

"She even showed me the key—right on her key ring. Seemed foolish to me, but she said the best place to hide anything was in plain sight."

Morgan asks for water, and Grady gets it for her. As she sips, he walks over to the windows, looks out once more at the Toronto skyline.

He wonders about Winnie's sudden enthusiasm for her long-gone gal pal.

Winnie must have known how much she and Morgan looked alike. Was she going to send Morgan into the Mexican bank? Let her smuggle the contraband back across the border?

With a little peroxide and some blue contacts, Morgan could take all the risk. What would have been Winnie's excuse? Standing guard? Acting as some sort of diversion? Keeping up appearances for her parents?

And then what would have happened to Morgan? Dumped? Or worse?

Grady sits down again, but this time in the chair.

"Then what?" he asks.

"I drove us back into town. She'd had way too much to drink. We didn't talk much, but she did ask me if I knew anyone who could sell the statuette. Like I told you. I said I didn't."

"Even though you did."

Morgan nods, eyes cast down. "I live kind of on the fringes of society. You meet people. Musicians, bartenders, other late night types."

"Why'd you lie to her?"

"I'm not sure. I guess because I was so uneasy about the whole thing. She didn't really care, anyway. Said she had some guy who could help her. She wasn't real comfortable with him, but she'd use him in a pinch.

"By the time we got to her place, I was hot. She'd been kissing my neck and feeling me up the whole way. It was all I could do to keep the car on the road. And then I couldn't find a parking spot. Her street was one-way, parking on only one side. We ended up blocks away. I kissed her as soon as we got out of the car, and she put her tongue practically down my throat. 'Leave your stuff,' she said. 'We'll get it in the morning.' So I grabbed my backpack and left the duffels.

"We walked to her building, went in through the street door and down the hall. By the time we reached the door to her apartment, I could hear music—heavy metal, not my kind of thing at all. I thought maybe she'd left a radio on so it would seem like someone was home. The building was as empty as I said, so it did make some sense. Anyway, she didn't seem worried, just unlocked the door and pushed it open.

"Winnie said 'Shit! 'How'd you assholes get in?' when she saw what was going on inside. But she didn't sound pissed. She sounded like it was a good surprise.

"There were four men in there. Sleazy looking guys. Real low-lifes." Morgan shudders. "They'd made themselves comfortable. There was a case of beer sitting on the hearth, and it looked like they'd been through about half of it.

"The tall blond guy—the one leaning against the wall. He was the one who answered. 'Not much of a lock,' he said. It was the first time I heard his weird voice. He sounded like someone was strangling him. It gave me the creeps.

"Winnie laughed. 'Meet my friends,' she said to me. Then she looked at the beer on the hearth. 'I need a real drink,' she announced.

"She walked through an archway hung with a beaded curtain, into the kitchen. I followed her. She tossed her purse on the kitchen table—she carried a big bag, kind of a tote, and I dropped my backpack right beside it. I couldn't believe she was going to let them stay. I thought we were going to be alone after all these months.

"'What are you doing?' I asked. She reached into the freezer and yanked out a bottle of vodka. 'Getting a drink' was her only reply. She pulled two glasses from the cupboard, sloshed in some vodka, held one out to me.

"I pushed it away.

"'I don't want it,' I told her, standing in front of her, blocking her path back into the living room. I was almost in tears. 'What about us? You and me? I thought...'

"'We will,' she said impatiently, brushing past me, 'later.'

"I couldn't stay there. I had to get out, do something to work off the adrenaline. But there was no back door, no discreet way out of that room. I pushed back through the archway, moving so fast the beads clacked as they fell back into place behind me, trying to ignore the men.

"I yanked open the door to the building's hallway and ran through it. I didn't slam it, didn't even close it. Hell, I hadn't even picked up my backpack. I could hear them behind me, hooting, hollering, 'Hey, baby, c'mon back.' Stuff like that."

"Where'd you go?"

"I just walked. For hours. Until my feet were sore. Until I was sure they'd be gone. It must have been three a.m. by the time I went back.

"The door was locked. And the music coming through it was even louder. I didn't have a key. So I knocked.

"Then I pounded.

"Finally, the little guy answered the door. He was naked. 'Hey,' he hollered. 'Reinforcements!'

"He yanked me inside.

"I couldn't believe what I found. There was Winnie on the rug in front of the hearth. Naked. On all fours. She was doing two of them—the one with dark curly hair..."

"Vassallo."

"And the big one. Or they were doing her. I've never understood the distinction." She erupted in a painful laugh that turned into a wretched sob. "The fourth guy—Billy—was still fully clothed, just watching, like I told you before."

Morgan is so upset that she doesn't seem to notice that Grady isn't shocked. He already knew that Winnie liked it rough. And he saw the story heading in this direction well before he had all the facts. Everything he had learned about Winnie said that her core was, if not rotten, certainly twisted. So one night at Goodtime Charlie's a few weeks after he got back from Ann Arbor, he primed the pump, got Davis to talk on the topic of the little blonde's character.

"Sometimes I fuckin' hate the crap I learn in this job," Davis confided over his fourth beer. "You remember Winnie, the one who died? Well, for starters, she was full of alcohol and ecstasy. Big deal, right? I mean, she was a college kid. Died on a weekend.

"But turns out that cute little girl was a sicko. She was into threesomes, foursomes, all kinds of weird shit. She especially liked rape scenarios. A gangbang was her idea of a fun Saturday night.

"So we get this bead on her, and then it's like we've hit the cone of silence. The scum she hung with don't talk to the police. They have 'privacy issues.' I don't envy the poor fucks who had to tell her mom and dad.

"Does it make it right that we don't know exactly what happened to her? No. And no cop likes to look like a schmuck, the guys in Michigan being no exceptions. But does it make it easier? I gotta admit."

Winnie's peculiar tastes might have made it easier for the cops to let go as the little blonde's death became a cold case, but the reality of her sexual behavior clearly still has the bite of fresh pain for Morgan. Her sobs accelerate, her shoulders shake. Each intake of breath is a gasp.

Grady wants the truth that erupts from this kind of emotional agony, but she's moving beyond coherence, edging into hysteria. He decides he has to do something to break the cycle. "Can I get you anything?" he says. "More water? A cup of tea?"

Morgan shakes her head, almost violently. "No. There's nothing you can do. Nobody can fix this."

He watches her force herself under control. She's still a mess, but he's brought her back to the present, to her story, to her predicament—and his. At last, she goes on with her story, putting herself back in that Ann Arbor apartment on that hot June night, picking up exactly where she left off.

"My mind was spinning. I was jealous. Hurt. I thought if she knew how I felt, it would make a difference.

"'Winnie,' I pleaded, 'stop, please stop. This is horrible. You have to stop.'

"Winnie paused. She took Vassallo's dick out of her mouth. Then she laughed. I couldn't believe it. I felt like she'd stabbed me. I was crying, almost hysterical.

"'How can you do this?' I sobbed. "'I love you.'

"She disengaged herself, stood up. Put her beautiful little body right in front of me. Taunted me.

"'Poor little baby,' she said. 'Thinks she owns me. Doesn't know that I fuck whoever I please. Thinks she's special. Thinks I l-u-u-u-ve her.'

"So I slapped her. Hard. Across the face.

"She put her hand to her cheek. She was shocked at first, I think. Then she slapped me back. 'Fuckin' cunt!' And she spit at me.

"The creeps were loving it. 'Cat fight,' one of them called out. They were whooping and hollering, egging us on.

"I socked her.

"'Good one,' one of them yelled.

"We were the same size, but I was stronger. Jogging, carting around all that luggage, I guess. And I was a lot more upset. She'd started out thinking it was funny. I was out of my mind with pain and fury.

"I hit her in the arms, the belly, the breasts. I hit every part of her I could reach, just as hard as I could. She was trying to fight me off, but she was too drunk. The big guy wanted to stop it, but Billy was enjoying it too much. 'Let 'em go,' he said.

"She pulled my hair. Grabbed me. I grabbed back. She pushed me. And I shoved her. With every bit of force I had, all the strength in my body."

Morgan's sobs break through again. When she can speak, she gasps out the words.

"She...she stumbled backward. Her foot hit an empty beer can. She lost her balance, fell. Landed hard. Hit her head on the edge of the hearth.

"'Shit!' I heard somebody say. 'Motherfucker!'

"I was sure she was knocked out, but before I could do anything, she sat up, rubbing her head.

"'Are you okay?' I asked. She was struggling to get to her feet, and I wanted to help her, but she waved me off.

"'Don't touch me,' she said.

"She used the hearth for balance and managed to stand. It took her a minute, and she didn't speak again until she was on her feet. Then she said, 'I think you should leave.'

"She meant me. That I should go. Her speech sounded slurred, but I knew she was drunk. 'I think you should...' And she went down, just folded like a rag doll.

"Her eyes were open. I waited for her to move. I was sure she'd get up again, ask why I was still here, scream at me to get lost. But she didn't. And she wasn't breathing."

48

"I thought I was going to throw up. Billy bent over her. He checked her pulse. He looked at her eyes, the back of her head. 'Dead,' he said.

"I picked up the phone, was going to call 9-1-1. But Billy grabbed my hand, pried the receiver out of my fingers, put it back in the cradle. How dumb was I? he asked. If I told the cops, I'd go to prison.

"'But it was an accident!' I insisted. I was fighting, he told me. They call that assault. Did I have a record? No? Then probably just manslaughter. Ten years. Maybe fifteen.

"I couldn't believe it. I'd never been in a fight before in my life. Never. And all I'd wanted to do was love her.

"I panicked. Didn't know what to do, didn't want to go to prison. I begged him to help me.

"Billy ignored me. He acted like he was getting ready to cut out. And I could tell that what Billy did the others would do.

"I tried to keep my head. 'You can't just go,' I said. 'You can't leave me here with her body.'

"'Just watch us,' Billy said. He nodded at Vassallo and the other two guys. They had pulled their clothes on, begun picking up the beer cans.

"'You don't dare,' I said. 'I can describe you. I'll say you did it. That it was a rape. It's my word against yours. And I don't have a record.'

"Billy just shrugged. He waved his boys toward the door. The Shrimp had his hand on the knob.

"I was desperate. So I said I'd make it worth their while.

"'How would you do that?' Billy sneered. I guess he was thinking I'd offer sex. But I was pretty sure he didn't care about that, at least not in any way I could imagine being involved with, and I didn't want any of them putting a finger on me.

"So I mentioned Mexico. Not much. But enough, I hoped. I even hinted that I knew where the key was. That it was hidden. That after they'd disposed of...Winnie, I'd take them to it.

"It seemed to work. They found rags and started wiping everything down. They knew how to get rid of a body, Billy said. No problem." Morgan gave a painful, almost hysterical laugh. "No problem."

"You dressed her." Grady makes it a statement rather than a question. It had to be his little imposter. Winnie had fallen and was clearly dead, irretrievably lost. But Morgan insisted on covering her nakedness. The building was empty. The main hall had a back door leading into an alley. So why dress a naked body? A woman's touch. A lover's concern.

Morgan nods. "Billy sneered at me. But he let me do it. He found a pair of rubber gloves in the kitchen and made me wear them while I pulled her clothes on. It was awful, wrestling with this...*thing* that used to be Winnie. And none of them would help.

"Then Billy took the rubber gloves from me and told me to get trash bags from the cupboard in the kitchen.

"And that's when I saw it in his eyes. As I went past him through the beaded curtain. He was a sick fuck. Clothed, like I said, while everybody else was naked. Getting his rocks off just watching.

"He had never intended to leave me in that apartment. He'd

been amusing himself, playing a game. Mexico hadn't been news to him. He was the one who was going to help Winnie sell the statuette.

"And he'd decided they didn't need me. That I was a liability. That two bodies wouldn't be much harder to get rid of than one.

"He might not have all the details about the town and the bank—I was pretty sure that Winnie would have told him just enough to get him on the hook. But he knew where the key was. She'd have enjoyed dangling it in front of him, just as she had with me. He wouldn't have any qualms about doing whatever it took to get the rest of the information.

"And once I gave it up, I was dead.

"It was almost funny. He was planning to get rid of me, but he still sent me on the errand into the kitchen. And that gave me a chance.

"My backpack and Winnie's purse were still sitting on the kitchen table. I grabbed my backpack. Then I realized that I didn't have any money, so I scooped up her purse.

"'Hurry up with those bags,' Billy called.

"'I'm getting them,' I said. 'They're under some stuff.'

"I used the kitchen chair to break the window. Then I was out and gone. It was dark, and it took them a moment to react. I was running, just running in the dark, not knowing where I was going or what to do. I couldn't go to the police. It was an accident. But Billy had convinced me that the law wouldn't see it that way.

"Winnie's car was parked a couple of blocks away. It took me a while to find it. I'd been in so much of a hurry to jump her bones that I hadn't paid much attention to where I was parking. But it started right up. And I took off."

Morgan's breathing is still fast and ragged, but Grady has the sense that she's pushing the emotion at this point, acting more than she feels, that he's lost the advantage of the shock and the flood of raw memories that followed. She's buttoned up again.

"From there, it's pretty much like I said. I didn't think about the fact that I had the key until I was deep into Illinois. And I didn't decide to go after the statuette myself until I was past St. Louis.

"By the time I reached Arizona, I didn't know how to feel. Free, like someone who's barely escaped disaster. Or grieving, like someone who's lost a lover.

"What Winnie did should have destroyed any illusions I had. But I kept remembering the good stuff, kept trying to resurrect that magical time in Traverse City.

"I felt raw, like someone had torn my skin off and even the air passing over me hurt, but almost reborn at the same time.

"I didn't have any real idea how much—or how little—Billy Oz and his boys knew until they found me in Tucson. I thought I was safe there.

"'You're the only one who has the whole plan,' Winnie'd said. 'I haven't told anyone else.'

"And I still believed her. So even if Billy and the others were looking for me, why in hell would they come to Tucson?"

Grady considers telling her.

"Let's go back for a minute," he says, buying time to decide. "Did you leave tracks on your way from Ann Arbor to Arizona? Send postcards, make phone calls? Anything like that?"

"No." Morgan seems genuinely perplexed. "And I paid cash everywhere I went." She pauses. "But, like I told you, I did use Winnie's ATM card once, in Ohio just across the Michigan line."

Grady just shakes his head. Decides to let her wonder.

"I never figured it out. But, on some level, I think I knew they'd find me—somewhere, at some point."

Grady remembers something she'd said—in her incarnation as "Clare," that night in his mother's kitchen, as she played with the ceramic kittens and his head. "I knew they'd find me," she said. "I just didn't think it would be so soon." Guilt, presumably. The often irrational conviction that one will be found out. And—on some level—an understandable lack of belief in Winnie's discretion. Morgan's subconscious was trying to prod her waking mind into acknowledging that it had, in fact, no way to determine how much of the plan Billy Oz knew.

Now, Morgan closes her eyes, leans her head against the back of the couch.

Grady has finally put the pieces together, but he has to admit they still make more than one picture.

Not about Winnie's death. Morgan's last tale, the one she has just finished telling after he confronted her with the photo, fits the physical evidence. The body was wiped before it was dumped at the airport. There were no fingerprints retrieved from the skin, no fibers from anything that didn't belong to Winnie or her apartment. But a few hairs and a lot of sperm remained, and those hairs and sperm matched The Shrimp, Taylor and Vassallo. Nothing from Billy. No surprise there.

But there were also two other hairs, dark ones that didn't match Vassallo. Hairs whose length said they might be from a woman. The official guess was another playmate, one who left before Winnie died.

Even the character of the bruises adds up. At least some of them were made by small hands, Andy told Grady. The folks up in Michigan were glad to assume it was The Shrimp, and Davis had no reason to dispute it.

But Grady kept his own counsel on the topic. By the time he heard this detail of the forensics from Davis over a beer, Luis had already done some work on the snapshot, and its story was starting to emerge.

So it's all come together, nice and neat. Up to the point that Winnie's head meets the edge of the hearth.

After that, things aren't so clear.

Grady believes that he now possesses the core, the essence, of the truth. But there's still the chance Morgan was more involved in the plot than she's let on.

What if Billy Oz and two of his boys went to dispose of the body and left Morgan and the remaining man—The Shrimp, say— behind to clean up?

What if she decided to go ahead on her own, gathered up the

backpack and safe deposit key, snuck out the kitchen window, took Winnie's car and headed to the Southwest?

As his beautiful piano player has said herself, when you're telling a really big lie, it helps to stick close to the truth.

"One more thing," Grady says. "That night at the Nelsons'. Who killed Vassallo?"

Her eyes stay shut. "Billy." Her voice is weary. "I told you."

Okay. Billy used the big knife. No disputing that. But he thinks again about the other wounds, the ones Davis told him nearly a year ago, when the cops were still puzzling over the murder of Vassallo at the Nelsons', when the case was cold but not quite dead. Something that haunted him then, something that's helping him now in his struggle—his determination—to stay icy cold at his core. He has a promise to keep.

Morgan didn't cut Vassallo's throat. Forensics established that early on. But what about the other wounds?

The injuries inflicted when Vassallo was dying were small, shallow stab wounds, made with something like a jackknife—or a paring knife. The "missing" one from the Nelsons' kitchen? Grady strongly suspects that the answer is yes, whether he can prove it or not. Vassallo was in agony, blood pouring from the open wound in his throat, and someone stabbed him, literally and repeatedly, in the back.

Grady believes Morgan when she says the fourth man, Taylor, wasn't there. For one thing, his gut says it's true. And Billy tended to use him as a lookout, maybe because he was good at it, maybe because he was built like a refrigerator, maybe because he'd seen too many movies and couldn't imagine a caper without a lookout. Whatever.

So somebody's behind Vassallo with Billy. Would have to be somebody small who could fit in up, under and between the knife-wielding Wizard and the struggling, mortally wounded Vassallo. The Shrimp was short for a man, but still he would have been crouching, bending. Not a physical impossibility, but close. Besides, he was busy guarding Morgan—and probably in shock that buddy A was slaughtering buddy B.

It had to be Morgan.

But why would she do it?

Revenge for Winnie's death? Vassallo was fucking Winnie right before she died. It was that sex act that turned Morgan's pain to rage and provoked the "cat fight."

Maybe that made Winnie's death Vassallo's fault, and if Morgan saw herself as innocent, perhaps, with her twisted moral upbringing, somebody else had to be guilty.

But the satisfaction of striking the blows against Vassallo would have been mostly symbolic. The damage was superficial.

He considered coercion, physical or emotional. Was she forced by Billy to wield the knife so that she'd be implicated? Did she take on the job knowing that Vassallo was dying anyway, hoping to convince Billy that he'd made a convert, that she was now on his side?

And there are other possibilities, including some so blackly evil that his mind wants to turn away.

How jealous was she?

Vassallo was the last man to have sexual contact with Winnie, to smash Morgan's illusions. Could she have agreed to give up the key and info for a price—his death?

She had no real power in the situation, but Billy might have been amused by the cold-blooded nature of the trade. Did she then double cross him by cutting out?

Grady's magician's trick—pulling out the photograph just when Morgan thought she was safe, just when she finished weaving what she believed was her last tale, shocked her into talking about her relationship with Winnie and Winnie's death.

But she had her catharsis, was drained but calm, by the time he asked her about Vassallo. Maybe she regained the emotional energy to get back in control, to lie. To make herself responsible for a tragic accident, but not the murder that followed.

What does he want the truth to be?

He opens his mouth to accuse her.

Then decides to make a statement.

Finally, all he does is ask.

"What was your involvement in his death?"

"Me?" she says. She sounds astonished. "Nothing. I don't hurt people."

She's finished. She stops, and he lets her. He's heard enough.

"There was another knife," he says. "A small one. Did you think I wouldn't find out about that? Billy was busy. And from what you've said, The Shrimp just stood there hardly able to believe what he was seeing. It was you."

"No!" she says. "No! I wouldn't, I didn't... It was the little guy. Billy forced him. I didn't want to tell you because I didn't want to think about it. It was too horrible..." She must be reading his face, because her words trail off.

They're both quiet for one minute, two, five. It's Morgan who finally breaks the silence. "Now what?"

Grady stands up, walks over to the window. It's full light by now. He's briefly stunned by the brilliance of a Toronto June morning.

He looks over his shoulder at the young woman collapsed on the couch. She's put a hand over her eyes. Like a little girl playing hide and seek. Grady thinks it's possible he's never seen anyone quite so tired.

His eyes go back to the world outside. It's big, complex. Like most people, he has spent the better part of his life trying to pretend it's simple, desperately trying to maintain some illusion of control.

He discovers what he's going to say next only as the words come out of his mouth. "I'm not a cop," he says. "I'm not even a P.I."

He hears her rise from the couch, come up behind him.

Then, she's standing beside him.

She smiles up at him gently. "Our thing," she says. Her voice is a murmur, reminiscent of the purr she uses when she hovers over a song. "Us. It wasn't just convenience. Or self-protection."

Grady wants to believe her, wishes he could.

She moves her hand to his arm, stands on her tiptoes. He draws her to him, holds Morgan/Clare/Winnie, so strange yet so familiar, in his arms. His lips touch hers. Her mouth is as soft, as sensuous, exciting, miraculous, as he remembers.

She finally breaks the embrace, takes his hand.

"C'mon," she says, moving toward the bed.

He lets her lead him. He is insanely aroused, blindly desiring. The bed is a golden invitation, a shining promise.

She leans over and turns out the lamp that is still glowing on the nightstand.

"Make love to me, Grady," she whispers.

Her hand caresses his chest. Her draws her into his arms again, kisses her deeply. Then he opens his eyes and looks into hers, gazes directly into those deep set, gleaming pieces of ebony.

"No," he says. "I don't think so." She looks at him, puzzling, despairing—he's not sure.

"She could have lived," he says.

He hears her gasp. He's still holding her, but now he's holding her up.

"The blow wasn't immediately fatal. If you'd gotten her to a hospital, she might have had a chance."

"You're lying." An accusation? Or a hope?

She breaks away and collapses onto the couch.

"Here. Read the ME's report." He reaches into his jacket and pulls out a sheaf of folded paper, part of the report he got from Luis, throws it at her.

She lets the pages fall to the floor, shakes her head violently. "No! No!"

"A good neurosurgeon, a little luck..."

"She'd have been a vegetable. She'd never have been Winnie again. It would have been worse than death. She'd never have wanted that."

Grady shrugs.

"How can you be so cruel?"

How can he. She's right. The odds of Winnie surviving her injury weren't good, and the odds of her surviving with her faculties intact were even lower. Almost infinitesimal, in fact. But...

"I was trapped. I couldn't... They wouldn't let me..." The words are right, but the hysteria seems forced.

Her voice is flat, her body calm.

"There was nothing else I could do."

She's just reminded him. Cruel is something Morgan deserves.

He reaches one last time into the inside right pocket of his leather jacket. His fingers grasp the roll of duct tape, move on—and momentarily stumble before they grasp the handle of the knife.

49

Grady lays his beat-up briefcase on Jill's kitchen table.

The house is silent. Charlie's on a business trip, and Sophie is sleeping.

Jill is thinner than ever, her shoulders skeleton covered by skin, her cheeks deep hollows.

She's offered him water, coffee, iced tea—but it's quick courtesy, done by rote. Grady can see her relief when he shakes his head. Every line of her body shows tension. She holds it in with crossed arms.

Time to get this over with, she must be thinking. Face it, confront her part in what was done in Toronto—she has to know she's responsible for it, that she was the force, he was only her weapon. These next few minutes will be bad, she must be telling herself, but what's done is done—and had to be done. Focus on what's next. Get to the important part, which is (she hopes) the healing of her daughter.

Grady opens the briefcase and lifts out the single white envelope. He undoes the clasp, pulls back the flap, then thinks better of it and puts the envelope on the table.

Jill stares at it. Grady places his right index finger on the envelope and slides it over to her.

She looks at him.

He nods.

She picks up the envelope, lifts up the flap, slides out the photograph—and gasps.

The photo flutters to the floor. Jill's eyes roll back in her head. Her legs sag, but Grady's there. He catches her and settles her on a kitchen chair.

"Head down," he says. "Between your knees."

Jill sits, limp, head between her knees.

Grady picks up the photo and slides it back into the envelope. He lays the envelope on the table.

After a long moment, Jill lifts her head. Silent tears track her cheeks.

"I had no idea," she says.

What can Grady say? Yes, you did? You knew? You asked for it? What did you think it would look like?

"That's horrible," she says.

Yes, it is.

Grady doesn't have to look at the photograph to agree with her. The image is burned into his brain.

Morgan, sprawled on her hotel bathroom floor. Big brown eyes open wide, but unfocused, seeing nothing. Arms pulled up over her head, wrists duct-taped to a leg of the old-fashioned bathtub. A red gash across her throat, a pool of red under her, around her, spreading across the white tile floor. The knife lying nearby.

Horrible.

He pictures Sophie dealing out her cards of death, adding Morgan's picture to the ghastly lineup. All he can do is believe Jill and hope she is right when she insists that this is the only thing that can bring Sophie peace. No, call it closure. There can be no peace from this much blood.

"Will it do?" he says.

Jill looks at him, shakes her head as if she doesn't understand his literal words, let alone comprehend their meaning.

"Will it do?" he repeats.

"I...uh...I...uh..."

"Will it help Sophie?"

"I...uh...I don't know."

Grady's voice is rising. He's somewhere between anger and pain. "Jesus Christ, Jill! That's why we did it! To help Sophie!"

Jill nods.

Now he's shouting, his voice a roar. "Well, will it help her?"

Jill comes to life. "Sssh! You'll wake her."

Grady manages to control the volume of his voice but not the tone. He is yelling in a wild, hoarse whisper. "Goddamn it, Jill, will this do the job?"

Jill just looks at him, straight on, right in the eye. He doesn't know if she's seeing a savior or a monster. Or maybe she's just realized for the first time that almost everyone is some of each. It's only the proportions that vary.

"Yes," she says, her voice shaky but her look determined, almost cold. "I think it will."

He lets himself out, leaving the photo and its white envelope on Jill's spotless table in Jill's shiny, granite-clad kitchen.

He guns the engine and even manages to lay a little rubber as he backs out of her driveway. But then he has to slow way the fuck down and crawl over the speed bumps between Jill's place and the Pergama gate.

Shit. Jill was perfectly willing to use him, to let his affection for her... No, call it what it is: love. He knows it, and she knows it, too, even though they have this fucked-up unspoken agreement never to talk about it.

She had no problem with letting his love for her turn him into a killer. She set him the task, she funded the hunt, she waited for him to bring home the goddamn bloody trophy. And when he did, she got all floppy. As if murder is ever clean, as if it isn't always an ugly, dirty thing.

The photo's delivered, his job's done. Move on.

He's through the gate, ignoring the wave from the guy on duty, almost to the turn for the main road when he swings a u-ey.

Cursing himself as a wimp, a coward and the most pussy-whipped creature to ever call himself a man, he's back through the gate and moving up the road, hitting the speed bumps at 30, letting the undercarriage of his wreck of a car slam into the cement at each one, almost hoping that he'll lose the oil pan or demolish some vital part that will stop him, keep him from doing what he can't seem to keep from doing any other way.

Then he's pounding on Jill's door, thinking even now, don't wake Sophie. Bell will wake her. Pounding won't.

He hears footsteps, and Jill's there, undoing locks. Not welcoming him, but letting him in.

She looks like crap. He's only been gone about five minutes. How could someone disintegrate that fast?

She doesn't say a word, just turns and walks down the hall, letting him follow, he guesses, if he wants to. It's as if she's conceding him the right to be there but doesn't give a fuck what he does.

They're in the kitchen, and he can see she's poured herself a drink, about half a tumbler of oblivion.

He caps the bottle and puts his hand over the glass, keeping it from her. "Jill," he says, "I didn't do it."

She doesn't even seem to hear him. She turns away, stands looking out the window at the back yard, the pool, the roof of the Nelson's house just visible over the tops of the trees. "I thought it would be worth it," she says. "For Sophie. But oh my God, Jack. Oh my God."

He walks up behind her. He's talking to her back, which doesn't seem right, or fair, but apparently it's the way things have to be. She should have to live with this. But he can't stop himself.

It's about what he did in Toronto. He could have gotten hold of a gun, even with Canada's stricter laws, but didn't see the reason. A knife was simpler, and there was symmetry in it.

It was easy to find what he needed. A Yellow Pages, a cab to a shopping district, then a walk to three stores. The one thing he couldn't buy retail, he'd brought along. It didn't take much space.

He was surprised that Morgan's seduction attempt went on as long as it did. He'd slipped a little something in her last cup of tea, a sizable dose of the drug he'd carried with him. But she was coherent even at the very end when he laid the hard truth on her.

He waited long enough to make sure she was out, then carried her into the bathroom. He arranged her unconscious body on the floor, tore off a couple of strips of duct tape, taped each wrist separately, and bound her wrists to the leg of the tub.

He picked up the knife he'd bought at a kitchen store, looked at it, the blade, her neck.

The next step was the blood. The bags were courtesy of one of Toronto's leading theatrical supply houses. As was the gash that Grady pasted across her exposed throat.

He "bloodied" the knife, then wiped the handle. Habit, maybe. Never any point having your fingerprints on something that might be mistaken for a weapon.

He took out the digital camera and checked the settings. Then, he pulled her eyelids open. Most people don't realize that it takes more muscle control to close your eyes than to keep them open. Grady knew that Morgan wasn't out so far that her eyes would stay open indefinitely, but her temporary coma was deep enough so that they would stay open long enough for him to get a shot.

He pressed the shutter, previewed the photo, adjusted her a bit, and pressed the shutter a second time. Had to pull her eyelids open again. The third shot was good.

He removed the duct tape from the bathtub leg and left her to sleep it off.

"Don't let anyone ever tell you that photos don't lie," he says to Jill's back. "They lie just fine."

She can search the Internet. She won't find any killing with the right description in the right city at the right time. And she won't find it because it isn't there.

Jill doesn't move. She doesn't cry, or storm at him, or tell him she's thankful. She just stands there. And for the second time that afternoon, he lets himself out.

50

Did he ever intend to kill Morgan? He did buy the knife, which wasn't absolutely necessary. A photo of a body needn't include the means of death to be convincing.

Maybe he was just keeping his options open.

Funny thing, though. Choosing to fake her death ended her legal jeopardy as effectively as actually killing her would have.

No choice there. Arresting her—or, rather, having her arrested—would alert Sophie that Morgan is alive. Almost unavoidably. Can't have that.

But what if he could find a way to turn her in to the police without jeopardizing Sophie's sanity?

Reality is that a conviction would be almost impossible. Even after all Luis's work, the meaning of the snapshot found in the duffel is still clear only to Grady—and Morgan. Understanding the story it tells requires interpretation and imagination. There's no chain of evidence. A prosecutor would be leery of depending on it. A defense attorney would crow in delight.

Morgan's involvement in the kidnapping? Nothing she told him would be admissible in court. She could credibly claim she was a captive herself and was forced into her role. And she did try to help

371

Sophie escape. That would support her.

And what if the system did succeed in taking away her freedom—which is pretty much all she has to lose. Is she going to commit some other crime?

Outside of smoking the occasional joint, probably not.

Has she suffered from her actions? Yes.

Has she suffered enough? Who knows.

Bottom line, he can't convince himself that imprisoning Morgan—whatever crimes she's committed—would accomplish a damn thing.

Is he rationalizing? Hell if he knows.

If he'd found the paring knife in the cactus between the Nelson's and Jill's house the first time he searched, when the crime was only a week old, the end might have been different. The rains hadn't started. There would have been fingerprints, blood...

Even if he'd found the knife months later, he might not feel this way. He looked several times after that first search, finally gave up only a few weeks before the Toronto trip.

Not that the knife would have meant much at that point as far as the law is concerned. Months of sun and a year's rainy seasons (one summer, one winter) would have destroyed anything that was forensically valuable. Oh, they could still have matched the size and length of its blade to the wounds. Depending upon how good the autopsy records are and whether anybody cared.

But Grady would have known. He would have known the knife wasn't lost in the garbage. That Billy Oz and his boys didn't use it or another small blade and take it with them. He would have known that Morgan dropped it there. And he might have done something more than just scare the hell out of her.

But he didn't find it. Maybe he did a crappy job of searching, with no tools, no help, too much prickly vegetation. Or maybe—and this is what he's betting his sense of justice on—the knife just wasn't there.

He thinks about judgment: Davis's judgment of the dead Winnie and what some might call her lifestyle, his own of Jimmy Q, and now of Jill. And himself, don't forget himself.

Cops are always making judgments. But, like he said to Morgan, he isn't a cop anymore. And there's something in most religions—maybe even all—about final judgment being reserved for forces greater than human beings, forces all-seeing, all-knowing, and, presumably, more wise, more just. Even more merciful. He remembers church from his youth, the last moments of the service, when the words "Go with God" would rain down on the bowed heads of the congregation in both forgiveness and inoculation. And, sinners all, they would leave the sanctuary for another week-long try at the world.

Morgan hasn't done well. No one can say she has. But under circumstances like Gina's—hell, worse than Gina's from what he knows—she's made something of a life. Not all straight, but not all crooked either.

By the time he reaches the turn off Sunrise, dust is skittering along the pavement, trees are whipping. There've been hints of an early monsoon this year. The sky is black to the southeast, clear to the west. Lightning crackles. He hears the first booms of thunder.

Grady's glad his flight landed hours ago, well before dark, has always hated lurching down into Tucson through shuddering air. It calls up his fears, every one of his demons. He remembers all the times on all the flights, clutching the arm rests as if his grip alone were keeping the plane aloft, expecting at any moment to plummet to earth. He'd think about his goodbyes, shakily compose farewell messages in his head, hoping, almost trusting, that some unseen force would beam them to their destinations.

At bottom, though, he's always known that this fear of imminent death by airplane—the reason for his goodbyes—is irrational. Morgan's terror was not. Whatever else happened, he has no doubt that she sat naked, totally vulnerable, on that sofa at the Nelsons', at the mercy of a sociopath who would not hesitate to kill. And she was alone in the universe.

373

He isn't. Under similar circumstances, he would need to say a number of mental and spiritual farewells. To Bear. His mother, Jill, Sophie. Davis to a certain extent. Even Gina.

His relationships aren't perfect. They're messy, not all that close. But each of these people is important to him. And that counts. This is a richness he has never before considered.

The first drops of monsoon rain hit the windshield. It looks like a good-sized storm. The trees, the brush, the cactus will drink it in. The morning's landscape will be visibly greener, brighter with the beginnings of bloom. The shrunken leaves of the prickly pear will fatten, become plump with moisture. The desert will throw aside its dry yellow veil and reveal its astonishing variety of life, its true beauty.

The rain pours down. It bubbles in the gutters and forms sudden, rapidly flowing rivers across intersections. Lightning rattles the sky, sends white-hot branching bolts from cloud to cloud, cloud to ground.

He punches a button on the dashboard. Ella's clear tones surround him. "Doobie doo," she sings. "Doobie doo. Doobie waa, waa, waa..."

The pavement glistens. He travels up a long hill. Black sheets of water stream down at him from the road ahead.

He turns the windshield wipers to high, punches a cigarette out of the pack sitting on the seat next to him and lights up.

51

Things are better. Sophie seeks her "cards" less and less, once or twice a day instead of nearly every waking moment. She's starting to sleep without drugs. A tutor comes to the house three times a week, and Jill can imagine that someday in the not too distant future Sophie will go back to school. She even has a little time to herself. Each Friday afternoon, an aide (a carefully screened aide, one who has made the substantial effort to gain Sophie's trust) comes to the house. And Jill drives away, shops, runs errands, does the kind of ordinary things that she hopes will let her begin to feel like a human being.

When she thinks about the price of Sophie's recovery, which she works hard not to do, she acknowledges to herself that it could have been steep. Her bargain with the universe was, after all, Morgan's life for Sophie's. A mother is a fierce creature. The world is nothing when weighed against her child. But she's wildly grateful that Jack found another way. He didn't just save Sophie; he saved Jill as well. And someday when she's gotten over her fury at his deception, she'll manage to tell him so. In the meantime, like Sophie, she is beginning to heal.

One of those respite Fridays, she's back from her errands but still working hard to enjoy the illusion of normality. She's putting away groceries while trying to hear NPR over the sound of the landscape maintenance going on outside. The noise is longer and louder than usual because their part-time gardener, Tom, is putting in a winter lawn. Lawns die in Tucson in the fall, and from November to April many neighborhoods look distinctly odd with their yellow yards and green palm trees. The Whitehursts try to be responsible about water use, have mostly cactus and other desert plants, but enjoy a small patch of grass. Charlie says he needs it for his eastern soul. So Tom is planting annual rye.

Jill has all but given up making out what the commentator is saying when the din stops, the radio blares into the sudden quiet, and the doorbell rings.

Tom stands there, covered with the dusty work of the yard. "I can't finish the dethatching today, Ms. Whitehurst. You know that place where we're taking out the century plant and extending the grass? I hit something. I'll have to get a new blade." He holds out the remains of a small knife, probably a paring knife, at one time of good quality, now bent and broken. "Hope this wasn't yours."

Jill looks at it, shakes her head. "Probably the first owner. Sorry about your blade."

"Risks of the job," he shrugs.

The least she can do, she thinks, is dispose of the thing that did the damage. She takes the broken knife from him. It's Messermeister, she notices, a high-end brand—but no good to anyone now. She carries the knife inside, folds it into an empty grocery bag so no one will get cut, and dumps the paper bag in the trash.

#

Forever after...

When Billy handed Morgan the knife—the other knife he'd had the Shrimp guy fetch, the little one with the pointed blade—something broke in her.

Her consciousness was entirely focused on wanting these men

never to have existed, wanting Vassallo not to exist. It was all their fault. They had robbed her of so much.

As Billy held Vassallo, she was striking the mortally wounded man, climbing his back to reach his vulnerable areas, striking him over and over, riding him down as he collapsed.

But even as he hit the floor, she turned her adrenaline to the service of self-preservation. Scooping up the key. Running, slick with blood, away and out, into the night. Proving she was a survivor and, perhaps, not so different from Winnie as she'd thought.

When you lose your core, grow up without an emotional home, maybe you're more vulnerable to moral slippage. She knew Winnie had used her, had known since that horrible night in Ann Arbor when Winnie told her about Miguel, Mexico, the statuette. And it was even more complicated than she told Grady.

That night at the Greek restaurant, Winnie told Morgan all about Billy Oz. She said she regretted involving Billy, had decided that she didn't need him, that she was clever enough to find an outlet for the merchandise herself. So she had figured out a switch, a neat little double-cross, to leave "The Wizard" where he belonged, way out in Oz.

Winnie would go to her aunt's in Tucson as expected. Morgan, dyed and clipped to look like her lover, would head straight to Mexico.

Winnie had even bought the blue contact lenses, had them in her purse. She waved them at Morgan over the uneaten Greek food and the ouzo.

By the time Billy and his boys arrived in Tucson, Morgan would have retrieved the statuette and be hiding out back in the good old U.S.A. Then Winnie would travel to Mexico as planned. She'd even let Billy talk her into taking one of the boys with her. Vassallo, if she could manage it. He was the least disgusting.

The man would have his own instructions from Billy. That was a given. Winnie would let Vassallo convince her that he should escort her into the bank. Together, they'd open the safe deposit box.

Together, they'd find it empty. She'd convince him the whole thing had been a con, that she'd had been a victim. He'd be pissed, but she'd commiserate with him, do what she had to, keep him from contacting Billy, and get him so drunk he'd be totally out of it, maybe even land in a Mexican jail.

Then she'd meet up with Morgan, and the two of them would be off to their new life with the whole pot. No splitting the proceeds.

Morgan wasn't a thief, didn't think of herself as a dishonest person. But she loved Winnie, and that shook her whole idea of who and what she was. If she didn't even know her own sexual orientation, maybe there were other things about herself she didn't know.

So she didn't say yes. She didn't say no.

But when she was confronted with the reality of Winnie's careless sexuality that was so cruel in its thoughtlessness... When she couldn't avoid realizing the implication of Winnie's games—that maybe Morgan herself was just another game... After her pain and fury resulted in her lover's accidental death... Well...

While she was driving Winnie's wreck of a car to Arizona, once the shock started to wear off, she couldn't help taking it to the next step, wondering what would have happened after she delivered the statuette to Winnie. Would she have died a death that wasn't an accident? Or simply been abandoned? Left broken and empty, unable to turn to anyone—especially the police.

Why not, she thought, do what she could to redeem the situation?

To her surprise she found she was capable of taking on a variety of personalities. It wasn't that different from putting over a song lyric. She'd seen all those black and white movies in all those hotel rooms over the years. And she modeled herself on the heroines (if you could call them that). Like them, she was a woman who wanted a different life, a life that required money. A woman quick to use her body to prevail over men. A woman capable of taking physical and emotional risks to get what she wanted.

She didn't let herself think about what happened in the last reel. That was old Hollywood, old morality. Not life.

But then she finally got to Mexico. And the safety deposit box was empty. Winnie's fiction was reality. Like a bad joke. And Morgan's illusions about her new hard-boiled self collapsed.

So she went on the road again, playing piano, smiling, sipping for hours on a watered-down drink while she sang songs written by people who died years before she was born.

She's back where she started. But sometimes she has a suspicion that no matter how many weeks, months or years she lives the life she led before, she'll never be doing more than going through the motions.

And in Toronto, when she reached out for Jack Grady... When she reached out in spite of the fact that he forced her to relive things she had worked so hard to forget... When she reached out at least as much from genuine feeling as from desperation...

Even that was too late.

She has no idea why he did to her what he did. She woke up stiff and foggy on the bathroom floor, rolled to her knees, clutched at the toilet to pull herself up—and saw the knife and the ghastly red pool she'd been lying in.

She became an animal, screaming, grabbing the sink, spotting her bloody neck in the mirror—her hands flying to the gash in her throat, attempting to hold in her life. She collapsed, almost fainting, thrashing around on the cold tile floor—until she realized it was all pretend.

Revenge of some sort, she supposes. Maybe for his ex-wife, or the little girl. Or maybe because she fucked him and left him once too often.

She knows it could have been real. The knife was no illusion. He must have left it lying next to her as a message. Watch yourself.

Does she dwell on any of it? No.

She didn't mean to kill Winnie. And she didn't kill Vassallo. Not really. He was dead standing there on his feet, even if he was still breathing. All she did was distract Billy, turn his blood lust away from her. Maybe let off a little steam.

But sometimes she has a suspicion. That if she has a soul, it is stained. And if she sold it, she received nothing in return.

And when she's dreaming, it comes back. Vassallo and Winnie. Hand in hand, shoulder to shoulder, naked flank to naked flank. Dented and bloody. Tracking her down in Toronto, New York, Atlanta, St. Louis...

She hears a moan, and it is hers, and she wakes alone to the darkness of the hotel room.

———

Excerpt – Next Jack Grady Novel: *Boiling Point*

—Available Now –

1

If he kicks the chair, he might get it dirty. But the fabric is dark, so prob'ly nothing will show. And his feet set a good back beat, though he can't hear it over his iPod.

He wishes his mother would let him play drums. Piano lessons are boring.

He taps the shiny surface of the end table with his fingers. Still not loud enough. He digs two pencils out of his backpack—gets a rhythm going on the table top, playing along with the song in his ears.

It's getting dark so he turns on the table lamp. December days, his mom would say, getting shorter and shorter as we move toward Christmas. Only a week from tomorrow!

Rat-tat-tat-thum-thum-thum, brrrrrrrr... Shsss! His mouth supplies the cymbal sound.

He hears the front door open at the other end of the house, quick footsteps coming down the hall, and then his mother stands there, jingling her keys.

"C'mon," she says. "We're late."

He grabs the backpack, catches up with her when they're already outside on the sidewalk. "So, how'd it go?" she asks. "It didn't," he says.

"Joshua," she says, "don't be clever. How was your lesson?"

"There wasn't one," he tells her. "I just sat there. She never came out and got me."

"You're kidding."

"No."

He slides into the back seat next to his little sister and buckles in. His mom hits the gas, pulls away from the curb. "Jenny's whiny," she says. "Get those things out of your ears and play with her." He has to, so he does. But when he puts the iPod in his backpack, he notices his math book is missing. He took it out to get at the pencils.

"Mom," he says, and tells her about the forgotten book. They'll have to go back.

Nobody answers the bell, but he's used to lesson rules: finding the door unlocked and just going in. And there's his book on the floor next to the big chair.

He's on his way out when he hears a moan. He stands there for a moment, listening. Another moan.

He walks over to the double doors leading to the music room. They're the glass kind, with lots of little sections and curtains on the inside. He can tell there's still a light on in the room like there was all the time he waited, but he can't see in.

He tries to turn the knob. The doors are locked.

His mom's annoyed. First, she says, there's no lesson. I drive you all the way over here for nothing. And now you tell me Miss Nancy's locked herself in her music room and she's sick. It's probably a TV, or a radio.

But Josh knows there's no way Miss Nancy would ever allow a TV or a radio in her music room. He also knows not to say this to his mother.

Watch your sister, she says. And she disappears into the house. He waits with Jenny in the car. She's fidgety, so he sings teensy, weensy spider. It doesn't help.

He unbuckles Jenny, helps her out of her car seat and leads her up the walk.

The front door's open. He walks Jenny down the hall to where it widens into the waiting area at the back of the house. His mom is standing there outside the music room holding her cell phone. "I hear something too," she says to him. "And you're right, the doors are locked. I'm calling 9-1-1."

Josh is scared, but he doesn't want to be a baby. He hangs onto Jenny, but she wants her mommy. She tries to pull away. He grabs at her, she falls back against him—and he stumbles. He lands hard against one of the double doors, and his elbow crashes into the glass.

His elbow's through the glass, and there's a piece of glass sticking out of his arm and jagged glass still in the frame, and his elbow's pushed the curtain aside.

"Don't move!" his mom says. She bends down to help him. He's looking at his elbow, but he can see into the room. And there's so much blood. Way too much for his elbow.

His mom carefully pulls some of the glass out of the frame, and the curtain moves a little more.

He sees two men, kind of crumpled against the wall. There's blood everywhere. Miss Nancy's right eye is a black and purple hole, and her long brown hair streams red.

One of the men groans.

His mom screams.

Friday

2

Ally's powerless, trapped in a damn middle seat, her long legs crammed against the row in front of her, wondering if there's any hope she'll get there in time.

If Paul dies or, even worse, if there's one of those ghastly decisions to be made and Marian has to pull the plug…

Ally has to be with her sister.

She tells herself that if Paul lives, it won't matter how long her plane keeps circling LAX. If she misses her connection to Tucson, she can take a later flight.

She wills the fog to break, the clouds to clear.

The intercom squawks. They're landing.

It's after noon by the time her plane pulls up to the gate in Tucson. Ally rolls her carryon down the long hall, ignoring the newspaper racks, avoiding what are sure to be screaming headlines in the local press.

But she has to stop at the ladies room, which is next to the bar. And when she comes out, she can't help overhearing the bulletin: "A University of Arizona professor and Oscar-winning composer of the hit song 'All Night Heartbreak,' is the primary suspect in yesterday's bloody killing near the U of A campus. News at 5:00."

She already knows what News at 5:00 will say. When Marian called the night before, the outlines of the horror were still sketchy. Paul had been shot in a home in the Armory Park area. There were two other victims: a young woman—a graduate student in Paul's department—who was dead, and a young man, unidentified, who was in surgery. Paul's condition was critical.

By the time Ally spoke with Marian as she waited for her connecting flight to Tucson, the other survivor had a name and a story. He'd come through surgery and had intermittent periods of consciousness. He said the shooter was Paul.

#

They're keeping watch, enduring—just as they have endured for hours. Ally has her arm around Marian's shoulders, has the illusion, the hope, that she's holding her sister together. Suddenly, the regular beeps flitting across the computer screen become a blat.

Paul's heart has stopped. People in scrubs flood into the space. A nurse moves Ally and Marian out of the room. But they know what's happening. They've watched too much TV.

They wait just outside the big doors leading to the ICU. Marian can't stay still. Her feet are planted, legs stiff, but her hands clench and unclench. Ally knows Marian is busy, bargaining with the universe for Paul's life.

A nurse appears. "Dr. Sanchez wants to speak with you." She leads them back into the ICU.

"Did he…?" Marian's voice is almost a whisper, as if she doesn't want to hear her own words.

They can see the room ahead. The stone-faced policeman still sits outside. "Please," Marian says, "tell me…"

"The doctor…" the woman begins, but then gets a look at Ally's face. "They got him back," she says. Marian nearly collapses with relief.

But within minutes, one of the doctors brings a woman to talk to them. Some sort of social worker, according to her name tag. She wears civilian clothes—cheerful colors, peach slacks and a pale yellow blouse. The doctor asks them if they want extraordinary measures taken if this should happen again. This? But they know. If Paul's heart stops. The doctor reminds them that his blood is no longer clotting. That his brain has been deprived of oxygen.

Ally reaches for Marian's hand, but her sister's whole body is clenched. She is a fist of pain and silence.

The woman in the Easter egg colors says how sorry she is, then presents the papers, neatly ordered on a clipboard. She offers a pen. Ally's arm is once more around Marian's shoulders, and she keeps it there while Marian signs the order: DNR.

But when the alarm rings again, Marian runs screaming to the nurses' station, begging them to help, do something, don't let him die. The team tries for 22 minutes by Ally's watch. Paul is pronounced dead at 5:08 p.m., almost exactly 24 hours after he was found. It's the delay that's made the difference, they're told, that crucial four to five hours between the moment the bullet pierced Paul's skull and the time help arrived.

Ally knows what everyone is thinking. That they—Marian, his children, his parents (if he still had any)—have been spared. They will not have to undergo the ordeal of a trial, the possibility of a death sentence, the years of agony while he sits on death row, the crises of hope and despair as lawyers appeal, and, finally, the execution. Marian, in particular, is lucky. What a joke.

What a horribly sick, incredibly painful joke.

"The kids," Marian murmurs, maybe to herself, maybe to Ally, maybe to God, "I have to tell the kids."

Saturday

3

Anyone can qualify to rent a piano, the saleswoman had said. But now she shakes her head.

"I'm sorry, Mr. Grady. Your credit score is much too low." She looks shocked, as if she's just found out he's an ax murderer.

He could protest, remind her that he has a truck, after all, purchased on credit. And that it hasn't been repossessed. But the "so far" would hang unsaid in the air between them. Truth is, he's come close to losing the truck. Twice. Both times his mom's chronic illness became crisis, and the cost of her meds skyrocketed. But the computer doesn't care about excuses.

The woman clearly knows she has a deal if she can just make the numbers work. She continues to play with her computer keys. "Hmmm," she says. "There is a Mr. Bear at your address. With acceptable credit. We could rent the piano in his name, if Mr. Bear would be amenable."

Mr. Bear would be amenable, Grady knows. The woman is assuming Mr. Bear is a roommate, or maybe a domestic partner. Grady knows that Mr. Bear, Mr. P. (for Papa) Bear, is his aging German Shepherd. When Grady took his current job working for a lot of rich people with too much time and the energy to bring up endless "issues," he put his home phone in Bear's name. Just one line, so a small bill, one he tends to pay on time. As a result, unlike Jack Grady, ex-cop, ex-husband, ex-a lot of other things, Bear is a solid citizen. A desirable debtor.

The woman taps a few more computer keys. "We can deliver on Monday," she says, tempting him further. "If he will just co-sign."

She holds out the paperwork, and Grady takes it. He can't devote any more time to this right now, anyway. Even though it's Saturday, he needs to go to work, such as work is.

Twenty minutes later, the guard at the entrance to Sungate lifts the wooden traffic control arm, and Grady winds his way, literally, up Sungate Drive. Sungate is nestled deep in the Catalina Foothills, north of the city proper. Old Tucson money, what there is of it, tends to cluster in the central Sam Hughes section near the university and in this, the oldest of the foothills subdivisions. Sungate has a mature golf course, an honest-to-god country club perched on a mini-peak overlooking the city lights, and a lot of quiet cachet.

Many of Sungate's homes are low, sprawling territorials, with multiple arches shading porticoes that front circular drives. A few heavily renovated homes are scattered here and there. To Grady they look like the false fronts of a movie set. And then there's the occasional new build, where an out-of-towner or speculating contractor has torn down an existing home and constructed a 5,000, 6,000, even 10,000 square-foot palace overlooking the fairways.

He makes the right onto Camino del Occidente, spots the address… What the?? He double checks it. Okay, they're renting. But there have to be better rentals than this. The guy won an Oscar. Where the hell is the money?

He's looking at one of the oldest, smallest homes in Sungate, a place that hasn't kept up with its neighbors for decades. The house has a flat roof, small aluminum-framed windows and a skimpy two-car garage. Its stucco is stained with dirt driven down from the roof by years of summer rains. The plantings look like plain old cactus plunked down in the caliche rather than "desert landscaping." Everything is faded, dusty.

For the moment, the street is empty. Grady parks in the driveway. As he pulls the keys out of the ignition, his eye falls upon the piano rental paperwork still sitting on the passenger seat. Odds are that a good percentage of houses in this community have an instrument many times better and more valuable than anything accessible to him—or P. Bear. And this house certainly does.

The doorbell echoes. He waits. The place is ready for Christmas. A wreath of faux pine boughs with a few gold cones and a red bow hangs on the door. Paper cut-outs of Santa Claus and striped candy canes decorate the sidelights. He can hear sounds from the backyard, children's voices. He pushes the button again. Still no response.

It's unseasonably warm, in the low 80s, and he's sweating. He's just about to walk around the side of the house and stick his head over the wall to get somebody's attention when he hears footsteps approaching on a tile floor. A disembodied female voice squawks from a speaker to the left of the door.

"Yes?" The voice sounds tired, even defeated. "Mr. Grady?"

The woman who opens the door and motions him in is in her mid-to-late thirties, African-American with a medium-dark complexion, of average height, slightly plump. She's wearing a short robe thrown on over a one-piece swimsuit of conservative cut and flip-flops. Her hair is pulled into a knot at the nape of her neck. Her sunglasses are perched on top of her head. Her eyes are red and swollen.

"We were by the pool," she explains, as if apologizing. "I'm Marian Ross." She waits, maybe expecting a reaction. "You don't know who I am," she says.

She's wrong. He was tied up for a day, responding to a call for help from his niece that seemed, for once, to have something authentic about it. Finding her a program. Again. Checking her into rehab. Again.

But since he surfaced, he couldn't have missed the story if he'd tried. It's all over the local media, hasn't even started to cool down. He's simply wearing his neutral, non-judgmental face. She has mistaken it for ignorance.

"Mrs. Ross," he says. "I'm so sorry."

She nods in response. He sees the tears start, registers the slight shake of her head as she regains control.

The entryway is as shabby as the outside. The tile is chipped and needs re-grouting. Wallpaper that imitates woven fabric is starting to curl at the edges. But he spots a grand piano in the living room to the right and a second piano, a console, in the den to the left.

"We'll sit back here." He follows her down a hall that runs the short distance from the front to the back of the house and opens into the kitchen. The low ceiling, avocado vinyl flooring and faux wood paneling in the eat-in area scream '70s.

A sliding door faces the backyard. Through the slices of view allowed by the vertical blinds, Grady can see two lounge chairs, their backs to the house, facing the sunny water of a pool. A straw hat pokes up over the top of one. Somebody's watching the kids.

They sit at a glass table that is outdoorsy in an ornate, wrought-iron sort of way, incongruous in the gloomy room. Grady wants a cigarette, but he knows these people won't be smokers. He glances around anyway. Nope. No ashtrays. Every home used to have at least a dozen. Are they all at the bottom of landfills?

Framed family photos decorate the walls. Dad, mom, a young son, an even younger daughter, whose wide smile shows two missing teeth. Paul Ross was a light-skinned black man with delicate, almost feminine features. The children appear to take after their father.

"I called the sheriff," the woman is saying. "But they told me they can't do anything. Not unless the reporters intrude in a way that's illegal or do some damage." She looks at Grady in disbelief. "It's been awful. Trucks with cameras pointed at the house. Those ghastly people ready to shove their microphones at anything that moves." One of the children has left an action figure on the table. Marian Ross's hands find it and bend it into an inhuman shape.

"I should have sent the children away," she says in a small voice.

"There's no one out in front right now," Grady comments.

The woman looks up at him, then suddenly seems to realize she's been torturing a toy. She pushes it aside and gives a small, rueful laugh. "Funny, isn't it? I finally crack and call the police—I've never done that before in my whole life. The police tell me I need to talk to you. And by the time the gate guard pages you and you get up here, two hours later, they're gone. Or hiding."

Grady doesn't attempt to justify the delay. He's learned long ago that he can never meet the expectations of his constituency. There is perfect, which is impossible. And there is falling short, becoming fodder for the conversations about the lack of good help and how everyone takes advantage. Even his rescue of a kidnapping victim not so long ago wasn't good for more than a brief pass.

"Have you talked to the person who's telling the guards to let them in?"

"Sherry Robertson."

"Yes."

"I called her. Well, not at first. At first, I didn't realize that I could do anything, that they shouldn't be here. I'm not used to a gated community. But then I phoned the front gate, and the man on duty told me what was going on." She takes a deep, shuddering breath.

"Sherry Robertson said she has the right. That she can let in anyone she wants. And if they end up somewhere other than her driveway, she can't control that. And then she just hung up on me."

The patio door slides open, and the wearer of the straw hat appears. "Can you watch them for a second, Mar?" she says. She holds up a large plastic glass. "I need more liquid."

Marian Ross moves over to stand at the open patio door, draws back the vertical blinds.

Grady can see a dusty back yard, with a patch of dried-up grass, a pool that needs both acid-washing and new decking. A curving slide. A few ratty palms. And the two children, a girl and a boy, perhaps six and eight years old.

The woman who has entered is late 30s, maybe early 40s, with a complexion that's about the same tone as Marian Ross's but somehow richer, healthier. Tall. Slender without being fragile or skinny, with a pair of shoulders that hint at a talent for sports, maybe swimming. She's wearing the straw hat that poked up over the top of the lawn chair, flip flops, a flowered bikini top and something Grady hasn't seen for years—genuine cut-off jean shorts. Her legs are terrific.

Grady finds himself sucking in his gut. Recently, a woman who happened to be occupying the next bar stool and was well into her liquor told him he looked like Harrison Ford. He felt pretty good for a moment. But then he thought, Harrison Ford is, what, 60? Even older? And I'm only 49?

Marian introduces the woman with the legs. "This is my sister, Allison. Jack Grady." The woman looks blank. "The security director."

Now, the sister gives him a look somewhere between a glare and a sneer. "Oh. You finally showed. So, Mr. Grady, what can we do?"

"About the press? Not a lot." There's a shout from the back yard, and Marian excuses herself to be with the kids. Grady finds himself talking to the sister. "You can go to the homeowners' association, and they can probably come up with some sort of sanction against the woman who's authorizing the guards to let them in. But it'll take a while. None of these people up here can agree that the sky is blue without appointing a committee and holding ten or twelve meetings. No offense."

"Hell, I don't live here." Her tone says not only doesn't she live here, she wouldn't live here.

"What's Ms. Robertson's major malfunction, anyway? Do you know?"

"Excuse me?"

"She's risking annoying the neighbors in a big way—and people up here aren't fun when they're annoyed."

"Well, Marian did mention that the woman was on the Music Association board."

"And Mr. Ross was involved?"

"I assume so. One thing about Paul, he was always involved."

Marian Ross steps back into the kitchen, eyeing the kids through the sliding door. "Look," Grady says to her. "This kind of nonsense won't last. The vultures will move on in a day or two."

It's the sister who comments. "Sometimes they don't."

If they've got their teeth into a whodunit, he thinks. And everyone knows who the perp was here. In deference to the new widow, though, he goes for a gentler slice of reality. "Only when there's a celebrity involved."

Marian Ross chimes in. "And Paul was a celebrity."

Huh? Does she mean because of the song? The man was a one-hit wonder, and that one hit was a long way back. Still thinking of her feelings, he continues to shade the hurtful truth. "Minor."

Marian Ross just shakes her head as if he's gotten it so wrong that there's no point in replying.

It's the sister who responds. "True. The Oscar was twenty years ago. And classical musicians don't sell tabloids. Usually. But…"

He finishes the sentence for her, and since she hasn't pulled her punches, he's just as blunt. "There's the race thing. A black college professor accused of murdering a white female student is still a story. But this isn't 1920s Mississippi. There's no lasting juice here for cable news. No missing bodies. No living suspects. It'll be a blip. Short term. And local."

The sister snorts. Grady feels as he's just tried to reassure the woman and has instead been labeled a naïve white boy. "Well…then, I guess you just can't help us." She says it in a tone that implies that Grady has turned out to be as useless as he looks.

Mrs. Ross reaches out to her sister as if a hope that's been keeping her afloat has just been snatched away and she's about to go under. "The kids need you," the sister says firmly but not ungently, almost pushing her through the patio door, back to the yard and the pool—away from Grady's presence.

Then the woman is waving him out, gesturing toward the hall, the front door.

He pretends he doesn't notice she's trying to get rid of him, and then curses himself for making the effort to prove he's not worthless even while the words are still leaving his mouth. "Look, I'm not sure what I can do, but…"

"You mean you actually *are* going to do something?"

Shit! Just what do you expect, he wants to say, a miracle? Fixing what is broken here is way beyond his powers, hell, beyond the powers of any mortal. But he's already committed. "I'm going to try."

The sister looks out through the open the patio door. Grady hears splashing and childish voices.

"Just show yourself out," she says. She turns her back on him and goes out to the yard.

ABOUT THE AUTHOR

Judy Tucker lives in Tucson, Arizona on a small lake that would be called a pond in wetter parts of the world. She spends most of her days working at a computer. This may be why Jack Grady is a technophobe.

Made in the USA
Middletown, DE
04 January 2019